The Weight
of Sound

PETER MCDADE

ISBN-13: 978-0-9797471-9-9
ISBN-10: 0-9797471-9-8
Library of Congress Control Number: 2017946602

Wampus Multimedia Catalog Number: WM-099

To receive a free download of this book's companion album, *The Weight of Sound: Original Soundtrack*, email *weightofsound@wampus.com* with the subject line "Free Weight" to obtain a redemption code. Offer expires December 31, 2017.

Jacket design by Erin Bradley Dangar (www.dangardesign.com).
Photos by Angela Georges (www.angelageorgesphotography.com).

www.peterjmcdade.com

For BLC

SIDE ONE

"A band is a dream, you know? It's a dream that you have, it's a dream that all your band members are having, it's a dream of another world, of some other place—a place that feels adventurous, that feels, I suppose, safe, where you feel you're accepted. A real band is a very, very particular and special thing."

—Bruce Springsteen, from an interview with David Remnick, 7 October, 2016

Arachnophilia

Philadelphia, 1987-1990

Sitting in the principal's office of his son's high school, Alan Ebster can hear the HVAC straining to maintain temperature. There's an unhealthy wheeze to the air flow, a smoker's gasping for breath. Two years, three, tops, he figures, and the entire system will need to be replaced. He has a sudden urge to head to the boiler room and investigate; anything would be better than waiting to find out what David did that was so bad the school called him.

Actually, they called Christine, who called Alan. He wishes he could be the one to say no, sometimes.

He's never been in a principal's office before. After watching what happened whenever one of his four older brothers angered their father, he'd tried to make himself as invisible as possible in school. He'd managed to do it, too, even though his own high school had been dark and claustrophobic: 400 students wandering narrow, airless hallways, thanks to the Midwestern aesthetic that abhorred natural light or wasted space. He'd never even made direct eye contact with his principal until he walked across the auditorium stage to get his diploma.

When Dr. Houston finally strolls in he looks younger than Alan expected—gray blazer and dress shirt, no tie, jeans instead of slacks. If he hadn't known better, Alan would have assumed he was talking to the art teacher.

Leaning against the edge of his desk, Dr. Houston casually details the fight that David had between second and third period. Alan might as well be listening to an account of aliens landing in the cafeteria. His son is so quiet, so passive: what could make him angry enough to actually throw a punch? "So, given Spider's solid track record, I think that a short suspension, a cooling off period, so to speak, will reset everyone's clocks. Let's bring him back day after tomorrow."

Alan's not sure the punishment is harsh enough, but nods, thanks Dr. Houston for his time, and stands to shake his hand. Nothing makes Alan more aware of his own calluses, built up over two decades of HVAC installation, than contact with the smooth palm of a man who's avoided physical labor. He adds something about having a talk with David when they get home, pointedly using the boy's given name. His son may have started calling himself "Spider" in sixth grade, but Alan refuses to. Christine does, of course, but she was also sure he'd drop it after a few weeks. Three years ago.

Out in the hall he finds his son sitting quietly on a couch with another kid, both staring at invisible spots on the ground. He expected something more uncomfortable for students in trouble, like backless wooden stools. David stands to follow him, and the two don't say a word as they walk out Central High's large, open entrance.

Once they're inside Alan's aging station wagon, David buckles his seat belt and turns on the radio, scanning the dial as if nothing's wrong. As if it's normal to leave school before noon. As if he hasn't done something so out of line his father had to clear his afternoon schedule and go sit in the goddamn principal's office. Staring through the windshield, waiting for the Volvo's engine to fully come to life, Alan imagines reaching over to snap the radio off and smacking the boy's hand. It's what his own father would have done: a car ride home clouded in angry silence, a few more smacks when they got home. His chest constricts as he inhales his old man's anger. Long after his father's death that anger lives on, hiding around the corner, puffing on a Camel and waiting for an opening.

When Alan glances to his right, though, his son looks impossibly small, and so thin his eye sockets form craters. His skin's as smooth as Dr. Houston's hands, except for the hair stumbling to life under his nose. Alan reminds himself that in addition to trying to push away his father's anger, there's another goal he's worked on every day since Christine gave birth: find the opposite. Ask himself what his father would do, in the face of some parenting challenge, and then do the opposite.

So he looks away from David and starts to back out of the visitor's parking spot. "Let's go to Friendly's. Your old man needs a milk shake."

"Now?"

"Now."

Alan worried the whole time Christine was pregnant. This new life inside made it hard for her to have enough breath for herself, hard to stand or walk or even sleep. It had taken them a long time to get around to getting married, and a long time to get pregnant, and he began to wonder if it was one of those things they just shouldn't have done. He continued to worry, even after she passed the various danger points the doctors had spelled out (please, God, let the kid stay in long enough to have lungs) and finally acquired that maternal glow he'd heard about.

Then his worry shifted to the idea that he'd have a daughter. He'd have to learn how to sit at a tiny table, drink pretend tea, and put up with passive Disney princesses. What he feared most was entering the kitchen, some day in the future, to find his wife and teenage daughter staring at him, their looks telling him he'd walked in (yet again) on a conversation about something he'd done wrong (yet again). "Christine can handle anything," he would mumble as he lay in bed, ashamed of the words as they came out, "but you know me, God. I need all the help I can get." He prayed even though he didn't understand how prayer worked; sitting inside a pristine church he felt none of the clarity he felt in damp and dirty basements. He could decode the jumble of an HVAC system's vents and tubes after a few moments of quiet study, but the nature of God was a mystery second only to Christine's arrival into his life. While he did not understand either miracle—Christ as both man and God, or Christine as this beautiful creature who continued to slip into bed next to him—he didn't want to examine either one too closely. Life without these miracles would not be life, but one of those dark foreign movies Christine liked to watch, subtitles going by too quickly for him to understand.

And then David Joseph arrived. Perfect. All his fingers, all his toes, wide-open eyes, Christine's natural smile, as easy a kid as neighbors and relatives and waiters and supermarket checkers had ever seen. On the rare occasions he did cry, you just needed to offer a reassuring smile, play a quick round of peek-a-boo, or toss him a ball, and everything was fine. For the first three years, Alan thought fatherhood was one of the easiest, most natural things he'd ever done.

They slide into a booth at Friendly's and don't say a word until the waitress comes to take their order. If she's confused by seeing a father and son among all the businessmen on weekday lunch breaks she doesn't show it. David raises his eyebrows as he holds the menu, as if trying to determine what his father will let him order. "Whatever you want," Alan says. "I'm getting fries and a chocolate shake."

When David orders the same thing the waitress nods and takes their menus away. The two of them sit there without saying a word for several long minutes, sharing the silence they create whenever Christine is not there to fill the gaps. "You look like you made it out OK," Alan finally says. He doesn't see any evidence of a fight on his son's face. "Where did he hit you?"

"It wasn't like we were really, like, hitting each other."

"Isn't that what a fight is?"

"Yeah. But it was like—wrestling. He sort of punched my stomach, but not much else."

"So why?"

"Is that what the fries and shake are all about? To get me to talk?"

"No." The surliness reassures Alan that whatever happened wasn't too traumatic. "The fries and shake are because I'm hungry. You have to talk because I'm your father, and you got kicked out of school. What happened?"

"He says I stole his guitar."

It's Alan's turn to be surprised. His son came home with a guitar yesterday, a beat-up acoustic that needed strings; he said he'd swapped his Game Boy for it. "The one you traded for?"

"Well, yeah." He's staring at the table, weaving his napkin through the tines of his fork. "I meant to trade for it."

"You meant to?" Alan exhales, relieved at the quick appearance of their food. He really needs a beer, but a chocolate shake will do. "Did you? Or not?"

"I wanted to." David creates a ketchup lake at the edge of his fries. "But I couldn't find the Game Boy."

"Where is it?"

Shrug. Fry dip into ketchup. "I dunno."

"You lost it?" The Game Boy had been a gift from Christine's mother. "I'll find it."

"You made a deal. No Game Boy means no trade. Give the guitar back."

"I can't."

"Can't? Or don't want to?"

"Can't. Won't."

His son is huddled over his plate like a kid at an orphanage protecting his only meal of the day, eyes suddenly close to tears. "So if the guitar means that much to you," he starts quietly, "why not just buy one?"

"HowamIevergunnadothat?" The question is a mumble.

"Save up your allowance?"

"Five bucks a week? Get my guitar when I'm what, thirty?" The number is spat out like the name of a cold, distant, alien planet. "Great."

"If it means that much..." Alan pauses. "I mean, how are we supposed to know it means so much to you if you don't tell us?"

"Like you'd buy me a guitar."

The boy's tone is a sharp knife aimed at an artery. If anyone had asked him, Alan would have said he's the kind of father his kid can talk to about anything, but with that single cut he realizes that's not the kind of father he has become. He's become Dad Who Says No. It had caught him off guard, his kid's Waves of Need—from the constant filling up of milk cups and dinner plates when he was younger, to the new shoes and clothes that drain their bank account now. He understands it's part of the package, but still he sighs and grumbles every time a new need emerges.

He's become the kind of dad he wouldn't tell things, if he was his own dad.

The table is silent for a long minute as they finish their milkshakes. Then Alan wipes his mouth, puts the napkin over his half-finished fries, and nods. Think of the opposite. "OK. Well. I can tell it means a lot to you. So." He pauses, unsure of how much it will cost, or what Christine will say—the boy had a fight at school, so we got him a guitar? "I'll buy you a guitar," he finishes, and as soon as he says it knows that whatever the financial cost, the look of wonder that washes across his son's face will offset it.

A tendency to obsess emerged shortly after David's third birthday.

The first time it was Mr. Rogers. That was fine, even if Alan thought Fred Rogers a little like one of those older bachelors you'd never let watch your children. The boy stared at the screen with an unnatural focus, but Alan never said anything to Christine. She thought even their son's bowel movements were far, far above average. When Elmo replaced Mr. Rogers, Alan considered it an upgrade, in spite of that annoying theme song.

The spinning-thing obsession soon followed, and that became much more of a problem.

It started with a red-and-yellow top that David's tiny fingers could just manage to get spinning around. He'd sit on the linoleum kitchen floor and play with that top for longer and longer stretches. Thinking about it later, Alan wondered if he and Christine were partially to blame for the problem; at first the moments of calm were so nice that they allowed the spinning, even handing their son the top when it seemed like he was about have a typical three-year-old's tantrum. Later, when they began trying to limit "top time," the tantrums became monumental, and even offers of more TV would not be enough to calm him.

Top time only ended when David found an old Wiffle ball and began to spin it. And spin it.

"Should we take him to the doctor?" Alan finally asked Christine.

"Why, so he can look at us like people who don't know what they're doing?"

"But I don't know what I'm doing, not with this stuff. Is this OK? Should a little boy really want to spin things more than he wants to hang out with other people?"

"My mother says it's a phase."

"Your mother. You don't mind asking your mother about this but don't want to ask the doctor."

"She's my mother. I tell her everything."

Alan refused to imagine what other private matters were included in the "everything" she talked about with her mother, a severe and humorless widow in Pittsburgh. In this case, Christine's mother was right, and the Wiffle ball phase ended, replaced by a much more intense obsession: watching records spin.

Alan's stand-alone stereo was one of the few pieces of furniture from his bachelor days that he insisted on moving into their new house—four-feet high, eight-feet long, and made of beautiful oak. Opening the top revealed a turntable and big knobs that controlled the solid-state radio. The speakers were built in at either end, a little bassy but clear and loud. It had a place of honor in the living room, despite Christine's occasional hints about how much more he could "enjoy his music" in the garage.

David had been completely uninterested in the stereo until one Saturday, when Christine was visiting her mother. Rain meant there was no taking the boy to the park, so Alan decided to break out the Beatles. Ever since he'd been old enough to imagine being a father, he'd dreamt of introducing his own child to the records that meant so much him, to the music that offered him a way to escape from his family. He laid out a selection of LPs on the dining room table, trying not to push David's fingers away too harshly. The boy still struggled to understand how to handle fragile things—just ask that Winnie the Pooh plate he loved so much it wound up in pieces on the kitchen floor.

"Which one should we listen to, buddy?" Alan waved his hands over the Beatles' first eight records, deciding that *The White Album*, and everything after, should wait.

The choice was instant: *Revolver*. Alan worried the cover might look scary to a child, but something about the mixture of line drawings and photos must have been appealing. That oh-so-British count-off and the classic "Taxman" riff caused a wide smile to break out on David's face. For the whole first side, he sat on the ground and stared at the speakers, repeatedly asking, "Who's singing now?"

When Alan went to flip the record, David followed to watch. That's when he discovered the thing making the music spun around in circles. David refused to allow his father to close the top of the stereo again; he wanted to see the record move. Alan didn't know if a four-year-old could resist reaching in and touching the LP, but he just watched, tiny body shaking more or less in time to the music. Father and son listened to *Revolver* four times that first day, and spent subsequent weekends working their way through the Beatles catalogue. Alan's friends marveled at his son's attention span and love of music, but he was never sure which his son enjoyed more: listening to the records or watching them spin around.

The name changes started the first day of kindergarten.

"I want my own name."

"What do you mean?"

"I want my own name."

"You have your own name. David."

"Daddy and Mommy gave it to me."

"Well, yes. That's what parents do."

"Want my own name. D.J."

"D.J.?"

As he said the new name the boy smiled so peacefully, so beautifully, that Alan just nodded. "OK. D.J." Another phase, he told himself. And besides, it wasn't like the name changed—it was just the initials for his given name.

The changes kept coming, though. In the first week of first grade he declared that D.J. was a "little boy's name," and he would now go by George, for his favorite Beatle. A few weeks later he said it wasn't right to "steal" George's name. He would be Stephen (with a "ph," not a "v"). Alan wanted to stop it right then and there, and explain that David was his name, and would always be his name, and that was that.

Christine urged patience. Christine was always urging patience.

"Let the boy be."

"The same way we let him watch hours of Elmo and spin that top around?"

"This is different. He's just trying to find his place in the world."

"He's six. His place in the world is first grade. Doing what his teachers and parents tell him to do."

"What's the harm? His teacher says it's not unusual for kids to try and figure out who they are. She thinks it even may be a sign that he's advanced. Especially creative."

"You talked to his teacher about this?"

"Well, yes, I—"

"Why didn't you tell me?"

"You were at work."

That was the moment he cracked Christine's parenting code. If there was a decision she didn't want him involved in, or didn't think he would approve of, she did it when he was at work. When it was something she didn't want to do, she would make him take off work to help her, or even handle it on his own. He did not call her on this, though, just sighed and accepted it. A marriage only survived if you allowed each other to get away with things occasionally, and this was one of those times.

For a while everything settled down. As Stephen, their son behaved well at school, discussed his day in complete sentences at the dinner table, and brought home a series of polite friends. Alan had little to complain about, as Christine frequently reminded him.

Even Will, one of the few dads in the neighborhood Alan could talk to about more than grilling techniques or the Phillies, liked to tell Alan how good he had it.

"Got called in about Dylan again today," he said on more than one evening, as they watched their kids ride their bikes around the cul-de-sac. "Lost two hours at work just so that tight-ass principal could make me feel like shit." Usually there was a beer in each hand when Will came out, one for him and one for Alan, but on days Dylan got in trouble Will would carry three, so he wouldn't have to go back in the house for a refill. "If he doesn't stop biting people I just may have his teeth pulled. Or pull them myself."

Alan would watch his skinny son zip around on his bike, in complete control even if it looked as if a strong gust of wind would carry him away. For a few years the name changes stopped, too. Perhaps, everyone had been right to tell him not to worry. At some point in fifth grade Stephen became Steve, but that seemed minor.

The start of sixth grade brought the big change. Alan came home one night and found his son and his wife on the couch, waiting for him. An ambush.

"Spider."

"Spider?"

"Yeah." He nodded, this Suddenly Almost Teenage boy whose hair drooped over his eyes, whose back seemed physically incapable of straightening. "That's my name."

"That's your name? Why, because you say so?"

"Alan." Christine's warning voice, the one she used to let him know she could tell he was about to get angry.

"So you think this is a good idea?" he asked her.

"I think it's his idea."

Alan continued to stare at his son, unable to understand how things had gotten to this point. Maybe he and Christine shouldn't have stopped at one child, no matter how hard the pregnancy had been. Maybe kids need a brother or sister to knock sense into them that parents can't. "And if he had an idea to gnaw off his leg, what would you say?"

His son stared at him in disbelief, shaking his head. "Oh, man, you are such a—"

"Come on, Alan," Christine interrupted. "It's not the same thing. Come on."

Alan left the room, wondering what name his son had been going to call him before Christine cut him off.

When they leave Friendly's, they go to Mad Matt's Music. Alan watches from a distance as his son wanders around the selection of guitars with a deadbeat hippie salesman, and doesn't blink at the boy's choice—a $200 Ibanez. David keeps it in his hands the entire car ride home, leaving the radio off and plucking gently at the strings. When they pull into the garage the back door opens immediately. There's Christine, eyes wide, her Worried Look in full bloom. It changes to surprise when she sees the guitar, but the boy's smile, and Alan's quiet nod, keep her from asking anything more than, "Is that a new guitar?"

The guitar doesn't just change his son's life—it transforms the entire household. David comes to breakfast carrying it, practicing chords between bites of cereal. When Alan gets home from work each day, his son is in his room, the same way he's been since he turned ten, but now that he's in there playing guitar there's audible proof he's doing something, making him more of an actual presence. The kid who used to sleep until noon weekends was up by mid-morning, a study in concentration on the living room couch, staring at his own fingers as they awkwardly tried out chord formations.

After a few weeks, though, Alan begins to worry. What if the guitar doesn't make David more social, but turns him into even more of a shut-in? "Shouldn't he be going out with other kids?" he asks Christine more than once. "It's Saturday night, for God's sake."

"You know how many parents are begging their kids to practice, right now, across this country?" Christine answers each time. "And you worry your son is playing too much."

"But he doesn't do anything else."

"He keeps up at school."

"Cs and Bs, when he could get As?"

"He's doing fine. And you can't tell me you don't hear his playing getting better."

That part is true: the kid definitely gets better quickly. As much as music has meant to Alan, he's never played an instrument. It never occurred to him, just as he'd never imagined trying out for the Phillies because he liked baseball. After just a few weeks, David is strumming much more smoothly, so smoothly that Alan can even tell what song he's playing most of the time—especially if it's a Beatles tune. "Yes, he's getting better. But doesn't he still need friends?"

Again, Will tells him he's crazy to worry. The men do their talking now on sporadic morning jogs, slow crawls through the streets of their neighborhood with no kids in sight. It's not that their children don't need to be watched anymore—if anything, teens need to be watched more than younger kids. What's more dangerous, a bicycle wipeout or getting into the liquor cabinet? No, it's just that their children now burrow into corners of the universe no one over sixteen has access to, leaving their dads to shuffle down streets alone, trying to magically erase the pounds that had begun padding their bellies after forty. "He's a good kid," Will says when Alan mentions his concerns. "Shit, I wish I knew where Chris or Dylan were most of the time. Some of the time, even."

"But he never leaves the house. He has no friends, as far as I can tell."

"He's fourteen, Alan. Last thing you want is him hanging out with other fourteen-year-olds, right? They're all dicks. Just like you and I were, at that age."

He nods, not sure Will understands how confusing it is to have a total stranger drifting through your house. He'd know what to do with an asshole teenage son. He'd know what to do with David's asshole friends, and would see right through the lies about what parents were going to chaperone the party. He got no training for this kid, who seems to exist in his own, solitary universe, this kid who gets up early in the morning to obsessively practice. And he's too old, and tired, to learn a new language.

He doesn't share his biggest fear: even though there have been no problems at school since the guitar arrived, and his son seems more awake, more engaged with the world, he thinks David is lonely. Will always be lonely. Will never have any friends. Will graduate high school but stay in the house with them, twenty-five and clutching that guitar whenever he's not bagging groceries.

And then he returns from a slow jog with Will one Saturday morning to find someone sitting next to his son at the kitchen table. The boys glare at him over their huge bowls of Frosted Flakes. Clearly they would make him disappear, if they only had the power.

Christine explains that the new kid is Owen, and he's come over to "jam." Alan can tell she's more relieved than she's letting on, and he is, too. Maybe David will actually make a few friends after all.

Owen doesn't come around more than a handful of times, though, soon replaced by a series of other monosyllabic boys of various shapes and sizes. Alan stops learning their names, because each vanishes within a few weeks. He finally asks his son about these disappearances as he drives him to buy new strings, even though he knows that David prefers his father never address him directly.

"What happened to that last kid? I thought he sounded pretty good."

"Tommy?" David scans the radio stations, as if searching for a hidden message. "Randall?"

"I don't remember his name. The one with the red hair that needed to be cut."

"Tommy."

"OK, Tommy. What happened to him? Playing with someone else now?"

"I dunno."

"Why doesn't he play with you anymore?"

"'Cause I don't want him to."

"Oh." Alan is embarrassed: he's assumed all the other kids had rejected David, not the other way around. "Why?"

"'Cause he's not right."

"Not right?" Audible sighing from the passenger seat, but Alan is curious. "You mean, like, not good enough?"

"Not right. Doesn't match the sound I need?" More sighing. "You wouldn't understand."

"Try me."

Groan. "I hear the music in my head. It's done, you know? Already there. Now I have to find a way... to make the sounds in my head, in, like, real life. Haven't found the right people to help me do that yet."

At the music store, Alan stays in the car and listens to AM radio news, which he always finds reassuring. Weather at sixteen past the hour, sports at twenty-one. Predictable. As the familiar stories wash over him he tries to imagine what it's like to hear music in your head all the time—never mind what the music in his son's head sounds like. He wonders if he'll ever actually hear any of it.

He hears that music for the first time early in David's senior year. Christine insists he come watch the Battle of the Bands.

"He's played every year since ninth grade, Alan. You've never gone, and your son has a gift."

He doesn't want to admit he's been waiting for David to ask him, or that he's afraid to go because he doesn't want to see his son crash and burn in front of strangers, so a week later he's hanging at the back of the gym with a handful of other parents. There's a group of moms clutching cameras, and some dads huddled in the back corner, discreetly passing a flask back and forth and laughing too loudly. Assholes who played football when they were in high school, Alan's sure of it.

The bleachers have been opened partially, but Christine prefers to stand— legs tapping nervously, hands fiddling with the snap of her purse. David didn't know when his band was going on, so they've been there since the first one started, a mercifully quiet acoustic guitar duo. Alan tries not to look annoyed when a second group of teens that doesn't include his son begins shuffling around the stage, setting up. They'll have to suffer through a set by Yes or Know, five lanky boys hiding behind long hair and one girl who would be singing, if she could even breathe in her tight jeans. It takes him a few minutes to recognize their first song, but when it turns out to be "Rock and Roll All Night" by KISS, he knows he has to leave the room. He taps Christine on the shoulder, motions to the hallway with his chin, and escapes.

As much as he hated own high school days, he would rather wander Central High than sit through a half hour of bad heavy metal covers. Maybe his school had been too small, he thinks as he turns down another of the endless series of wide hallways. Maybe if he hadn't needed to use up so much energy hiding he would have had more time to find a crowd of his own. He passes football and basketball team photos and plaques, band photos, even photos of various clubs, some with as few as two members. Calculus Club? Good luck, kids. At least they've found each other.

None of the photos or lists include David Ebster, though. When he graduates it will be as if he was never here at all. Maybe he is like his old man.

When Alan returns to the gym new clusters of teens have popped up all across the floor. Christine points to the stage, and there, standing in the middle of all the activity, barking out instructions as he unravels a guitar cable, is their son. He looks taller, and not just because he's standing on the temporary stage that's been set up. It's his back, Alan decides: his back is straight in a way it never is when he slouches through their house.

After a few minutes of noisy chaos—banging drums, piercing feedback bursts at random intervals, jagged guitar strums—the lights dim, and David's band is introduced by whatever teacher has been stuck with the emcee gig. He doesn't remember hearing the name before, and he has to give the kid points for cleverness: Arachnophilia. He also doesn't recognize any of the other musicians, or the kids suddenly filling the space between audience and stage. He's known his son must have friends, somewhere, but seeing him toss a wave at people in the crowd makes him feel like he's watching the end of some cheesy thriller on TV. The mysterious, silent character who's spent the entire movie in a wheelchair is suddenly standing, striding across the room to deliver a dramatic speech. It turns out he could walk all along.

What surprises him most, though, is the way his son controls everyone onstage. As soon as the teacher who's introduced them starts to walk away from the mic, David turns to the band and loudly counts to four. His voice is so clear and commanding it doesn't just sound like a different version of his son's voice: it sounds like a different person. A different species. And that control continues for the next half hour. The other guitarist stands off to the side with his eyes locked onto David's hands, which move in a series of fluid gestures. A little upward motion and the band gets louder, downward makes them play softer, and a quick circle means they repeat the section again. Someone has replaced his quiet, barely sentient son with a musical drill sergeant.

They play six songs, all written by David, according to Christine. For most of the set no one in the band speaks to the crowd, though David and the bass player both smile and wave after some songs. The acoustics of a high school gym make it hard to decipher the words his son is singing, but Alan can hear enough of the melodies to know that the tunes are pleasant, even catchy.

David approaches the mic just once to address the crowd. "This is our last one, so thanks for coming out." He pauses, offering a smile that reminds Alan of the look on his son's face when he'd picked "D.J." as his new name. "And remember—love your spiders!" With that he gives another four count and the band is off. The song is louder than any of the preceding ones, more aggressive. He can hear "TV" and "ghost," and something about someone being "screwed," but not much else. Whenever the band hits what turns out to be the chorus, though, Spider sings loudly and clearly enough to be understood, even through the weak PA:

> You want me to be
> What you want to see
> But you can't make me
> What I'm gonna be
>
> I don't want or need your help
> Only I can change myself
> I don't want or need your help
> Only I can change myself

The song has a big rock ending, with David conducting the other three as they slowly hit the last chords. Alan doesn't have to be the father of the lead singer to know the applause is louder, and more sustained, than it had been all night. David turns to face the crowd, exhales, and then offers a deep bow. The rest of the band mimics the bow, poker-faced until the applause starts; then the four teens turn to each other and grin, as if watching the successful completion of some secret plan they hadn't been sure would succeed.

Alan turns to look at Christine, staring at their son with pride and wonder. He wonders if she figured out that David was singing that last song to him.

Two weeks later David turns eighteen, and Alan and Christine take him out to the restaurant of his choice. The Birthday Dinner is a family tradition that started when David turned eight, but they were surprised when he agreed to go. He'd boycotted the dinner on his sixteenth and seventeenth birthdays, and seemed to enjoy their presence even less this last year. He chose Bella Luna, a high-end Italian place neither of them had been to before.

They make it halfway through their entrees before there's any tension, and might have made it longer if Alan could have resisted asking about college. Thanksgiving is less than two weeks away, though, and all the other parents with high school seniors talk about nothing but whether their kids will take the SAT a second (or third) time, and the most polite way to stay on top of people writing recommendation letters. David refuses to take the SAT, even once. Hasn't asked to see any schools. Hasn't even gotten blank applications to pretend to fill out. Christine preaches patience, the same sermon she's been giving Alan since the kid was born, but sometimes waiting patiently just gets you left behind.

"So I have to ask. What's the college plan?"

"Well," David begins, tearing off another piece of bread, "I'm not going. That's the plan."

Alan looks over at Christine, to see if this is another secret the two of them have cooked up, but he can tell by the look on her face that she's just as surprised as he is. Exhaling slowly, he tries to pretend he is one of those TV fathers who never worries because he knows all problems get solved in thirty minutes. "OK, then. What will you be doing after high school?"

"Don't worry, Dad. I'll be out of your hair."

Christine grabs Alan's wrist: clearly, for her, not going to college is one thing, but leaving home is another. "Your father wasn't saying you had to move out," she says quickly. "I think he's just—"

"Just making sure I have a plan, I got it. And I do." He dips his bread into the marinara sauce pooled around his chicken parmigiana. "I'm gonna take the GED in January, and then head to Athens."

"GED? Not graduate with your friends?" Christine asks, her face drained of color.

"I need to get out of here, Mom. You know that."

Alan is more worried about the announced destination. "Jesus, David. Why Georgia?" It's like the boy has said he's going to the moon. By way of *Deliverance*.

"You wonder why I don't tell you things when you can't even call me by the right name."

"Just because you make up some ridiculous nickname for yourself doesn't mean I—"

"Ridiculous nickname? Thanks, Dad. Your support means so much to me."

"Will the two of you stop, please," Christine says, her voice just above a whisper. "We didn't come here to fight."

"No, we sure as hell didn't need to pay twenty dollars for a plate of spaghetti to fight," Alan says. "We can fight at home for free." He's unable to keep the comment in his head, forgetting the one lesson he should have learned from his old man: sometimes saying less is more. Staring at his son and wife as they poke the remains of the dinner none of them will finish, he realizes that for all the energy he spent developing a parent strategy different than his father's, he's only managed to create the same results.

The entire family falls through a fun-house mirror after the Birthday Dinner. Alan and Christine sulk through the house, barely talking to each other or David. Their moody son, however, is replaced by his Happy Doppelgänger. New David eagerly checks the mail, starts to clear out excess crap from his room, and regularly chats with selected members of the large posse the Doppelgänger maintains.

Books about the GED not only appear—they also get read. By David.

Another senior appears on Saturday mornings, someone who helps with math prep in exchange for guitar lessons. David's idea.

Magazines from Georgia arrive in the mailbox, and get scoured for ads for rental shares and possible jobs. New David even asks Alan for advice, for the first time since second grade. "Pay less and have two roomies, or pay a little more and just have one?"

"The fewer people there are the less likely it is you'll find something to fight about," Alan says, more pleased than he shows when his son nods thoughtfully, as if his father has finally managed to say something useful. As stunned as he still is by the idea that the boy will be gone by February, he also can't help but wonder if David has figured out something his parents have not.

He wants to share these observations with Christine, this feeling that the boy might actually be right to try his hand at a music career—it's not like the kid ever cared about anything else, anyway. But she is so busy with a new series of stray causes and projects, it's clear she does not want to discuss their actual life.

Fleece blankets for homeless women.

Alphabetization of the spice rack.

Scrubbing all the baseboards. Twice.

It's not until the night before the boy's scheduled departure that the two of them talk about what's happening. When Alan gets home from work the house is quiet and spotless, all surfaces polished until they glisten in an unnatural way. He imagines himself in some *Twilight Zone* episode. Maybe he just dreamed having a wife and son. What was that song David used to play all the time? "This is not my beautiful house, this is not my beautiful wife..."

He finds Christine sitting at the kitchen table. Aside from the empty tea mug in front of her, the kitchen is free of clutter. That omnipresent stack of mail they needed to go through, the morning's paper, any pot or pan that still needed to finish drying: all gone. Even the placemats have been put away.

"Where is he?"

"Last night in town. Said he had friends to see before he left."

He can hear the hurt in her voice, and smell the pot roast in the oven. The boy's favorite.

"It's OK," she says, still not looking at him. "I understand."

"Dinner smells good." When she doesn't answer, he continues to stand there, keys in one hand and briefcase in the other. Is he supposed to go to her? Or silently leave the room? "You OK?" he finally asks.

"OK. You want to know if I'm OK."

Her tone makes it clear he asked the wrong question, but there's no way to take it back. "Yes. Are you OK?"

"How could I be OK?" she asks quietly. "Tomorrow he heads out into the world. Alone."

"Christine."

"And you want to know if I'm OK? Jesus, Alan."

"Kids go out in the world. It's what they do. We did it."

"But he's not ready. You're letting him go before he's ready."

He almost lets it slide. Maybe he should, knowing how much pain she's in. But why, he decides, should she get to blame him for all of that pain? "What do you mean, I'm letting him go?"

"You know what I mean."

That's when she finally looks at him. Her eyes are tired, discolored, and half-shut. His own father's eyes, those few times he dared talk to the old man after his nightly cocktails. Knowing it's from crying, not drinking, does not make it any easier to bear. Again he almost lets it slide, almost walks out of the kitchen to disappear into the TV. Having this conversation now feels like hitting both of them when they are down. But if they don't talk about it now they'll never talk about it, and he worries about the damage an extended silence could generate. "No, Christine, I don't know what you mean."

"You're his father. It was your duty to make him do the right thing." She turns her head away again, focusing her eyes on her tea mug. "Instead you just checked out, the way you always have."

"You know that's not fair." He wonders if he should take her hand in his, try to remind her how much they've been through already. Convince her they will get through this, too. He decides to keep his distance, afraid she will leave the room if he moves any closer. "I love that boy, Christine."

"Then why are you letting him go?"

"Because he's always been a stubborn kid who did what he wanted. And now he's eighteen and stubborn, and we can't stop him anymore."

"You could have."

"How, exactly? I didn't see you throwing yourself in front of the car, or slashing the tires. You packed him a lunch for the drive."

"Because I worry about him."

"And I don't? I've been worried about him since before he was born. Mr. Rogers, Elmo. The top? And Jesus, with the name changes. How many times did I want to put my foot down about this stuff?"

"And the one time it matters, the one time you should do something, you won't." Her eyes narrow. "Why did you ever buy him that fucking guitar?"

And there it is, her real complaint, with a rare Christine f-bomb thrown in for emphasis. If only Alan had never bought that guitar. If only he'd just grounded the boy after that fight in school, come down hard on him the way his old man would have—maybe their son would have given up on music. He has no answer for that; for all he knows, she could be right. Maybe he could have broken his son's obsession with music, once and for all.

But would the three of them have been any happier?

They don't eat dinner, don't watch TV. By eight the pot roast is packed away in the refrigerator, and they head upstairs to brush their teeth, apply their ointments, and take their various pills, unflattering rituals performed openly for either to see. After all these years together there are no more secrets, no denying that they are both much older than they ever imagined they would be. He watches her finish her nightly routine out of the corner of his eyes, as he lies in bed and pretends to read *Newsweek*. When she's done she doesn't say a word, just turns out the light on her night stand and lies down, as close to the edge as she can get.

He turns out his light, even though he's not really ready to sleep, trying to offer a sign of solidarity. She doesn't speak, doesn't even reach a hand out for some minimal contact. He listens to her shallow breaths and knows she can't shut herself off forever: after tomorrow morning it will be just the two of them.

They're all up by six. Alan can't remember the last time the three of them had breakfast together. No one talks much except for David, rambling through the various highways he'll take to Georgia, how the trickiest part will be getting to the Turnpike. Alan suddenly remembers a piece of advice his own father gave him that could actually be useful here: "The trickiest part of any trip is the beginning," he says. "After that you'll be fine."

David nods, but keeps rambling about gas prices and fears of a flat tire. Alan offers benign reminders to never eat anything fried or called a "hot dog" when you're on a long road trip, and to take lots of breaks. There's nothing for any of them to say, and they all know it, but he hopes his bland comments somehow offset Christine's grief and the boy's nervousness.

He expects as much from Christine, but seeing his son's nerves exposed catches him off guard.

It's still dark when they walk out to the car. David is silent, but Christine is softly crying. Alan goes to hold her hand, or even lay a palm upon her back, but she resists, determined to go through this alone. She squeezes her son tight and hard, frantically whispering something in his ear. He mumbles, "I know, Mom," in response, and then she heads for the house at a jog without looking back.

Which means it's just him and his son. He can't remember the last time that happened, either. He stares into the eyes of the young man in front of him, startled to see a glimmer of the same fear he saw in Christine's the night before. He's only eighteen, Alan thinks, but then he reminds himself that's how old he was when he left home.

So: his boy is eighteen. How did that happen?

"Your mother will be OK," he says. "It's hard for her, but she'll be OK. For the love of God, though, call her when you get there."

"I will."

"It's hard for me, too. But." He takes a deep breath—he doesn't have a big goodbye planned, but he can see the kid needs to hear something. The Oscar winner caught by surprise, no speech prepared. "Your mom would kill me, hearing me say this. But I think you're making the right decision."

"Really?" His eyebrows raise. "You really think so?"

Alan nods. "Music's the one thing you've really cared about, Spider. And you're lucky—it's also the thing you do best." He realizes he's thought this ever since the shock of hearing the plan wore off, and wonders why it took him so long to say it. "I think you should go see what happens. Your mom's worried you're too young, but I'm glad you're not waiting until you're too old."

His son leans into him, the keys in his left hand pressing hard into Alan's back as they hug. He didn't get, or want, a goodbye from his own father when he left, never mind a hug. This tight clutch is proof history didn't repeat exactly.

He watches the Chevy Nova until it disappears, and then heads slowly back to the house. When he gets inside all the lights are off. Christine has gone back to bed. The house already feels quieter than it has since the first time they brought the boy home, walking slowly and carrying him as if he was a rare and fragile thing that would break if they made a single misstep.

Alan Ebster pours himself another cup of coffee and heads back outside. Standing on the front stoop, he feels his own fears about his son's journey fade, ever so slightly, as he watches the sky gradually awaken. It's light enough now, he thinks. The boy should be able to find all his turns.

Behind Door Number Two

Athens, 1992

There are forty or so people watching as Spider steps on to the stage, though "watching" might be an exaggeration. Tuesday night at Broadway Pizza means $4.99 Pasta Plates, with unlimited refills. While you eat you can scan the TVs scattered across the dining area, screens filled with sports games, sports highlights, and men in suits talking about sports. Spider knows that he's the free peanuts, something easily ignored unless it's right in front of you; maybe you take a handful, out of boredom, or curiosity, or maybe you don't. He recognizes a few faces tonight, at least. They might have come on another Tuesday, since he's been here every week for six months now, or he could have seen them at one of the gigs he played with his band, Monkeyhole.

Or maybe Athens is just a small town.

"Hello, Pizza People," he says, stepping on to the 8 x 8 wooden stage the owner sets up for the weeknight acoustic acts. "I'm Spider, and you are now my captive audience." Broadway Pizza isn't the kind of place teenage Spider imagined playing when he lay in bed at night, too stoned to shut his brain off, but he refuses to take it lightly. That's not always easy, but it's not as hard as trying to pass algebra, or studying for the fucking GED. He moves the stool that A. J. Dobronski, the blonde with big boobs who plays before him, likes to use. It's cheating to sit and play, unless you're B.B. King, but it works for A.J. When she sits her acoustic becomes a resting spot for her ample breasts, so for her thirty minutes of competent covers all the horny undergrad eyes are actually on the stage. Even the women's. Hell, even Spider watches her play, waiting for the night when her football player boyfriend doesn't show up. The goon carries her guitar, helps her work the electric tuner, and then spends her entire set scanning the crowd, a tense Secret Service Agent expecting the worst. Spider is more than qualified to take his place.

For these Tuesday gigs, he likes to open with a cover. He refuses to play any in a Monkeyhole set, since he has so many original songs ready to release into the world, but in this setting, an interesting cover can help pull attention from *SportsCenter* to the stage. Tonight he's worked up a shortened, slowed down version of "Wanna Be Startin' Somethin'." The level of chatter remains constant during the intro, but he takes a dramatic pause before that opening chorus, and that causes a few heads to turn his way; he's just beginning to harness the power of unexpected silence. By the time he gets to the outro, slapping the side of his Gibson in time to that ridiculous and brilliant chant, he actually has the table of girls in the back trying to sing along. "Ma ma se, ma ma sa, ma ma coo day! Ma ma se, ma ma sa, ma ma mumble say." He catches their eyes and nods encouragement, relieved when none of them shoot him an angry look. After two years in a small college town, it's getting harder and harder to avoid all the girls he's somehow offended.

When he finishes, the applause is louder than anything A.J. or her boobs got all night, satisfying his competitive urge. The challenge now is to keep them from drifting away. Before the applause can fade out completely, he launches into "Change Myself," the only song from his life in Pennsylvania that he still plays. It's fast and angry enough to hold most of the crowd's attention; most college kids still want to remind the world that only they could decide who they were going to be—even if they're putting off trying to figure it out for as long as they can.

He just dropped the song from band gigs, though, and tonight he wonders if it's time to drop it from his solo sets. A part of his brain turns sixteen whenever he plays it: sitting in his bedroom in Logan, door locked, trying to get the Ibanez in his hands to sound the way he wanted it to. The music in his head was his escape from the rest of his life, perfectly formed songs that started appearing to him around the same time he realized certain girls had a smell he could not define or resist. He'd always loved music, so hearing melodies he'd never heard before, but felt like he'd always known, made sense. In fact, he assumed everyone had channels of music in their brains, playing all the time; it wasn't until he confided this idea to Lee, one of the guitarists he burned through in high school, that he understood how different his head was from everyone else's.

It was one of the many days he was frustrated Lee wouldn't just play what Spider told him to. He always insisted on trying other parts, and when he was stoned he thought they all sounded "fucking amazing." Finally Spider muffled Lee's strings and said, "It may sound amazing to you, dude, but it's not the sound in my head." Lee looked even more confused than usual when Spider tried to explain that his head was a radio, with two or sometimes three or four different songs for him to tune in to. Lee said all he heard was his father bitching about his grades, and Ann Marie Bunsa moaning his name.

After he finishes "Change Myself" he pauses to plug the upcoming Monkeyhole gig at the Rockfish Palace, pleased to hear a few claps when he drops the band name. He plays four in a row from the standard Monkeyhole set, and "Pay Me Now" works especially well. He's eager to get to the end of his thirty minutes, though, because he's going to close with "Behind Door Number Two." It'll be the first time he plays it live. It's less than a month old, but already feels like an important song.

"I'm gonna finish up with a brand new one," he says with a grin. "So let's all hope I remember how it goes." He's especially proud of the opening riff, which doesn't sound like anything else he's written—it's like he's moved up a level in a video game. Most of the words came to him all at once, which is always a good sign, though he still doesn't know what it's about. That's a good sign, too, he's decided. It's time to stop writing about his father or needing to get laid.

> I used to see you
> Even when you weren't clear
> Could feel you touch me
> Even when you weren't near

As much as the song excites him, Monkeyhole has yet to master the feel of the groove. The band sounds too stiff, and the whole thing lumbers when he imagines it soaring. Epic: he hears this as an epic, especially when it hits the chorus, but they haven't achieved liftoff yet. It's a failure that serves as the final bit of proof Shannon is never really going to be their bass player—something about the groove eludes her, and probably always will. Spider knows now Shannon should never have been in Monkeyhole in the first place; this time, his fondness for pursuing women just out of his league intersected with his dream of having a woman in the band, and that combination convinced him she could work out. And then he kept her around for too long, determined to sleep with her before she was fired. Now that he's done one, it's time to do the other.

As he gets to the chorus he spots Paul. He must have arrived after Spider started; the two of them are supposed to head out after his set and meet a new weed connection Paul's made. He used to come to all of Spider's solo sets, but he's started boycotting these Tuesday gigs. He thinks it's beneath Spider to play here, but the band needs all the publicity it can get. Spider also feels a loyalty to the first place in town to give him a regular gig.

> Where have you gone, my friend
> Now where are you?
> Behind door number one
> Or behind door number two?
> Tell me where I should go

What I should do
To make sure this message
Will get through to you?

By the time Spider rolls into the bridge, he's more confident about the song than ever and wonders if Paul feels it as strongly. He tries to make eye contact again, but Paul's drifted to the back table of undergrad girls. And, in the night's first bad news, the girls have been joined by a redhead Spider recognizes. He quickly shifts his gaze to the other side of the room, to the safety of a table of awkward geeks.

Tiffany: that's her name. She didn't seem crazy the first couple of nights they'd hung out, but then he broke his Two Times Rule. He'd figured out that as long as he didn't spend more than two nights with the same girl, the relationship couldn't be thought of as so serious that it required some sort of breakup talk; he could just stop returning their calls, and they would give up. Tiffany didn't turn crazy until he got stoned and lonely enough one night to ask her over for a third time. He made it worse by letting her stay the night. After that, she began to call him every day. She'd even wait for him at the house, or show up at his Wuxtry shift. Always so happy to see him in that first instant, and then immediately getting angry at him when his excuses for not seeing her were deemed inadequate. He'd finally had to have the We're Not Doing This talk.

He hates that talk.

The applause after "Behind Door Number Two" is sustained enough to satisfy him; he's lost some of the casual listeners he hooked with the Michael Jackson cover, but the first few tables have filled in with people who paid attention for most of the set. He thanks everyone one more time, gives a final plug for the Rockfish show, and then quickly grabs his guitar case. He's hoping to get out the back door before Tiffany comes over.

"Good set, man. Might sound even better with some fucking drums."

Spider closes the Gibson's case, looks up, and nods at a grinning Paul. "That joke. I mean maybe if you keep saying it, maybe it'll get funny? Maybe?"

"I don't know, I thought it was funny."

Tiffany. Spider tries to look calm as she walks up to the stage, holding a can of Budweiser and wearing a black Ramones T-shirt that makes her pale red hair look fiery. It's the same shirt she wore the night they met at the Globe, except she's scowling, instead of smiling in a flirty way. And now he knows she couldn't care less about the Ramones: she just likes the shirt. "Oh, hey, Tiffany." Casual. Unconcerned.

"Your friend here has been cracking me up," she says, pushing the Bud into Paul's chest.

"Good," Spider says calmly. He can tell from Paul's eyes that he's just realizing he's been talking to a live hand grenade.

"But you're the real funny one, right?" Tiffany steps up onto the stage, her voice rising enough to make a few heads to turn to see what's going on. "I'll call you, ha ha. We'll do this again, hee hee. Of course you're special, ho ho ho. Funny as Jerry fucking Steinfeld."

He knows he shouldn't engage, but he can't help himself. "It's Seinfeld."

"Jesus, I know," she says. "Which means I'm Eileen and he, this poor guy, he's fucking George."

Spider picks up his guitar and points to Paul. "You ready, George?"

"George? I can't be Kramer?" He turns to say something to Tiffany, but Spider hops off the stage and pulls him to the back door, Tiffany's shouts chasing them into the alley.

As Paul drives them to the Color Box, where his weed dealer is playing a gig, Spider starts to fill him in on the Tiffany backstory. He doesn't get very far before Paul holds up his hand. "Stop it, man. I get it. Heard this one before, but it was about Jessie. Or Mandy. Or Sue Ellen."

"Oh, I guarantee you, there's been no Sue Ellen. I have my standards."

"You need to slow down your burn rate on these women," Paul says. "Or there's not gonna be anywhere safe for you in this town."

"All the more reason to get out of town," Spider says. "Hurry up and graduate, so we can leave before I get killed."

Mentioning Paul's struggle to finish his junior year gives him reason to complain about his classes at UGA, a topic Spider is tired of talking about. Paul promised his parents he'd finish his degree, and Spider has given up trying to convince him he could just go ahead and drop out. His refusal to do so worries Spider, makes him wonder if Paul is getting a degree in case the band doesn't work out. People with back-up plans always use them. He feels better when he tells himself that Paul's loyalty and sense of commitment will transfer to the band, and remembers the checks Paul's parents send him for expenses, which allows Paul to throw down for more than his share of food and beer.

Spider values loyalty in the drummer above all other players, because he's learned that having the right drummer is the key to having the right sound. In high school he'd worried most about finding a second guitarist, then realized what a mistake that had been when he just grabbed a bass player and drummer to fill out the rest of the band. The core of the band was the drummer and the guitarist: that's where he should have started. Bonham and Page formed the connection that made everything else possible. With the Stones, same axis, held in place by Charlie and Keith.

So when he moved to Athens, his first goal was to find the right drummer. He hit the clubs several nights a week, befriending as many doormen as he could; they usually let him in for free in exchange for the occasional joint, since they knew he'd take off after a song or two. He only needed to hear a few minutes to know if the drummer was a possible match. He wanted someone good enough to show off and roll around the kit if he needed to, but who was smart enough to know it was rarely necessary. A drummer who could generate, and stay deep inside, whatever groove the song needed. Everyone saw Bonham as this big old heavy hitter, but his secret weapon was the light touch he deployed when the song needed it. "Fool in the Rain," "Down By the Seaside." He could make Zeppelin swing.

So: he was looking for some love child of Bonham and Ringo. Nothing like searching for the impossible.

After months of frustrated hunting, Spider found Paul because he needed to take a dump. He was on his way to the 40 Watt, planning to check out the Hummingbirds and some hot-shit drummer they supposedly had, when the leftover Mexican he'd scarfed down on his way out the door demanded immediate escape. He ducked into Jilly's, a pizzeria on Broad that hosted lame cover bands but usually had a clean bathroom. On his way back out he recognized the first verse of "Feel Like Makin' Love," one of the worst, and longest, songs ever written, a song that usually made him want to break into a run.

But, Jesus. The thing actually had a groove.

So he blew off the Hummingbirds and stayed for the whole set. Even "Radio Free Europe" and "Best Friend's Girl" were listenable, as long as he ignored the out-of-tune guitars and the way the singer insisted on shouting "Take it, Bill!" before each half-assed guitar solo. Watching the drummer float above the others was like watching a pro quarterback playing in an exhibition game with local amateurs. He kept throwing perfect spirals, and they kept getting dropped.

When he talked to Paul between sets and discovered he was as well-versed in Television and Berlin-period Bowie as he was in Zeppelin, Spider knew he'd found his drummer. He just needed to convince Paul, who was used to judging a band's worth by how much money they made, even if they made it playing crappy covers. By the next afternoon the two of them were working out arrangements of Spider's songs, and after an hour of that, Paul had agreed to drop his other band.

Spider never understood why he had to move from Philly to Athens to find a drummer from Boston. He was just glad Jilly's kept their bathrooms clean.

Nearing the Color Box, Paul slows down to look for a parking spot and asks Spider about the 40 Watt. Again. It's the most legendary club in

Athens, and Paul is desperate to play there. Spider wants to play there, too, but he wants to play there more than once—and he's not sure the current line-up is good enough to get them a second gig, even if he talks his way into a first. It's not just Shannon he's worried about; lately he's been wondering if Newt, Monkeyhole's other guitarist, is too good. Having a lead guitarist who's been too good for too long leads to solos with too many notes, far busier and more complicated than they need to be. It also means the guy is playing in three or four other bands, panning for gold in as many rivers as he can access. Spider had insisted his two previous lead guitarists quit their other bands, but Newt had refused, and Spider had gambled he would be worth it.

"I think we're ready, man," Paul says again as they get out of the car. "It's time."

"I don't think so. We don't even have a decent demo."

"We have that board tape from the Rockfish."

"Jesus, that sounds like—"

"And we add a song or two from the Arachnophilia tape."

"No way." Spider shudders at the memory of making his first "real" recordings in high school. Fucking Tim Zito on guitar, an awful player who was only in the band because he had a four-track machine. Another lesson learned—recordings are permanent, so only make them with the right people. "No fucking way."

"I think it all sounds good enough," Paul says. "Maybe we should vote on it."

Spider wishes they hadn't run out of weed. He and Paul could already be stoned and listening to music, instead of hitting this same dead end. "Not everything gets to be voted on," he says. It's as close as he ever wants to get to spelling it out for Paul: a good band can and should look like a democracy, as long as everyone knows that one person calls all the important shots.

They're quiet for the rest of the short walk to the Color Box, one of the tiny clubs that seem to pop up almost weekly in Athens. Sometimes they close within a month, sometimes they last just long enough to be missed when they disappear. And in rare cases (OK, the 40 Watt) they become institutions. There's nothing particularly special about the Box, but Spider likes its vibe and hopes it can stick around for a while. The two of them get in for free, since Paul got them on the guest list, and head for the bar in the back. Spider is bummed to see Leave Greta Alone, the weed dealer's band, is still onstage. He'd been hoping to head straight to the dressing room, score a free beer, pick up the pot, and get the hell out of there. At least Paul buys them each a Heineken while they wait.

There's thirty or so people in the club, and maybe half are actually paying attention to the band. As he takes his beer from Paul, Spider focuses on the stage for the first time since they arrived. He quickly dismisses the singer, aimlessly mumbling into the microphone—if you're not going to take ownership of the show, no one in the crowd will want to buy it from you. The guitarists are capable enough, but their lack of confidence is embarrassing, the two kids up there are clutching their matching Strats like any minute someone's gonna come along and take them, like they know they haven't earned the right to keep holding them. Maybe that's why the drummer is hitting too hard: trying to be the one person on the fucking stage who plays like he has to be there.

But off in the corner, invisibly holding all these clashing parts together, is the bass player. He's keeping a watch on everyone in the band, especially the drummer, as he lays down a solid groove, adding just enough flourishes to make clear he could play a lot more if he thought it was necessary. The song they're struggling through sounds like a reject from *Green*. It's not even bad enough to be memorable, and the chorus really is "I love you like the sun." The bass line, though, works against the melody in an interesting way, while also locking in tightly with the drummer. It's a miracle of playing Spider can't get enough of. He only looks up when the song ends and Paul taps his shoulder.

"You haven't heard anything I've said, have you?" he asks. "Don't tell me you like these guys."

"That you can even think that depresses me," Spider says, taking a long swallow of Heineken as the lead singer attempts some between-song banter. "To make up for that insult, tell me which one is keeping me interested."

"The bass player's not bad."

"He's more than not bad."

"Doesn't look like a dealer at all, does he?"

"He's your pal with the good weed?"

Paul nods.

"Well." Spider finishes the beer and tosses it into an oversized garbage can at the end of the bar. He wishes he could fast-forward through rest of Greta's set; he's heard enough to start imagining how much fuller his own music will sound once he steals this bass player with pot connections. The band would be easier to listen to if they were worse, but they're cursed with competence. The songs bleed into each other, varying only slightly in tempo, but at least Paul throws down for a second round of beer. Their last song turns out to be their best, by a distance Spider can't even measure: a faithful version of "Into the Mystic," with the bass player cutting loose and the drummer not hammering the groove to death. Ending the set like that means that the band is dumb, as well as dull; you should never end with a cover that makes it clear just how weak your originals are.

Afterward, Spider and Paul head to the tiny backstage area. The next band is All God's Chickens, a terrible white funk group Spider poached a lead guitarist from a few months ago. Asher proved to be allergic to actually practicing, and was quickly replaced by Newt. The guys in Chickens still haven't forgiven Spider, so he ducks his head and stares at the graffiti on the wall of the shared dressing room as they shuttle their gear back and forth. When only the Greta guys are left in the room, Spider continues to hang back for a while, watching the the bass player, Danny, interact with the rest of the band. Everyone else seems more excited about how the set went, which Spider is relieved to see: a good player also has to have good taste, and he's hoping Danny realizes how average Leave Greta Alone is. He's also relieved that only the two guitarists really seem like they're friends; it's much harder to steal players when they're emotionally invested in their current band.

When Paul motions, Spider goes over to join him and Danny. "Great playing," he says, shaking Danny's hand. "Really. You held the whole thing together. Fucking Elmer's Glue."

"Thanks," Danny mumbles, like he doesn't know how to respond to compliments. Is it possible he doesn't know how good he is? "Paul's been telling me how much fun it is to work with you."

Spider shrugs casually. "I have my moments. Just wish we had a real fucking drummer, you know?"

Danny smacks Paul's shoulder. "Well, you know the easiest way to find a drummer in Athens, right?"

Spider grins, always ready for a new drummer joke. "No, how?"

"Call Domino's."

The banter continues for a few minutes, and then Paul seems to sense Spider is ready to move things along. Anticipation: another good skill for a drummer to have. "We were just wondering where we could go to test Danny's new... toys."

Spider grins. As if any of them, in the dingy dressing room of the Color Box, had to speak in code about getting stoned. "Well, we can go play with his toys at my house," he says.

Spider helps Danny load his gear into his Oldsmobile, casually bullshitting about the music scene's ups and downs, while Paul gets his car so they can caravan to Spider's place. He's trying not to ask too many questions too quickly; he doesn't want the night to begin to feel like a job interview.

That's what it is, of course, and Paul knows it. "You're really gonna replace Shannon, aren't you?" he asks, as soon as the two of them are alone.

Spider shrugs. "We've had this talk before."

"Yeah, but I thought she was, like, still on trial."

"Really? You really think she can get where she needs to be? And not just her tits, but her playing?"

"She might get there."

"You want to gamble on that, Mr. Play-the-40-Watt-now?"

Paul groans, checking the rearview mirror to make sure Danny is still behind them. "She quit two other bands to be exclusive for us, man. I feel bad."

"Me, too," Spider says. He mainly says this to sound nicer than he really is. "But don't you want a better bass player to lock in with?"

"Yeah. But I'm tired of firing people. Brad, John, Eddie." He lists the names of their previous bass players sadly. "Now Shannon? And what if Danny doesn't work out?"

Spider doesn't admit he probably couldn't have named all the bass players they've tried. "First we need to see if he even wants it."

"And if he does? And quits Greta, and then you decide he's not good enough?"

"Then I guess we look again." Conversations like this add to the worry Spider had about Paul's pursuit of a college degree. Does Paul think they can get what they want and be nice to everyone? "This is more than just a good time, right? This is my life. And I thought you wanted it to be yours, too."

Like every drummer, Paul taps when he's nervous, and his fingers are pounding the steering wheel around 140 bpm. "I just hate screwing people."

"So do I. But I hate the idea of fucking this band up even more," he adds as they pull up to his house. How come drummers never know when to stop talking?

The house is one of those small, rectangular ranches that spread across Athens in the 1950s. He lives in what used to be the dining room, but it's cheap, and he sees no reason to pay more just to have a closet, or a door instead of a curtain—not as long as his housemates keep letting him use the basement for practices. All their neighbors are also in bands, or so old they don't hear very well, so there's not even a cut-off time for loud noise. So, while there's a faint smell of mildew whenever he enters the house, and none of them has ever run the vacuum cleaner that came with the place, he's never felt so at home.

It's hard for him to remember how nervous he'd been on the drive down from Philly. He was hoping to find a world of geeks and misfits, all inspired by the R.E.M. explosion, but what if he just met the same assholes who walked the halls of Central High? Listening to mixtapes he'd made just for the trip, he worried, for the first time, about his own music. What if he got to Athens and he found out the music in his head wasn't better than the music other people heard in theirs? Dylan, Strummer, Costello, Mitchell,

Lennon, even Stevie Wonder: all through the long drive, none of his heroes offered solace, only taunts.

His anxiety wasn't eased when he arrived at his first apartment. The guys who lived there had sounded cool on the phone, but in the real world, they were three months behind in their rent, and spent most of their days fighting with each other, their pot dealers, and the angry woman in the apartment below. For two days Spider hid in his room, afraid his loser roommates would pawn his guitars and amp as soon as he left. His father, of all people, saved him. The letter arrived on day three, slid under his door by one of the stoners. It took him a moment to place the handwriting—had he ever seen more than just a few words of his father's scrawl?—and the letter itself was so boring Spider grew annoyed. Talk of lawn care, business at his fucking HVAC company? Who takes the time to write this shit out? But it ended with a sentence about how proud his father was of Spider for striking out on his own, how he knew Spider had made the right choice. Between that sentence and the enclosed check, Spider knew his old man had come as close to showing actual emotion as he could.

And the check allowed him to pack up and leave, skipping out on his agreement to stay for six months. He moved into the Travelodge and started looking for somewhere new to live. There were cockroaches in the hallway, creatures so large they should've had to pay for their own rooms, and their existence made him wonder if Georgia could be a place anyone could actually survive. Hanging at the Globe one night, though, he started talking to Ryan, one of the bartenders, and learned he and his roommate were looking for someone willing to rent what was really a small, unused dining room. He knew he'd found the right place as soon as he examined their extensive, and relatively well-curated, record collections. (Bonus points for *The Hissing of Summer Lawns* and *Sketches of Spain*, but the lack of any Sly Stone was a crime, and the chaotic filing system was depressing; the record collection was the one part of the house you should devote time to keeping organized.)

Once he could stop worrying about where he would live, he felt the rush of having complete control of his life for the first time. He slept as little or as much as he wanted. No longer forced to live according to the ridiculous schedule the rest of the world created (teens in class by 7:30 a.m.? Really?), he discovered his personal day started around noon and ended somewhere around 4 or 5 in the morning. And since the record store he worked at didn't open until noon, that was perfect. He also learned he could eat pizza several times a day and not gain any weight, and that twenty hours a week at minimum wage, combined with stray checks from home, could give him enough money to live. Ryan, the more stable of his two new roommates, also taught him how to scrape the resin from a bong.

When he walks in with Paul and Danny he's relieved to see that Ryan and Lisa—the latest in a rotating series of third roomies—are both out. Ryan would have just bogarted the pot, and his staring would probably have freaked Danny out: skinny, dark hair, clean-shaven, and quiet, Danny was just Ryan's type. Ryan kept saying he was bi, but Spider had never seen him with a girl. Spider didn't mind, though, not when he could earn a few extra days to pay his rent just by smiling a lot and walking around in his boxers.

Lisa would have caused the opposite problem: she was so adorable Paul and Danny would both have been obsessed with impressing her— even after Spider introduced her as Lisa the Lesbian. Spider still tried, too, even though he knew he had zero chance of scoring. Why are lesbians always so fucking cute?

Spider leads them into the living room. Paul likes to be in charge of prepping the weed, and takes his usual spot in the middle of the couch. Eagerly getting his rolling papers and lighter out of his pockets and laying them on the table, he looks like a surgeon assessing his tools. Spider's job is to select good music and keep the pitcher of cold water full. So while Danny and Paul inspect the pot, Spider cues up *Marquee Moon* on the turntable. It's a record he could listen to any time, sober or stoned, but he also wants to test Danny. Anyone who doesn't know Television, and who can't appreciate the way they merged guitar craziness with intense lyrics and melodies, would be hard for Spider to take seriously.

Paul always makes a big deal of examining a new bag of pot closely, as if he knows what the hell he's talking about. Danny looks a little uncomfortable as Paul rambles on about consistency and texture, though he does give a nod of approval when "See No Evil" begins. Spider can't tell if Danny's uneasy because he's a nervous pot dealer, or because he doesn't know Spider, or because he doesn't think the Leave Greta Alone gig went well. He's just hoping Paul shuts the fuck up soon, because he wants Danny to relax, and hang out.

Luckily, the mood lightens as soon as the first joint is passed around; the pot is as good as Danny said it would be. By the time "Friction" starts blaring in the background the whole room tilts, and the three of them are unable to stop laughing about the fact that they're all laughing so hard. Spider asks a few questions about Leave Greta Alone, open-ended and bland, but intended to help him figure out whether or not Danny is happy. It sounds like his six months with Greta is the longest Danny's stuck with a band, but it also sounds like he's just trying to talk himself into thinking they're good, with phrases like "getting there" and "working some shit out."

"Well, all I can tell ya," Paul says, "is that you know when it's right. I mean, when you're playing with the right people?" He grins, and then exhales and closes his eyes. "Fuck. It's better than..." His voice drifts off.

"Than fucking," Spider finishes.

"Than fucking, yes. Exactly."

They lapse into silence after that, everyone aware that the title track, the last song on side one, is working through its third chorus. They're less than a minute away from Tom Verlaine unleashing one of the best guitar leads in rock history. Spider watches Danny's face during the breakdown that serves as runway for the solo, and he knows that look: it's the look of someone who wants to be a part of something bigger and better but doesn't know how to get there. It's the look Spider's pretty sure he wore until he met Paul.

Spider's been so lost in thought he's surprised when the singing comes back in, that last verse that magically fades out. He loves the idea that the band is still playing the song, in some alternate, better universe. It seems like the record just started, and it also seems like it's been hours since that guitar solo began. Music can do that, he learned as soon as he began really listening to it: music can create this vortex of time, where things can speed up, or slow down. Or sometimes both, simultaneously. Looking at Danny and Paul he can tell by their dazed eyes and slouched bodies that they've also been somewhere else. He waits until he hears the click of the cartridge return before he speaks.

"Supposedly that was a first take."

"Fuck me." Paul sits up and reaches for some water. "Really?"

"I believe it," Danny says. He's still leaning back, rubbing his eyes. "I love how it almost falls apart a couple of times, but never, like, completely falls apart. Like they know they can let it all hang out, since it's only their first swing."

Spider nods. He loves talking about the way songs he loves were recorded, but those same stories just make him anxious to get into a real studio with a real band. Soon. "That's it, man. You can hear them all walking out to the ledge, peering over, but never letting each other fall."

"I know it's great to be here, now," Danny says, "but I also know it'll never be fucking New York in the '70s. Can you imagine?"

"Jesus," Paul says, nodding. "Going to CBGB's and seeing these guys in their fucking prime."

"Thing is, as great as it is to be here now," Spider says, "I also think the time will come to move on. You know? Not New York," he continues, carefully hinting at the plan he's started working out in his head the last few months—a plan he's still trying to sell to Paul. "But, like, Boston. Close enough to play New York. Closer to the center of everything."

"You'd do that?" Danny sounds interested, if a little nervous.

"Maybe?" Spider shrugs. No need to get into too many details yet; every time they'd poached a new bass player he'd been sure they had the missing piece, only to be proven wrong. He's still angry at himself for

Shannon: he'd always worked so hard to keep his dick from screwing up his music. "First we have to get this line-up fixed, record some fucking music."

"It's like the Manhattan Project, your fucking band," Danny says, laughing. "Like you're building some A-bomb to drop on the world."

Spider laughs. "You just wrote the first marketing slogan, man. Thanks."

Paul drains his glass of water in a single, extended swallow, burping as he slams the empty glass down on the coffee table. "Jesus. That is some good fucking weed."

Danny grins. "If I'd known how strong this shit was, I wouldn't have sold it to you assholes."

"So we should roll another?" Paul says, laughing as he reaches for the bag.

"Not for me, man," Danny answers slowly. "I am fully scattered, covered, and smothered."

Spider grins. Must be a Southern boy, with a smooth Waffle House reference. That's why Boston scares him a little. "I think I'm good, too," he says.

"OK, then, flip to side two? Got any beers?"

Danny shrugs, as if he's agreeable if nothing better comes along, but Spider has a better idea. "No, man. You're thinking small. After a song like that? All I wanna do is play."

Danny's face lights up. "Yup, same. I wish I could play right now."

Paul bursts out laughing. "Dude, you know we practice here, right?"

Danny looks around. The main floor of the house isn't even 1000 square feet. "Where?"

"Downstairs," Spider says. "Everything's all set up."

The idea of playing makes all three of them move faster, like they'd suddenly found a good line of coke to snort. The limp, stoned feeling gives way to sharp, quick actions. Paul leads Danny downstairs, to get him set up, and Spider calls Newt, to see if he can come over. He knows this is the last step in Danny's audition and wants to hear how he sounds with the whole band. Newt's roomie says he's playing a frat party, though, and Spider hangs up the phone a little depressed; given how talented Newt is, it's as big a waste as filling the party kegs with expensive champagne.

His mood lifts again as soon as he gets downstairs. It should feel like cheating on a girlfriend, seeing Danny wear Shannon's bass, and watching him fiddle with the settings of her amp, but as soon as he starts tuning it's obvious how much more ownership he has of the rig. Even with everyone stoned, there's already more focus than he usually feels in the practice room.

Or maybe it's just that he doesn't want to sleep with Danny, so his own mind can be a little clearer.

"So?" Paul says, stretching his arms as he sits down behind the kit. "What should we play?"

Danny starts riffing on the "Taxman" bass line, and Spider grins at the vivid flash of memory he has every time he feels that low D rumble in his stomach. Sitting with his father, listening to those Beatles records over and over again.

"Jesus," Danny says, pausing to tweak his tuning, "that always sounds so good when I'm stoned. One of those licks that was, like, alive before the world started."

"Then let us honor that lick," Spider says. He grins, and does the one-two-three-four-one-two opening, a piece of mimicry he has always been proud of. They roll into the song like a well-practiced tribute band, Paul in command of that not-too-fast-not-too-slow groove, and Danny completely nailing the McCartney bass lines. The next two-and-a-half minutes of music are among the best Spider's had since he moved to Athens. Standing inside the sound as if it were a glass elevator hurtling up into the dark night, he knows this feeling could be caused as much by Danny's pot as his bass playing. But it's so satisfying it doesn't matter either way. Danny even steps up to Newt's mic to do the call-and-response: "If you drive a car-car... " The only challenge comes during the guitar solo, when Spider has to decide how to fill in the gap. For a split second he thinks of just scatting the lead, but everything is sounding so good, he doesn't want to go for comedy. So he does his best to just play a solo himself, something he rarely does, and he's surprised at how satisfied he is with the result. Messy, and chaotic, but also kind of sharp and intense. And why not? McCartney plays it on the record, after all. Once again, a guitar lead from someone who isn't a guitar virtuoso serves the song best.

As they hit the last chord, Paul does a little tom roll, and all three of them slam down at the same moment. Yeah, it's a cheesy rock cliché, but Spider knows that when everyone actually ends at the same time by instinct, it's a good sign. He doesn't even miss Newt; turns out, a three-piece can sound quite full, even during a guitar solo. Wasn't the strongest geometric shape the triangle, anyway?

Paul and Danny can feel it, too, he can tell. Danny's screwing around with other iconic bass lines, seeing what else they can just play without thinking about it, and Paul's nodding along in encouragement. Spider feels like it's already time to move on to the next part of the audition, though. He starts playing the opening riff for "Behind Door Number Two" and looks at Paul. "What do you think, Paulie boy? Wouldn't it be nice to hear this one with some real bass?"

There's just the slightest bit of hesitation in Paul's eyes before he nods. That loyalty, even to Shannon, even this late in the game. It's good to know it's still there, and also good to know Paul knows when to say goodbye.

"I don't know that one," Danny says, turning to study Spider's hands, fingers already drifting to root notes he can grab hold of. "Who's it by?"

"It's one of mine," Spider says, grinning. "And I can't wait to hear how it sounds."

Listen Again

Boston, 1995

No one listens to drummers when they're not behind a kit. Paul has known this since he was twelve years old and playing in his first band, but it still pisses him off. It's happening again as he sits in the cramped control room of Cheap Sh*t Studios, sharing the worn-out loveseat with Danny: it's one in the morning, and for over an hour no one's taken anything he's said seriously.

Paul, Danny, and Spider have spent more time talking about "Pay Me Now" than playing it. All of them agree the track isn't working; even Stanley Gaines, the anemic engineer included in the studio fees, knows it isn't working. What no one can agree on is why.

"I just think it sounds... stiff." Spider has been repeating this message for over an hour.

Stanley nods slowly, like he's just heard something new and insightful. "Stiff. Yeah. I see where you're coming from. Thing is, it sounds just fine when you're in there playing." He points a black Sharpie through the glass window to the studio where Monkeyhole's gear is set up.

At first Paul found Stanley's faux Zen insights illuminating, but now he's convinced that the man never actually says anything. He repeats his own suggestion. "Why don't we just try a take without the click?" They're tracking the songs to a click track, to keep the tempo consistent, but on songs with lots of drum fills it's harder to make that sound natural.

"No click?" Stanley repeats. "I see where you're coming from."

Danny shakes his head. He's been a pain the ass all night, as far as Paul is concerned. "I don't think the click's the problem." Even when he talks, he doesn't look up from the *Rolling Stone* he's been holding since they came in from their last take. The cover photo of Michael Jackson and Paul McCartney only gets more annoying, the more Paul has to look at it.

Spider nods. "Danny's right. The tempo's fine. All the parts are fine. It's just sounding, you know. Stiff."

"Well, that's why we should loosen it up a bit," says Paul. Being exhausted doesn't help a circular argument like this straighten itself out.

They all come straight to the studio after a day at their various dead-end jobs to take advantage of the studio's reduced night rate. Even with this "cheaper shit" time, as Spider calls it, they only have enough money for six recording sessions to track and mix the five songs planned for their first EP. The pressure of such limited time is increasing the tension. "Pay Me Now" is one Spider keeps calling "extra important," because he imagines it most likely to get some radio play. With each take, Paul can feel the pressure growing. Now everyone's too worried about fucking up to relax and just play the song.

"We've tracked everything else with a click," Spider says. "So that's not the problem."

"No, but time works differently in this one," Paul says. "The groove needs to drive a little harder in the chorus, but, then, like, the bridge is a little more... floating." He pauses, wishing he could explain things to everyone else as clearly as he can to himself. "If we don't speed up and slow down just a little bit at some points, like, breathe, then it's not gonna sound natural."

"Time works differently. Speed up and slow down to sound natural." Spider shakes his head, as if in disbelief. "Yeah, maybe. Or maybe we just haven't played it right yet."

Paul leans back as far as he can. "Fine. I mean, what the fuck, I'm only the drummer."

"Oh, please." Spider rolls his eyes. "I said 'we' hadn't played it right— not just 'you.'"

An awkward silence follows. The only sound is Stanley tapping his Sharpie against the mixing console, softly mumbling "Stiff, stiff." Paul is just about to suggest they call it a night when Stanley asks, "What do you call a guy that hangs around musicians?" He's already laughing at the punchline.

"What?" Danny asks from behind his magazine.

"A drummer," Stanley says.

Paul groans. Stanley only has one way of dealing with studio tension— a collection of drummer and bass player jokes—but Paul has to admit it usually works. He decides to see if the night can still be salvaged. "How do you know it's a drummer at your door?"

Stanley, still laughing, asks, "How?"

"The knocking speeds up and slows down."

That one gets Danny to put down *Rolling Stone*, and even makes Spider smile. He spins his chair and stares down at the sixteen-track recording console, wearing the fully engaged look he has onstage. "Stanley, Stanley," he says, tapping the side of the console. "What do you say we listen to this motherfucker again?"

Paul Wells was sent home with a note from his teacher at the end of his first day of first grade. Mrs. Pinkham prided herself on her orderly classroom, so these annoying habits of young Mr. Wells—the constant tapping of his fingertips on his desk, to say nothing of his insistence on turning freshly sharpened no. 2 pencils and watercolor brushes into drumsticks—had to stop. Immediately.

"I don't remember tapping," Paul insisted. His mother and father stood in front of him, passing the note back and forth. He would always remember how unusual it felt to see the two of them standing together; by the time he started kindergarten they were rarely in the same room, preferring to send messages from one end of their brick ranch house to the other via their only child. "I don't remember doing it."

His father reached out and grabbed Paul's hands with his own. "Damnit, you're doing it now," he said, twisting Paul's hand.

Paul was startled to see his thumb and pinky tapping against each other. Staring at his hand in disbelief, he heard, for the first time, a rhythm playing in some deep corner of the back of his head. His fingers were keeping time to a soundtrack he hadn't even known he was hearing, as if they were operating separately from the rest of his body. Had they been doing this his whole life?

From that moment on Paul became very aware of his hands. Even when they weren't moving, they wanted to, sometimes so desperately they hurt. He learned when it was safe to give in to those urges: the fantastic release of recess, for example, and Tuesday and Thursday art class, when there was so much noise he could let his fingers ripple across the bottom of the desk. He also learned when it was not safe—above all during story-time, which Mrs. Pinkham took very seriously. During story-time Paul sat on his hands, trying to ignore their throbbing.

There were moments when his mind wandered, however, and he lost control. Such moments led to more letters sent from Mrs. Pinkham to his parents, more talks about what he should and shouldn't do at school. By the end of first grade, his hands and Mrs. Pinkham's frayed nerves collaborated on what would prove to be the epitaph of Paul's entire educational experience: *Paul's mind is sharp but prone to wandering*, his teacher wrote on his final report card in perfectly shaped cursive writing. *His constant fidgeting is a challenge to himself and his fellow students.*

Luckily, Paul had what every fidgety child should have: a funny uncle. When Uncle Joe entered a room he immediately swooped down to pick up whatever child was closest, using his arms to swim that lucky kid through the air as he made appropriately goofy noises. Not only did he have dozens of bad riddles and puns to share, he had an endless appetite for whatever bad riddles and puns you had come across since you'd last seen him. He laughed out loud even if they failed to make sense, as Paul's often did.

Q: "Why did the road cross the road?"

A: "To visit his friend, the road!"

Uncle Joe also had a tendency to do the opposite of whatever his brother-in-law—Paul's father—wanted. When he heard about the problems with Mrs. Pinkham, Uncle Joe said that "fidgety" just meant energetic, and energy was a thing to encourage in a boy.

Halfway through Paul's long battle with Mrs. Pinkham, Uncle Joe told Paul he was taking him out for dinner on his birthday. This meant a trip to Pistilli's: spaghetti with meatballs, fountain Cokes that tasted sweeter than bottled, and chocolate ice cream in a cold silver dish for dessert. When the day finally came, Paul was annoyed to learn of a surprise side trip on their way to dinner. As they pulled into the strip mall that held the town's ShopRite and post office, he feared the worst. "This will only take a minute," he imagined his uncle saying, "a minute" for adults always translating into what felt like hours. Instead, however, his uncle parked in an empty spot in front of Fast Freddy's Music and turned to Paul. "Well, you better get in there," he said.

Paul stared at the neon sign above the door. "Fast" seemed to glow brighter than "Freddy's," and "Music" barely glowed at all. "Go in?" he asked, suddenly nervous.

"Your first drum lesson starts at 5:00."

Paul turned to his uncle.

"That's right." His uncle pointed to Paul's hands. "We have to find something for those to do that won't get you in trouble."

Paul looked back at the door. "But you're coming with me, right?"

"Oh, no." Uncle Joe leaned his car seat back. "I'm gonna take me a quick nap, dream of Pistilli's."

Paul would always remember how it felt to walk in by himself. Opening the door was terrifying, he was so convinced that everything he said and did was going to be wrong, but the first thing he saw were drum sets, ready to be hit. That feeling, like he'd somehow found a place he was supposed to be, would stay with him longer than any of the specifics of his first lessons. In fact, it hadn't taken Paul long to realize that Scooter Owens, the acne-pocked teen who taught him for three years, couldn't keep proper time if his arms were covered in new Rolex watches. That hadn't mattered, though. Scooter taught Paul how to hold his sticks, and to never be afraid of the drums, and that was all he needed to learn.

After another listen and a quick game of ping pong to blow off steam, Spider gives in and they try recording "Pay Me Now" without the click track. After two takes they call it a night, since Paul thinks it sounds much better, Spider doesn't, Danny no longer answers any questions, and Stanley can see where everyone's coming from. What they all agree on is the need to take the next night off, so they can come in and listen with fresh ears.

When Paul walks into the apartment he and Danny share, he's suddenly lonely. Yes, Danny was a pain in the ass all night, but Paul still wishes he hadn't gone to his girlfriend's. His head is filled with the kind of questions you need to say out loud to make them go away. What if the music they're recording is not what they want it to be? God, what if it sucks? Or, what if it's great, but no one listens? What if they're spending all this time working so hard on something that's just going to come out and get ignored? They all keep saying they're in this for the Music, but would they really keep killing themselves if some genie from the future came and said, "You know what, guys? No one gives a shit. No one *ever* listens."

Paul likes to think he would, that the Music is really all that matters, but there are moments he's not so sure.

He hits play on the blinking answering machine and walks over to the fridge. The machine, which came with the apartment, is so old it sometimes goes days without working, but when it does work, it allows people to leave as long a message as they want—if there's blank space on the tape, the person on the other end can keep talking. Spider went for five minutes once. When Paul hears Leila's voice, he shuts the refrigerator door and stares at the picture of Nixon and Elvis that Danny taped up. "Hey Paul, it's me. How's life in the Little City? Listen, give me a call when you get this. And no, I don't care how late it is. Just call! K?"

Leila. He slowly moves to the kitchen table and sits down just within reach of the phone. Leila was the one woman he pursued in all his years in Boston, albeit in a style Spider declared "So subtle it's oblique," which is probably why they never went on anything resembling a date. Six months ago she moved to New York City for a job at one of those expensive magazines devoted to the insider gossip and numbers that drove the music industry. She hadn't called since, though he had twice. Each time they talked about him visiting "once she was settled," but he stopped calling when he realized he felt worse after each conversation.

Leila. She answers on the second ring, and promptly scolds him for taking so long to call her back. When he tells her he's been in the studio, she feigns interest. "Really! How's it going?"

"Great, great," he says, wishing he had a more exciting word to use. Leila never approved of Paul's devotion to Monkeyhole. As the two of them stood together in various Boston clubs talking about music, off and on for two years, Leila went from quietly observing that Spider wasn't your classic front man—"A little too geeky, right? A little too awkward or something, you think?"—to loudly urging Paul, the night before she left town, to consider all his options.

"Well, look, I can't talk long," she says. "I have a few people over."

"Oh. Sorry." For the first time he notices a Marvin Gaye record playing in the background, amidst the sound of clinking wineglasses and giddy chatter.

"Thing is, you need to get up here tomorrow. Need to. There's a 9:35 Amtrak that gets you into Penn Station by 1:50. That'll give you enough time to get to Irving Plaza by 3:00."

It's the invitation he's been waiting for, but something in her voice makes him wonder about her motivation. She sounds too adamant, even for his fantasies. "Tomorrow? Why tomorrow?"

"The drummer for Ebenezer's Screwed went into detox." She speaks quickly, and Paul imagines her being tugged back onto the dance floor by Marvin Gaye himself. "They hired a studio guy for a few gigs, but they're gonna need someone long-term. Rest of the tour, maybe the next record. The manager owes me a favor, so long story short, you have an audition tomorrow at 3:00."

To allow himself a chance to digest all that information, he stalls with a short cough. Ebenezer's Screwed is one of the Bands of the Moment, thanks to the video for "Kids Are For Tricks." The animated bunny from the old Trix cereal commercials plays a starring role, chasing after the photogenic band members in an increasingly threatening manner. The bunny's image is now all over Ebenezer T-shirts, helping them sell out clubs across the country.

"You there, Paul?"

"I have to work." Sadly, it's the first thing he thinks of. To survive until the band starts making steady income, he works at Data Duty, typing details from police reports into databases accessed by insurance companies. The best thing about the job is that he's allowed to wear his Discman. While the horrific police reports unnerved him at first—husbands and wives assaulting each other, hit-and-run drivers steamrolling small children—they now wash over him, as his fingers move to the music filling his head.

"Come on, Paul. Think no one in America is going to call in sick tomorrow?"

"But I have a band," he says. Even having the conversation feels like having an affair.

"Listen. Paul. I know you have a band, and your loyalty is adorable. But you need to decide if you want to be a typist or a drummer."

By the time he entered high school his classmates all knew Paul was a drummer, the same way they knew that Valerie Bischoff had told her English teacher she wanted to be a nun, or that Sherri Ferguson had let Stanley Reagan unzip her pants and touch her red underwear. School became a bearable place, thanks to discovering other kids who could analyze the newest Elvis Costello record in ways they never could analyze *The Scarlet Letter*.

These were also the kids who'd become guitarists, or bass players—or at least were willing to play bass, given the excessive number of guitarists. They formed a series of bands with shifting, incestuous lineups, and devoted themselves to learning the songs of their musical heroes. Paul filled his notebooks with doodles of potential logos, and possible set lists for the shows they all assumed would someday happen.

Like most teen males he was initially drawn to the Canadian rock trio Rush, with their dramatic, overly complicated music. Rush's drummer, Neil Peart, became Paul's first drum hero, so his first band, the six-piece Mona Moonshine, played lots of Rush. Mona Moonshine also played lots of the Who, allowing Paul to flail around his drum kit like Keith Moon, only pausing his steady stream of tom fills and cymbal crashes to play a basic backbeat when his arms got tired. In his senior year, the softer touch of Stewart Copeland, drummer for the Police, opened up a whole new rhythmic world. He ditched Mona Moonshine for Colt 45, a hyperactive trio that learned the first two Police records in their entirety; finally Paul understood that there was actually a lot of music to be made even if you stayed on the hi-hat for more than a few bars at a time.

The one constant drumming influence was John Bonham. Paul hadn't paid any attention to Led Zeppelin until he heard about their drummer dying, but once he started listening he couldn't stop. Even "Stairway to Heaven," which didn't have drums for what seemed like forever, revealed more on each listen than Paul had ever learned at Fast Freddy's. From its simple-but-brilliant intro fill, which *always* lasted a beat longer than you expected, to those crazy syncopated snare riffs at the end, the performance was one huge lesson in how a drummer should serve the song. It took Paul hours of practicing—his headphones secured by an old tie so they wouldn't fall off—to master it. The playing was heavy yet light, toying with time in ways you could only appreciate when you listened closely. Time moved in mysterious ways on Zeppelin records, seeming to speed up and slow down ever so slightly at just the right moments, and you could tell that Bonham was the one pushing time forward or holding it back.

During his last year of high school Paul also discovered some of the other joys of playing music, thanks to Colt 45's performance at the senior pool party. That night Anne Babyak was so impressed with his jazz-like fills during "Walking on the Moon" that she later let him unhook her bra— amazingly soft and covered in little flowers—and use "those wonderful hands" on something other than drums. His ego later received another boost from Uncle Joe, who had agreed to serve as a chaperone when the party looked like it was going to be cancelled by some nervous parents. He hung around the far fringes of the pool house, where Colt 45 set up, but the next time he came over he made a point of sitting Paul down and telling him how good, how really good, he had played. Years later, at Uncle Joe's funeral, Paul heard that conversation again so vividly in his head that he wondered, for the one time in his life, if there really were ghosts.

In spite of these minor triumphs, Paul's parents did not like his plan to play drums for a living. Even the average students from his high school were expected to go to college, a fact Paul's father spelled out clearly during one of their post-divorce dinners. In response, Paul delivered one of the longer monologues of his seventeen years, explaining that he was tired of classes and studying and feeling like an idiot for forgetting things he had just heard an hour ago in a lecture, and just wanted to work on something he was good at: playing the drums. His father calmly put down his Kentucky Fried Chicken leg and wiped his cheek. "You're going to fucking college," he said, slowly and clearly. "Now hand me another biscuit."

The Biscuit Incident, as Uncle Joe called it, became the stuff of family legend. The biscuit Paul hurled at his father had a greater impact than planned, thanks to the muscles built up by years of drumming and the biscuit's density, no doubt the result of over-kneading by an apathetic KFC worker. The size and exact hue of Paul's father's black eye varied with the telling, but all agreed that there was a black eye. After a series of loud phone calls, Paul promised to get a college degree and his parents promised to stop telling him what to do after that.

So Paul went as far as his disappointing 2.06 GPA and his surprising 1370 SATs would take him. In the summer of 1989 he drove Uncle Joe's old Dodge Dart Swinger—loaded up with his Gretsch drum kit, one suitcase of clothes, and four boxes of records and cassettes—to Athens, Georgia. He had never been to the South, but he had every R.E.M. record and figured there had to be a million bands floating around their hometown.

After Paul hangs up with Leila he restlessly wanders the empty apartment. He's only considering going because he knows he'll never get the job. He really wants to see her, and can't imagine turning down an actual request to come visit, but it still seems like cheating on a girlfriend. He already has a band. He's the drummer for Monkeyhole.

A band, he hears Leila's voice replying, that dicked him around all night in the studio. A band that might never make a dime. As he brushes his teeth he avoids making eye contact with himself. Not just because he knows he will go tomorrow, but because he wonders, for the first time, if he's really a drummer at all. Maybe the problems in the studio tonight were his fault—maybe what he wants to be and what he really is are two different things.

When the alarm wakes him up the next morning, Danny still hasn't come home, but Paul doesn't bother to leave a note. Last night's self-doubt has been replaced by anger at the way he was treated, and he figures it's better to just take the whole day off from everything Monkeyhole. When he calls in sick his news is accepted easily, and he takes that as further evidence he's doing the right thing.

On the train to Penn Station he listens repeatedly to "Kids Are For Tricks," the song Ebenezer's Screwed wants drummers to audition with; luckily Danny had the CD, in the stack of promos he got from his job at Planet Records. It follows the classic Nirvana formula, alternating quiet verses and loud choruses. It's not awful, even if he forgets it as soon as it ends. As far as the drumming goes, his first concern is tempo. The much louder, much more manic choruses of "Kids" will tempt everyone to speed up when they play it live, though the recording sounds mechanical. While some bands expect the drummer to serve as an anchor, holding the tempo in place, others prefer to occasionally speed up at the end of a fast song, and excite the crowd. Time works differently for everyone onstage; he'll have to figure out what the guys in Ebenezer want by watching their body language. Guitarists who twitch their legs usually like things to speed up a little, and bass players who stand rooted in place usually like to lock in on a tempo and stay there.

The other big question is style. The song wasn't recorded the way Paul would play it—spots where a simple snare fill would be enough are overwhelmed by complicated rolls across too many toms; unnecessary cymbal hits clog the verses; and even the basic beat is cluttered with distracting hi-hat flourishes. It reminds Paul of being a high school freshman, so anxious to show how much he could play that he didn't listen first, to hear how much the song needed him to play.

After half a dozen listens he hasn't decided exactly how to play the song, but calms his nerves by reminding himself he doesn't even want the gig; as long as he doesn't make a complete ass of himself in front of Leila, and she gives him a few hugs, the whole trip will be worth it. Paul puts *Zoso* into his Walkman, skips to the last track, and closes his eyes. Bonham always has the answers. "When the Levee Breaks" comes on, and the enormous boom of the kick drum and crack of his snare drown out all his doubts.

Paul leans his head against the window of the train. He can feel the rhythm of the tracks reverberating on the glass, creating a complicated counter-rhythm to Bonham's pounding. He wonders if he'll ever be on a record someone listens to when feeling alone, his playing literally wrapping around their head. "If it keeps on rainin', levee's goin' to break," moans Robert Plant. "When the levee breaks I'll have no place to stay."

Paul met Spider his second year in Athens. They didn't meet in a Physics or British Lit class, or in the bedroom of a girl they were both unknowingly dating, though Spider would later enjoy making up these variations of the story for anyone who asked. They met at Jilly's Pizza, where bands played on mismatched pieces of shag rug, shoehorned between an old Ms. Pac-Man machine and the hallway leading to the bathrooms.

Sophomore year Paul played in Kudzu, who had a regular Thursday slot at Jilly's. One night in January, between sets, Spider walked up and began to talk as if he already knew Paul.

"So tell me, man—what the fuck are you doing with these losers?"

Paul looked across the pizzeria at the other four members of Kudzu, all of whom were devoting their break to working a table of blonde freshmen. They'd asked Paul which one he'd wanted but he'd passed, already weary of young Southern girls whose names invariably ended in "i." He knew he should be defending his bandmates, but he also knew they were no better than the sea of other average musicians who'd migrated to Athens. "They're OK," he said, turning back to Spider.

"No," Spider said. "They're not. Any grown man who bothers to learn the chords to 'Feel Like Makin' Love,' never mind sings those words in public..." He shuddered before downing the rest of his Budweiser. "Well, anyone who can do that can't be a real fucking musician."

"Ah, people love that shit," he said, pointing at the decent-sized crowd. He liked to think a lot of them had come to see Kudzu.

"Oh, please," Spider said. His hair hung off his shoulders in a series of knots and tangles that rustled softly whenever his head moved. "These assholes won't even remember who they sleep with tonight, never mind you guys."

"Well, no one's making you stay," Paul said, sliding his foot in front of the beer cooler when Spider reached down to grab one.

"You're making me stay, man." Spider slapped Paul on his back again. "And for a drummer to keep me interested during 'Feel Like Making Fucking Love,' never mind yet another raping of 'Radio Free Europe,' is nothing less than a miracle." He shook his head. "A goddamn miracle."

Paul would later admit to Danny that he thought Spider was an asshole the first time they met, but he didn't mention that he kept talking to him only because his compliments had boosted Paul's ego. After Spider stayed for the third set and helped Paul load his drums into the Swinger he seemed like less of an asshole, and by the time he mentioned his current obsession with Television's *Marquee Moon*, an album Paul could never get anyone in Kudzu to listen to, Spider had become someone worth hanging out with.

The next day he dragged his kit over to the basement of the house Spider shared. He soon learned Spider had a much better voice than his name or hair would suggest, and, even better, he'd written a dozen songs that showcased that voice very well. Paul's hands knew exactly what to do during those songs, even though he had never heard them before. For the first time he wasn't trying to remember some other drummer's approach, deciding what to mimic and what to change, but writing his own parts. He and Spider played for hours that afternoon, and even without a bass player Paul knew that the music they created matched those distant, previously incomprehensible rhythms he'd been hearing since Mrs. Pinkham's class.

Spider already had a name for his band: Monkeyhole. There was no talking him out of it, either. "Monkey plus keyhole. Easy to remember without meaning anything!" He hadn't moved to Athens for UGA, but to find the rest of his band. For Paul, joining Monkeyhole meant trading the moneymaking Kudzu for a group that had never booked a gig—one that didn't even have a steady bass player yet, or a lead guitarist—but he didn't care. The music made him feel like he was a member of a band, not just a drummer. Like he belonged.

Spider also revealed to Paul the genius in Ringo Starr's playing. Poor Ringo, the butt of so many smart-ass high school musicians' jokes. Ringo, with his funny accent, stupid rings, and small drum kit. Six months into Paul's time in Monkeyhole, Spider was trying to explain the feel he wanted for a particular song when he suddenly snapped his fingers and said, "You know, like Ringo. Play it like Ringo would."

When Spider realized Paul thought the idea anyone would want to play like Ringo was hilarious practice immediately stopped. The two of them and their current bass player—an acne-pocked kid Spider poached from an R&B cover band, a decent player who would soon grow tired of not being paid—went upstairs to blast the Beatles. To silence Paul's specific criticism—"Ringo? He never rocks"—Spider started by playing the reprise of "Sergeant Pepper." This little two-minute song had always washed right past Paul, not much more than a stall before "A Day in the Life," but after two separate listens, with Spider pointing out how solid the groove was, and how much the drums sounded like they were right there in the room, in spite of the totally outdated recording equipment, Paul grudgingly admitted Ringo could sort of rock. With this new understanding, the fills in "Day" sounded more impressive, revealing layers he'd never noticed before. Ringo used the toms to deepen the groove at key points, sometimes even sounding like he was purposefully falling slightly behind the beat. And the shift in beats when McCartney sang "And I went into a dream" displayed a soft touch that Paul had never noticed before. He was a completely different drummer than Bonham, but they both found a way to stretch time when they needed to. When he said this, Spider nodded enthusiastically. "Because he plays the song, man," he said. "He doesn't play the drums: he plays the song. Some songs need more time."

Finally, in the summer of 1993, Paul Wells finished his degree at UGA with an unsurprising 2.2 GPA. While his graduation was as much a relief for his parents and their respective new spouses as it was for Paul, they didn't travel to Georgia for the ceremony. Paul didn't mind. All he wanted was for his father's check to clear, something the last two birthday checks had failed to do, and for his parents and step-parents and everyone who had ever urged him to try to "do better" to keep their end of the deal: now that he had a degree he could stuff in a box and forget about, he just wanted to go play the drums.

So Paul also skipped his graduation ceremony. The day after his last final, he, Spider, and Danny—the best bass player they'd ever had—loaded up a 1982 Ford van, purchased with the money from selling their own cars, and began the long drive to Boston. After four failed attempts to add a second guitarist they had decided they were a trio, perhaps the coolest form of all rock bands. A friend of Spider's knew the guy who booked some club called T.T. the Bear's Place, and they had a slot on a Wednesday night. As Spider said, lighting a joint when they crossed the Massachusetts border at three a.m., careers had been launched with much smaller first steps.

When he walks into Irving Plaza, Leila is waiting at the back bar for him. She's let her hair grow long, and her leather jacket looks like it organically sprang from her mocha skin. When they hug hello he lingers, enjoying the feel of her shoulders under his fingers and the press of her chest against his. Not until she pulls away does he look towards the stage. The guys in Ebenezer, their guitars hanging limply around their shoulders, are huddled in a small clump on the left side as four or five roadies mill around. On the drum riser is a tall, thick-bodied kid laughing a little too loudly. He can't be older than nineteen and looks strong enough to bench-press all three members of Monkeyhole.

"Is he the first or second?" Paul asks.

"Second."

"How was the first?" He's surprised by how nervous he suddenly feels. He doesn't want the gig, he reminds himself—just to play well and hug Leila at least one more time, when they say goodbye.

"Nothing to worry about," she says, wrapping her two hands around Paul's left arm and pulling it close to her chest. "They didn't even ask him to stick around for the show." She leads him to the back corner of the bar and quickly launches into a complicated story about apartment-sitting for her new boss. The sound of her voice, and the feel of her hands casually rubbing his arm as she talks, are enough to convince him he made the right choice in coming.

Just as Paul turns around to see what's happening onstage an unimposing figure he'd assumed was a roadie grabs the microphone at the center of the stage, then issues a loud four count to kick off "Kids Are For Tricks." Everything instantly sounds great. The surprisingly agile Muscle Drummer has learned the song note-for-note, including all the busy fills; the band is loud and assured. The lead singer, Ex-Why, goes full throttle for the empty club, holding his arms out during the chorus as if he truly expects a nonexistent mob to sing along.

When it's done, everyone quickly turns to offer the drummer handshakes and smiles; the kid's worked up a healthy sweat in four minutes, and looks ready to pose for his first press photo. Paul groans, lowering his head onto Leila's shoulder.

"Oh, he wasn't all that good," she says, rubbing his back.

"Not good—just perfect."

A booming voice calls out from the stage, in an almost comical British accent, "Leila, love? Is your mate here?"

"He's here, Conrad," she says, waving her arms. "Good luck," she whispers quickly before sending Paul off with a kiss on his cheek.

Taking a deep breath, he heads to the stage. He's introduced to a series of people whose names come much too quickly, and time begins to spin out of control; Paul can hear Spider warning him not to get caught in "the Vortex," his phrase for that moment when everyone in the band gets so hyper that their playing speeds up. He feels better as soon as he hides behind the drum set. He fine-tunes the set-up of the snare, stool, hi-hat, and bass pedal—as long as those are all in their proper positions he can play any set. As much to calm himself as to test the arrangement, he takes a deep breath and begins thumping out the opening to "When the Levee Breaks." The kit creates a deep, satisfying echo in the empty club, and he shuts his eyes to soak in all that volume and power. He's surprised to hear the bass and guitar come in at just the right moment, and opens his eyes to exchange smiles with the two Ebenezer members who'd started playing. They play the whole intro, only stopping when the other band members appear from the wings. Ex-Why's the last to take the stage, and after giving Paul a quick nod he counts off "Kids Are For Tricks."

The song locks in effortlessly. That minute of Zeppelin had allowed Paul to read the bassist's style (rock-steady, but not as locked-in as if playing to a metronome), and the rest of the band follows the rhythm section faithfully. He decides to just play the song as he hears it, skipping all the excessive fills and bringing the dynamics down in the last verse. Like Ringo, he thinks, a bit startled by the way that insight leads to a stray and fleeting image of Spider, happily lost in the moment onstage. "Like a dress fitting just right," he'd said. "With Ringo it's not always a fancy dress, you know? But it always fits right. Besides, the dress is just a way for you to dream about what's underneath."

The last chorus speeds up slightly, but the enthusiasm of the others onstage makes it clear they enjoy cutting loose. As the main riff repeats one more time, to end the song, he takes a chance and slows down just slightly. They all follow, and as the chords and cymbals ring out he suddenly realizes he's played a song with another band for the first time in... four years? When the bassist and guitarist come over, grinning, he feels a sudden rush of confidence, like some girl he'd been eyeing has just looked at him and smiled. After Paul thanks them and they begin to shuffle offstage, Ex-Why steps up onto the riser, cellphone in his hands. "Good job," he's saying as he dials. "Can you stick around for the show?"

His parents never timed their rare visits to Boston to coincide with a Monkeyhole gig. In truth, that was a relief for Paul. The kind of success they would understand—a spot on the *Today* show, or at least a gig at a clean, sold-out theater, over by ten—still eluded the band, and the last thing he wanted was to reignite old debates about what he should or shouldn't be doing. Uncle Joe did come to see him play, a few months before the band went into Cheap Sh*t Studios. By the end of the night, his uncle had moved down to the front of the stage, jumping in place with the other hundred enthusiastic fans, and Paul was glad the one family member he felt close to had seen him onstage.

Then, over breakfast the next morning, Paul learned Uncle Joe wasn't actually a relative.

They met at Cere's, Paul's favorite local coffee house, and Uncle Joe repeated all the praise he'd lavished on Paul just after the show. "I loved how you guys worked together—it was like the three of you would be playing even if the audience wasn't there. That's when I understood that you've found... your place, you know? You figured out exactly where you're supposed to be, all on your own. Well done."

That morning, with the lingering buzz of a good show ringing in his ears, and Cere's house blend warming his chest, Paul understood his uncle was right: he had found his place. "Thanks, Uncle Joe," he said. "It means a lot to me, you know. That you came to see me." He paused, and then added a thought he'd been hoping to have a chance to say for years. "I'm glad you're in my family."

His uncle grinned. "Well, that means a lot to me, Paul. But." He sighed. "You should know. I'm not technically a member of your family."

Paul's first thought, he was ashamed to remember later, had been that the incoming revelation must have something to do with him—that he was actually adopted, or the result of some accidental baby mix-up that had just been uncovered.

"Your mother's always called me her brother, but the truth is we're just friends. When my own family disowned me, your mother became my family."

"Wow. That sucks. Why did they... ?" Paul stopped. "No, you don't have to tell me." He kept his eyes focused on the man next to him, the man who'd not only understood Paul was different but had urged others to embrace that difference. "It doesn't matter. You're still my family." He smiled. "I mean, without you I might not even be playing."

"I know—your mother keeps reminding me." Uncle Joe smiled as he clasped Paul's arm. "I'm just glad you're so good at it. Otherwise I'd have a helluva lot of guilt to deal with."

After they finished their coffee, they strolled Paul's neighborhood of funky clothing shops and used bookstores for hours. The next time he saw his mother, at Uncle Joe's funeral, she'd told him how excited Joe had been when he called to tell her about his visit, how he'd reassured her that Paul was doing just what he needed to be doing. After the service, as he helped his mother serve Entenmann's and coffee to the dozens of people who squeezed into his childhood home to share funny stories about his funny Uncle Joe, Paul wondered if Joe's "real" family had any regrets. Later, helping his sad and slightly drunk mother up to the bedroom she'd spent several miserable years sharing with his father, he didn't have to wonder if she had any regrets. "I grew up hating my father," she'd told him after all the guests left, "and then I wound up marrying him."

The night of Joe's funeral was the last night he would sleep in his childhood bed. Lying there, listening to *Dark Side of the Moon* on his Discman as he tried to fall asleep, he decided the best you could hope for was that the family you happened to be born into didn't fuck you up so much you couldn't go out and find a new family of your own.

Before the show, he slips away for a slice of pizza with an excited Leila. She insists that his audition had been the best, and promises to grill Conrad, the manager, for information. When he asks her if she's dating Conrad she laughs, as if he'd asked if she planned to take up space travel. Moving to New York has given her a whole new language, one he doesn't quite understand; he wonders if he would if he spent more time with her. Which means he wonders, in spite of himself, if he would spend more time with her if he was playing with Ebenezer. They must be constantly coming to New York, to play, meet with their label, do press stuff... . For the first time since he'd walked out the door in the morning, he imagines taking the gig if it's offered. A wave of guilt passes over him, but he washes it away with a long swallow of Rolling Rock, and the memory of last night's painful recording session.

Backstage, he tries to act casual—talks Zeppelin and R.E.M. with the bass player, tries to be appreciative but casual when the guys in the band compliment him on the audition. A shocking number of roadies are camped out over the buffet, which includes cold cuts, beer, chips, and several plates of Hostess Snacks; for every band member, two or three gorgeous girls are milling around, fiddling with their ALL ACCESS laminates as if they're Golden Tickets for Wonka-land; and several band members are either talking on cellphones or to reporters with microphones. Monkeyhole certainly didn't tour in such a style—less popular bands were lucky to have a dressing room at all, never mind one big enough to actually get dressed in. A dressing room and a twelve pack meant someone in the club likes you. Touring like this would be a whole new experience, Paul realizes, another new language to learn. Opening his second package of Yodels, he understands how powerful the language could be.

He watches the show from several different points in the club. The kids in the crowd are rabid, thrashing around in constant motion, barely pausing to breathe between songs. The band is tight, and the drummer filling in is clearly a pro, but most of the show is lifeless. When Ebenezer finally plays "Kids Are For Tricks" to open their set of encores, the crowd's singing drowns out Ex-Why during the chorus. Paul's mind wanders frequently, though, and he can't help but think the same is true for a portion of the crowd—and even some of the band members, who all disappear in the shadow of Ex-Why.

After losing track of Leila, he finds her at the back bar, drinking a martini. She kisses him on the cheek and assures him the job is his.

"But what if I don't want it?"

"Of course you want it." She reaches up to rub his chest with her non-martini hand, as if scrubbing away a stain from his shirt. "You're here."

"But I have a band." He wants to add, "I really came here to see you," but he knows how pathetic it will sound.

"Listen, Paul." She looks directly into his eyes as she talks; if she were speaking in slow, romantic tones the scene would fulfill one of his most common and intense fantasies, but her sentences are sharp and blunt. "You guys will release your EP, on your own or maybe, maybe on some small local label. Fine. Congratulations. Some cool college kids will play it on their cool college station. Some of those same kids will work at cool record stores and make a few of their friends buy it. And then, Paul? And then. It will disappear. And you'll be back to typing." She takes a sip of her martini and shrugs, her shoulders' quick rise and fall telling him the truth is hard but necessary.

Paul knows this is his chance to defend Monkeyhole to Leila and to himself, to remind them both that some independent records manage to break through, and besides, what's really important is the Music, right?

Instead he turns back to look at the stage, where Ebenezer's Screwed is finishing their second set of encores. Ex-Why is ripping his sweaty T-shirt into pieces and flinging them into the crowd, inspiring throngs of young girls to push each other to the ground.

After the show Paul wanders around backstage, wondering what to do next. The last train will be leaving soon. It occurs to him he could just get his backpack and take off, and no one would even notice. In the dressing room he finds the young muscle drummer gushing drunken praise to Ex-Why and the keyboardist, and he can't bear the idea of going over and trying to sell himself like that. Besides, the smiles and backslaps from everyone else in the band make it clear that they have found their new drummer. His answer provided—not good enough for the gig; hopefully still good enough to play with Monkeyhole; two hugs but no more from Leila—he hangs his backpack over his left shoulder and turns to leave.

He feels a tap on his shoulder and turns to see Ex-Why staring at him. The singer looks older offstage, more serious. "So, mate. What'd you think of the show?"

"Oh, great, great," Paul says, the word sounding as lame when he says it as it does when people say it to him after a show.

"Really?" Ex-Why's eyes widen. "Thought we were all on OK, then?"

As Paul tries to decide if Ex-Why is really British, or if the accent is some sort of weird act, he also has to decide if the singer wants unqualified praise or some more honest answer. He notices the keyboardist, a quiet figure who spent most of the night playing just outside the glare of the lights, is standing next to Ex-Why, and figures they have come to say goodbye. Thanks, but no thanks. In that case, there's no reason to try to act any part, no reason not to just tell them what he really thinks. "Well," he says, "to be honest things kind of lagged in the middle of the set."

"Really?"

"Seems like the focus was lost, some of the intensity, you know? And I know the drummer is just temporary, but he seemed almost too solid, like he was afraid to let things go sometimes. But," he quickly adds, not wanting to be that guy who only talks about the bad stuff in a set, "I thought everything snapped back during 'Close to You.' And the encores had the place exploding." A ska-punk version of a Carpenters' classic wouldn't have been his first choice of cover songs, but he doesn't mention that.

Ex-Why pauses for a second, sipping from the large bottle of red wine held to his side. "Alright then," he said, slapping Paul on the shoulder. "Thanks for coming out."

Paul watches him walk away and say something to Conrad, standing in a far corner of the room. He's turning around one last time when Conrad signals for him to wait, and then walks over.

"Leila says you need to get back tonight, then, so we got you a cab. We'll get you to Amtrak in time for that last train."

"Thanks for having me," Paul says, trying to make it seem as though it was just another night in New York for him.

"Don't mention it," Conrad says, pushing the door open. "Now, who should I be calling?"

When Paul steps outside he's surprised by the small, hard raindrops that hit his face. "Calling?" he repeats, turning sideways to look at Conrad.

"Who do I send the contract to?" Conrad looks down the alley behind the club. "Mind you, standard wording—liability and termination clauses, all that."

A contract? Paul realizes that not only is he being offered the job, it's assumed he'll take it. Instead of asking for time to think it over Paul just nods, as if Conrad's assumption is correct. The feeling coating his chest reminds him of the first time he took acid. He can see the Hendrix poster he was staring at as he chewed the small piece of paper he'd been offered without asking anyone just what, exactly, would happen next. It was much easier to act than to think.

"Or, we can just e-mail it to you to forward along? Leila has your info?"

"Sure, thanks." Paul wonders if Leila knows a cheap lawyer he can use.

"Now, mate, just so we understand. We're just signing you up for the rest of this tour. Four months, maybe two more if Europe works out. Not a member of the band proper, or anything, right? Sometimes new mates get a bit confused about what's on the table."

"Right," he repeats, though he had never thought about people in a band just being employees, and not full band members.

Conrad squints down the street again as the drops of rain begin to fall heavier. "Don't get me wrong." He turns back to look at Paul when the lights of a car begin to drift toward them. "Good drummer like you, there shouldn't be any problem in terms of salary and renewing and all that. But at this point only Ex-Why is technically a band member. Too many cooks fuck up the pie, right?"

"Yeah, yeah," Paul says. Another new language, that of a high-powered manager, a language that needs to talk about European tours and "pies" made out of money.

"Good. First things first, gotta get you up to D.C. in a week for a few practices, and then the tour kicks up again. After that, we'll talk about playing some tracks on the next record."

"As long as I stay out of detox, right?"

"Detox?" Conrad looks confused for a moment and then laughs, slapping Paul on the back with one hand and grabbing the door of the slowing cab with the other. "Ah! Yes, the last drummer. That's what we're telling the press, right? But truth is Ex-Why was a bit tired of the chap. Best to move on."

Fired: just like a bad typist.

In what seems like seconds, he's on the train heading home, unable to remember the cab ride. He leans his head against the window and fishes around in his backpack for his Discman. The idea of quitting Data Duty is exhilarating, and all the questions that come with his new job overwhelming—Does he move? How much money will he make?—but the thought of telling Spider and Danny looms ahead on the Amtrak rails, like some big animal moving too slowly to get out of the way. Leila must be right, he tells himself, he must have wanted the job all along. Why else would he audition?

He presses "play," wishing it was a magic button with the power to erase the next week of his life and make this the train ride to D.C. he'll take to join up with Ebenezer. Not only isn't the button magic, though, it doesn't play the CD he expects. Instead of "Black Dog," *Zoso's* opening track, his head is filled with "Kids Are For Tricks," the first song on the Ebenezer CD. He decides to listen anyway, taking it as an omen—he can listen as a band member now. OK, technically an employee, not a full member, but to anyone else he'd certainly *look* like a member.

Paul shuts his eyes in exhaustion. He imagines playing in front of large crowds, traveling on buses. His mother can watch his band on MTV, a measure of success even she will understand. He can hear her asking where he is in the video, but he'll smile and say, I'll be in the next one. Not adding: as long as I'm not fired first. His father will ask again how much money he's making, and for the first time he might have an acceptable answer that doesn't involve lying.

It isn't until "Kids Are For Tricks" ends that Paul realizes the whole song has washed over him—he hasn't paid attention to it at all. He wants to chalk that up to how tired he is, but he has to admit that the same thing had happened during his audition. He'd paid attention to the drumming, and followed the cues and other players so that he could perform his own parts, but the song itself left his head as quickly as it entered, not unlike the police reports he typed, day after day. Forgettable, competent rock; a song that looked better on video than it sounded on CD.

He switches CDs, anxious for Zeppelin to drown out the other thoughts in his head. This time, however, not even "When the Levee Breaks" offers an escape: "Don't it make you feel bad," Robert Plant sings, his voice a harsh sliver of pain being jabbed into Paul's ears, "When you're tryin' to find your way home, and you don't know which way to go."

He walks through the door at 8:20 a.m., almost exactly twenty hours after he left. His stickbag makes a hollow echo when he throws it on the kitchen table. It doesn't look like Danny's been home at all.

Next to the sink, the answering machine is flashing red, the fast and inconsistent blinking that always drove his inner metronome crazy. One message.

"Hey hey hey, Paulie boy." Spider's voice is slightly wobbly, a sure sign he had a few drinks or joints—or both—before calling. "Just heard 'Feel Like Makin' Love' on the radio, man. Listened to the whole damn thing, even that endless fucking fade out—I mean, kill the song already, you know? Or give me the butter knife, so I can kill myself." Burp. "Anyway. You know what I was thinking about, right, the *whole* time that song played? Seeing you with that lame-ass band. What was their name? Mildew? Honeydew? Man, I couldn't believe it. A drummer good enough to make listening to the rest of that shit bearable." After that there's a pause, and Paul heads over to the cupboard.

"OK, back," Spider continues. "Had to get a Tootsie Roll. Needed a Tootsie Roll-o, now-o." The sound of unwrapping is followed by an audible sigh of relief. "Anyway, as I was saying. That night. I knew I'd found the first piece of my band. The most important piece: the fucking drummer." Loud belch. "And that's to keep this from getting too goddamn Hallmark for any of us." Belch. "Now, about tomorrow."

Paul stares into the cupboard. His cereal's gone, but Danny's got some Frosted Flakes.

"Tomorrow we're meeting at Zito's for a pepperoni pie around six, and hitting the studio around seven. And, now, don't be mad at me, Paulie, but Stanley and I listened to 'Pay Me Now' tonight. I had to, man, just had to. I dragged that fat bastard off his couch and made him play the tape for me. No forty bucks an hour, either. One joint, one listen." Another pause, filled by the sound of another Tootsie Roll being opened. "I'm telling you man, never get rid of this answering machine, it lets me talk forever. Where the fuck are you, anyway? Movies?" Belch. "OK, so 'Pay Me Now.'"

Paul takes his bowl of cereal over to the kitchen table, chewing quietly.

"*Had* to listen. Had to, and glad I did. Stanley and I, man, after like, thirty fucking seconds of that last take, we both looked at each other and smiled. Shit, the drummer was right. Go figure. The drummer was fucking right. That second take? That's it. We're done. You were right, you asshole—time works differently. We need to speed up and slow down a little, need to breathe. The bridge finally works for me, you know? It floats, just like you said." Burp. "I taught you about time, too, listening to Ringo, and then I forgot. Stuck my head up my ass, so worried about this fucking record, and how it needs to be right... Shit. But you remembered, you motherfucker. Time works differently in each song." Pause. Belch.

"So tomorrow night we'll move on, cut another basic track. Maybe tackle 'Door Number Two'? I don't know. And, well, and now I gotta piss, so you think about it, and I'll see you at six. And remember, Paulie," he added, dramatically pausing before starting to sing, "'When I think about you, think about loooooove.'"

Paul looks at his watch. The message lasted more than two minutes: impressive, but not record-breaking. If he limits himself to just one more bowl of cereal and washes his face and hair instead of taking a full shower, he can still make it to Data Duty on time, and only wind up losing one day of work. And if he calls Leila on his lunch break, she'll be at work, he'll get her machine, and he won't have to tell her directly he's turning the job down. He'll just have to deal with his memory of hugging her, and the knowledge that it probably won't happen again.

All this means he'll be tired as hell when it comes time for the studio. Spider sounds buzzed and happy on the answering machine, but he'll pick some new tiny fight tomorrow night, and Danny is probably not done with his moody phase, but the music will still sound great. Eventually. And then his reward will be the hard sleep that comes to those whose bed is in the right place.

MNKYHL

Los Angeles, 1996

There are things you don't learn about being on tour until you go on tour. Danny was keeping a mental list as the band worked through its longest stretch of shows yet, both in terms of time—three weeks—and distance— all the way to the West Coast and back. He was learning helpful lessons about food (no buffets, ever, and nothing fried until after the gig) and hotels (never say how many are really sleeping in one room), but the lessons about time were the most powerful. Time could speed up wildly or come to a complete stop; hours spent sitting in the van dragged on, especially when it was your turn behind the wheel, while the forty minutes you had onstage clicked by at triple speed.

Danny checked his watch. 11:45. The hours between the gig and getting paid, it turned out, went by even more slowly than time spent on the flat highways of Texas. Nutz on Sunzet, the first club they had played in California, had made it clear that no one got paid before midnight. Spider had wanted Danny to get the money hours ago, since Monkeyhole had played at eight and was getting only two hundred bucks, but Paul supported Danny's decision to wait. They'd want to come back to L.A., and the first step toward a better time slot was not pissing off club managers—in this case a moody alcoholic named Rat. After their set they'd gone to In-N-Out Burger, bought some postcards to prove to friends and family that they'd made it, and then headed back to the old Econoline van to wait.

And wait.

From the passenger seat, Paul called out, "OK. Bassists."

Danny tapped the steering wheel, thinking. The "Only Pick One" game they'd started somewhere in Colorado was the latest time killer. No official scoring system had developed yet, but bragging rights usually depended on answering faster than the other two guys, or going last and coming up with what everyone agreed was the perfect choice. They'd worked through most TV and movie categories, and were on to musicians. "It's obvious, but gotta say McCartney."

"You mean you gotta 'Say, Say, Say,'" Spider sang cruelly. He was stretched out as much as he could be on the old leather couch that served as the back seat.

"His bass playing is still flawless, even if he's sold his soul," Danny said. The choice was safe and undeniable, but he'd forgotten how angry Spider was at Sir Paul. His love for everything Beatles fueled his rage at the music McCartney was making now.

"John Paul Jones," Paul said. "As good as Bonham was, Jones made him better."

Danny was working on his argument for McCartney over Jones, something about the bigger role McCartney's licks played in those tight arrangements, when Spider growled again from the couch. "You guys are so fucking predictable. Give me Duck Dunn."

Of course, Danny thought: how could he have forgotten Spider's recent obsession with all things related to Stax Records? Their next album would probably be influenced by that obsession, so Danny had been trying to get caught up. Ever since he'd started playing with Spider and Paul he felt like he'd walked into a class on Music History halfway through the semester.

"Fuck. Duck. For the win," Paul said.

"And it's five to twelve," Spider added. "Please tell me it's not too early to go ask the nice man for money."

"OK, OK," Danny said. He stretched, slowly pushed the van door open, and stumbled out onto the uneven pavement of Nutz's parking lot. He'd only taken two steps away when Paul leaned his head out to shout a final instruction.

"And remember, no talking about his brother."

Danny nodded impatiently. "I know. No talking about Springsteen. No whistling 'Born to Run.' No questions about Asbury Park." Before they'd left Boston, they'd heard about Rat from the manager of T.T. the Bear's Place, their home base and monthly rent gig. Frankie had told them that Rat was the washed-up older brother of the Boss himself, but that you should never, under any circumstances, mention Springsteen. Bruce and Rat each did his best to pretend the other didn't exist.

Danny could hear Paul singing "Dancing in the Dark" as he resumed his walk. Shards of glass flickered in the lights, and off to his left a steady stream of cars rumbled down Sunset Boulevard. Los fucking Angeles. While most of the other Boston bands they knew were still sitting around the bar at T.T.'s, talking about really going on the road someday—not just hitting New York or Philly, but really logging some miles—Monkeyhole had done it. Ever since he'd joined, the three of them had focused on what needed to get done next, and then worked to get it done. Like moving to Boston, as soon as Paul graduated. Not quite as cutthroat or expensive as

New York, but still in that Northeast touring corridor, with lots of cities within a few hours' drive. His family was surprised when he announced the plan, since he was twenty-four and had never been further north than Chattanooga, but he'd been telling anyone who'd listen that he was going to be a musician. Either they weren't paying attention or they hadn't believed him.

In just over a year, Monkeyhole had gone from opening for other local bands to headlining weekends. What they'd all focused on most, though, from the moment they started playing together, was making a record. It's what bands did: make records. When all of the demos they sent out to any record label they could find an address for were ignored, they paid for the whole thing themselves—not quite a full-length album, but a five-song EP was still a finished product, a piece of evidence that they could offer as proof that they were a real band. They sold the first 1,000 copies themselves, found a manager, and made another 1,000. Small-scale, but they got college radio play in little pockets across the country. That radio play, and a few good reviews from college journals, allowed them to string together two weeks of shows along the West Coast, from Long Beach to Seattle. They booked gigs in St. Louis and Pittsburgh on the way home, but on the way out they'd driven for three days, with breaks at Motel 6 and Denny's. Danny had been worried their first set would feel stiff, especially since there were only ten people in the club when they started, but they'd torn the place up, earning genuinely shocked praise from the house soundman. By the time they played their homecoming show at T.T.'s, they should be tighter than ever. Their manager was trying to get some labels out for that gig.

A real label. With a real label, they could hire a tour manager and Danny wouldn't have to get paid after gigs. He hated trying to shake money out of clubs, with business offices hidden in some dark corner, and managers that were usually drunk, stoned, assholes, or all of the above. He did try to come across as energetic and grateful, so they could play these clubs again—he'd bullshit enough to be polite, even though all he really wanted to do was watch bad cable and go to sleep.

He'd offered to start handling all the money when they moved to Boston. He needed to find some way, besides singing backing vocals, to contribute as much as Paul (who helped Spider with production and arrangement) and Spider (who wrote and sang all the songs). After almost four years, he still felt like the new guy. Spider and Paul had played together longer, and seemed to know so much more, about everything from music to drugs to women. They'd also both been born and raised in the North, so the move to Boston was like a return to home turf, while it had taken Danny a few months to adapt to the fast pace and constant chill in the air.

As great as it would be to not have to handle the money anymore, he'd start worrying again about not being involved enough. Spider often had bass parts fully formed in his head by the time he brought a song to the band, so Danny's role was limited to the occasional bass lick or arrangement tweak. Paul mapped out the routes on tour, using some huge road atlas his uncle had given him, and accepted no help. Even the setlist was off-limits to Danny: Spider took care of that, too. Danny made a suggestion for their first LA show, but that only led to one of those circular arguments Spider always wound up winning. Spider wanted to close with "Gardenia," a new song that wasn't even on the EP they were promoting. It was gonna be a great song someday, but Danny thought it sounded like they were still learning it, and it had this tricky not-too-fast, not-too-slow tempo that Paul struggled to nail sometimes. Danny wanted to end the set with something faster, like "Pay Me Now," the song off the EP that got the most radio play. Since they were the opening act for all these shows, their audience would be biggest for their last few songs. Crowds always got into "Pay Me" by the time the second chorus rolled around, and it had a sharp ending that Danny thought would be a perfect way to make a lasting impression. Spider wanted people to walk out humming the chorus to "Gardenia," though, and while the two of them went back and forth Paul was driving, pretending the streets of L.A. were so tricky that he couldn't give an opinion. Spider finally said, "We're gonna close with it," and no one said a word for the last half hour of the drive to the club. Spider got his way, and Danny got reminded that he wasn't really an equal third in the band. And probably never would be.

When he finally made his way back inside the club, past the long line of people and the doorman who thought he was trying to sneak in for free— "You played with who?"— his focus was pulled to the band onstage. A few hours earlier the club's high ceiling had made Monkeyhole sound boomy, but now that people stood shoulder-to-shoulder in front of the stage the music sounded sharp and clear, and so loud it felt like the guitar amps were right against his ears. Lower Level Love was almost as established as the night's headliner, the Krush Tones; their name on the club marquee was as big, and they were on the road with two full-length indie releases behind them. It was impossible not to become jealous as he watched, both of the size of the crowd and the techs floating around the edges of the stage. He reminded himself that Monkeyhole could—would—get there soon. Next time L3 (as their fans liked to call them) came through Boston, Danny could go see them at T.T.'s, maybe get a chance to bullshit with them before the show. He'd nod real slow and say, Yeah, I think we played in L.A. together. Last November, maybe December? Nutz's? He'd say it just like that, tilting his head like he had to think real hard to separate one L.A. gig from another.

Danny forced his way through the crowd hovering around the back bar to shout at the bartender: "Where's Rat?" The lineman opening two beer bottles at once had the same blank look on his face he'd had that afternoon, when he finally opened the back door after Danny banged on it for fifteen minutes. He'd asked what the fuck Danny wanted, leading to the day's first lesson: no one shows up for soundcheck on time at Nutz's. Four o'clock meant five at the earliest, and bands lower on the bill, like Monkeyhole, didn't check at all. "Where's Rat?" Danny shouted again, and the bartender motioned over his right shoulder.

Danny squeezed behind the back wall of the bar, and headed up the narrow staircase. At the top, a hallway stretched out to his left; he squinted into the harsh light of a half dozen or so bare bulbs, unnerved by the sudden silence. It wasn't a peaceful quiet, though, as much as a spooky stillness. Walking slowly down the hall, squinting in the pale yellow light, he heard no sound other than the squishing noise the carpet made when he stepped.

He tried not to think about why carpet would make a squishing sound.

Danny was starting to think the bartender had steered him down a dead end when he saw a door ahead on the right. His knock forced it to swing half-open, and an angry voice called out, "Yeah?"

After hesitating long enough to make the voice call out again—"Who the fuck is it?"—Danny stepped into the office. His face was slapped by an acrid smell, instantly familiar; it was the same mixture of mildew, old food, and male body odor that had saturated Duffy Newman's basement. Dark and dingy, concrete floors, no windows, stray pieces of furniture deemed unfit for the rest of the house. Nonetheless, he and Duffy had gladly endured it countless teenage afternoons, drawn by the pinball machine and ancient copies of *Playboy*. As he was adjusting to the much brighter light, Danny noticed a man on a swivel chair staring at him. His face, in spite of its pock-marks and uneven black-and-gray stubble, was nearly an exact duplicate of Bruce Springsteen's. In his lap was either a young boy or a flat-chested woman, shirtless, with short red hair and an IRON MAIDEN tattoo across the right forearm. Danny cleared his throat. "I'm looking for Rat."

"You got me, Wyatt Earp." Rat raised his hands as if a gun were pointed at him. "Move it or lose it, Kiki," he said, dropping his knees and forcing the androgynous figure off his lap.

"Can't lose what the good Lord gave me," Kiki said, landing so gracefully that Danny decided she must be female. After a tug on Rat's curly black hair she shot Danny a quick salute and a wink, then disappeared behind a low doorway she had to bend down to walk through.

"Have a seat," Rat said, motioning to the faded yellow couch across from his swivel chair. "You were in one of the bands, right?"

Danny nodded, ignoring the damp sensation he felt through his jeans when he sat down. Rat's voice reminded him of the people in the anti-smoking films he'd seen in high school health class, wheezing out warnings between sad puffs of smoke. "Yeah, Monkeyhole."

"Monkeyhole." Rat twisted his chair around and began shuffling through papers on the desk behind him. "Monkeyhole," he mumbled again, absent-mindedly patting the pockets of his worn jean jacket.

"Thanks for having us, really," Danny said. He reached out to accept the money he assumed Rat was about to hand him, and then casually dropped his hand to his knee when Rat turned back around with nothing but a pack of Pall Malls. "The stage sounded great, and everyone—"

"Hey, take a breath. Relax." Rat shook a cigarette loose. "You guys from New York, right?"

"Boston."

"Boston! Bah. What's Boston but a fucking suburb of New York, right?" Like a seedy magician, Rat seemed to pull a lighter out of thin air. He lit the cigarette and inhaled deeply. "How you like L.A. then, huh?"

"My first time here. It's been all everyone said it would be, you know?" He paused, waiting for Rat to say something else, but Rat just wheezed as he took another drag on his Pall Mall. "I wish we had more time," Danny continued, "but we gotta head out to San Francisco." He paused again, wondering if he should have said 'San Fran,' but Rat still didn't speak. "We'll be back end of the week, though, to play Long Beach."

"Long Beach!" The words came out buried in a deep cough. "Fucking cesspool." Rat dropped the pack of cigarettes down on the desk behind him; when he swiveled back his eyes focused on an ambiguous point on the ground. After a short silence he jerked his head up and squinted at Danny. "You want a drink? Margarita?"

Danny waved nonchalantly, like he drank so much he could afford to pass one up every now and then. "Actually, I just need to get paid," he said, trying to give Rat a serious look. There wasn't any point in trying to schmooze: Rat was so out of it he wouldn't even remember talking to Danny.

"Course you fucking do. Working man, on the move. Call me the working man, guess that's what I am." Rat rubbed his pock-marked face with the hand that held his cigarette. He stood up slowly and looked around, as if searching for a street sign. "One second," he mumbled, before folding himself in half to walk through the same door Kiki used.

Danny wondered if he should follow. Leaning against the back of the love seat, he nervously glanced at his watch and decided to wait a few minutes. If Rat was really going to get the money, they might still be on the road by one, and time could start moving at its normal pace again.

He started fantasizing about the giant Snickers he'd buy himself when they stopped for gas, and planning how he would describe their first California gig when he called Linda, his girlfriend, the next day. She was a huge Springsteen fan, so it'd be fun to tell her he met the Boss's brother.

The night before he'd left she'd come right out and asked him: Were they still going to be a couple, even as the band started to travel more? Caught off guard, he'd given the answer he thought would leave them enough time for goodbye sex: Of course. Linda translated "of course" into a demand for daily phone calls, lots of postcards, and a vow of fidelity. After four days, four phone calls, and countless sightings of attractive West Coast women, Danny had to wonder if those conditions would be possible to maintain for another two weeks.

Of course, he wouldn't be too surprised if he fucked things up. Linda had seemed out of his league from the first moment he met her in Atlanta and she was dating Bob, one of his friends. She'd been right to dismiss him as not worth her time, but then they'd somehow met again in Boston. She looked better than ever, and this time she actually noticed him. Luckily for Danny, she'd come to see a Monkeyhole gig, one of those great T.T.'s shows where the band and the crowd both performed just as they should. And just like that, he had a girlfriend and a really great band: just the way his teenage self had imagined, sitting alone in his bedroom imagining a better life. What he hadn't imagined was how hard it would be to have both at the same time. He planned to hold on to Linda for as long as he could, to do whatever he needed to in order to keep her from escaping, but he also knew the unspoken rule of being in a band, a real band committed to making it—the band always won.

So if it came down to doing something Linda needed, or doing something Monkeyhole needed, he would have to do the thing for the band. Would she feel better, if she knew that everything else in his life could—might, at some point, have to—lose that contest? It had always been that way for him, too, from the first band he joined. Nemesis Theory, freshman year of high school. One of the few ideas he and Duffy Newman ever came up with, during all those days they hung out in that basement, that had actually been realized. They'd just discovered the Rolling Stones, thanks to a VHS tape of a concert movie that Duffy's sister owned, and Danny made Duffy watch it over and over. He decided that it was Keith's rhythm guitar, more than the leads or even Mick's singing, that made the Stones sound like the Stones. And all he wanted, from that moment on, was the chance to be Keith Richards. He borrowed his older brother's beat-up Martin, and the *How To Play Chords* book Rob had never bothered to open, and started to teach himself.

Rob had moved on to drums from guitar, and that's what gave Danny the idea, one he was able to sell to Duffy: we'll start our own band. Duffy didn't care as much about music, and would always have chosen a *Star Wars* movie over the Stones, but he did like girls. Once Danny pointed out that a guy who looked like Mick Jagger scored with women just because he sang in a band, Duffy was on board as the singer.

With Rob on drums and their friend A.J. on guitar, they just needed a bass player. Mike Miller had a perfect garage for band practice, complete with a PA from his dad's wedding business. He didn't play an instrument, but Danny figured he could learn how to play bass. Mike insisted on guitar, though, so Danny switched: playing bass was better than not being in a band at all. Rob turned out to be a great drummer, but the rest of them were awful. Danny still pushed everything else aside—no more soccer, no more chess club—to focus on keeping the band together.

The five of them slowly got good enough to play at parties and in their own back yards for friends. They'd even started to play some songs A.J. and Duffy had written—they all sounded like "Jumping Jack Flash" and were always about needing to get laid, but they were their own. Rob was a year ahead of them, though, and went off to the University of Georgia, even though Danny begged him to wait.

"Why would I do that, man?"

"For the band."

"The band?" Rob looked confused. The two of them were alone at the start of a practice; once again, everyone else was late. "Dude, this band is just something for us to do until we get the hell out of Stockbridge, right? I mean, you're not gonna stay here any longer than you have to, are you?"

There were 20,000 people in Stockbridge, Georgia, more or less, and Danny thought maybe half a dozen of them were bearable—and Rob was one of them. That afternoon Danny imagined, for the first time, what the house would be like after his bother left, with just him and his parents sitting in awkward silence at the kitchen table. And that's when he decided he would also leave town as soon as he finished high school.

A week after graduation he got as far away as he could. Athens was only ninety minutes by car, but it felt like he'd used hyper-drive to jump into another universe. The Stockbridge-type jocks and rednecks were still there, laughing in sports bars and stumbling towards UGA for the occasional class, but the town was big enough for Danny to avoid interaction with them for most of his time in Athens. He could go entire days without seeing a mullet, entire weeks without hearing Lynyrd Skynyrd or Molly Hatchet.

It didn't take long to settle into a new routine: keep an eye and ear out for bands that needed a bassist, wait tables at the Grit, and dabble in a little weed-dealing, all while reassuring his parents that eventually he would sign up for some courses—of course he would. He sometimes wondered if Rob had any idea how much he had changed Danny's life. He owed Mike Miller a thank you, as well, for being a dick and refusing to play bass. Danny was better at bass than he'd ever have gotten at guitar; he heard rhythms others didn't and could create the kind of groove that pushed a song along without stealing attention from the melody. Best of all, bass offered him the chance to play a big role without most people actually noticing, and he'd grown to value that.

As good as life in Athens was, though, he'd only worked his way through a string of average bands until he met Spider and Paul. He knew Monkeyhole was different the first time he played with them. He'd finally figured out what a good bass player needs to succeed: a good drummer and a good songwriter.

He checked his watch again. Rat had been gone for fifteen minutes, and he'd been in the club for almost half an hour. The couch was slowly swallowing him, like some bad science-fiction movie creature. Much longer, and Paul and Spider would think he'd fucked up and come looking. Paul would list things he'd have done differently, and Spider would ask, in that annoyed voice that always reminded Danny of his father, if he needed to do everything in this fucking band. He took a deep breath, crossed the room, and walked over to the door Rat and Kiki had disappeared behind.

Giggles from the other side, intermingled with music. Unbelievably, Danny recognized a song from *Darkness on the Edge of Town*. "When we found the things we loved, they were crushed and dying in the dirt... " He knocked but no one answered, so he slowly opened the door.

A disembodied voice shouted at him to close the door; when he did so Danny felt like he'd stepped into one of those dark rooms at the aquarium, swimming in muted blues and reds. Blinking to regain his bearings, he saw the only light came from a large, old-fashioned jukebox to his left, flashing random patterns of red and blue as it played. To his right were three blurry figures, one of whom waved and called out in a raspy voice, "Yo, Monkey Man."

"Hey," he said, taking an uncertain step towards the figures. "Sorry, but—"

"Where you been? Come the fuck in, already."

Relieved, Danny smiled and started walking in the general direction of the voice. As the room came into focus, he saw Kiki and Rat sitting on two stools in front of a low counter, the bartender from downstairs leaning across it. All three of them had cigarettes and drinks, and Kiki had put on a Dodgers Jersey—STRAWBERRY 44. The new look made Danny think Kiki was actually a guy.

"Drink, Monkey Man?"

Danny shook his head. "No, thanks. I just—"

"Come on." Rat playfully slapped Danny's back. "Chip, grab the man a Hiney-kin."

"Done." The hulk behind the bar nodded and disappeared through the small doorway.

"Really, thanks, but the guys are waiting for me. I—"

"The man wants to talk business. Fair enough... " His voice drifted off and he stared at the ground again. For a second Danny thought he'd made him mad, but then the pock-marked Springsteen blew a thin trail of smoke at Kiki and grinned. The action magically transformed Rat's face, morphing him from the weary and isolated Bruce of *Darkness* to the Bruce of *Born to Run*, smiling and leaning on Clarence and looking ready to take over the world. "Can you go check on that asshole Chewie, babe?"

Kiki nodded on the way out, winking at Danny.

"Have a seat," Rat said, thumping the stool next to him as he turned to watch Kiki leave. He turned back to Danny and grinned again. "Is that a nice piece of ass, or what?"

Danny paused, trying to decide if Rat had really just asked him if he thought a young guy was attractive. And who was "Chewie," and why did everyone in this place have such ridiculous names? The flashing lights on the jukebox were making him a little queasy, and the start of "Candy's Room" had never sounded spookier, all hi-hat and half-spoken Springsteen mumble. "Heh," he said, forcing out a non-committal laugh.

Rat looked satisfied, as if that was just the answer he was expecting. "So, Monkey Man," he started, rubbing his face as he talked. "What do you play?"

"Bass." Danny tried not to look disappointed as he realized Rat hadn't seen their set. What would Rat really remember about tonight, anyway? Everyone said the house soundman was who you wanted to impress, and they had done that.

"Ah, bass." Rat left his cigarette in his mouth and reached out, taking hold of Danny's right hand with both of his. "Yeah, pretty damn good fingers for a bass player."

Danny managed to mumble a thank you, wondering how long he had to leave his hand there. Rat leaned close enough for Danny to smell an odd mixture of alcohol, cigarettes, and baby powder.

"Now, look at these fucking sausages." Continuing to hold Danny's left hand with his right, Rat grabbed Danny's right with his left and lined the fingers up. "You can see why I couldn't play a fucking thing. My luck to be the one in the family stuck with Ball Park Franks for fingers." He grinned again, still holding Danny's hands. "They plump when you cook 'em, right?"

Danny forced a smile as he politely studied Rat's fingers. They were enormous, though he didn't think Rat really wanted him to say that, and so dirty they seemed to have a completely different skin tone. Most unnerving of all was how smooth the fingers felt, like they were coated in an excessive amount of lotion. Danny knew he should try to make a joke, but what he really wanted to say was, What the fuck are you doing holding my hand? For once, not even Springsteen, growing louder and more desperate, offered any solutions: "And what (what) she (she) wants (wants) is (is) me."

After a long minute Rat let go. One hand reached for his cigarettes on the counter as the other picked up his glass and tossed down the rest of his drink. On the jukebox the opening piano riff to "Racing in the Street" started, a sound so sad it always made Danny's insides sink. He watched Rat swirl the ice cubes in his glass, as if desperately trying to free a few more drops of alcohol, and began to get nervous—was he going to have to turn down some sort of awkward pass? It could be a funny story, later, about that time Springsteen's brother made a move, but for now it would just make getting paid that much harder.

The door opened again. Kiki walked back in, and came over to mumble in Rat's ear. "What the fuck," Rat said, slamming his glass on the counter. "That fucking fucker." He didn't even look back at Danny as he bounded over to the door in three unsteady steps.

This time Danny followed, determined to keep him in sight. By the time he reached the door, Rat was halfway through the office, moving at a speed Danny would not have imagined possible. Breaking into a near jog, Danny closed the gap to a few feet when he reached the hallway. A tall man in a three-piece suit leaned against the wall, walkie-talkie in one hand and a cigar in the other. "You said you had this covered, Rat," the man said in a condescending voice. "You'll be covered in your own shit unless it's fixed."

Rat was already moving toward the stairs by the time that threat was issued, Danny just a few steps behind. The hallway seemed much shorter on the return trip, and Danny was surprised at how quickly he found himself back downstairs. By that point, he had caught up to Rat, close enough to tug on his ragged jean jacket as he called his name. Rat ignored him, though, and all Danny could do was follow the opening Rat made in the crowd as he headed toward an obese man in gray sweats standing at the sound board. Slapping him on the back, Rat started talking loudly. "What the fuck, Chewie? Contract says first song at one. It's quarter after and there's no one on the fucking stage."

So this is Chewie, Danny thought to himself. And: if it was after one, he'd been in the club over an hour. Spider and Paul were gonna be furious. "Rat," he said, daring to slap Rat's back, though not as hard as Rat had slapped Chewie. "I need to get paid."

He turned around, looking stunned to see Danny there. "Monkey?"

"Who the fuck is this?" Chewie looked up from the sound board and pointed to Danny with a flashlight. "You can't come and talk to me on your own? You need to bring Doogie Howser?"

"I need to get paid, Rat." Danny focused on maintaining his professional voice, trying not to let the Doogie Howser comment get to his head. "Now."

"You stiffing the bands, Ratty? Do I need to get everything up front?"

"You need to get your band fucking onstage and playing," Rat said. "Been almost an hour since L3 ended. Too much fucking dead air, and I don't want to pay overtime for the fucking crew."

"I can't put them onstage if you're not gonna pay us." Chewie grinned. "I mean, if you got no candy money for Doogie, what's that mean for my boys?"

Danny was surprised at how much smaller Rat looked out here, being bossed around. He could tell Rat just wanted him to go away, so he pushed one more time. "We need our money, Rat."

"Yeah. Sure." Rat casually pulled a thick wad of bills out of his front pocket, unfolded it, and peeled a fifty off the top.

Danny froze. As ludicrous as it seemed to actually get paid after all this time, it was even more ludicrous to only get fifty bucks. "But on the phone you said two hundred."

Rat waved him off, the fifty still flapping in his hand, and tapped his watch as he turned to the Krush Tones's soundman. "So whose tiny dick do I have to suck to get your boys on the stage?"

The soundman didn't even turn around this time, just scratched his butt through his sweats.

Danny swallowed. Rat had been out of it all night. He just made a mistake, and all Danny had to do was explain. Forceful, but professional. "You said two hundred on the phone," he said, speaking louder. "Rat. You said two hundred."

"Fucking five more minutes, Chewie. Then I go onstage and start pissing on all that fancy gear." He turned back to Danny and looked surprised to see the fifty still in his left hand. "You still here, Monkey boy?"

"You said two hundred. The guarantee—it was supposed to be two hundred."

"Two hundred? You're saying two hundred?"

"Yeah," Danny said, ashamed at the way his voice shrank. "Two hundred."

The lines on Rat's face deepened. "Why the fuck would I pay you two hundred dollars?"

Danny became conscious of the muscles in his cheeks, and the way his arms had stopped moving. He was hoping Chewie would turn around again, that maybe that would pressure Rat into giving him the money

Monkeyhole was due, but he'd put headphones on, and was staring intently at the flashing lights on the mixing console. "When I called to book the gig—"

"There's no way I'd pay the goddamn Happy Hour band two hundred bucks. My mother could come here and sit on the stage doing needlepoint for all I care, as long as I can put 'Show Starts at Eight' in the ad."

Danny didn't say a word. Everything he'd been about to say was drowned out by the echo of the phrase "Happy Hour Band." Of course— that's what they'd been. When he'd asked for two hundred on the phone and Rat said yes right away it wasn't because he'd liked their EP so much. He'd only given them a slot as a favor to the manager of T.T. the Bear's Place. He'd never intended to pay them more than fifty bucks. Probably lucky to get anything.

Happy Hour Band.

From behind Rat's head he could see the soundman, now talking to someone on the stage through a microphone. Between the mixing console and the stage the floor was packed with people all waiting for the band they'd paid to see. None of them, not even Rat, had seen Monkeyhole. All Danny could do was take the fifty and get the hell out of there. It wasn't like anyone at the club had ever signed and mailed back his homemade contracts.

He closed his eyes and slid the money into his pocket. Fifty dollars. It would cover gas to San Francisco, but in his mind he'd already spent the rest of their "guarantee." First show of the tour, and already they were a hundred and fifty bucks behind.

Danny pushed his way past the random clusters of drunk people standing outside the club. As he passed the Nutz On Sunset's sign, he stopped to take one last look. They were listed up there, all right, down at the very bottom. MNKYHL. When Spider had complained their name had been spelled wrong the bartender shrugged. "Too many vowels tonight. We ran out after the first five bands. What the fuck, though, right? No one reads the vowels, anyway."

Spider was so angry he threatened to cancel the gig, but Danny and Paul managed to joke about it.

"I haven't wasted time reading vowels since, like, fifth grade," Paul had said.

"Besides," Danny had added, "we got a 'y.' 'Y' is a vowel sometimes, right?"

Danny should have known right then what kind of night they would have. His first clue that their big L.A. debut would be essentially nonexistent—a ghost show for ghost crowds and ghost pay—and he'd missed it.

When he got back to the van, Spider was curled up in a ball on the couch, his face resting against the peeling leather, and Paul had leaned the passenger seat as far back as it would go, a T-shirt over his eyes. Danny shut the door quietly and slid his key into the ignition. Running his tongue over his lips for moisture, he wondered where he would find the energy to start driving.

"Danny?"

He didn't answer Paul in a whisper of his own until he'd started the van. He checked the rear-view mirror to make sure Spider was still sleeping. "Thought you were out."

"I was. I think." Paul took the T-shirt off his eyes and yawned. "You get paid?"

"Yeah."

"Took fucking forever." Paul stretched his arms and then folded them across his chest.

Danny rubbed his face with both hands, listening to the van's idle smooth itself out. "Tell me about it."

"He give you a hard time?"

He wanted to turn the experience into a Story they could all share, but he also didn't want to sound like he was complaining. Or to tell them they only got fifty—Spider would try to go get the rest, Paul would insist on taking over, and the next two weeks would suck. "Nah." The lie came so easily he could almost imagine believing it someday. "Just took a while to find him. Then he kept wanting to fucking talk, and offering me beers."

Paul shrugged. "Well, I guess you couldn't be a dick about it."

"Yeah. Who knows, we may actually wanna come back here." Danny stared at the steering wheel, knowing he should put the van into drive and start moving. "The place is packed now. Maybe we can go on a little later next time."

"What do you figure, drive for an hour or two and find a motel?"

"Yeah." Danny flexed his fingers. The series of calculations he made—the time they needed to arrive tomorrow, minus the total distance they had to drive, factoring in how long he could safely drive before falling asleep—were reassuring. Concrete questions with concrete answers. "That would leave four hours to drive tomorrow. Load-in at five."

"Sleep until check-out. Sweet."

Danny was just about to shift the van into drive when Paul spoke again.

"So, what'd you think of the show? Really?"

"The show?" Danny didn't know what to say. The show felt like it had been played days ago. "Well, it was hard going on so early," he said softly, anxious to keep from waking Spider, "but I thought the few people who were there were into it."

Paul grinned. "I'm talking about the playing. I mean, who gives a shit about the crowd when you take the stage at eight, right? I was just glad the place wasn't empty."

"Right." Danny forced Rat and Kiki and Chewie out of his head, and focused on the way his fingers had moved just the way he wanted them to, the notes in lockstep with Paul, Spider's guitar floating above them. They knew their job, as rhythm section—allow Spider the security to go as far into the stratosphere as he could manage. "I think Spider was right about 'Gardenia,'" he said reluctantly. "It worked great as a closer." As much as he wanted to rock at the end of the night, the last choruses of "Gardenia" had really soared, in a way they never had in practice. It was like he finally heard the song Spider kept describing, when he explained how he wanted it to sound. And Paul realized, singing "gardenia" over and over at the end of the night, that he felt closest to Spider when the two of them were singing harmonies. The applause had been warmer and longer than any other time during their set.

"I hate it when he's fucking right." His gaze drifting out of the window of the van, Paul continued, "I was worried about that one, too. Tricky to get the feel of it just right, you know? Not as easy as bashing through something. Still not sure I have control of it."

Danny was surprised to learn Paul could feel any kind of concern about his own playing; he seemed so full of confidence, any time he sat behind a drum set. "No, no, not at all," he said. And it was true—the fill Paul played when he came in was just right, and locked in the perfect tempo. "Felt good to me. Felt better than it had before, really." He nodded for emphasis.

"Good." Paul shut his eyes again. "Twelve shows in fourteen days— that's what this is all about. Playing. Working ourselves into better shape than we've ever been, out here in some strange fucking new world where no one's even heard of us. Like playing on the moon, or something. Can't wait to see what it does to the music."

"You're right," Danny said, angry that he'd let himself forget that. The guy who'd booked the show in San Francisco said dinner was free; that would help. If they could find a cheap hotel and keep getting decent mileage, he just might be able to spread the missing money around the next few days and balance things out.

"So, I gotta know. Did he look like Springsteen?"

Danny felt a thin smile creep across his face. "Like some sort of through-the-fucked-up-looking-glass Springsteen, yeah."

Paul laughed quietly. "One degree of separation, Danny m'boy. One fucking degree."

"Christ, you dicks, Springsteen doesn't have a brother."

They turned to look at Spider, still curled up on the couch. "What?" Danny asked.

"He doesn't have a goddamn brother. One sister. No brother. That's it."

"No brother?" Paul repeated. "But Frankie back at T.T.'s said—"

"No fucking brother," Spider said. "The house guy told me Rat just says that shit so everyone thinks they're related, and then makes a big-ass deal about no one talking about it."

"Why didn't you say something before?"

"Jesus, you both pop such big boners for the Boss, I figured you knew his birth sign and favorite color, never mind how many fucking brothers and sisters he has."

Danny and Paul looked at each other and laughed. "What a loser," Paul said. "How pathetic."

"Now let's get going," Spider said. "And stop at a Kwik-E-Mart pronto, 'cause I gotta take a huge fucking whiz."

Danny looked at Paul and shrugged as they turned around again. "Sure as fuck looked like him. Was even playing a Springsteen record."

"Really?" Paul asked. "Which one?"

"*Darkness.*"

Paul nodded respectfully. "Well, at least he played the right album."

"Yeah." Danny eased his foot off the brake and backed the van out of its parking space.

Draping the T-shirt back over his head, Paul started laughing again. "Man—what a pathetic way of dealing with your shitty life."

"These badlands," Danny started singing, "you gotta live 'em every day." He paused to look both ways before easing the van onto Sunset Boulevard.

Dígame

Chicago, 1997

It's a perfect afternoon for a game so Wrigley Field is packed, even though the Cubs suck. I settle into the upper regions of the bleachers with the guys in Monkeyhole and Nickel, our soundman. The opening weeks of the band's first headlining club tour have been solid—only one real disaster, some fucking diner in Columbus that refused to turn off the big-screen TV behind the drums—so spirits are high. After a few months of opening for a wide range of bands in venues big and small, I can tell the guys like carrying the weight on their own. I'm remembering again why I prefer tour managing for bands on their way up more than bands on their way down, even if the venues (and paychecks) are smaller.

I take a sip of Diet Coke and dangle my feet over the miraculously empty seat in front of me, sun on my face and bratwurst in my hand. I feel like I'm still a real Chicagoan, not someone who escaped as quickly as he could after high school.

My own drinking days may be done, but I buy everyone else a second round after the Cubs finish their first at bat. After I got clean I worried about being around people doing the things I couldn't do anymore—like drink a cold, refreshing beer on a perfect summer day at a ballgame, that layer of foam coating your lips before the thick malt slides down. Yes, there is a sharp tug somewhere just below my ribs, a tangled guitar cable being yanked the wrong way. After almost nine years, I can usually loosen that feeling with one of my tricks, though, like pretending I'm just watching people in a movie have a drink, like it's just a two-dimensional image, not the real thing. Or I just look at the tattoo on my left wrist: 12/31/88. It's my sober date, and it sure would be a bitch to have to get it taken off.

The hardest part of staying clean was finding a new, comparatively harmless addiction; I've settled on Diet Coke and just refuse to read about any tests on poor lab rats. And socks. When I'm on the road, I go through three or four clean pairs a day. Feels like putting a new coat of paint on an old chair.

Danny's sitting next to me and trying to explain baseball to Spider, who swears he's never seen a game, a rare chance for a bassist to teach a guitarist something. Next to them, Nickel has started waging a series of small bets with Paul—a dollar if the next out is a grounder, five bucks if Paul can get the blonde two rows over to wave at him. Like most good drummers, Paul is inherently laid-back. Whenever I needed to find drummers of my own, I knew guys who were low-key offstage worked the hardest and played the best once they were onstage. Of course, Paul's also a little defensive, the way all drummers are, the result of being made the scapegoat too often, but the occasional reassuring nod or kind word keeps him happy.

Nickel's up ten bucks on Paul when Spider pukes. Spider's still on his second Bud in the third inning, a pace he should easily be able to handle, but I notice his pasty white skin is even paler than normal. First guess: food poisoning. He'd insisted on wandering off to find a "good local joint" for breakfast, and it looks like he got more local flavor than he'd bargained for. By the time I get us back to the hotel lobby, panic has replaced the good vibes we'd been soaking in just a half hour ago.

I should have known I'd have to leave the game early—it happened the other two times I went to Wrigley.

The first was with my father, 1970. Summer after my mother died. I'd just turned fourteen, and I guess my father felt like he and I should do some bonding. Turns out sitting with thousands of strangers can't change people who don't have anything to say each other. We left right after Harry Caray sang "Take Me Out to the Ballgame," because Dad wanted to beat the crowd. On the way home, I begged him to buy me a copy of *Let It Be*, and we never went to a game again.

Second game: 1974, summer after high school finally ended. Malkie was with me that time, of course. We grew up together, learned how to play guitar together in seventh grade, discovered drugs together the summer before tenth grade. By the time we'd graduated we'd formed our own band. Malkie switched to bass and we called ourselves Dígame, a name that sounded cool and played off the fact my last name is Gonzalez, but I look like I could be planting bombs for the IRA. Burned through drummers like skinny joints and played any back yard that would have us. Cheryl was at the game, too; I discovered her a year after I discovered the guitar, and managed to hold onto her for longer than I ever would have guessed. This amazing girl with soft blonde hair, tortoise shell glasses, and a 4.0 GPA also swore like a sailor and made the first move.

She liked to surprise you.

That trip to Wrigley should be a fonder memory than the one with my dad, but I just remember feeling tense. Now that we'd all graduated, it was time for What Happens Next. Cheryl was off to the University of Wisconsin-Madison, and was going to meet all these smarter, more attractive guys. Malkie and I were headed for a clean start in Austin, which we'd heard was a great music town. Despite my brave talk I was a little freaked out about leaving home. Dad and I had pretty much stopped talking by my junior year, but it was still the only house I'd ever lived in. How the hell did you pay bills, anyway? And what if we never found a drummer who could keep time? I felt so wired I even imagined Malkie and Cheryl were having more fun with each other than they were having with me, trying to make up new rules to make the game less dull.

All of which probably explains why I drank so much so quickly that day that I needed to leave in the sixth inning. Two weeks later Cheryl was in Madison, starting work on her English degree, and Malkie and I were driving to Austin in a 1962 VW bus, starting work on our doomed career.

Everyone keeps asking how Spider could get sick here in Chicago, one of the most important dates on the whole tour, but I'm not surprised. I keep reminding the guys I've been on the road long enough to learn most of the key lessons: Never stay at Motel 6; watch out for women with wrists thicker than yours; when the record company says "We're all behind you, boys," you know things are really bad; and everyone will get sick at least once. And it won't happen in Boise, or Iowa City, or the Other Jacksonville, the one in Alabama—someone's gonna get sick in some important city where lots of radio and press and record company dweebs are expected to be at the show. So I wasn't surprised a health crisis hit just in time for a key gig, and by the time we're at the hotel, I'm ready to empty my bag of tricks.

First, you isolate the Carrier. Luckily, I've been going to the Days Inn on Diversey for almost twenty years now. It's known as "The Rock and Roll Days Inn" since so many bands on tour stay here, thanks to its great location, decent price, and free breakfast until noon. It's nice to bump into old friends rolling into town as you're leaving, shooting the shit in the room with the continental breakfast, surrounded by framed band promo shots of all shapes and sizes. When we get back from the game, Sammy, the 300-pounder who's been behind the desk for as long as I've been coming here, gets me a deal on an extra room.

I send Paul and Danny to shower and get ready for soundcheck, and drop Spider off in his new room. Shades shut, AC on, blankets piled up. I need him comfortable enough to sleep, but also want him to sweat out whatever vile bug he swallowed at breakfast. When I finally get to the room I share with Nickel, he's already left for the venue, which means I can take my time in the bathroom. I really have no problem surviving on these low-budget tours, with their stops at Denny's and twenty-dollar per diems, but no man in his forties should have to share a bathroom with anyone he's not having sex with.

Another Cubs Curse: two of the people I went to games with are dead.

I had to show up for Dad's funeral but skipped Malkie's. I was on the road, flogging one of the last incarnations of Dígame. Late 1985, two years after I fired Malkie and Pedro, at least three years since the band's golden age. I'd booked my current line-up into some restaurant in Las Cruces, determined to prove to the world, or at least to myself, that I could still play. Cheryl managed to track me down, making herself enough of a pain in the ass to the bartender that he called me over to the phone while we were waiting to soundcheck.

"It's me, Jimmy."

"Of course it is," I said, trying to act as casual as possible. "What's up?"

"It's Malkie. He's gone."

For a moment I thought she meant he'd left her. It would have made me happy, I admit, if he'd left her the way she'd left me, but I knew it wasn't possible. He'd waited for her for too long. "Gone?"

"He told me he'd stopped. Said it was for good this time."

Oh, she meant "gone." For the first time in years, I wished I was in the same room with her, wished I could somehow find a touch that would comfort. "Fuck, Cheryl."

"I believed him, too."

I could hear her crying, and was actually jealous; I don't think I'd ever made her cry.

"I need you back here for the funeral."

"Oh. Cheryl. I don't know. I'm not good at stuff like that." I hadn't spoken to Malkie in years, but I still couldn't bear the idea of seeing some box and knowing he was trapped inside. "At dead shit."

"Fuck that. Just tell me you'll be here. I need to stand next to someone big, Jimmy, someone who can hide me from everyone's stares."

"They're not gonna stare, Cheryl. No one's gonna—"

"Of course they are. I'm the bitch who let him OD."

Behind me the coked-up soundman called, "Yoyoyo, Jimbo to the stage-o."

"Cheryl, I—"

"I know, I know, you gotta go. Go play, Jimmy. Just tell me you'll be here. Friday. Noon." And then, to make sure I'd say what she need to hear, she added, "You owe me."

"OK, OK, I'll be there," I said, knowing full well I'd never find the energy to line up all the dominoes I'd need to knock over: cancel gigs, find money to pay the lame-ass rhythm section I'd hired, and then make my way back to Chicago by Friday at noon. "I'll be there," I repeated. "I promise."

When I head back to check on Spider he attempts to sit up, but after depositing a gob of phlegm onto his blanket he lies back down. When I ban him from soundcheck and he doesn't even fight me I know he's really sick, but I still hope a few good hours of sleep and another round of vomiting can take care of it. I decide not to take him to the doctor yet; a trip to an office full of sick people's the last thing he needs.

So I gather up Danny and Paul to head to the club, cracking jokes and downplaying Spider's condition. They're trying to act like everything's fine when we walk into the Metro, tonight's venue, but Nickel instantly tunes in to the high-pitched tension in everyone's voices. "No Spider?" He's decked out in the same sweats, fanny pack, and lanyard he's been wearing since Omaha. "We got no fucking Spider?"

"No, but don't worry, he'll be OK for the gig." If Nickel is gonna be Nervous Stage Mother, I need to be the Calm Dad. "He just needs to sleep."

"That's OK for him, Jimmy, but what I need is to have this band fucking check. Tonight—"

"I know, man, I know. I'll check his rig."

Danny and Paul think the idea of me playing is hilarious, even though I string, tune, and strum all of Spider's guitars on a daily basis. Instead of getting pissed off at their lack of confidence in my chops I ham it up, try to lighten the mood. I make it sound like I've tuned up wrong, strum the guitar like I have a bad case of arthritis, and play some classic riffs with godawful timing and crazy, jerky leg stomps. Being a good Road Manager means everything from getting hotel rooms with more than three TV channels, to counting heads at the club so the band doesn't get screwed out of that extra fifty bucks, to keeping label assholes happy, to—most importantly—maintaining balance. I need to be heavy if things are too light, and fly like Sandy fucking Duncan if things get too heavy. If it helps to play "Back in Black" like an awkward teen trying to show off at the local music store, well then, that's what I do. When I hear the guys laugh, and even see Nickel crack a smile back at the sound board, I know it was the right move.

Finally Nickel gets on the talkback mic and demands that we play a real goddamn song. I turn to the guys and grin. "So, what song is it you wanna hear?"

"Gotta be 'Pay Me,'" says Danny, laughing.

"Yeah, man, you're gonna have to sing it tonight, right?"

I shake my head. "Pay Me Now" is the band's first single, the song their label made sure was played on Chicago's key radio station by buying lots of ad time, the song that's supposed to put a couple of hundred people, minimum, in the Metro tonight. I love the song, even feel a little jealous of Spider for writing it—classic pop formula, one of those "You think you've heard it before" songs you want to hear again as soon as it's over. I've heard it enough to fake it by now, but I don't want them checking anything they'll really play; it will just remind them that Spider is not here. "Too fucking fast," I say. "I'll need an oxygen tank." I strum a few chords as I talk, suddenly aware of how much I'm trying to calm my own nerves. Now that the joking is over, and we're about to actually play a song, I'm filled with a desperate urge to sound as good as I did when I was the same age as the guys onstage with me, but to pull that off I'd need to have full control of my fingers, and I lost that a long time ago.

I casually move towards Spider's mic, set up just slightly stage left. The Metro is a great club to look out onto from the stage, with a high balcony and a wide-open floor, a space that invites you to fill it with sound. I take a deep breath, and for a long moment focus on the energy, the physical force, that emanates from standing on a good-sounding stage with lots of expensive equipment behind you and a tight rhythm section to bullshit with. It's almost a powerful enough energy to make me forget how nervous I am, how much I don't want to suck in front of these guys. My fingers feel especially tight; I hold guitars all the time, but it's the first time in years that people will be listening to me playing a song, not just noodling around to make sure everything is in tune.

I'm beginning to wonder how long I've been standing here, if I'm just freaking Danny and Paul out more with my weird silence, when I hear guitar coming out of the PA. Nickel's moving faders behind the soundboard, and motions for me to play louder. My fingers are picking, not strumming, and I recognize the melody: an old Dígame song, emerging from a distant part of my brain. Our first release, actually, a single we recorded a year or so after we moved to Austin. I switch to chords, to give Nickel a little more volume to play with, and see Danny's walking over to me, following my hands. It's not rocket science, as Malkie used to say, and Danny's nodding as he starts to map positions out on the neck of his bass: he gets the A and B first, and then loops back to the Em. As he starts to play along I can hear Paul finding his own path—just kick and hi-hat at first, until he gets a feel for the groove. I flash back to all those other temporary rhythm sections I'd had to quickly teach our songs, once I'd fired Malkie. It never sounded as good without him, and how could it? He'd been there for so long, next to me, that when he was gone the best I could do was awkwardly stumble along, a three-legged dog that only kept moving because there was no other choice.

Malkie never came up with music out of thin air, but without him I'd never have written a song. It makes sense, I guess—we pretty much did everything together, from the first time we met. When I wanted to start writing our own stuff, so we could go and make our own records, who else was I going to do it with?

What he was good at was song titles. He'd call them out while I sat there with an acoustic guitar, both of us drinking or smoking whatever we'd managed to get a hold of. Sometimes the titles were just jokes, sometimes they were more serious, sometimes they sounded like jokes but I had this sense they were more serious—thinking back on it, these nights were as close to sharing any sort of real inside stuff as we got. I'd have done just about anything for Malkie, up until the moment when I couldn't stand to be near him, but we never sat down and asked how each other was doing or anything.

It was much easier to light a joint and listen to music.

We wrote a lot of songs when we first moved to Austin, working our way into new clubs and desperate to record as soon as we had enough money.

"Smell My Love?"

"You're not even trying," I said.

"Mutual Blonde?"

"Better. But 'Mutual' is gonna be hard to sing." I strummed an open G, trying to get those syllables out clearly.

"Linda's Legs?"

"Good alliteration, but Cheryl would kill me." I started finger picking, something I was trying to get better at. I was determined to keep Dígame a power trio, just me and Malkie and whatever drummer we could stand to be around, so I was always working on ways to get new sounds out of one guitar. "Give me something long," I said. "Shake it up."

He was silent for a while, working on his rum and Coke. "I Missed the Boat So I Bought a Bike?"

"Clever. Maybe too clever. And too many Bs."

"One Too Many or a Hit Too Few?"

When the title felt right to me, it was almost like the song was already there, and I'd just needed the title as a kind of a key to unlock the door it was hiding behind. My fingers started picking a nice mid-tempo, and a melody was there—no words, at first, just a kind of mumble. Malkie nodded along, and a half hour later we had a basic verse and chorus down. Words came easily to me back then; I never sang about myself, just pretended I was someone else, and told their (usually sad) story. After another joint the song was done, and I knew the first time he and I ran it down that it was a good one. It wouldn't have existed without him, none of them would have, but he never took any songwriting credit when I offered it. Said he was just happy to be along for the ride.

He only asked me for something once, so how could I have said no?

Onstage at the Metro, I wait for Danny to get a handle on the basic verse chords, and then run through the chorus. It's not ideal to soundcheck a brand-new song, and I can see Nickel talking to himself as he works on bringing the bass into the mix. Dígame's songs were never complicated, though. By the end of the chorus I can tell Danny has it, so I turn to Paul, who's already keeping time on the hi-hat. I motion to the floor tom, and he settles quickly into a solid mid-tempo groove.

We're humming along pretty well, considering I haven't played the song in fifteen years and these guys have never heard it. Even Nickel's fretting over channel levels and scratching his hair a lot, which means he's feeling in the zone. After the three of us run through a full verse and chorus, though, Nickel makes the talking motion with his hands, meaning I should start singing. I kick myself for not picking a song Danny could sing—he does backing vocals every night, so he could have just moved to Spider's mic while we played some simple cover song. We're here, though, and I don't want to bring things to a halt just when I had everyone distracted from the day's challenges. So I reluctantly move back to the mic, and this time, when we return to the top of the verse I start singing:

> At my best when I just don't think
> Just rely upon my own instinct
> I can pass any kind of test
> Just by using my reflex

Once I hear my voice mixed in with my guitar, riding along with a solid rhythm section, I realize my fingers are moving the way they're supposed to, creating the sound my brain hears. I can feel them again. I have such control over my fingers I allow them to wander off on their own, so I can focus on the rhythm of the words in the chorus.

> But now it's getting late, and I'm kind of confused
> Maybe I've had one too many, or maybe just a hit too few

By the time we hit the end of the second verse, we're already better than any of the patchwork, post-Malkie versions of Dígame. Maybe that's why the words hit me in a new way:

> She wants me to be Bogart
> So I try to learn the part
> Light a cigarette or two
> Slash a joke and look real cool

For the first time I realize who the poor schmuck I was pretending to be really was, and who his Bacall had been. How had I missed it, before?

After the last chorus the stage sounds great, and I can tell from Nickel's bounce that the room is tuned. We could stop playing, but since my fingers are awake they want to take a turn at a solo. I tell myself Nickel would want to check the lead volume on Spider's amp, anyway, so I turn to Paul and Danny and signal for them to just ride the verse out. Both hands are fully loose now, for the first time in years. The stage feels draped in a heavy layer of moisture, and my brain snaps and crackles as if I'd just snorted a line of coke off the taut belly of a twenty-year-old dancer. I'm suddenly living in a science fiction movie, and someone just showed me what life is like if more than five percent of my brain is engaged. There's a clarity I have not felt in a long time, but it's not like a flash of clarity that hits me and then vanishes—it's a lingering clarity, wiping off an entire layer of film I did not even know had crept across my eyes.

I finish with my back to the empty club, Danny and me forming a tight triangle with Paul at the center. The last chord rings out reluctantly, my fingers dragging the sound out as long as I can, until all the remaining noise melts into the ringing cymbals. The three of us grin at each other.

"Not bad, old man," says Danny.

Paul emerges from behind his kit to slap me on the back. "Decent song, too. Who wrote that?"

I hesitate, before saying, "Friend of mine, a lifetime ago."

Nickel's walking out from behind the soundboard, doing that slow clap thing. "Not bad, guys, not bad," he says. "Now if you can just lose the fat guy in the middle of the stage, you could have something... "

For a few minutes it felt like I was in a band again, like I was one of the guys everyone else works for, but that fades as soon as Paul and Danny head off to check out the dressing room graffiti. Doing the math as I get things ready for the opener—rolling up guitar cables and marking spots on the stage with duct tape—I realize I've been a crew member for longer than I was a band member. After I got rid of Pedro and Malkie, I kept hiring replacements, clinging to the name Dígame even as I started changing rhythm sections. Nothing worked, and although I knew the problem wasn't lame drummers, or the changing tastes of asshole fans, I still couldn't admit what was really wrong.

Finally, I went ahead and hired myself out as an extra guitar player. Not a bad way to make a living, really; you're still onstage, you're still making music, you don't have to haul shit, and, while you don't get the best girls or drugs (those are for the *real* band), you do better than the roadies. To make a living doing that, though, a guitarist has to have his brain and his fingers hard-wired. I didn't have those, anymore, which meant my reputation went from something that got me hired without an audition to something that meant my calls were never answered. At that point I was qualified to become a short-order cook or a fucking roadie.

Luckily, I'm a good roadie, because I'm a terrible cook.

I lost my fingers in Albuquerque, standing in the alley behind some dive Dígame was headlining. Summer, 1983. Pedro was there, chain-smoking the way he did before every show, and so was Malkie. Until I fired him, I'd never imagined life without Malkie—it'd be like imagining life without music. This was the tour when he never stopped wearing that great leather jacket he found in Santa Fe, the tour where we ate at nothing but Waffle Houses, and the tour when he asked me if I minded if he made a play for Cheryl. I guess he figured two years was long enough for me to go back to her if I wanted to. I sure wasn't happy, imagining the two of them getting together, but that was the one time he asked for something, and I couldn't say no. Not just because I owed him so much, but because I couldn't risk losing him. The band mattered more to me than Cheryl, and always had— one of the sins she was right to accuse me of.

So I was in that alley, strumming the Les Paul and trying to remember the chords to the song Neil Young wrote about Albuquerque. It's on *Tonight's the Night*, and like that whole record it sounds like the band is so fucked up they can barely play, but at the same time they sound like they have to get this song out or they'll die. When he sings "Albuquerque," he makes it sound like it has a dozen syllables, like it's the longest, saddest name for a city you've ever heard. As I struggled to find the chords, Malkie began to riff on the way the club guy had pronounced our name when we showed up for soundcheck—"Dig-a-me," he said, laughing so hard he struggled to roll his patented airtight seal, "like we're a bunch of fucking Italians."

I started laughing, too. Malkie finally finished the joint, took a hit, and passed it to Pedro. Then he started roaming up and down the alley like he was some lame-ass Italian trying to score with American chicks. "Dig-a-me," he said, "Please-a-please. Touch-a-me. Suck-a-me."

Behind me I could hear things in the club beginning to pick up. The opener—local kids so young Malkie called them "preschoolers"—was onstage, doing all that last minute bullshit. Strumming loud chords, whacking drums, trying to make each other laugh like they're not nervous. In my head, I finally heard the opening chords of "Albuquerque," so I started to play, my fingers walking across the body of the guitar like a child finding his way to his bed, like they'd been doing for more than twenty years. When I looked down, though, my fingers weren't moving the way I wanted them to. I watched for several long seconds, trying to figure out if the fingers were moving faster or slower than I expected them to, but they were just moving—differently. Wrong. Like they weren't connected. My ears were catching up by this point, and I could hear that nothing sounded right.

"What the fuck, man," Malkie said, slapping my arms. "It's like you never heard the song."

"One too many or a hit too few." Pedro grinned at his joke.

"Look, just give me Crazy Horse, and I'll be fine," I said, as if having Neil Young's backing band instead of my own would solve the problem. At that, I laughed it off, like I'd been fucking it up on purpose, and asked Pedro to roll another joint.

An hour later we went in and played a no-more-than-decent show, one of those shows where everything was too fast or too slow. I felt it, and I could tell Pedro and Malkie felt it, and the crowd just didn't feel anything. I shook off any fear that it was more than just one bad show with a couple of lines of coke provided by one of the waitresses. A few hours after we played we were back to being three guys ripped and having a good fucking time on the road, even on nights the gigs weren't great. We knew exactly what we were—a great band that had played many great shows before and would do it again. I tried to forget that all night long I'd had to think about my fingers in ways I hadn't since I was ten years old, and by the time Malkie and I were passed out in the waitress's living room—and Pedro was still awake in the waitress's bedroom—I'd managed to do it.

We had another two weeks out there in that desert, bouncing around Arizona and New Mexico and Texas. None of the shows was better than that night in Albuquerque, and a few were much worse. After that we headed back to Chicago, where we were supposed to finally finish up our second album, and play a few showcase gigs to find a new label to replace our bankrupt one. Instead we got home and bitched at each other like a three-headed couple married too long. Not long after that I fired both of them, saying we all needed a fresh start. Pedro went out to LA looking for studio work, Malkie moved in with Cheryl, and my goddamn fingers never worked right again.

Any leftover buzz from soundcheck is erased when I get back to the hotel and make sure Spider is getting ready. He's watching an old *Fantasy Island* with the sound off, and his voice cracks when he tries to speak.

"OK, then," I say, "time to get going."

He shakes his head, his eyes empty and dark, and that's an even bigger source of worry than the fact that he looks and sounds like crap. Spider is usually pure ego and confidence, the way all frontmen need to be. "Can't do it, Jimmy."

"Of course you can." I turn off the TV with a dramatic snap of the remote. "Hit the shower, get dressed, and you'll start feeling better."

"What if I don't?"

Spider's taller than me by a good six inches or so, but since he's lying down and I'm standing up, I loom over him for once. And he does look like shit, his baggy eyes and sunken cheeks making him less a skinny frontman and more a heroin addict who's gone too long without a hit. I've been with the band for a few months now, long enough to feel protective of them as a unit and as individuals, so I wonder if this is what it feels like to walk into your kid's room the morning he's gotta go to school no matter what, because he has a big test or has to play the lead in *Our Town* or something. How hard it must be to not give in, to not just feel their sadness and discomfort and say, Screw it, you can stay home. "Well, the truth is, even if you still feel like shit after you shower and eat something, even if you still feel like shit when you get to the club and put on that guitar—you still have to go play the show. Not only that, you have to be good. Can't cancel this one, man. They all need you to pull it out."

He shakes his head. "Fuck that, Jimmy. I have to think of myself, man. And I feel like shit."

"Yeah, I know you do." I keep my voice casual, like I'm not telling him anything he doesn't know. Fronting a band is just another kind of addiction, after all, so I can speak the language, and play up to his ego. "But we both know you're the leader of this band. You guys play at democracy pretty well, but you're the one everyone else—everyone else playing, everyone else watching—keys off. You're the one everyone knows really makes all the decisions. And you guys need this gig. So, you're gonna go out and play this show like it's the only thing you wanna do. The only thing you can do."

"Aargh."

"Yup."

He moans again, and slowly sits up.

"That's it, baby. Welcome to stardom."

"It's days like this I understand how people start doing some serious fucking drugs."

I may have hidden my own musical past from the guys when they hired me, but I was open about my drug problems; it makes it easier, to not have to explain every time I turn down a beer. "Wish I could blame all my bad habits on eating shitty eggs the day I had to play a gig," I tell him, shaking my head, "but it started long before that."

He throws off his blankets with a melodramatic flourish, and for an instant he looks like the Spider I've seen take control of a stage. "I'll go take your goddamn shower, Jimmy, but I don't know how much it's gonna fix this voice."

"We'll get you some pineapple juice, break up the phlegm. Tune everything down a half-step. No one'll notice, and you'll crack a lot less. Now, hurry the fuck up," I say, pointing to the shower.

I order an energy-building supply of food from Room Service (chicken noodle soup, of course, a small plate of pasta for some carbs, and a piece of apple pie, in case nothing else gets him to eat), and then walk over to stare out the window. Chicago. After my escape, I had no idea I'd be back so often. Or that the city could always make me feel as weird as it does. Luckily there's only one spot remaining in the universe where I still feel like a fucked-up teenager.

As I stand there my hand reaches into my jacket pocket and grabs my cellphone. I haven't had a phone number for Cheryl in years, but I suddenly have this overwhelming urge to see if I can remember her mother's. It's a number I dialed a million times as a teen, one of the few I've never forgotten. I can still remember the sound of Cheryl's mother answering—because it was always her mother, like some guard at the gate—and how excited I would get once she was done forcing me to make small talk, finally saying, "OK, I'll go get Cheryl."

As I listen to Spider slowly croaking his voice back to life in the shower, my fingers start dialing, as if testing the new life they've been feeling since soundcheck. I tell myself I'll hang up when it starts to ring, but as soon as the connection is made, I want proof I have the right number, proof I still have some piece of our time together, and the next thing I know I'm hearing that voice again: Cheryl's mother, this time on her answering machine. As dry and to-the-point as always. I still don't hang up. Having gone this far, I leave a message, explaining that I'm in town, staying at the Days Inn on Diversey, and would love it if she could call back with Cheryl's number.

I know no one's gonna call back; her mother hated me even when we were together, and even if she does give Cheryl the message she has no reason to call me. It'd be nice to blame the drugs or the booze for the way things ended, but I know it was really because I—me, Jimmy fucking Gonzalez, a man who now prides himself on being able to solve every crisis, from knowing how to fix a snare drum with a shoelace to how to jump a dead Ford back to life on a deserted highway—didn't have the right answer when I needed it most.

I lost Cheryl at the end of 1980. Dígame had just released its first record for a small label in Texas. We did well touring in pockets throughout the Southwest, and, thanks to a large group of old friends with big mouths, we could usually pack small clubs in Chicago and Minneapolis. Malkie and I shared a tiny place in Austin, and Cheryl and I were splitting a studio apartment in Chicago, once she moved back to start her PhD at Northwestern. After managing to hold on to her for all those years, I'd drive sixteen hours up to see her whenever we had a week or two off, just to show her how far I was willing to go, literally, to keep her close.

On one of those long weekends, we finished my traditional welcome-back-to-Chicago dinner—a take-out deep-dish pizza with a bottle or two of red wine—before she told me she was pregnant. I remember thinking to myself, as I wiped tomato sauce off my chin: So that's why she didn't have any wine. I don't remember much of the rest of the conversation, though, only the end. It all seemed out-of-focus, like I was trying to play along to a song I thought I knew better than I really did. When she finally asked, point-blank, "So what should we do?" I thought she was waiting for me to say what I'm pretty sure we were both thinking. I had no idea she'd later throw this phrase back into my face.

"So, we can't—we can't keep it, right?"

Those were my exact words. She and I agree on that much. What we don't agree on is what I meant by them. She swears she heard them as a demand, from me to her, to go get an abortion. But if she really heard that, why the hell didn't she say something at the time? Instead she just nodded, slowly, like I'd said what she'd been thinking.

All I meant was that I didn't think the two of us could raise the kid. Who would have argued with that? We were twenty-four, but while our parents may have started pushing out kids when they were that age, we sure weren't ready. Was she gonna stop work on the PhD and get a job, so I could wander around the country in an old Ford van and play small rock clubs? Or was I gonna give it up and go flip burgers, maybe? There were other options, like finding an adoption agency, right? I figured we'd talk about them next time I came back into town.

I was back in Chicago a month later to play a gig. We'd had phone calls but never talked about the Thing We Should Talk About—I figured I'd wait until she brought it up. Malkie was the only person I'd told about this, and he said to just let her be, that some women needed to deal with shit on their own. I thought I was earning future bonus points for down the road. Instead, she told me, just before we hit the stage, that she'd taken care of "the problem."

"What do you mean?"

"That problem you never want to talk about." When she took a sip of her Tom Collins I realized she'd been drinking during dinner, too. And I hadn't noticed. "The baby."

"Oh, Cheryl," I said, finally realizing what she meant. "Why didn't you—"

"You'd made your vote clear, Jimmy."

Behind us the club was playing the title track from *Aja*. I'm not mad at Cheryl for much—she did what she felt was right through most of this, I know—but I'm still pissed at her for ruining that song for me. "Shit, Cheryl." I swallowed. I could tell by looking at her she needed to hear something, but wasn't sure which of the million somethings I had in mind would fix her. Just apologize, or explain? Tell her I acted the way I thought she wanted me to, or would that just make her feel worse? "I didn't mean to—"

She just waved me away with her hand. "Go play, Jimmy."

There's lots of things I could have done. There's a million ways to write a set-list—hell, there's a million ways to play the same lead break, when you think about it. Instead I just did what I always did before a show: I kissed her on the forehead and rubbed her back before walking to join the others getting ready on the stage. I never told her I rubbed her back for good luck, that having my hand come into contact with her body brought it to life; now I wonder if telling her that would have changed anything.

I'd like to say it was impossible to play that night, but when you're in a band everyone else depends on you to do your part, no matter what; this is especially true for trios. Everyone's more exposed, everyone needs more help from the others. So I played, and played well. The other guys were in high spirits, so I rode that wave for an hour or so. When we finished, she was gone, and by the time I got back to the apartment, she was gone from there, too. Left a note saying she'd gone to her mother's, and I knew things were bad if she went there instead of staying with me.

I've only talked to her once since.

Monkeyhole slams the Chicago show, and I couldn't be prouder. Spider plays and sings as if he's just woken from a long and peaceful sleep, like he's got so much energy the stage, the club, even the goddamn city can't hold him. Paul and Danny back him up beautifully, working harder than anyone in the audience can notice. That is the lot of the rhythm section: when they do their best it means the average listener isn't aware of them. Spider and the songs need to be the focus, and tonight they are. The label assholes are drunk with excitement backstage, talking about finding more money to push this single, and planning what the next one should be.

I've met enough of these industry executives to have my doubts about about how much of the night's enthusiastic talk will turn into action over the coming weeks; big labels expect ninety percent of these indie college bands they're signing to fail, as far as I can tell, like one of those old-school farm families that had lots of kids because they knew so many would wind up getting sick, or dying. As good as the band is, and as great as the record sounds, the odds are still steep. I don't say anything to the guys, of course. It's all part of the game: the whole industry revolves around image, so the band needs to act as if they believe they are going to be part of the lucky ten percent that makes it, in order to have any chance at that happening.

We're walking back through the hotel lobby, talking all at once on top of each other like giddy high school kids, when I see her standing by the front desk. She's swapped the tortoise-shell glasses for sleek wire frames, but the outfit—jeans, simple blouse, leather jacket—could have come out of her teen closet. I keep it cool, casually remind everyone of tomorrow's departure time, and then walk over. I'm still trying to think of what the hell I can say when, as usual, Cheryl comes up with something first.

"You look clean."

I'm surprised. "You mean I used to look unclean?"

"Of course. Your eyes used to sink much deeper into your face." She smiles. "You look better than I thought you would. You look good."

"Oh." I'm proud of myself for not buckling too noticeably when she smiles. "Well, that's good, I guess. I mean, I am clean." We stand there for a second, and then Sammy comes out from the office behind the check-in desk; I guess the guys woke him up with all their excited chatting. He lets me and Cheryl into the room they use to lay out the free breakfast spread so we can have a place to sit and talk.

It's weird to be back here at night, with just a single light on by the front windows. We sit at one of the tables and start talking about things neither one of us really wants to: weather, the Cubs, how our tastes for cereal changes when we get older. Finally she shakes her head and sighs— the kind of "Oh Jimmy, what have you done now?" sigh that I never thought would be so good to hear.

"I gotta say, I was more than surprised you called."

"I didn't expect your mom to tell you."

She stares at me a second, then smiles to herself and shakes her head. "Mom's been gone for a few years now."

"Oh. Sorry to hear it."

"That was me you left a message with. I got the house when she died."

"No shit."

"I know. I even sound like her now, right?" She laughs at that, the first real laugh since she showed up, and I instantly feel better. "If you'd've told me I'd be moving back into that house, someday. Goddamn, Jimmy, I would've had you kill me." She takes out a pack of cigarettes and a lighter and throws me a guilty look. "They're not gonna kick me out if I smoke in here, are they?"

"Nah. Sammy's good to me."

She's lit up before I even finish answering. "You need one?"

"I need one, but I gave them up."

"Get the fuck out—really?"

I nod. "The beer and cigarettes were the worst—harder than the coke, or even the weed."

"It all had to go?"

"All or nothing, just like the stupid Lifetime movies." I move my arm closer to her side of the table, and turn my hand so she can see the tattoo on my wrist. "It did work, though. And I look at this any time I think about fucking up again."

For a moment her fingers linger above the tattoo of my clean date, as if she's about to touch it. "This doesn't mean," she says, pulling her hand back away, "you're all full of Jesus or anything, does it?"

"Not full. But I did have to accept the idea that there are some things more powerful than me."

"Jimmy. Clean. Something I never saw coming." She slouches down in her chair. "I didn't see your call coming, either. Such a shock I had to come here and ask: why now? Really."

"Why did I call?" I take my hands off the table and stick them in my pockets. "Just wanted to, I guess."

"Fuck off, Jimmy. Don't try and blow that past me. You must have had a reason."

I don't answer, just stare at her. It's good to have someone like this around, I realize, someone who calls you on all your cop-outs.

"How many times you been through here working shows since Malkie—I figure, what, two or three a year, on average? Forty, fifty times?"

"Yeah, easy."

"So why today?"

I pause. It still feels like I don't know the answer, but she's right to push me: it's gotta be in there somewhere. I close my eyes and feel my fingers moving, still reaching out to touch anything, even the lint in my pockets, they're so glad to be alive again. I trust my instinct and say the first thing that comes to my mind. "Is it lame to say because some kid guitarist puked on me at the Cubs game?"

She's just staring, the way she does when she knows there's more to tell.

"And that I played guitar today, really played for the first time in years. One of the songs Malkie helped me write... "

"Which one?"

"'One Too Many.'" I'm about to add that I understand, all these years later, what the song is really about, but I hesitate. So here I am again, not telling her everything I want to. She nods, though, like she has enough of an answer.

"Good choice. Probably your best." For the first time since she showed up, she smiles like I've just said something that made her happy to hear. It was always a rush, that smile; seeing it became just as addictive as the applause of a crowd. "I'm not sure any of that's the real reason, but it sounds like something you'd tell yourself. I'll settle for that." She pauses. "I'm glad I came. It really is good to see you clean."

"I'm glad I called," I say.

She puts her cigarette out but doesn't reach for another. "But I didn't come to just ask that. I came because I figure it's my last chance to ask you something that's been bothering me for years."

"Last chance?" I hadn't planned on her showing up, but now that she's here I don't want her to leave.

"Yeah, Jimmy. But I figure it's lucky in a way, most people don't know when it's their last chance." She looks at her watch. "And I gotta hurry up about it. For some of us the workday starts at eight, not noon."

I nod. It seems cruel, to see her for just long enough to remember how much I miss her. "Fair enough. Besides, I figure you..." I skip a beat, but decide to say it, even though I'll sound pathetic. "I figure you got someone waiting at home, too."

She shakes her head. "Not the way you're thinking. Just me and Mac."

"Mac?" I feel an inner shudder, terrified by the image of Cheryl wandering around her childhood home with an aging and overweight cat. "Who's Mac?"

"I can't call him Malkie, I just can't. So." She breaths in, like she's still puffing on a Marlboro. "So I use the other nickname for Malcolm. Mac."

I have no idea what to say to that. A kid—a young Malkie out there. My hands come out of my pockets and start playing with containers of sugar and Sweet'N Low on the table.

"He's almost twelve now, and still a pretty good kid, all things considered."

"Good luck with the teen years."

She nods. "Yeah, I remember what assholes teenage boys can be."

After that, we're both silent for a while. I'm trying to imagine how Malkie would have dealt with a son—would it have been enough for him to clean up? "Damn, Cheryl."

"Damn? It's not a life sentence, Jimmy." She smiles that fucking smile again. "I mean it is, you know. But in a good way."

"Of course." I break her stare and glance at some of the promo shots filling the walls around us. It used to impress me, how many of the bands on the wall I had some part of—extra guitarist, or roadie or tour manager— but now I realize no one else will ever know. I'm not actually in any of the pictures. "It's gotta be hard doing it by yourself."

"Oh, it's exhausting." She flicked her wrist to check her watch. "And I gotta have him out of bed in less than six hours. Can I go ahead and ask my question?"

"Of course," I say. "Ask anything you want."

"How come you didn't show up at the funeral?"

The question comes out in a fast, steady rhythm, like she's practiced it. "You came all this way just to ask that?" I stare into her eyes for as long as I can bear to, and then look down at my hands. My fingers are still tingling from playing earlier in the day. I wonder if they'll be back tomorrow, when I wake up, or if I'll lose them again when I go to sleep.

When I look back up at her, she's still waiting for me to say something. "Yes, I came all this way to ask that," she says. "I needed to watch you answer."

I tell myself there's no reason to hide anything, since this will probably be the last time we'll talk. "I was embarrassed. Ashamed."

"Ashamed? Of what?"

"How I'd just fired him, like that." I bite the side of my tongue. "How I'd let him down."

"He always figured you fired him because of me, you know."

I nod. "Well, Malkie knew me, all right. Always did." I exhale, surprised at how much the breath hurts when it comes out. "I fired him because I was being an asshole, and when I heard what happened, I knew." I would like to stop there, but both of us need me to finally say it. "I knew that he'd have made it if we'd kept playing together. That if we'd kept playing together we'd both have made it, one way or the other. The way we always had. So. If I hadn't fired him," I finish quickly, so I can finally say it out loud, "he wouldn't be dead."

She lays her hand out on the table between us, to where it's almost touching mine. Almost, but not quite. "You and your ego, Jimmy. The only thing that would have changed, if the two of you kept playing together, is that you'd both be gone now." She shoots me a half-smile. "Though you still should have been at the funeral, asshole."

"I'm sorry. You're right."

Her hand retreats to grab her purse. "It's twelve years late, but I accept your apology."

"Thanks." I take a deep breath. "So did he know?"

"That I was pregnant? Yeah. Stayed around long enough to find out it was a boy."

I try to decide if that makes everything less sad or more sad. As if she's reading my mind and has the same question, Cheryl shrugs. "Sometimes I think he did it on purpose, you know. Like he knew this was better than him hanging around, too fucked up to help."

With that she stands up, and I can't think of anything to say to keep her from doing it. I get up and follow her, the two of us walking wordlessly through the lobby. Back on the street we stop. She lights another cigarette, and it's almost impossible to keep from asking for one myself. Instead I force myself to think of Malkie. "So," I say, "Mac."

"Yeah." Her face makes a kind of smile I'd never seen on her before. "Mac."

"Good kid?"

"Good kid."

"Does he play?"

She laughs. "Of course. He has to, right? It scares me, how good he is already. He's got his father's fingers, for sure."

"Lucky kid." The phrase comes out before I realize how wrong it could sound, but she touches my hand—the first time we've touched since she's shown up—to stop me from apologizing.

"It's OK, Jimmy." Her hand slides up my arm for just a second; after a quick squeeze of my elbow her touch falls away for good. She drops the just-started cigarette onto the ground and smashes it, like she's just realized she needs to be somewhere else. "You look good like this. Clean. Keep going, OK?"

I want to think of some magic last thing to say, but all I can do is bend down to kiss her on the forehead and rub her back one last time. As she turns to walk away, my fingers hang in the air, feeling the empty space she's left behind.

It's a Dirty World

Atlanta, 1998

"Titties, Dave. Titties."

Standing in front of me—much too close, to be honest—is Crazy Eyes Calhoun, the enormous creature who serves as both morning DJ ("Keeper of the Morning Zoo Crew!") and Music Director for radio station 99X. As he talks his huge hands rub his meaty man breasts. "Titties," I repeat slowly, trying to make it sound like going to a strip bar is a brilliant idea no other radio guy has ever come up with. The truth is, every time I offer to take him out after a show one of my bands is playing, as a way of making sure he actually comes, he makes the same request. Using the same word.

"Fuckin'-A-OK, Dave. Who doesn't like titties, right?" He slaps me on the shoulder and belches.

I try not to read too much into his last comment. I hope it's just a rare rhetorical flourish, not a hint that he knows something I don't want him to. "See you at dinner," I say, flashing a thumbs up before I head down the hallway.

I'm here to get 99X to play "Drive Into the Sky," by the band Monkeyhole. Their debut album, released last fall by Mountain Records, got some traction in the Northeast and Midwest with its first single. The holiday season knocked all the new bands off the air, but Mountain just green-lighted a second single, and freed up some money to push for more national radio play. Since I'm Mountain's radio promo guy for the Southeast region, it's my job to get airplay east of New Orleans and south of Richmond. The key to all that is Atlanta. The key to Atlanta, for a band like Monkeyhole, is 99X.

And the key to 99X is Crazy Eyes. He's an Atlanta institution, his voice having moved up and down the FM dial for over ten years: country, talk radio, classic rock, top 40. He switched to "Alternative Rock" when that became a lucrative format for record companies, and with this last move came a promotion to Music Director. He'll be the one to decide whether 99X adds "Drive Into the Sky" to its rotation. A station can "add" a song in heavy, medium, or light rotation; while I would be thrilled to get medium, which is ten or fifteen plays ("spins") a week, 99X is such an important station, in a region the band has not yet cracked on radio, I'll settle for light (five spins). So I will treat Crazy Eyes as if he is powerful and intelligent, even though he is, underneath his boisterous veneer, nothing more than a cog in the machine, one more mid-level bureaucrat just trying not to get fired. Given his drift through musical styles, I'm not even sure what he listens to when he's alone.

Does he even like music? He must have, at least when he started out. It's possible he no longer thinks of songs and bands as music, but products he must evaluate in order to make a living, a grocery store manager trying to decide what should be placed near the cash register for impulse buys. If so, did he notice when that change happened? As his voice follows me down the hall, excitedly listing all the strip bars and trying to decide which one he'll make me take him to, I wonder if I'll notice when my own love of music starts to fade. When do chefs stop eating at their own restaurants?

Above Crazy Eyes in the station's hierarchy are representatives of the corporations that own the bandwidth; below him are the idiots who talk on the radio. All those voices—the wacky morning guys and their sycophantic female sidekicks; the heavy metal dudes who rock the daytime hours; the silky smooth sirens who tease you at night—they're all low-level employees, housed in bland office buildings you drive by without even noticing. Filling out the rows of cubicles in the station's offices are marketing people and sales people, a sea of business degrees turning the immeasurable gift of music into numbers they can crunch.

They might as well be selling time shares in Florida.

99X pretends to be cutting-edge by including some formerly underground indie bands on its playlist, but it's really just another example of the way Corporate Rock dominates FM radio. Even to get on the elevator that brings you to their floor, you have to sign in with the rent-a-cop at the front desk, so all fantasies of young musicians hand-delivering demo tapes to hip DJs and getting them played that afternoon—"Kid, this stuff is terrific! Hope you know what color you want your Cadillac in!"—are hereby dashed. A young band like Monkeyhole has to pay to even get on that elevator; since direct cash payment is no longer legal (see: Payola scandal), Mountain Records purchased commercial spots for the band's show tonight. One corporation shifted money to the other, and we gained access to the ninth floor so we could shake hands with Crazy Eyes. Before the show, the label will pay for dinner for key staff members; after the show we will pay for Crazy Eyes and a few of his fratboy interns to see some "titties." The only avenues open for young bands these days are toll roads, but at least Monkeyhole has Mountain's loose change to spend—for now.

Walking down the station's hallway to catch up with the band, I'm impressed once again by the parade of platinum discs on the wall, handed out by record companies as tokens of gratitude. Nirvana's *Nevermind*, Pearl Jam's *Ten*, and R.E.M.'s *Monster* attest to 99X's solid history, scalps hung up for all to see. For more than five years, the station has helped bring indie rock into the mainstream, and now you need 99X behind you to sell records in the Southeast. They're what I call a lemming station—all the other stations in the region follow the path they cut, even if that path leads straight off a cliff.

Unfortunately, the more successful 99X becomes, the more cautious they get. More and more songs in the carefully programmed playlist come from major record labels, not independents, and fewer new songs are worked in each week. This causes playlists everywhere to freeze as nervous stations wait to see what everyone else is playing. My job is to try to convince all the stations in the region that everyone else *is* playing my label's bands, through exaggerations and/or lies. Any kind of add I manage to get from 99X can be used for leverage, to get other stations to also play "Drive." More stations playing the song should lead to more records being sold, but my job performance is measured in spins, not sales.

Even for music it all comes down to numbers. Welcome to Capitalism.

Out in the lobby, I'm happy to find all three members of Monkeyhole managing to look interested as they schmooze two DJs and an intern. If their song is added, they'll need these grunt workers to make sure it doesn't get lost in the shuffle. "Alright," I say, slapping Danny's back. "I gotta get you to soundcheck."

The guys nod, say goodbye, and bound after me as I head to the elevator. This is my first chance to spend any time with them, and I'm glad to learn that, while young, they're also savvy enough to not start talking about what the station visit means until we're alone in my Accord. As I pull out of the parking lot, Spider turns to me. "So what do you think, David? They gonna play it?"

I pause, staring at the red light that lets us back onto Clairmont Road. Usually when a band asks that question, I just say, "Of course!" and leave it at that. I like these guys a lot, though, and have ever since I heard the record: the music is melodic and polished, but with loud, rough edges. I've also heard their self-produced EP, which initially drew Mountain's interest, and I'm impressed with their transition. The move to a major label, with its bigger budget and increased pressure, is when many indie bands get nervous, and jettison the unique parts of their music that got them noticed in the first place. Monkeyhole's record still sounds like they mixed their parents' Beatles records with their big brothers' Clash records, and, most importantly, it still sounds like a record they had to make or they would explode. Just the kind of stuff I want on the radio, and the kind of record I used to dream about breaking when I still believed I could break any record, as long as it was just good enough. All of which makes me want to answer as honestly as I can, while still sounding optimistic.

The light turns green. "I sure hope so," I say. "But it's gonna be tough." I look in the rear view mirror and see that even Paul is paying attention to me—how can you not like a band who even has a drummer that pays attention? "Bringing some of the staff out for a big dinner will help, a good show tonight will help, and treating Crazy Eyes to 'titties' will help."

"Titties?" Paul echoes.

"Yeah. Atlanta's famous for its strip bars, and Crazy Eyes can't get enough. Whenever I ask him what he wants to do after the show, that's always his answer."

Spider shakes his head. "And he really used the word 'titties'?"

"Oh, yeah," I say, grinning. "He was even kind enough to grab his own, to make sure I understood."

"Jesus. Thank God I missed that." Paul shudders, and turns to Danny. "Titties."

The guys laugh and start talking about other radio experiences they've had working their way down the east coast. I'm impressed by how well they get along. I wonder if they know they have a four percent chance of selling more than 10,000 copies of their record, and only a one percent chance of selling more than 50,000 copes—which *still* might not be enough for Mountain to pick up their option for a second record.

Even if they knew, I suspect it wouldn't matter. They'd plow ahead, assuming they could beat the odds, just like the rest of us.

Mountain Records is an imprint of Timeless Discs Inc., which is owned by MCA, which I think is owned by someone else. Mergers and consolidation happen at levels far above mine, and while some of my co-workers follow the industry gossip closely, I try not to. Paying attention to that level of activity only reminds me of local weather forecasters who spend all that time charting winds and fronts and pressure systems. No one watching really understands, or cares about, the details—all they wanna know is if it's going to rain. I move through my day as blithely as I can, and figure when I die, I'll get to meet the single sentient being in charge of all cultural production in America. I just hope it's not like *Soylent Green*; I don't want to be eaten and then regurgitated in the form of a New Kids on the Block doll.

Five years ago, I stumbled into my job at Mountain the same way everyone in the music world does: I wanted to get laid. When I was at the University of Michigan, my roommate had a band called the Flour Children. I went to watch Tim play just about every weekend, telling myself it was because the band was so good. They always played the same set at the same club, mixing covers of R.E.M. and U2 with Jim's earnest originals. The truth was, the Flour Children were derivative without being charming, a terrible combination, and Tim was gay but in denial, an even worse combination. The two of us never talked about his band's stalled career, or the drunken fumblings we allowed ourselves when Tim was between girlfriends. He moved to New York to pursue his dream of rock stardom and I moved to follow my dream of Tim-dom. Both dreams died when Tim settled for a job on Wall Street and a girlfriend with a cool Brooklyn apartment.

Tim left me with more than just a lease to deal with, though. All those nights in clubs across the city, helping him beg for gigs, left me with enough names and numbers to land a low-level record industry job. At first I just called record stores to make sure they had enough copies of Mountain releases in stock, but after a few months I was talking to radio stations, setting up promotions and helping get our bands airplay. A year later I got offered my own region, the Southeast. I eagerly accepted, even though it meant leaving New York, a place I'd grown to love for its unique combination of opportunity and anonymity.

I actually bumped into Tim two years ago, when I came back to New York for the College Music Journal festival. We talked about my job with Mountain ("Wait, you're working the South?" he asked, "Like *Deliverance*?"), the pros and cons of having a keyboard player in a band ("Hassle versus reward, man"), and his girlfriend's unexpected pregnancy ("Oops"). The complete lack of sexual tension between us made me wonder if I'd imagined that aspect of our relationship, until he'd had a couple of beers and asked if my hotel room was nearby. It thrilled me to almost turn him down. I viewed it as a sign of growth.

Soundcheck. If you've never sat through one, you can't imagine how dull it is, at least until the last ten minutes, when the band plays a few songs full throttle and, if everyone has done their job, it sounds so good your ears crackle. Today I will have to hang out the whole time—from the monotonous checking of the kick drum to that final ten minutes—so I can shuttle Monkeyhole back to the hotel to clean up, and then to dinner with people from 99X. The thought of watching Crazy Eyes tear into a piece of veal already has me unnerved.

When we get to the Point, the small but hip club the band is headlining, they head to the stage to see if the roadies are ready, and I head to the back bar. I need to set up the tab Mountain will run to keep the record store managers, local press, and everyone from 99X happy with free drinks. As I wait for the manager to emerge from whatever dungeon bar managers hide in before darkness falls, I'm surprised to see the television turned to MTV; I thought TVs in southern bars were required by law to be tuned to sports, day or night. "Closing Time," by Semisonic, a power trio from Minneapolis, is playing, and I'm thrilled. When I champion Monkeyhole to people at the label who are more skeptical about their chances, I point to this song as an example of how to break a power trio: clever video, catchy chorus, nice guitar break.

If "Closing Time" offers optimism for Monkeyhole, though, the next video offers the opposite. Cobraslap is another Mountain band, and has a chance to be one of our biggest hits. If their record really breaks, there could be even be a bonus at the end of the quarter, so I should be thrilled to see them getting MTV play. If only I didn't hate them. The budget for the "Bannister" video is bigger than the entire recording and promotion budget for Monkeyhole's CD, all so we can see a pretty woman cleaning a house and singing suggestive lyrics while her bandmates glower from behind a wall of cheesy effects. But what I really hate is how catchy the song is, and how part of me is imagining what I could do with a nice bonus check. The better Cobraslap does the bigger that bonus could be, but the harder it will be for me to get anyone at the label to pay attention to Monkeyhole.

The manager finally comes out and runs my company credit card, and I escape to the club's narrow balcony just as the VJs start gushing about Cobraslap. I have a seat and watch the guys onstage, bantering as the soundman checks the mic lines. I call the New York office to make sure they fax the finalized guest list to the club. An overeager frat type named Sandy does my job for the Northeast region—the job all radio promo people want. When you work the Northeast, you travel to Boston and Philly and D.C. and have your home base in Mountain's main offices, mixed in with the other Timeless Disc offices on Fifth Avenue. Atlanta's been easier to adapt to than I'd imagined, but I've missed Manhattan since the day I left.

Sandy does not answer, though. Instead it's our boss, Monica. "Hi, David. I was just thinking about you."

"Really? I'm flattered." I listen to Paul administer a series of slow, even hits to the bass drum. Since she hired me, I've talked to Monica in person less than a dozen times, so I know her just well enough to be intimidated. I imagine her smoothing her short, black, always freshly styled hair, and try not to worry about why she was thinking about me.

"You're in Atlanta today, right?"

"I'm at the venue now. Just reminding Sandy to fax the guest list."

"Right in front of me. Looks like you worked hard on this one."

"It's a good record," I say. Paul is checking the snare drum, sharp cracks bouncing around the Point's high ceilings. "Want to get some folks out to see them."

"Hit 99X already?"

"Yeah. Got Crazy Eyes and a few others coming out for dinner before the show."

"You really think we can get the add?"

I begin pacing nervously, trying to decide how honest to be. I want her to think I can do anything, of course, but Monica's also quite familiar with the taste and texture of radio-guy bullshit. "It's a good fit for them. Just need to push Crazy Eyes off the ledge."

"I hope you're right. We just heard from WNEW."

New York City's WNEW, the biggest station to add Monkeyhole's first single, started playing "Drive into the Sky" three weeks ago. Like most big stations, WNEW runs weekly phone surveys. They call a random listener sample and play twenty-second snippets from the songs in rotation—yes, twenty-second—to see how people react. Those twenty seconds go a long way towards supporting, or destroying, all the work it took to get that song on the radio. Monkeyhole was part of this week's survey. "What's the word?"

"Not so good, I'm afraid." I hear her shuffling papers as she talks. "They're sticking with it for now, but knocking the spins to light."

"Damn." I lean against the balcony wall, watching Spider and Danny, laughing about something as Paul monotonously hits his floor tom. If the biggest station playing the song starts decreasing airplay too quickly, the second single could already be doomed. And then promotion of the album would officially end.

"So we need 99X this week, David."

"I'll do what I can," I say, wishing Crazy Eyes was still as "crazy" as he was two years ago, when I could talk him into taking more chances.

"And," she adds, "when you see Crazy Eyes tonight, mention Cobraslap."

Paul is now playing his whole kit, so I step into the narrow hallway behind the balcony to hear better. Mountain has occasionally tried to get Top 40 airplay for a band that first had success in Alternative Radio, but we've never gone the other direction. "We're crossing Cobraslap over to Alternative?"

"I just finalized plans today," Monica says. "Going for adds in two weeks. It's a natural fit: bold young woman, not ashamed of her body, singing about empowerment, unique production touches."

Suzy fucking Suze, a symbol of empowerment? "It's a dirty world/you need a real strong girl"? Up until now, even the Mountain records I didn't like were at least artistically legitimate. The problem is, Mountain has not had a lot of big sellers, aside from a few regional hits and one fluke platinum record (a five-piece, Pearl Jam-like band whose lead singer killed himself during the making of their first video: tragedy plus marketing equals money). While being part of MCA means there's money to take chances on young bands like Monkeyhole, there's also pressure to have enough hits to turn a profit. The idea of trying to get Cobraslap played on alternative radio, after they started out on Top 40, reminds me how good Monica is at her job. Getting airplay in multiple formats is a great way to sell lots of records, and most programmers for alternative radio came out of classic rock. They're male and straight and full of lust for young Suzy. And if I pitch Cobraslap with a comparison to a band like Garbage, say, who gets a lot of alternative airplay, the programmers can justify the add.

Talking about "Bannister" on this visit, though, could make Crazy Eyes think the label wasn't serious about Monkeyhole. Before a station commits airtime to a new band, they want to be confident that the label is also committed.

Lemmings don't like to go off cliffs alone.

"Crazy Eyes has already mentioned them," I say, and it's true. I don't add that the discussion centered around whether the lead singer is of legal age.

"Good. Feel him out about an add. I'll fax this guest list down."

"Thanks." The bass is done being checked, and Spider is strumming loud power chords. "It's about to get oh so loud here, Monica."

"But you haven't even asked why I'm sitting at Sandy's desk."

Openly mentioning Sandy catches me off guard. "I figure you'd tell me if you wanted to."

"Let's just say that I'm thinking of ways to get more out of this department. It's time to start selling some fucking records."

"Sales are a good thing," I say, as if offering some Zen insight.

"I'm a big believer in moving up or moving out, David. If we want to sell more records, we need more airplay in the Northeast. I need to find someone who can get the job done up here."

Most of Monica's conversations have layers of hidden meanings, so I'm wondering if this one is as obvious as it seems. After a moment of silence on my end, she makes her point even clearer.

"Get me 'Bannister' on 99X, David, and we'll get you up here to talk about how you might work the Northeast differently than Sandy did."

Leaving the more ominous thought unsaid—what happens if I don't?—she hangs up. I swear I can hear the silence ringing from her end, even as the band launches into "Drive Into the Sky."

I step back into the balcony and collapse into one of the chairs, switching my focus from Monica to Monkeyhole. This is the first time I've heard them play live, and it will either be much better or much worse than I expect: I've done this long enough to know that's always the case. From the drum fill that kicks the song off, I'm instantly relieved. I had worried more about the guitar than anything else, always the trickiest part of playing live as a trio, but Spider's more than adequate, smoothly switching between the key riff and strummed chords. More importantly, even at the half-energy level of a soundcheck, his voice carries across the empty club with power and confidence, and his look—kind of half-interested intellectual, brainy but sexy—works better onstage than in the real world. The recording of the song is loaded with backing vocals, more than they can reproduce live, but Danny's voice is full-sounding, and confident.

Confidence. Monkeyhole has it when they play. The casual listener can hear when a band lacks it, even if they don't use that word to describe their dissatisfaction. They'll drift away in the club, or hit a different preset on the radio station, because there are few sounds less satisfying than the sound of someone who doesn't even believe in himself.

By the time the guys hit the second chorus their energy is picking up, even though it's just a soundcheck. In spite of how good they sound I am still thinking of Monica's call. It's making me realize just how much I want to make it back to New York, this time with more money and no Tim. How much I want to live there—need to, really. As much as I hate spending time with radio assholes, it's something I've learned to do well. I can get them to see things the way I want them to, a talent that probably says more about me than I want to know. It's also one of the few jobs that can be powered by love of music, short of being able to play it—something I've never been able to do.

There's always "record store guy." Last time I went to visit Gary he suggested that I get a job in one of those hip Athens hang-outs, maybe open my own someday. After almost two years together we still weren't close enough for me to tell him that's one of my nightmares, like waking up as one of those three-hundred-pound men who can only wear sweats, or spending my last years in a nursing home, fighting over the remote and waiting for Jello Thursday. I wish he'd been able to figure out just how much I would hate being the clerk who forces some obscure CD in your hands as he dismisses the band you came in looking for, the guy who makes no secret of the fact that he knows more than you do.

He meant well, I guess, and it is sweet that he wants us to live in the same city. The truth is, I like being an hour away. I did offer to have him move in with me a few months ago, in a moment of bedroom optimism, but later decided my bravery came from knowing his reaction. Born and raised in a series of small towns, Gary considers Athens as big as a city needs to be, and he looked as if I'd suggested he move to Moscow. When I sang, "Darling I love you but give me Park Avenue," he pointed out that Eddie Albert won that fight, and they moved to the country.

If I lose my job, the pressure to move in with him will increase. If I move to New York, the choice will be made for both of us.

The band finishes the bridge, passing my last test when Spider nails the solo. Having a lead break with a three piece can be tricky, since there's no rhythm guitar, but Danny and Paul play aggressively, to compensate, and the lead lick cuts through the club sharply. The bridge into the guitar solo is my favorite moment in the song, and the part of the song that I wanted WNEW to use for their audience test. Monica overruled me; she always likes to test the chorus. Trying to figure out why the WNEW test went poorly, I wonder if I should have pushed harder for "Gardenia," the other possibility considered for the second single. Monica and Sandy wanted to go with the faster and shorter "Drive," but "Gardenia" has the record's best chorus. Everyone decided it would work better as a third single, the traditional slot for slightly longer, more mid-tempo songs, but if there never is a third single, we let the band drown without giving them their sturdiest lifeboat.

When the song ends, there's no applause—there never is at soundchecks, unless someone's girlfriend or mother is in the audience—and the guys huddle in front of Paul's drum set, stretching and laughing. Somewhere below me broken glass is being swept up, and the shards scratch against the cement floor.

Danny looks up towards the balcony and catches my eyes. "Hey," he calls out. "How'd it sound?"

"Good," I say, nodding. "That's my favorite."

"Ah, spoken like a true label rep," Spider says, laughing.

I hold my hand over my heart. "It's true, it's true."

"Where we going for dinner?" Paul calls out from behind his kit.

"Spoken like a true drummer," I say, pleased at the laughs I get. When all else fails, use a drummer joke. "Italian. Classy place. Wear something clean."

More laughs, and then they all turn to focus on their soundman—chubby, sweat pants, old T-shirt from some eighties Stones tour: the quintessential soundman, in other words—when he comes over. I'm on my way down the balcony stairs when my phone rings.

"This is David."

"Yeah, can you play Misty for me?"

I smile, and turn to walk out the back door. It's Friday afternoon, so Little Five Points, the faux Bohemian part of Atlanta that is home to The Point, swells with yuppie shoppers. "Well, maybe if you hum a few bars," I say, knowing full well that Gary will. He does, and I smile some more. A song that people don't get tired of hearing every day is said to have a "slow burn," and it occurs to me that a good relationship can thrive on the same repetition. Needless to say, no one at Mountain knows about Gary. He accuses me of being ashamed of myself, and of him, but I just hate giving away an advantage. If I'm going to advance, I need to be called on for trips to titty bars like anyone else.

"You know, like that," he says. "And maybe dance around in a French maid outfit?"

"Aren't you supposed to be at work, young man?"

"Yeah, but the server went down."

"The server?" I say. "I'm no computer-type genius, but isn't that *your* job?"

"Well, I found a way to blame someone in another city today, so we all got to go home."

Soon we are naturally talking about nothing much at all, one of my favorite things to do with Gary. I pace a small circle and wonder, as I often do when things feel right, why we don't see more of each other, why I don't just move to Athens. Through the door I can hear the end of "Gardenia."

"So what's the dinner plan?" Gary may prefer small-town living, but he longs for Atlanta's restaurants.

"Veni Vidi Vici."

"A fine choice. Sneak some of that bruschetta in your jacket pocket for me. You can eat it tonight when you call me, and I'll live vicariously."

I open the club door enough to peek in, and see the guys gathering their coats. "I think they're done, so I need to get them cleaned up for dinner."

"Ooooh—you get to wash them all by hand?"

I feel like I'm still blushing when Paul spots me, and leads Danny and Spider my way. "Gotta go," I say, hoping he can tell I'm smiling.

"Don't forget my bruschetta."

At the hotel the guys go off to get ready and I hang out alone. My own apartment is an hour away if the traffic is bad, and Atlanta traffic is always bad, so I burned some of Mountain's money on a room for myself. I should plan my approach to Crazy Eyes, or nap for half an hour to store up some new energy, but instead I lie down and flip channels, thinking about Monica, and New York.

I still remember the first time I saw Central Park, and Times Square, the first hot dog I'd bought off a cart. Everything was on this intense new scale, so much more beautiful and ugly than any place I'd ever seen, or imagined. Tim and I were so overwhelmed we actually kissed when we first walked into our hotel room, even though it was still daylight out.

It was the only time we kissed in full light.

At first, city life was perfect. We searched for an apartment, and hugged like lovers when we found one. We scoured the *Village Voice* for bands who needed singers or guitarists. Our fumblings became more intense and involved less alcohol. We went to clubs we thought would book

Tim, and I found myself able to convince people his various bands were worth booking.

And then things were not perfect. The more convinced he was of future stardom, the harder Tim began to look for a girlfriend. At least we resigned ourselves to our fates quietly; by the time he'd moved out, I'd found a few gay clubs where I felt comfortable, where I didn't need to tell people it was "David, not Dave," because my name there was usually Paul. Or John. Or George.

My ticket back will have to be paid for by Cobraslap, though, punched only if Crazy Eyes agrees to play their song. Monica will be happy with a Monkeyhole add, but "Bannister" is the meal big enough to feed us all. As I watch Martha Stewart fold egg whites into a soufflé, cupping the expensive bowl against her chest and working her spatula like a magic wand, I try to stop thinking about how important the next few hours might be, for me, or Monkeyhole. Or Gary. I'm putting on a show as much as the band is. Thinking too much won't do any of us any good.

Crazy Eyes brings two interns and two DJs to dinner: two more people than I expected, but at least he showed up. I handle things with the maitre d', and work so hard to keep the large circular table covered in food, everyone's wineglasses full, and the conversation flowing smoothly, that I barely eat myself. Luckily, the Monkeyhole guys are once again naturals, spreading themselves out around the table and sharing road stories. When I pick up my credit card I slip a piece of bruschetta into my pocket, wrapping it in a nice cloth napkin to keep it from staining my jacket.

The boys play well, and I'm especially happy to hear them start with a ferocious version of "Drive Into the Sky." With the help of a low door price (a $4.99 special thanks to Mountain buying that extra block of ad time on 99X) and the fans the guys still have in Athens, the club is almost full. Better yet, the crowd likes the band, and the band genuinely enjoys the crowd, a rarer confluence than you might expect. I spend the second half of the set hovering around Crazy Eyes and Scooter, whom I peg as the intern most willing to come with us to the strip club later.

I also catch myself thinking of ways to get Cobraslap on 99X. I can't help it: part of my job's appeal is puzzle-solving, and Monica has given me a tricky puzzle to solve. Direct appeals to Crazy Eyes' lust for the "Bannister" maid would probably work best. There must be contests the station could run in honor of the song—after all, this is the man who created a bikini contest for pregnant teenagers back when he was a country-station DJ. And I try to reduce my guilt about cheating on Monkeyhole by telling myself if Cobraslap's record hits really big, it might help us bankroll another Monkeyhole album.

Cheetah III, tonight's strip club of choice, is packed. Crazy Eyes's bulk and determination, combined with Mountain's cash, clear a table in front of the largest runway. I corner Spider and explain that the band members should rotate up to the front table two at a time, since it can only hold four people. I secure another table further back, close enough to make money flow as quickly as needed, but far enough away to hide my lapses in concentration.

Paul takes the first shift at the back table with me, firing questions about how the show went as he keeps an eye on the stage. At Cheetah, each group of dancers performs three songs by the same artist, taking off their pasties for song two and getting nude for the finale; the girls onstage dancing half-heartedly to "Walk This Way" still have two more songs to go. By the time "Love in an Elevator" begins I've reassured Paul about the gig—drummers are an incredibly insecure bunch, so always tell them they rocked. As Crazy Eyes and Danny begin to air-guitar the riff, I wonder if anyone is thinking about the deeper implications of a bunch of horny guys sitting very close together, staring at naked girls dancing to a song performed by guys who look like girls.

I assume Paul's paying much more attention to the stage than to me, so I'm surprised when he asks, "So how quickly does this get unbearable?"

I continue to feign interest in the dancers and try to figure out what he means. Is he talking about strip clubs in general? The music industry? I volley. "Oh, come on, Paul." I say, turning to him with the most natural grin I can work up. "Who doesn't like titties?"

He shakes his head. "But doesn't it suck? To come to clubs like this and pretend to be straight?"

I take a sip of beer. I've understood "gaydar" since the sixth grade, when Trevor Faulkner and I eyed each other warily from the playground shadows, each somehow aware the other understood, even if we weren't sure what we understood. I know mine has not failed me now: Paul is straight.

"It's cool, David." He shrugs. "My uncle's gay."

Behind us Steven Tyler is screaming "going dowwwwwwn," and I can only imagine what Crazy Eyes is doing as he anticipates the next song, when the dancers will be fully nude. "Having one gay family member means you can tell who else is and isn't gay?"

He holds up his hands. "I didn't mean anything about it, man. I just thought it might be nice for a minute, to know you didn't have to fake it."

He's right, but I still don't offer any confirmation. As much as I like Paul, I've only hung out with him for a day, and need to know there's no other agenda here.

"My uncle got me my first drum lesson. I mean, without him, I don't think I'd be here, part of a band, you know? God knows what else I could do."

The Aerosmith set is ending with "I Don't Want to Miss a Thing." I breathe a little more easily and decide to go ahead and enjoy the chance to be myself for a few minutes—if I can remember what that feels like with anyone besides Gary. I am a little worried, though. Am I just more obvious than I suspect? And if I'm bothered by that, does that mean I'm just another stereotypically self-hating gay guy? "Well, your uncle sounds like a great guy. But I'm already involved."

"You pull it off fine," he says, as if reading my mind. "Don't worry."

"Thanks," I say, so reassured the air moves into my chest easier, and the dingy lights over the strippers' runways have sharper edges. For a moment, the world slips into a sharper, clearer focus. It soon passes, though, obscured by a ring of smoke from the guy puffing on two or three Camels in front of us. I need to practice reacting to people learning my secret; they're more likely to lose faith in a promotions guy who can get flustered than one who's gay.

"And, I wasn't looking to set you up." He starts to slowly spin his bottle on the table. "He died, a few years ago. My uncle."

"Ah, that sucks." I don't dare ask what he died from.

"Yeah. It's like, he was the one member of the family that got me, you know? So it was like I lost my whole family, when I lost him."

"At least you had one member of the family that got you," I say, talking before I can think about my words.

Paul nods, still watching his bottle as he spins it. "Yeah. As hard as it was to, like, come out as a drummer in a non-musical family, it must have sucked even more for you."

"Well, I've decided to just avoid the whole coming-out thing. I mean, why should I have to go through this extra step?" A rare family photograph, of me and my parents and my twin sisters, illuminates in some distant corner of my brain. And then disappears, as far away as Dallas should be. "Why do gay people have to expose themselves? Most people never tell their families everything, so I'm just gonna keep quiet about it."

"But you're dating someone, right?"

I nod, wondering what Gary's doing. Is he still awake? Waiting to see if I get back to the hotel in time to call him?

"And don't you want your family to meet him?"

"Not so much. In a way it's easier—the few times I do go home, I don't have to suffer through awkward meals." I imagine Gary and my mother, hanging out in that cavernous suburban kitchen. If she ever got over the fact that he was a man, she'd probably think he was the ideal daughter-in-law.

And if dogs ever figured out how to talk, we'd know when they needed to pee.

"Fair enough," Paul says. He stops spinning the bottle and leans a little closer to me. "So they gonna add our record, or what?"

I pause. Back at the Point, Crazy Eyes paid attention to Monkeyhole's set, but so far I have the impression he's come along mostly to enjoy two desserts and a couple of lap dances on Mountain Records. (Which, of course, really means on Monkeyhole, since the day's expenses will be charged against any future royalties they make.) "I think Crazy Eyes genuinely likes the song."

"But."

"But the more successful the station is, the less he calls the shots—the more the big money behind the station decides things. So Crazy Eyes doesn't want to make any sort of bold move and have it blow up in his face." When the waitress drops off two more beers, I hand her a ten and push my bottle to the center of our tiny table. "But I can call him on Monday, after your visit, your good set and turnout, this trip to Tittie-land, and try to get him to spin it a few times next week. Maybe even just late-night spins—that's not as much of a risk for him, but it'd still count as an add. Then I can tell X-Rock in Birmingham that 99X is playing it. The programmer there loves it, but he's new to the market, so he needs someone else to go out on a limb first. Then he can add it, hopefully in medium."

Paul grins. "And then you can tell 99X that X-Rock added it."

"Exactly."

He takes a long drink, still grinning when he puts his bottle down on the table. Brown hair that probably curls no matter what he does to it; one of those bodies that sneaks up on you, with its hidden muscles and subtle definition; and a tendency to be quiet—sexy and silly and all at once open and mysterious. I bet his uncle was cute.

"The record's really great," I say. "It's my job to tell everyone that, but you should know this time I mean it."

"Thanks."

Being open for a few minutes has given me the energy to get through the rest of the night, like I've peeled a layer of plastic off my skin. Would it be possible to be out in the open in New York? That's an advantage to the move I hadn't thought about.

The Aerosmith set is ending; the dancers are picking up their discarded G-strings and collecting the last singles from the drunks at their feet. I see Crazy Eyes look around for a waitress and then awkwardly push his way toward the bar. I tell Paul I'll be back and head off to meet Crazy Eyes so I can pay for their round.

At the bar he grins and roars like a drunk bear. I nod enthusiastically, saying "Oh, yeah," as I take out a twenty.

"Those are some great fucking guys you have there," he says, screaming over the ZZ Top song that begins as the new dancers come out. He's in no rush, knowing that the second and third songs are the ones to watch.

"Damn straight," I say. Crazy Eyes looks so happy, and seems to like the guys so genuinely, that I decide to push now. Away from his office, after hours of drinking, he might feel more like gambling on something just because he likes it. "So you gonna add their song or what?"

"Oh, man. Why you gotta ruin this with business talk?"

"Come on. It's perfect for you guys. Loud drums, catchy chorus, good lead break. And all in two fucking minutes." I pause, thrown by what seems to be genuine appreciation in his eyes—he actually likes the song. "It's like, the best R.E.M. song anyone's written in the past ten years."

"I know it and you know it, but there's no room at the inn. Our playlist is full full full."

I take a deep breath and glance at the bartender. He's busy dealing with a couple of angry frat boys, so I have a few extra minutes to do what I can. "Five spins next week, that's all I'm asking. Give me the add and five spins." I don't always talk this directly to Crazy Eyes, or to anyone else in the business, and I'm hoping it gets him to pay attention. "Five fucking spins."

He belches and turns to look at the stage, bobbing his large head to the chorus of "Legs." The split second of musical bonding we had is gone, replaced by our more traditional whore-and-john relationship. "What'll you give me?"

He's responding to my direct language with his own. At the edge of my field of vision, I can see the girls onstage, moving even more slowly and out of time than they usually do. A distasteful liquid seems to leak into my chest, some combination of Italian food, Heineken, naked women, and shame: I suddenly have this image of myself, not holding the band's CD, but clutching a brochure for some time share condo in Florida, a great investment opportunity, just listen to this offer...

I shake it off, and think of Monkeyhole, whose fate may already have been determined by WNEW's survey results, but who deserve one more round of good news before reality hits. I could offer Crazy Eyes more ad buys, but there's no guarantee that'll be enough. I think of New York City, and how much easier it is to expose yourself there than to hide down here in the South: this part of the country has never really escaped its history, making it harder to escape your own. I think of how desperate Monica is to get "Bannister" on 99X, and how desperate Crazy Eyes might be to see that little maid up close, and how that combination is so much easier to sell than

Monkeyhole. I tell myself I am just doing my job; it's not my fault my role in the universe is limited. The bartender finally meets my eyes, and I hold up four fingers and point to an empty Heineken bottle sitting on the bar. "An on-air interview with Suzy Suze when she comes to town," I say. "Passes for the show, for staff and on-air giveaways."

He turns back to face me. "The maid in the snake band?"

I smile broadly, glad this part of my life is not being filmed for the historical record. "The one and only."

"Shit, Dave. This mean you're bringing the maid to alternative?"

"Yes, yes we are. So you give me five Monkeyhole spins this week and an add for Cobraslap in two weeks, and I'll have her spend a morning in that tiny booth with you when they come to town."

"Will she be in the French maid outfit?"

I hold my hands up and raise my eyebrows, as if to say I can't promise, but why not?

The first song is ending. I shuttle two beers from the bartender to Crazy Eyes, keeping two to walk over to the band myself. I can see him struggle through a series of inner calculations. It's his turn to consider all the ramifications of all the trade-offs. I try not to think of how similar his calculations are to the ones I just made. "Think of the contests you guys can have," I say, horrified to hear myself but thrilled with the idea of getting two adds at once. "French maid contests. *Wet* French Maid contests."

He grins and takes a big swig from each beer. When our eyes meet, I get a brief but vivid glimpse of the hard-assed Southern boy who worked his way to the top of a powerful radio station. "OK, Dave. Five spins for your boys, but no promises after that. An add for the maid in two weeks, but I want tickets for giveaway and staff, I want 99X banners at the venue, and I want her in the booth on the day of the show."

I nod, as ZZ Top assures me, "Every girl crazy 'bout a sharp dressed man." We shake hands. "It's a deal, big man. It's a deal."

The last thing I tell the guys, as they're heading into their hotel room, is that we have the 99X add. It'll be a great ace to play tomorrow when we hit Birmingham, so we should get X-Rock to commit, as well. I don't tell them about the limited number of times it will get played, or that there's no commitment after the first week. If time is really moving as quickly as I think it is for their record, there's no reason to deny them one night of staying up late and talking about their second single maybe taking off in the Southeast.

Lying on my bed in my boxers with the still-wrapped bruschetta next to me, I turn on the TV but mute the sound. The channels flash by me, but I'm seeing the future unfold more clearly than anything on the screen: when I deliver adds for Monkeyhole, and, more importantly, Suzy, Monica will fly me up to talk about the Northeast position. Slam the interview, and I might even be up there before the quarter is out. By that point Monkeyhole's record will already be done, having sold a few thousand copies. The option for their next album may not even be picked up.

When I find a Soloflex infomercial I put down the remote. I wonder if the abs on the model would look as good in real life as they do on TV. It's after two, so Gary will be sound asleep, and as much as he'll protest later, I know there's no point in waking him up. I'm hungry, but the bruschetta has grown soggy; I throw it into the empty trash can next to my bed. Gary will stay in Athens, and while he may come visit once or twice, we will not wind up on the farm together, the way they did on *Green Acres*. Watching the faceless Soloflex boy work hard enough to coat his abs in a thin layer of sweat, I hope that the muted pangs of guilt I feel in my own—much less toned—stomach are a sign of growth.

SIDE TWO

"Life in the hive puckered up my night
A kiss of death, the embrace of life
Over there I stand 'neath the Marquee Moon
I ain't waitin', uh uh"

——Tom Verlaine, "Marquee Moon"

Getting In or Getting Out

Boston and Phoenix, 2000

Standing in Room 24D of Sunshine Homes of Arizona, Linda really wants a cigarette. If it weren't such a cliché (stressed daughter needs to indulge in bad habit) or so ironic (what better way to escape the heat than smoking a cigarette?) she would have disappeared to buy a pack. Instead she stands awkwardly by the tiny sink in her father's new home, 250 square feet of bland beige carpeting. It's the room he'll probably spend the rest of his life in, watching TV and looking out two small, square windows. They did spend the extra hundred dollars a month for a view of the courtyard, complete with sporadically functioning fountain. As she waits she tries to perfect a smile that convinces everyone she thinks this move is a good thing, but the panic she can feel seeping into her eyes is making it hard to focus. If her father's brain began to spring this many leaks before he turned seventy, what does that say about her own future?

Phoenix. Jesus. Whatever happens in her future, it better not happen here. A dry heat, don't worry, it's a dry heat. She's heard that bullshit since she landed. A dry heat? In the way Mars must be dry, yes.

Her father's wheelchair arrives at the doorway, pushed by her younger sister, Claire. Her mother and the doctor trail closely behind, everyone's face shaped into a forced look of blank calm, hostages trying not to alarm the viewers at home as they read a list of demands. Just as she is working up the strength to greet her father in the cheeriest voice she can summon, her cellphone rings. She curses loudly, her default reaction to any surprise, causing her mother and her sister to exchange knowing looks. They've been angry with her about one thing or another since she arrived from Boston, as if she should somehow have done more than clear three days off her calendar and fly across the country. And Dr. Something, whose name Linda has been told at least twice but still can't remember, actually tilts his head and looks at her over the top of his glasses with disdain and disappointment, as if she's been letting him down not for a morning, but for a lifetime.

At least her father doesn't look angry. Of course, he's not looking at her at all, doesn't look directly at anyone not on TV these days, so that may not count.

She begins to dig through her purse, growing more frustrated with each ring, and with each new useless item she finds. Enormous Liberty Bell key chain without keys? Thick address book that's now superfluous, thanks to this new fucking phone that's supposed to make life easier? She curses again when she grabs the phone just in time to see the "Missed Call" message appear. Danny.

Now she's not just embarrassed, she's worried. He knows what she's doing today, and wouldn't call unless there was a crisis. She's debating whether she should duck out of the room and call him back—how much angrier can everyone get, anyway?—when the phone starts ringing again. This time she turns around and answers quietly. "What's up?"

"It's over." He sounds like he's been crying.

"Over? What's over?"

"Spider's breaking up the band."

"What?"

"Done. No more shows. Giving up on the second record. Going out on his own."

"Oh, Danny. I'm so sorry." A lot of other things she wants to say pop into her head—how she never really trusted Spider, how she always knew he would let Danny and Paul down someday—but she keeps them to herself. Being the girlfriend of someone in a band is a lot like being the confidante of someone in a volatile relationship; it's always best to keep your opinions to yourself until you're certain they won't just get back together. Behind her the doctor is explaining something to her mother, and she can feel Claire's eyes drilling angry holes into her shoulder blades. Danny's news is bad, but no one's dead or in jail. She needs to get off the phone.

"Jesus, Linda. I mean, what am I supposed to do?"

"We'll figure it out," she says, even though she has no idea what an unemployed bass player at the edge of thirty should do next. "And I hate to say this, but I have to go. They just brought my father back from his intake tests."

"I know, I know. I shouldn't have called. I just. I wish you were here."

"I wish I was there, too." She promises to call soon and switches the phone to mute. When she turns back around her father is being settled into his beloved La-Z-Boy, the one piece of furniture that made the journey from his old home. "Sorry about that," she says. "Bit of a crisis at home. Never just rains, am I right?"

Dr. Something stares at her coldly. "We just finished going over your father's intro assessment." He nods in the direction of her mother, as if

Linda needed to have "we" clarified. "His vitals look great," he continues, flipping pages on his clipboard. "He's got the heart of a man half his age. And..." The doctor's voice drifts off as he looks over at her father.

"And?" Linda prods. Even on her best days she hates the moments people waste trying not to say the things they have to say.

"And," he continues, turning back to look at her, "I don't want anyone to worry if he exhibits some... agitation during his transition period. You're making the right move. We'll be able to monitor his treatment, get him acclimated to his new surroundings. Increase in-room assistance as necessary."

Linda's mother continues to stare at the doctor even after he has stopped talking, as if waiting for some final reveal, some bit of information that will somehow wipe out the hell she's been through this last year. It's so hard to see her mother like this, to see the woman who never met a challenge she didn't rise to and conquer easily shrinking by the minute, that Linda turns to Claire. Their father's illness may not have made them friends, but it has rejuvenated the unspoken communication they'd mastered when they were eight and six, wordlessly planning their line of attack to get their parents to give them more TV time or an extra dessert. Neither one needs to speak to understand what each is thinking as their eyes meet: they're fucked. Their father's brain will continue to drip away, even as his healthy body plans to stick around for a long time, trapped in room 24D.

She survives the next forty-eight hours in Phoenix by staying in constant motion. She's especially eager for any errand that needs to be run—after avoiding Walmart her entire life she goes three times to buy various supplies, learns the names of the entire Sunshine Homes maintenance crew. Volunteering for any and every task allows her to contribute and, even better, have a few minutes to herself, to enjoy the silence or talk to Danny. It does sound like the band has really broken up, which means that she'll have to become Supportive Girlfriend when she's done being Dutiful Daughter.

What she's really trying to do, she knows full well, is avoid actual conversation with her sister and mother. If she were fifteen again, the bond those two had forged would have made her crazy with jealousy, but now she's just grateful to be ignored. Ever since Claire had married—a lawyer, Claire? Overkill much?—and then quickly provided the first grandchild, she'd clinched the Favorite Daughter Contest their mother had been silently running since Claire's birth.

So of course Claire arrived a day earlier in Phoenix, and plans to stay a day longer, even though she's the one leaving a young child behind. Build on their lead—that's what winners do.

But Linda is happy to concede Claire's victory and get back home. When she first arrived in Boston, after finishing undergrad at Emory, she wasn't sure she would survive the year she'd allowed herself before going to grad school. The city seemed too cold to survive in, literally and figuratively, after Atlanta. She became more comfortable once she understood that the coldness was the result of an increased intensity. Life in Atlanta felt friendlier because generations of heat and humidity had laid a damp layer over everything, slowing the pace down and removing the rougher edges. Boston was cold and sharp, but those sharp edges pulled life more clearly into focus. The constant need to move to stay warm meant that after one day in Boston she felt as if she'd lived a week in Atlanta. Once she adjusted her speed to match the city's, she felt more engaged and alert than she'd been in years. And horrified by the idea of living somewhere less intense.

She'd relocated for an entry-level job at an ad agency, something she imagined to be so far removed from her "Real Goal" (as yet undetermined: Medicine? Social work?) that she would be able to leave once she'd picked a graduate school. She never expected to be as good at it as she was, or for the pay to rise so quickly. Watching the balance drop on her student loans was so much fun that one year off turned into two. Seven years later she finds herself so high up the scaffolding of DD&G that she no longer needs to convince consumers they need to buy something: she just needs to convince companies that they should hire DD&G to convince potential customers. Give her time to construct a PowerPoint and practice her witty banter enough to make it sound offhand, and Linda can close a deal. She earns increasingly large annual bonuses, and calls from high-ranking men whose names appear on the company letterhead.

So she's not sure when or how it happened, but Boston is home.

Danny is part of that, as unexpected a success as her advertising career. He's the first boyfriend she's lived with since she was an undergrad, playing house with Bob the Drop-out. She now saw Bob for what he was all along—one of those college habits she can't believe she ever had, like eating frozen pizzas for breakfast, or watching Nickelodeon while stoned—but at the time it had seemed so serious. So intense, to be "living together." It's odd, then, to think of how less serious things with Danny felt, even after they moved in together. By then she was old enough to understand that relationships started and ended, and everyone eventually recovered and moved on. She assumed that would happen with Danny, as well, after the sex became less fresh or the money issues more complicated. Walking down the hallway to their apartment, bleary-eyed from the early-morning flight, she's a little overwhelmed at the fact they've been living here for more than four years.

Four years. As long as she'd been an undergrad. Longer than Nirvana made records.

There'd been a few minor crises, but only one major trauma. What surprised her wasn't the trauma itself—is there a modern relationship that doesn't have to deal with some sort of cheating, at some point?—but the fact that she was the guilty party. She'd been so convinced Danny would be unfaithful when the band was on the road that she indulged in pre-emptive flings of her own. As each fleeting encounter happened she pretended she was watching a bad movie about someone else, instead of living her own mistakes. That pretense proved easy to keep up, since she didn't tell anyone, even Paul's girlfriend Rachel, the one person who would understand the challenge of being left alone when the band toured. She edited the events out of her sporadic journal entries, threw away all restaurant receipts, deleted phone numbers of men she vowed never to see more than once. Or, at most, twice.

So when Danny found out what she had been doing, she shared his disbelief. She'd managed to hide the worst part of herself from herself; having it suddenly exposed left her fairly incoherent and inconsolable for days, to the point that Danny had to comfort her. Whenever she made mistakes as a child, her father used to say "We are all works in progress," but that was only reassuring if you believed that someday the work would be complete. Danny refused her offer to enter couples therapy, and insisted, after a tense period where every touch and word seemed weighted down by hidden meanings, that he'd forgiven her. But how could she believe that, when she'd spent her twenties telling anyone whose boyfriend cheated to dump the loser? "Cheaters never change," she and her posse would chant at any member of their group who tried to justify sticking by their wandering boyfriends.

As she climbs the third flight of stairs to their apartment, her legs begin to wobble. Phoenix has left her more exhausted and emotionally drained than she expected, and she can feel her confidence curdling, bad half-and-half hiding inside a safe-looking carton. When these moods strike, she wonders if the infidelities were a way of telling herself to break up with Danny, to escape before their lives became so interwoven that neither of them had the energy to separate all the threads. After he forgave her, though, she couldn't even consider ending it, couldn't imagine herself as being that cruel. Which means her subconscious attempt to end the relationship could prove to be the action that kept them together?

Logic loops like this make her head hurt, the same contorted ache she feels watching one of those time-travel movies Danny loves. She pauses outside 322, inhales, then exhales as slowly as her lungs will allow. She's not in Phoenix: her father with the fucked-up brain, her mother and sister with their grudges, are not waiting for her on the other side.

When she opens their apartment door she's greeted by a wall of Lysol so thick it coats her cheeks. She steps gingerly onto the carpet, so recently vacuumed there are track lines. It's like she's stumbled onto a sanitized movie set of her life instead of the life itself. She's dated Danny for six years, lived with him for almost four, and she's never seen him clean anything; the band's break-up must have hit him even harder than she imagined. Shutting the door softly behind her, she puts her luggage down and tells herself not to worry, to just enjoy the extra layer of calm that settles upon a spotless house. She's reminded of the old Woody Allen joke, about the woman with the crazy brother who thinks he's a chicken. We can't take him to the doctor, she explains: we need the eggs.

"Danny?"

He comes jogging into the living room, Edith Bunker voice fully engaged. "Welcome home, Archie," he says, wrapping his arms around her in a vise-like embrace. When they first began dating his enthusiastic hugging caught her off guard; not only was it different than the casual-to-indifferent Boyfriend Greetings she'd grown used to, it was unlike the rest of Danny's low-key demeanor. After this trip, though, she is especially grateful for the way she can feel each of his fingers dig into her back.

She curves her face so their lips can meet, pulling away only after a long minute of contact. "Hey, dingbat," she says, smiling because he's wearing a button-down shirt that looked like it had actually been ironed, not a T-shirt that looked like he'd picked it up off the floor. "Did you go out and imprison some poor immigrant to clean our apartment?"

"Mon cheri," he says, bowing. "That was all me. Turns out loud Zeppelin makes anything possible. Even cleaning."

After she changes out of her work clothes, they take a leisurely walk along the Charles and devour plates of tapas at Sweet Devil Moon. She'd avoided all discussion of her father during their phone calls, but at dinner she talks about everything that happened at length. The depressing sight of her father staring off into space, the fear the same fate might await her. The tension with her sister and mother, and how it made her feel like once again she would never be good enough. Danny seems eager to talk about anything but the band, so she just keeps rambling.

When they get back to their apartment, she sees just how wiped out he is. He collapses on the clean couch, as if the unseen strings controlling his actions have just been cut. Linda bends to kiss him on the forehead and heads into the kitchen for the last bit of that Shiraz they started before they went out, emptying the bottle into a single glass for them to share.

When she returns he's holding up the stereo remote. "Is it maudlin to want to listen?"

She knows what he wants to hear. "I don't think so."

He holds out his hand for the wineglass. "I know, way to feel like we're at a fucking funeral. But I need to hear it."

"Of course," she says, swallowing a yawn. What she really wants is to sit in silence with him, finish the Shiraz, and then go to sleep. Waiting on her laptop is a half-hearted presentation on the rollout strategy for the new Motorola cellphone, a needy child she will have to deal with before nine a.m. He listened to her unload after her awful time in Phoenix, though, so she sits down next to him.

He's playing the rough mixes of the band's second record, the one they now know is never going to come out. When the band finished it he'd never sounded more proud to be a part of something, but the record company rejected it, and dropped Monkeyhole from their contract. Spider's decision to go out on his own came after six months of looking for a new label. She tries to pull her thoughts away from her father staring into space in Room 24D, and why people need to buy a new Motorola; she tries to focus on how hard it must be for Danny—he's been in this band the whole time she's known him, and considers Paul his best friend.

The first two songs play without either of them saying a word, just silently draining the wineglass. The writing doesn't seem as strong as it was on *Behind Door Number Two*; it's like she can hear Spider's frustration with the first record's poor sales coming through too clearly, the sound of someone trying too hard to connect with too many people. The worst ad campaigns, she always reminds the eager kids she supervises, are the ones that try to hit too many demographics at once. When the third song starts, though, her thoughts stop wandering. "This is my favorite," she says. "Something about it—it almost sounds like a new band." She turns to him and smiles. "I mean, not that I wanted you to be a new band."

He's nodding. "We put it together in the studio, without worrying about how we'd play it live. Or whether radio stations would like it. Spider just started playing this cool old keyboard he found lying around the studio, and Paul and I worked out a groove. 'No fucking guitars,' Spider kept saying. 'Not on this one.'"

She closes her eyes. Knowing the song will never be released intensifies the melancholy she hears in Spider's voice.

What room was best to hide in
When you needed to
A corner invisible
Safe for only you

What do you remember most about that old house
Was it harder getting in or harder getting out

She'd always planned to ask Spider what he was singing about. The two of them never had much to say to each other, so it had been nice to think they might have an actual conversation the next time they were forced to hang out together at some band function. Is the narrator in the song Spider, or someone else, some character he's imagining? And who is the narrator talking to? This time, as she listens, she wonders if the singer is speaking to himself, asking questions he'd been avoiding. It's one of those songs whose interpretation can change and shift with the listener's moods, more subtle and interesting than most of the others on the record. And Danny's bass, she notices this time, almost works like a lead instrument at points. No wonder he wanted to listen.

As the song ends, she understands she'll never get to ask Spider her questions, because she'll never talk to him again. Danny was never close to him the way he was close to Paul, and that was before he was fired. The thought doesn't make her sad, just reminds her that people really do just disappear from your life.

The next morning she wakes up smelling coffee. Good coffee, being brewed, in their apartment.

She didn't even know they had a coffee maker. They walked to Bleak Street Bean every morning, and she has to admit, as she puts on a robe and goes to investigate, that she's been looking forward to their Cafe Au Lait since she got on the plane yesterday. When she stumbles out to the tiny kitchen, Danny is humming along to Fleetwood Mac—one of those odd songs from *Tusk*—and warming two mugs with boiling water.

"Hey, hey," he says, leaning forward to give her a kiss. "You timed it just right."

She watches him push the plunger down on a French Press. "I didn't know we even had one of those things. Never mind how to use it."

"We didn't, but when I was cleaning I found a couple of partially used Macy's cards. Turned 'em all in for this puppy and a good grinder. Paul's a fucking coffee snob, and he swears this is the way to make it at home." He smiles, pours a healthy dollop of cream in her coffee, and then passes the mug to her, handle out.

"My little shopper." She stares at the coffee, marveling at the perfect shade of light brown.

"Is something wrong? Cream, no sugar, right?"

She wraps her hands around the mug and smiles. "No, it's perfect. I just didn't know you knew."

"Oh, I've been watching." He pours a cup for himself, takes a sip, and grimaces. "I hate it when fucking drummers are right. This is great." He smiles and puts his mug down on the counter. "So," he continues, clapping his hands together, "what can I get you for breakfast? You want eggs and toast? Some good brain food, before your presentation?"

"Would you be offended," she starts slowly, again torn between being charmed and unnerved by this New Danny, "if I told you I was shocked you even knew I had a presentation today?"

"No. I get it." He looks into his mug for a second, and then back up at her. "I put the band first. A lot. But it's what I thought I had to do, what we all had to do, if it was gonna work."

"So I'm what you get when the band breaks up." A statement, not a question, said with a more bitter edge than she intends, but he's the one broaching a heavy subject so early in the morning. "I'm the consolation prize."

"Is that what you think?"

He sounds hurt by the suggestion, but she lets it sit there, between them.

"That's my fault," he continues after an awkward silence. "Because you're so not the consolation prize. At all. You're the thing I never thought I'd be able to keep. And now I want to figure out how I can."

She takes another sip of coffee. There are worse things than letting him try to impress her in new ways. "Yes, eggs would be great."

While it makes sense, given her lifelong love of music, that Linda wound up dating a musician, she never would have expected it to be Danny Cutrino. She met him for the first time in Atlanta, when he was a stoner buddy of her then-boyfriend. His frequent, unannounced visits, his eyes permanently tinged in a red marijuana haze, drove her crazy, but they were far from the only problems she and Bob had. When she met Danny again in Boston, though, he looked so different she didn't recognize him at first. More than his arms (were they always so toned?) or his hair (shorter, washed), it was his eyes—they were so much more focused than she remembered. Maybe that's why she noticed, for the first time, how deep their green was. He was a natural behind the register at Bleak Street Bean, bantering with everyone in line, and the smile he threw her the first time he saw her was warm and genuine, as if he'd really forgotten, or had never cared, how mean she'd been to him.

For the next two weeks she found herself pleasantly excited whenever Danny was working. She was always running late, so they could never chat for long, but that was part of the fun: a few minutes of eye contact, some light banter, nothing more expected from either of them. Then one Friday he mentioned his band was playing T.T. the Bear's that night, and that she should come out and watch. Much to her surprise she heard herself say, "Sure, sounds great."

Her friend Andrea was always up for any adventure that might involve seeing single men, so Linda dragged her along. Monkeyhole was headlining, and Linda made sure they arrived after the first band; she wouldn't have to make awkward, pre-show conversation with Danny in a mostly empty club. She only remembered the band from its days struggling in Atlanta, so she was shocked to find the place packed. She and Andrea forced their way to a comfortable spot along the side wall, and she saw Danny onstage, fiddling with amps and tugging on cables. Instead of having to keep him from hovering around her, she found herself annoyed by the fact that he didn't even seem to be looking around, wondering if she'd made it.

"Which one is he?" Andrea asked.

"The bass player."

"Oh?" Andrea peered over toward him and nodded approvingly. "He's not bad at all."

Linda examined Danny as objectively as she could. He'd strapped his bass on and wore it low, which she always liked. The sleeves of his black T-shirt had been cut off, making his arms look even better than they did when he poured coffee. Not bad at all, and maybe even better than that. She also liked the way he seemed so comfortable wandering the stage, joking with the other band members and the stage crew. The old Danny, the one from Atlanta, had never looked confident. About anything.

The house music stopped abruptly, and Spider approached the mic. "Alright, motherfuckers," he said with a grin. "Let's see if we can make everyone's life much better. Especially ours." Even before he'd stopped talking the drums began, playing a beat that reminded her of a Pretenders song, that great one that ended their first album. The collective crowd started bobbing their heads along—as hard as it was for her to imagine, it seemed like a lot of them knew what song was starting. After letting the drums go long enough to get the people closest to the stage clapping, Spider began to sing in a strong, confident voice. "Let me tell you how it begins... "

That was the night Danny morphed from Cute Coffee Boy she liked flirting with into someone worthy of pursuit. She stayed to the end of the set, long after Andrea had disappeared with a frat guy from BU, and liked the way Danny smiled when he saw her. He grilled her about the show, asking which songs had sounded best and how she thought the crowd reacted. When he asked her to sing her favorite parts, she confessed that she didn't sing. Ever. For anyone. Just mouthed the words to "Happy Birthday" at parties, her singing voice was so inadequate. He ran his fingers along her throat, as if to coax the sound out of her vocal cords, and the charge she felt reminded her of being in high school and making out, when the sensation of being so intimate with someone turned your whole body into this raw, exposed nerve.

A week later they went to a Krush Tones show, but left for her place halfway through the set.

The cafeteria salad she carries back to her desk seems pathetic after the omelet Danny cooked her for breakfast, its slightly wilted greens and generic packet of Italian Dressing making her lonely. She wants to call him, just to hear his voice, but she worries about setting a precedent. She's never called him before on her lunch hour—will he start to expect it every day? The break-up of the band means they're making new rules for their relationship, and she doesn't want to screw things up.

So she calls Rachel, to see how Paul is coping.

"Jesus, he keeps making these goddamn lists."

"Lists?"

"Things to do to the apartment. Places for us to visit. Places for us to move. Bands to try out for. Ways to save money. Every day I get home from work he's there, waiting, some new list in his hand. He needs to get back out on the road soon or I'm going to kill him."

Linda's spent enough time with Rachel these last few years to see the look on her face clearly, even over the phone: narrowed eyes, crinkled forehead, pursed lips. She's also learned that Rachel is happiest wearing this Annoyed Look of Disbelief. "Well, Danny's cleaning."

"Himself?"

"The apartment. Not only that, he made me coffee this morning. And breakfast. Real breakfast, Rachel, with eggs and his own hands and the stove and everything."

"Jesus. Is this what PTSD does to people?"

"I guess so." Linda takes her first bite of salad and wonders if it would be taking advantage of Danny's unsettled state of mind to ask him to make her lunches. "The strangest thing of all? He remembered I had a presentation today. Even asked me questions about it."

Rachel snorts. "OK, that's some crazy shit, but maybe you should just enjoy the ride as long as it lasts. I'm not even sure Paul knows what my job is."

Spider, who seems to be always dating yet terminally single, calls Rachel and Paul "The Lockhorns," after an old comic strip about a bickering couple, and they wear the title like a badge of honor. They've been together even longer than Danny and Linda, and she long ago stopped trying to understand their relationship. It made sense for her and Rachel to kill some of their nights together, when the guys were on the road, but Linda knows the two of them would never have hung out so much if it wasn't for their shared Musical Widowhood.

She began to make excuses for not going out with Rachel, as the band stayed on the road for longer stretches of time. She enjoyed the chance to revisit the rituals she'd developed during those stretches she wasn't dating anyone seriously: watching marathons of *Law & Order* and *Sex and the City*, having cereal and frozen pizzas for dinner, and buying more Entenmann's products than she would ever admit. She often wound up restless, though, too eager to accept dinner invitations from co-workers that turned into visits to bars later on. And sometimes turned into more than that, each mistake met with a vow that it would be her last. When the next mistake was made, she had a list of rationalizations ready to go. It's not like she was married to Danny, she told herself, and she certainly she didn't imagine him acting like an Eagle Scout around drunken fans after gigs.

She had the Iron Horse in Northampton to blame for the two of them realizing just how much she'd fucked up. The club had its power cut off a few hours before Monkeyhole was supposed to play, so Danny decided to surprise her by driving home for the bonus night off. When she finally stumbled into the apartment sometime after three, he wasn't sitting on a chair in the middle of the room, like an angry TV spouse. He was in their bed, pretending to be asleep. So she pretended to sleep next to him.

They didn't have it out until the next morning, but she decided to break her rule about never staying with anyone she had a shouting fight with. It didn't seem fair, since she knew she was the cause. A year later, she finds there are long stretches where she forgets what she did, forgets to check his eyes for signs of distrust. She wonders if he ever manages similar stretches of forgetfulness.

After she hangs up with Rachel she throws away most of her salad, feeling guilty about the wasted food, and about the way she will never be as good a friend as Rachel would like. Jesus, what is she truly good at these days? She played the sister and daughter roles spottily at best in Phoenix, and the girlfriend role is feeling the stress of all this change.

It's not Danny's constant presence that feels odd, because when the band wasn't touring there were long stretches where he was home all the time. There was always a predetermined ending, though, some moment when he would go to record again or get back out on the road. This time there's no foreseeable end. She finally asks what his next musical move will be, but his mood grows so dark that she doesn't bring it up again.

Which means they spend a lot of time working hard to not talk about anything more than a day or so into the future.

Linda is determined to celebrate Danny's thirtieth birthday in style, though, and makes reservations at Blue Ginger. Rachel and Paul come along, and seem oddly determined to get along for the night. She finds out why they're so happy halfway through the meal: Paul's just gotten a new road gig, and will be leaving in a week for rehearsals. "After that," he says, filling everyone's wineglasses, "who knows. It's at least three months, and then there's talk of a swing through Australia."

"Australia!" Danny looks at Rachel. "Would you fly out to join him for that?"

"Hell yeah," she says. "For that, I'd break my no girls on the road rule. And just think," she continues, looking at Linda, "if Paul had talked Danny into trying out as well, the two of us could go down under together."

"I know there's a dirty joke to be made there," Paul says, "but I can't find it."

Rachel starts to hum "Land Down Under" and Danny makes jokes about "shrimp on the barbie" in a terrible Australian accent, and everyone seems to be floating on that magic buzz of good food and strong wine— just the kind of fun night out Linda wanted Danny to have. She wonders, though, all the way through the rest of their entrees, the shared desserts, and the brandy, why Danny didn't want to audition with Paul. He didn't even mention the opportunity. The two of them never had the chance to talk through the pros and cons together, and she'd imagined their incessant togetherness would make it impossible to keep secrets.

But that's just it, she decides, watching everyone else enjoy themselves: they're all sitting here with secrets. Things they know about each other but choose not to share. Hanging out more doesn't mean fewer secrets—it means more.

By the time they get back to the apartment, she knows she's too drunk to start a serious conversation, but she can't stop herself. She doesn't even wait for Danny to take his coat off.

"Why didn't you tell me Paul wanted you to audition with him?"

"What, the Ebenezer's Screwed thing? God, they're awful."

She drops her purse and coat on the coach in an unseemly pile. "I thought you missed playing with Paul."

"I miss playing our music. With Paul. But playing that shit with him every night would be worse than not playing at all." He hangs his coat up and turns back to her. "If I get offered a chance to apply for NASA, or to start driving big rigs, I won't be mentioning those, either."

They're standing awkwardly in the living room, five feet apart. "It's not the same thing, Danny."

"So you want me to go and get a road gig, any road gig?"

"No, no. I just thought that music meant a lot to you."

"It does. It was my life."

She rubs her head, as if a little massage now will keep the morning hangover away. Or allow her to drift back in time and not start this conversation. "But it sounds like you're giving music up. Are you?"

"I don't know. I think so. Maybe?" He shrugs. "I can't think of any other band I'd want to sacrifice everything else for."

"So, then." She tries to think of the nicest way to ask the question she has to ask next. "What else would you do?"

He shrugs. "I'm thinking I could go to school."

"College?"

"Yeah. I thought I'd go off and figure out what I want to be, when I grow up."

I've already lived with an undergrad, she thinks, and it wasn't so fun. In fact, she had vowed to never do it again. And why are they still standing? It's like they're both afraid to move from their spots. "You want to grow up? Now that you're thirty?"

"I've been thinking that this is, like, a new start. And I wanted you to be there, with me."

"Wanted?" She wonders what else he's been thinking about. "Past tense?"

"No, that's not what I meant—not past tense at all. Is it past tense for you?"

"Not at all. But," Linda adds, "is it future tense?"

Now he's rubbing his forehead. "How did this get so confusing? I mean, what are you talking about? If we'll still be together tomorrow? Next week?"

"Yes. And longer. Like, years down the road."

"Married?"

His question catches her off guard. While it could look like they already are married, in some ways, it also feels impossible to imagine. One step closer to becoming her mother.

His next question is asked more quietly. "Have you thought about it?"

"Yes, I have," she says after a long pause. "At some point, right, anyone living together thinks about it?"

"How romantic."

"I mean, it's more than that. But there was always the fucking band, right? So I knew there'd always be a record, or a tour, just around the corner."

"But the band's gone."

"Right. I know. I just—I want to make sure you're making these decisions for the right reason. And not just because you're afraid to go back on the road."

"Afraid?"

Standing in a dark room after too much wine is probably her only chance to ever say it. "Afraid of what I'll do when you're gone."

"That." He seems to deflate. "That's over. You said it's over, so I trust you."

"Do you?"

"If I didn't trust you I wouldn't be here. But if you can't believe I trust you, then that's as big a problem, right?"

She can tell he believes he's telling the truth. He believes he's forgiven her. She doesn't know if it is the truth, though, or one of these things people tell themselves over and over hoping it will become true. And when they finally stop talking and head to the bedroom, naturally reaching for each other's hand, she can't tell whether all the shit they just worked into the ground beneath them will do more good or more harm.

The next day Linda heads back to Phoenix, one of four weekend visits she has planned for the year. Danny gets up to make her coffee and eggs, the two of them honoring some unspoken agreement to not talk about the things they said. Not yet.

She hopes to find her father settled in, the popular new arrival already wandering the halls with a posse of other charming old men. The second visit proves even more dispiriting than the first, though. Watching his focus drift in and out over the course of their four-hour visit she understands how unrealistic her expectations had been. She knows enough not to dream of a medical miracle, but she has been hoping for the kind of resolution that comes at the end of a TV show: the scene when the kindly doctor comes into the room and sees her chatting pleasantly with her somewhat coherent father, everyone fully adjusted to their new lives.

Instead she witnesses two angry outbursts, two crying jags, and one bout of incontinence. Thank God for the brief stretch when he was focused enough to relate a series of funny stories about his own father, an Irish pub owner she never met, or she would have needed to go find a medicine-dispensing doctor of her own. Her mother seemed much less flustered by everything, but that also made Linda sad. Less than a month in, and her mother was already accepting the worst.

Jesus—or maybe what Linda watched wasn't the worst?

On their way home her mother pulls into a Chili's. Neither discussed this plan beforehand, but they are both so tired it makes perfect sense.

"So how is Danny doing?" her mother asks as soon as they sit down. "Has he found a job yet?"

Linda would usually hear such an immediate question as an aggressive opening, a way to discuss the inadequacy of her life in Boston, but tonight she senses her mother is just desperate to talk about something besides her father. "No, not yet. I don't think he has any idea what he wants to do."

"Another band? Is that how it works? Like secretaries, looking for a new company?"

"It could work that way, if he wanted it to, but... he was excited about that particular band. I don't think he could join a band he didn't care about."

"So what will he do?"

"I don't know." She shrugs, pretending to carefully consider the glossy menu. "He mentioned college."

"Thirty-year-old freshman. Well." Her mother fiddles with the salt and pepper shakers. "No income there. How are you going to get married?"

"Maybe we're not." She puts down the menu, having settled on a Caesar Salad. Hot food in Phoenix seemed unbearable. "It was easier, in a way, when he had the band to keep him distracted. Now I worry about him expecting too much if it's just the two of us."

"Expecting too much?"

"Yes. I'm not like Claire. I can't always meet everyone's expectations."

"You shot your way up in a male-dominated industry. A timid wallflower you have never been."

Linda is startled. That could be the nicest thing her mother has ever said to her. "Working has always made more sense to me than being alone with other people. Especially men." She pauses so the waitress can take their order. "I just don't know that he's the one. I mean, for forever."

"I was thirty when I married your father. And in those days, people had given up on me ever finding someone. And here you are thinking it's too early."

"It's different now, Mom. People don't have to..." She stops herself before saying the last word, but it's too late. Her mother knows her too well.

"Settle? You think I settled?"

"That's not what I mean."

"I think I know what you were about to say."

"But, not for you. For me. Am I settling for Danny?" She wishes that you could order your wine on the way to the table, so it could be there waiting, before you had to say a word to the other person.

"That's too vague. What specific issue makes you wonder if you're settling?"

She's reminded of the way her mother would grill her and her sister at the dinner table every night, always pushing for more concrete details. "Good" was never the right answer to "How was your day?" You had to provide details, supporting evidence. The flush of annoyance she feels at remembering those cross-examinations fades, though, when she wonders why this is the first time she's connected that childhood memory with her ability to make an effective presentation to a room full of strangers.

Is everyone's adult life really shaped by the crap they deal with as kids? And if that is the case, is that depressing or reassuring?

As if sensing her deep need, the waitress delivers their glasses of wine before Linda has to answer her mother's question. She takes a long sip, never more grateful for an average Merlot. "Well," unsure even as she starts how much more detail she will give, "there's been infidelity."

Her mother laughs, a genuine laugh from the belly. "Now you sound like you're from my era. You guys aren't even married yet—how can there be infidelity?"

"But I worry about what that... means. For us. That it happened."

"It means that he had sex with someone else. It doesn't mean any more than that, unless he leaves you. Men have sex as much as they can. If you're not in the room, and someone else is, that's how it happens."

Of course her mother assumes Danny cheated on her. She plays along, lacking the strength to turn down the road of Full Honesty. "That's depressing."

"It's biology, and best not to overthink it." Her mother drains half her Zinfandel in two quick swallows. "Did he love her, this other woman? Or women?"

"No," she says. True: Linda never loved any of them.

"Then it was just sex. And it's not pretty, or what you bargained for, but it happened. And ended, right?"

Linda nods.

"So what good does thinking about crappy stuff that's over do either one of you?"

Something in her mother's voice makes her call an obvious truth out of its hiding spot. "So Dad cheated on you?"

Her mother stares at her silently before answering. "Oh, I don't feel comfortable talking about your father. Not with him sick, Linda. It's not fair."

She wonders if her mother would be more forthcoming if she told her the truth, that she's the one who cheated. That she's the one who needs to know if this will be too much for a marriage to overcome. It makes her feel ten years old to admit it, but she can't bear her mother knowing the truth. "It would help me, Mom," she says, deciding she will edge closer to the truth without touching it. "I don't know what to do."

"How would talking about our past, about our personal—" Her mother looks surprised, not a look she wears comfortably. "How would that help you decide whether or not you can marry Danny?" Her eyes narrow, and Linda can see her brain working through the questions. "Oh. You don't know whether you can trust him."

She nods. It's the truth, albeit not in the way her mother thinks: she's not sure that she can trust Danny when he says he trusts her.

"There's just two questions you have to ask yourself. Can he stop, and can you forget?"

Linda switches the pronouns in her head as she cuts a piece of bread for her and her mother. They both need something to soak up the first glass of wine so they can hurry up and have another. "So how do you forget?"

Her mother shrugs. "For me, it's like exercise. Daily exercise. Remember the good, push the bad away. Each day aim for more good in, more bad out." She takes a bite of her bread. "It never seemed like too much trouble, because we were so much better together than we were apart. So maybe that's a third question: are you a better person with him?"

She imagines jogging in the mornings with the new Danny, the one who doesn't travel, the two of them making their best selves stronger. Is that how it worked? You picked the person you think you can become better by being with?

"Though I have to tell you," her mother adds, holding her empty wineglass up so their waitress can see it, "if he ever calls me some other woman's name, dementia or not, I'll punch him. Hard."

Linda flies home Sunday afternoon, so she can get in to the office in time to salvage Monday afternoon's presentation. One of these days the job will stop coming as easily to her as it does now, and she'll be screwed, but in the meantime she knows she can watch bad movies on the flight instead of working.

If only she could convince herself as easily as she convinces strangers. If only she could sell herself the things she needs. But what? If she just knew whether the product was Getting Married or Staying Single, she could write the script.

Linda closes her eyes and imagines herself delivering a PowerPoint to her fellow passengers, something to replace the much less useful instructions for the gas masks whose actual appearance would be so terrifying that no one would be calm enough to put them on properly. The first image projected on the big screen behind her would be a large photograph of her parents on their wedding day. She knows the shot well, can see it clearly on her closed eyelids: her mother, wearing a classic white dress and the kind of wide-open smile Linda never saw her flash in real life, has her left arm curved around the back of her father. He's leaning down to look at her, oblivious, as he so often was, to anything else but her. The title of the talk, *Things I (Don't) Know About Love*, is superimposed on the photo, and after spending a few moments pointing out interesting things in the picture (this was still the sixties, people, so yes, that hipster in the bell bottoms and turtleneck, off to the side there? That was the priest), she'll click her pointer and change the background and the tone.

New slide: *No One Else Can Ever Understand Someone Else's Marriage.* Photo: her mother in that terrible kitchen with the pale yellow linoleum floor, hands on hips and eyes full of rage, pointing at someone off camera.

"This is the same woman, maybe ten years later. I took the picture, with the cheap Kodak camera I'd gotten for my birthday. I thought I was being smart and clever—young reporter, documenting the world around her. Just out of the frame is my father, absorbing whatever blows my mother throws his way.

"I watched this marriage, close-up and from a distance, and never understood why he put up with her anger, her mood swings, and her general inability to ever appreciate him. The one clue I ever had, the one piece of evidence that might have explained what it was she offered, was his laugh. I grew up hearing this deep, booming laughter through the wall separating my bedroom from theirs. It never failed to catch me by surprise.

"What surprised me wasn't the fact that he was laughing—my father laughed and smiled his way through my whole childhood. What surprised me was that it had to be my mother making him laugh like that. This wide open, pure laughter that somehow the two of them shared when no one else was around."

We Hide Ourselves From Everyone Else. Photo: Linda's mother, staring directly at the camera. Her eyes are angry again, but there's also a visible sadness.

"How could the woman who scowled her way through my universe make him laugh so loudly? Sometimes in the morning I would watch my mother for clues, for signs of that other person, the one who was so funny that she could make a grown man cackle like a little boy. All I ever saw, though, was a woman who seemed annoyed that the rest of us were there, a woman determined to get us all out of the house every morning as quickly as possible."

All Marriages Follow the Same Pattern, But No Two Marriages Are the Same. Photo: her mother and father, looking young and frazzled, both staring at a lump of baby in his arms.

"One of the rare times the two of them looked at, and saw, I think, the same thing. That's me, some tiny infant keeping them awake all night, according to legend, and sleeping all day. Couples have babies so they won't run out of things to say, and that was true for my parents. They disagreed about almost everything that had to do with our upbringing, but I think that's why my sister and I are so good at reading people. And finding different ways to try and get what we want."

At the End, What You're Left With Is Each Other. If You're Lucky. Photo: her parents as they are today, in Room 24D of Sunshine Homes Complex 2044. He can't stare at her the way he used to, but for once she has her gaze fully focused on him. She won't need to say anything for this slide, just let it sit there for a full eleven seconds.

Eleven seconds, she has learned, is the perfect amount of silence to have when you want to make a point sink in. Long enough to be powerful, not so long it gets awkward or too weird.

No Spouse Is Perfect, But You Must Find the Perfect Spouse. Photo: A gray box with a big white question mark. If she's selling herself on the idea of

Danny as Perfect Spouse, then this should be a photo of him—perhaps onstage, mouth wide open as he sings some backing vocals, those beautiful fingers frozen in motion on the strings of his bass?

But if that's the Danny who's the perfect spouse, what happens when Musician Danny stops existing? Who does he get replaced with? Is it the same Danny, just with a different outer casing? If that were true, then she could maybe live with College Student Danny. Maybe even marry him. But isn't it inevitable that he'll be changed by the process of reinvention?

Maybe she's asking the wrong questions. Maybe she's really just much more self-obsessed than she wants to admit. Maybe what she's really worried about is the change she'll have to undergo, as a result of his changes.

By the time she gets back to the apartment, it's almost midnight. Danny is in bed, curled on his side, so sound asleep he doesn't even move as she lays down next to him.

Sleep should come easily, but Linda feels herself struggling. The last sight of her parents—her mother sitting next to her father, her hand tightly covering his, their eyes drifting blankly toward different spots in the distance—proves hard to shake. How hard it must be for both of them to be there.

And how much harder it would be to be anywhere else, alone.

A sudden leg twitch wakes her up. She doesn't remember falling asleep. She turns to stare at the clock: 2:06. She feels so wide awake that she would have believed the clock if it read 7:06.

She rolls onto her side and stares at Danny, to make sure he is indeed still there, that she did not dream his presence when she returned home. How long has he been the stronger one? Probably all along. It's like watching the end of a well-put-together mystery; the solution quickly morphs from unbelievable to obvious. What would she have done, if the career she expected to keep doing for the next ten, twenty, thirty years, had been suddenly taken away? And how would she have handled it, if he were the one who failed the fidelity challenge?

She chides her inner thoughts for phrasing the problem in cold business speak. How about, if he was the one who justified his own weird self-image issues by fucking other people?

He's on his side, facing away from her. If he can sense her watching him, she decides, she will know it is time for her to stop wavering. She'll know it's her turn to make the move. To get on bended knee, if that's what it takes.

Commit.

But what happens if he doesn't notice her? The thought makes her chest collapse, as if she's spinning on that amusement park ride where the floor falls away while you're pinned against the wall. She decides to start stacking the odds. A quick poke of his shoulder, a slight touch of his hip with her so-slow-it's-barely moving hand. As he begins to stir she clears her throat, ready to sing for the first time since she auditioned for, and was rejected by, the fifth-grade chorus. Leaning down close to his ear, she tries to sing a line familiar to them both in a new way: "Let me tell you how it begins... "

This Next Station

New Rochelle & New York City, 2004

When I walk into the kitchen the only light is coming from the digital clock on the stove: 3:06. I quietly slip off my shoes and jacket and stand perfectly still. Mom and Dad aren't sitting at the kitchen table, ready to confront me over my lies. I didn't even get a single panicked call from them. Everything worked out just as Amy had planned.

Well, almost everything.

I walk to the refrigerator, hoping I'll know what I'm hungry for when I see it. I reject anything I think Beau will want, so I don't have to deal with him later. A shake of the orange juice carton tells me it's almost full, so I take a long swig, then a second. I put it back and move over to the pantry. Maybe something salty? I'm staring at the bag of Lays when my cellphone vibrates. I flip it open to see a text from Amy: *I know what u did asshole I wasnt asleep*

I close it quickly, as if that can somehow erase the words.

The phone's still in my hand when another message buzzes in, this time from Cameron: *sorry.*

Buzz. *lying faggot fuck u*

Buzz. *reallyreally sorry things got fuckd up*

Sneaking in to the show had been Amy's idea. She didn't even like Monkeyhole, the best obscure band I'd uncovered in all my hours of surfing music sites. *Behind Door Number Two* was twelve perfect pop songs, sad and angry and catchy at the same time. It was their only CD, released more than five years ago, and the fact that not many people at the time cared or noticed made the music more beautiful and tragic: a thing's more valuable if it's a secret. I played her the CD after we'd been dating for a month or so, and she looked disappointed from the opening song on. I'd built it up too much, I guess, raving about this amazing, incredible lost record only a few people knew about. "It's good," she said, after three songs. "But can we listen to the rest later?"

I was bummed. It was the first time I'd shown her something that really meant a lot to me, and I'd imagined us both liking it so much we started making out, not stopping to watch TV. Later, though, I felt a kind of relief. Monkeyhole could keep being my secret, a band that only I, and a few select others, appreciated.

But a month later, sharing the record with Amy did pay off. "So my brother loooooves them," she said, rubbing my arm as she talked, the way she did whenever she was excited. We were slowly pushing our way through the halls of Madison High, one of those annoying couples who insisted on walking side by side even when it was crowded. I loved that. "When I told him you'd made me listen to the CD a million times, you went up, like, ten levels in his eyes "

That was good to hear. Amy's brother studied film at NYU, and I'd always worried he didn't think I was worthy of his sister. I couldn't imagine being twenty-one, living in New York City, going to classes where you talk about movies. It almost made me think life really would get better once high school was over, even though there were only a few months left before summer and I was still on the waiting list for my top three colleges. My parents kept saying a year or two at community college, living at home, saving money, would that be so bad?

How many words were there in the English language for "yes"? Beau might be happy on the See How Long You Can Live At Home Plan, but I needed to get out.

"Did he dock you points when you told him you thought the CD sucked?"

"Silly! I told him it was great, of course." We stopped outside her algebra class, where we always waited until first bell. That left me just enough time to rush to bio. "But get this—one of the guys is in some new band playing in the city next week. Next week!"

I shrugged. "I know." I'd read everything I could find about Stackd Souls, the new band Monkeyhole's lead singer had started. An EP was coming soon, and they'd started touring the East Coast. "But you have to be twenty-one to get in."

"Oh, come on, Andy. You have to stop worrying about the small stuff." The first bell rang, and she gave me a final hug. "We'll talk more at lunch."

I moved quickly through the halls with the other trying-not-to-be-lates, wondering how I'd managed to become one of those guys who raced against the bell because I had to walk my girlfriend to her class first. As a freshman and sophomore, I'd been noticed only as Beau's little brother; three years ahead of me, he'd left such a golden trail of testosterone and trophies that everyone who met me had the same question. "Andy Achenbach? Are you related to Beau?"

Yes, yes I am, I always answered, understanding their confused looks. Sure, I'll tell Beau you said hello. But no, I'm not going to play basketball or football or baseball or any of the other crap sports he played so well. In ninth and tenth grade my belly poked out over my belt, no matter how baggy my pants were. Thank God my mother had been right about one thing: I finally did grow three inches taller, and that simple change pulled my body into focus. I remained one of the Mostly Invisible High Schoolers, but not being noticed sure beat being seen for all the wrong reasons.

I walked into biology just as the late bell rang. Beau was probably right, when he told me Amy only made a move on me last summer because I finally looked OK in a bathing suit. I didn't care. It sure was better to be one of the almost-late kids than someone who sat waiting for class to start because he had nowhere else to be.

Amy came up with a believable cover story: we were going to meet Cameron and his girlfriend in the city, where we'd have dinner and see a foreign movie. When Amy's parents worried about the two of us taking a late train home, Cameron offered to ride back with us. That closed the deal; Amy's parents were always bugging Cameron to visit.

A week before the show he e-mailed me, to go over all the details. He included a link to a clip of Monkeyhole playing some club in LA right after their record came out. You could tell the small crowd had never heard of them, but they sounded great. They looked so young—not that much older than me and already out there in the world, doing something. I wrote back to thank him, and the day before the show he sent me an MP3 of a new Stackd Souls song: "Hope they play this one tomorrow!" I wanted to send an e-mail talking about the song, because I liked it so much, but I didn't want to come across as some overeager kid.

Amy and I rode Amtrak to Penn Station after school that Friday. She talked about drama with her friends and I nodded at the right times, but it was hard to focus. I was excited to see Spider's new band, but couldn't stop worrying. What if our parents found out what we did? Even worse, what if Cameron couldn't get us in, even though he said he had it all worked out?

I felt better as soon as Amy and I stepped off the train and onto the platform. The world is a brighter place every time I arrive in New York City; a layer of film covering regular life gets peeled off, and all the colors and noises intensify. Walking with Amy I could imagine watching the movie of my own life and thinking, just for a second, that the guy holding that pretty girl's hand looks happy. He looks together.

As soon as we climbed the stairs to the lobby, Amy spotted Cameron in the middle of a large cluster of people. It's a little freaky, the way she can sense when he's close. Once, we were walking around Hartford, killing time before a movie, when she insisted we head to a nearby diner. There he was, having pancakes with one of his college buds, and Amy didn't even know he'd left the city. When she ran into his arms in the lobby of Penn Station the two of them looked like one of those snapshots from WWII, men and women reunited after years apart. His hair was so much darker they looked more like a couple than brother and sister. I hung back, giving them space, and watched Cameron bend down to whisper in Amy's ear. She grinned, whispered back, and all I could do was marvel—would I ever have secrets to share like that with my brother?

Would I ever sprout wings and shoot rain through my toenails?

When they separated, I walked over, holding my hand out for Cameron to shake. I was surprised to get a hug instead, a hearty embrace with hands pressed flat on my back. "Great to see you guys. Bonnie and Clyde, breaking out of the 'burbs for a night on the town."

"Good to see you, too," I said.

"Is Carrie going to meet us at the restaurant?"

"No can do." Cameron shook his head. "Had to go to her mom's in Long Island. Can't make it."

"Not even the show?"

I could tell from Amy's voice that she was disappointed, but the idea of a "double-date" had always been more exciting to her than me. I met Carrie when she visited Amy's parents over the summer, and she and Cameron looked like a bad match. She didn't laugh very much, and never seemed to look directly at me or Amy—she tried not to talk to us at all, and if she had to she kept her head turned, like she didn't want anyone to know. Even worse was her constant complaining, about the weather, the lack of cable TV, and all the other horrors of small town Connecticut. I was afraid she'd hate Monkeyhole and make us leave early.

"God, that sucks." Amy's eyes got narrow, the way they did whenever she was upset. "I wanted to see her."

"I know, but it's cool." Cameron glanced at his watch and then squeezed between the two of us. "We're gonna have a great fucking time," he said as he steered us through Penn Station's crowded lobby. "Italian food and loud music, man. It's why New York was invented."

Cameron led us to a small Italian restaurant, one of those places that didn't even look like a restaurant from the outside. Amy worried about how close the tables were, but I loved the way the hostess recognized Cameron, and showed him right to the only empty table. We didn't even have to order— Cameron had set the whole thing up in advance, and plates of pasta just started appearing. Along with a bottle of wine we all shared, without anyone asking for our IDs. Even Amy had to admit, once the food arrived and she'd had a glass of wine, that everything tasted amazing.

Cameron talked for most of the meal, summarizing the movie we'd told our parents we'd come to see—a Spanish film called *Talk to Her* that sounded so weird and confusing I wanted to come back and see it for real. I kept asking him to go back and clear up something about the characters or the plot, and worried that Amy wasn't paying enough attention. She was probably right, though, it wasn't like any of our parents were ever going to see some movie about women in a coma. She and I had to just more or less talk about it the same way when asked.

"So what are you gonna say?" I asked, sopping up the last of my bolognese with a slice of bread.

Amy shrugged, and then looked from me to Cameron. "That I thought it was boring, but you two brainiacs loved it."

Cameron clapped his hands together, a satisfied look on his face. "Now that sounds perfect," he said. A few minutes later he motioned to the hostess, nodded, and then stood up. "OK. Time to claim a good piece of real estate at the club."

"Don't we have to pay?" I asked, thinking of the crisp twenty dollar bills I'd gotten.

"Taken care of, my friend," Cameron says, slapping my back playfully. Just when I didn't think he could get any cooler, too. "It's all been taken care of."

To get to the club we took a taxi, one of those rides from the movies where the cabbie plays weird music, curses all the other cars on the street, squeezes between buses, and tries to run over any pedestrian who dares to use a crosswalk. I sat in the middle, bouncing back and forth between Amy and Cameron. It kept me from worrying too much about how Amy and I were going to get into the club. As much fun as dinner was, and as in charge of everything as Cameron seemed to be, I knew I'd start sobbing right on the streets of New York if I got this close to seeing a musical hero, only to be turned away.

We stumbled out of the cab and followed Cameron down the block. The street was dirtier than the one the restaurant was on; it had that smell of garbage and cigarettes and spilled beer found in parts of the city my parents pushed me through quickly, whenever we visited.

"Three tickets," Cameron said, taking them out of his pocket. "I also have three IDs."

"Three IDs?"

"Of course, there's three of us, my man." He smiled, patting my shoulder with his empty hand. "I'm gonna hand them to the doorman and kind of push you guys through. You just walk on in, like you own the place, OK?"

"That'll work?"

"Trust me. This show's not gonna sell out, and they need all the bodies they can get on a Friday night. Long as we got something that looks like an ID and a ticket, we're in."

I wanted to ask what the name on "my" ID was, in case the doorman quizzed me, but Amy slipped her arm through mine and pulled tight. "Just relax, babe," she said, leading the way, as always. Waiting for the couple ahead of us to find their IDs, I thought of all the other things she'd taken care of. She'd asked me out. She'd initiated our first kiss. She'd even taken her shirt off and put my hands where she wanted, when I'd had no idea if it was time to make the move, or even how to work the logistics of girl clothes.

It turned out Cameron had the same power to make things happen. As he handed the bored-looking doorman the tickets and IDs, Amy and I walked past. A few seconds later Cameron was putting his arms around each of us. "Welcome to Brownies," he said. "Now, you go grab one of those spots along the right wall, while I get us all some beer."

Amy and I found an open piece of graffiti-covered wall. The Ramones were playing over the PA, and the people milling about all looked the way I imagined the music geeks I talked to online would look: lots of untucked button-down shirts, more than a few half-assed beards, and not many girls. I was about to say how much I loved the place when Amy made a sour face. "Not the cleanest dump in the world, huh," she said, still holding my arm.

I shrugged. "Could be worse, right? No dead people on the floor or anything. At least I don't think so..."

She slapped my arm. "Don't even joke about that!"

I was still riffing on the dead body joke—Wait, is that pale guy over there even breathing?—when Cameron came back with three Heinekens. "Thanks," I said casually, trying to make it look like I took brews from buds all the time. The coldness of the beer felt good going down my throat, but the taste was so harsh it was hard to fake a "that's great" smile.

Amy took a quick swig from her bottle and then placed it down on the narrow ledge running along the wall. "I have to go hit the bathroom before they start."

"Yeah, probably best to go now," Cameron says. "The line for the women's room is always, like, a million times longer than the one for the guys."

As she walked away I tried not to feel nervous. I'd been alone with Cameron before, waiting for Amy to get ready, or at some gathering when everyone else drifted away for a moment, but this felt different. Maybe it was the e-mails; it felt like he knew much more about me now, but it was also weird because we'd never really talked in person without other people around. I was glad he started talking first.

"Did you get that last e-mail? With 'This Next Station'?"

"Yeah! Thanks. I think it's my favorite new one."

"Right? I knew you'd like it. You think he'll do any Monkeyhole stuff?"

"I hope so," I said, drinking some more beer and deciding it wasn't as awful as I first thought. "I always wished I'd gotten a chance to see them live."

"I did, once. Drove to Boston with a bud when we were both still in high school."

"Wow. How was it?"

"Amazing, man. They owned that place. I was sure they were going to be, like, huge."

"I can't believe they just made one record."

"It's crazy. I've tried to explain it to other people, how great that CD is, but no one gets it..."

"I can't explain it, either," I said, remembering that disastrous listening session with Amy. "Each song just feels like it's important, though, you know? Usually there's just one or two like that on a CD, but on this one, it's like they all fit together. And even when I'm not sure exactly what he's singing about, it's like I understand, anyway? Like I know what he's feeling, if that makes sense." I looked down at my hands, suddenly embarrassed. There's a reason people think I'm a dork when I talk about music, and if I kept going I was going to lose whatever cred I'd built up with Cameron. "I'm sorry. I talk too much about this shit."

"No way, man. It's great to hear someone get as into it as much as I do. Most of my friends zone out when I start to talk about music."

"Mine, too," I said, surprised to hear myself adding, "at least, the few friends I do have."

"Fuck high school, man." Cameron smiled at me. "Fucking losers."

It was nice to have someone not tell me just to tough it out, high school would get better, blah blah. "It can really suck."

"Of course it sucks. You're made for college, man."

"So it is different? In college?"

"Jesus, yes. It's like, I know more people, I see more people, but I have fewer friends—but that's OK, because the friends I do have are better than the friends I had in high school."

"That would be... great." I tried to not to have a panic attack right there, imagining none of the waiting list spots opening up for me. Wouldn't community college be just like high school? "I just can't imagine finding the right place."

"Why not?"

"I don't know. I mean, my brother had sports, you know? And would always talk about how great it felt when he was playing basketball or baseball or whatever, how the field was 'his home.' But I never feel like that." My head started bobbing, and I realized it was because "Alex Chilton" was playing over the PA. That made sense: this was just the kind of club the Replacements would play. I was aware of my right leg shaking in time, and wondered if this was what being drunk felt like. How much wine had I had with dinner? "It's like the only place that really feels like home is my room, when I'm listening to music." I put my beer bottle, which was suddenly almost empty, back on the ledge next to Amy's. When I made eye contact again with Cameron I was relieved to see he wasn't laughing at me. "Sorry, that was stupid."

"Not at all. That makes total sense. It's pretty much the same for me, man. I could tell you got it, in our e-mails." He grinned, and for the first time I noticed it was the eyes that made it obvious he was Amy's brother—the same shade of blue that seemed to lighten when he smiled. "So let's keep at it, OK? You send me any cool music you find, OK? And I'll do the same."

"OK, thanks." Then, just as we both started to say something at the same time and then both stopped at the same time, because we were laughing, Amy came back.

"Jesus," she said, picking up her beer and taking a long swallow. "We can never talk about that bathroom, OK?"

I tried not to feel too disappointed that she'd come back. That was easier to do when I saw how happy she looked—I loved the way her face opened up wider when she was happy. We picked up our beer bottles and clinked, and once again I couldn't believe she was going out with me.

Stackd Souls was the second of three bands, and Cameron had timed our arrival just as the first was getting their gear off the stage. The club was less than half full, which wasn't surprising; Spider's new band had just put out an EP on their own label, and the headliner was a Minneapolis band that even Cameron hadn't heard of. He went off to get another beer for Amy and she continued one of the stories she'd started on the train ride. I tried to listen, but it was impossible not to be distracted by watching the band set up. There was another guitarist, a female bass player, a keyboardist squeezed into a far corner, and the drummer, who was listening to something on headphones as he adjusted the height of his seat. Spider came out last, holding a red guitar and a beer. He put his bottle down on an amp and said something that made the bass player laugh so loudly the drummer took off his headphones to see what was going on.

"Holy shit, there he is," Cameron said when he came back, cutting off Amy's story. He grabbed each of our hands and started edging toward the stage. The crowd had been growing more dense, but Cameron walked at a steady pace, looking straight ahead, and soon had us standing less than ten feet from the stage.

"Can we do this?" Amy asked, looking at the people now behind us.

"Of course," Cameron said. "Everyone paid the same price, right? We just wanted to be closer more than they did."

I never would have pushed up to the stage on my own, but it was amazing to be able to see the stubble on Spider's face, to read the tiny Beatles button on his guitar strap. Cameron and I were trying to guess what song they would play first when the club music abruptly stopped.

"Hello, people made of Brownies!" Spider held his hand up high and then saluted, drawing a loud cheer. "We are here to eat you up," he said, dramatically stretching out the last three words. Then the drummer played a quick fill and the band launched into "Drive into the Sky." My experiences with live music had only been in bigger places—like an awful U2 show at some arena that swallowed up every quiet moment—and in the small club the sound was physical in a way I had not expected, a force pressing against my chest. And when the crowd sang along with the last chorus, it was as if I'd found a way for the music to get even bigger than it sounded in my head, when I listened late at night in my room.

I'd never thought that possible.

They started the next song while the crowd was still clapping, and then played two more in quick succession, new songs I'd never heard before. It was like watching a great TV show without commercials, or listening to one of those records like *Dark Side of the Moon*, where one song bled into the next. I was more aware of my body—the way my arms and legs were moving as much as they could in my tiny square of space—but also beginning to feel like I was somewhere else, like my brain had finally left my body behind. When I looked at Cameron he also seemed lost to the music, eyes darting from one musician to the next, but Amy looked bored. She smiled when she saw me watching her, and gave my arm a quick squeeze, but she also mouthed "I can barely breathe!" I worried that she might expect me to offer to leave, and looked away before she could signal to do so.

After the fourth song the band finally stopped, and the whole room seemed to exhale. The other guitarist and the bass player bent down to check their tuning, while the drummer and keyboardist reached for bottles of beer. Spider smiled at the applause and stood at the microphone. "I don't care what the rest of the world says, you're alright, people of New York. Every time I come here I get all warm and fucking fuzzy, you know? Fucking Mayberry come to life. With a little extra trash, for flaaaaavor." As he talked he strummed a single chord twice, and as soon as I heard it I knew what song would be next. I turned to whisper the title to Cameron, and when I turned back to the stage I saw Spider watching me.

"What's that, College Boy? You think you know what's next?"

I was too nervous to speak, but could feel Cameron's fingers poking me in the ribs. "Answer him," he whispered. "It's Spider! Talking to you!"

"Yeah, I can see it allllll from up here, College. Something you wanna share with the class?"

"I, I'm not in college, yet," I said.

Spider held up a finger to his lips before he bent his head to watch his tuner as he plucked his strings. "Quick, someone get this kid a beer before he gets tossed out," he said, smiling as the crowd laughed. "So Not In College Yet," he went on, strumming his guitar quietly again, "what do you think's next?"

As he finished the question he stared directly at me, grinning. I was no longer invisible; I'd become part of the show. In fact, it felt like the whole club was watching me, but I wasn't bothered. I'd been noticed for something I was proud of—how well I knew this music. "'This Next Station,'" I said, so determined to be heard this time it came out more as a shouted command than a guess.

Spider smiled at my answer. "You sure, Not College? Final answer?" I nodded, he gave a four count, and the song kicked in, just as I'd predicted. And I swear he winked at me as the first verse began.

> It's a hard lesson to learn
> A truth nobody wants to know
> The things we work the hardest to earn
> Are never in our control

I heard some of the people behind me singing along to this song that hadn't even been released yet, and when I turned to watch the scene I saw the club had filled up quite a bit. I joined in the singing, too, so loudly I could hear myself over the crowd—something I'd never done outside the safety of my room, and even then only when I knew no one else was home. When the first chorus started the sound came from the stage with such force that I had to press back against it, to keep from losing my balance. I leaned forward, into the crowd and the stage and the music, feeling stronger than I could remember ever feeling before.

On the walk back to the train I tried to explain how amazing it was, to see Spider live, to hear songs that meant so much to me played right in front of me, so big and loud I could literally feel the music hit my chest—but Amy didn't get it. "I don't know," she'd said, "don't you like listening at home better? No stupid drunks, no club smell. And God, I think my ears are, like, broken." I wanted to keep trying to get her to understand, to make her appreciate the way the sound became something you could touch as well as hear. I was afraid it would come out all wrong, though, and then she'd get confused, so I'd get frustrated, and that would just make her annoyed. So I let myself grow quiet, and tried not to think it might have been more fun if she hadn't come.

The ride into the city had been thick with an excited vibe, people heading in for a night on the town, everyone anxious to see what would happen. On the 1 a.m. back home there were fewer people, and they were either trying to sleep, sprawled out in uncomfortable positions, or talking quietly. I leaned my head against the window, Amy to my left, her hand holding mine. She was speaking quickly, and a little too loudly, to Cameron, sitting across from us. I remembered she'd solved her boredom problem by watching the last half of the set from the bar, where she'd had at least one more beer. I ignored their conversation, which was full of that shorthand only the two of them understood, and examined my Stackd Souls EP. I bought Cameron a copy, too, insisting on treating him for once.

As we got closer to the New Rochelle station Amy grew quieter, and the next thing I knew she was leaning against my shoulder, her eyes closed.

"So," Cameron said with a grin, "do you think the two of us can carry her to the car?"

"You think she's really asleep?" As I asked she snorted, and then began snoring.

"Oh, yeah," he said. "Ever since we were kids, man, the moment she falls asleep nothing can wake her. My guess? She's out until lunch tomorrow. When she finally wakes up, she'll have a hell of a headache, and my parents will kill me if they figure out how drunk she got."

He was right: when we got off the train the two of us had to struggle to get her into their dad's Honda. "Don't ever tell her I said this," Cameron said as we collapsed in the front seats, "but she could stand to lose a few."

"You'd better hope she didn't hear that." I turned around and looked at her, stretched out across the back seat.

"Friend, she won't remember any of this. Take it from a guy who's been this drunk himself a few times." He smiled and started to slowly steer us out of the parking lot.

For once I didn't want to turn on the radio or put in a CD; I just wanted the music we'd heard to keep ringing in my ears. The first few minutes of the car ride were quiet, except for Amy's deep breathing, but it didn't feel too awkward or weird—it felt like we were both just thinking about the night. "Thanks for working all this out," I finally said. "The tickets, getting us in... the whole thing."

"Oh, man, no worries. I mean, that was amazing, am I right?"

I nodded. "Amazing."

"They're gonna be huge, I just know it." He grinned, and then playfully slapped my shoulder. "I'm so glad that you were there. It meant a lot more to go with a friend who's a real fan, you know?"

"I know." He'd just called me "friend" twice, and I realized that was something else that happened at the show—we'd become friends. He was really the first music friend I'd made in the real world, and not just on some website. "Amy puts up with me talking about music so much, but I just don't think she gets it."

"I hear you," he said. "Even with the all the great people I've met at NYU, it's hard to find someone who understands music the same way I do. The same way you do. I mean, a show like that? I'm gonna feel great for weeks. None of the crap weighing me down is gonna have as much power."

I couldn't imagine what could be weighing him down, and wondered if he wanted me to ask him about it. "It's like I feel inspired to do... more. To be more, somehow."

Cameron slapped the steering wheel with the palm of his hand. "Yes, that's a perfect way to put it: to be more. To be more me, you know? If that doesn't sound too dumb."

"No, I get it, I do." We turned down my street, and I was sad the night was ending. "Sorry Carrie couldn't go."

"Oh, it's OK." Cameron sighed, peering over his shoulder at Amy. Her snoring was slow and steady. "I mean, I didn't want to bum Amy out or anything, because she really likes Carrie, but we broke up a few weeks ago."

"Really? Man. That sucks. Sorry."

He slowed to a crawl as we reached my house. "Don't say anything to Amy yet, OK?"

"Sure. Of course."

"To tell you the truth, it's probably for the best. This whole relationship thing can really wear me out." He turned to me. "Sorry, don't mean to be a bummer. You and Amy are doing OK, right?"

Were we? Doing OK? I didn't think about it in those terms. It was better to have a girlfriend than to not have a girlfriend, that much I knew. It was nice to have someone to do things with, even if it was the things she wanted to do. But wasn't that how it usually worked? Since I'd never had a girlfriend before, I didn't really have anything else to compare to being with Amy. I also didn't know if the out-of-tune moments I felt were all part of dating. Like, those occasional flashes that we were just two people pretending to want to be with each other, because we thought we were supposed to. Or times I responded to a random text from Amy telling me she was thinking about me by writing, "Me 2!" even when I wasn't.

"I probably shouldn't have asked that, sorry." He put the car into park, its low idle merging with the sound of Amy's snores. "I mean, she's my sister, so I guess it'd be weird to talk about that."

"No, it's not that." I dropped my voice to more of a whisper. "I mean, it's more I just don't think about it, all that much. How things are, with us."

He smiled. "I knew you were smart, Andy. That's the best way to go about it. I get myself in trouble by thinking too much."

"Maybe I don't think enough. Amy's my first real girlfriend, you know. Kind of making it up as I go along."

He leaned his back against the door and his eyes grew wide. "Your first girlfriend? Really?"

His disbelief was flattering. I was almost ready to believe him, that I could be smart, that I could be a cool friend, if I just met the right people. "Yeah, high school pretty much sucked until this year. And it still sucks, just less."

"Just remember what I said: you're gonna fucking love college. And for the assholes who made high school hell for you, college is gonna suck. They're gonna flunk out, and then go check your bags at the airport."

"I want you to be right. I really want that." I was horrified to feel that warm feeling in the back of my throat, like I was about to cry. And still I kept talking, saying the kind of thing I would normally leave buried in my own head. "It's like no one sees me, except to make fun of me."

"Man, Spider saw you tonight."

I grinned. "He did, didn't he?"

"And Amy, Amy sees you."

I nodded, but something about the lingering adrenalin from the show made me confess more than I normally would have, even to myself. "Sometimes I wonder if even she really sees me, you know? Or does she just see me as something she wants me to be, right? I mean, if we can go to the same show, like this, and have two such different reactions..."

"That's the struggle, right? Fuck, to get someone to see you, and see the world the same way you do?" He glanced into the back seat, where Amy had rolled over, her face pressed into the back seat. "Thank God for music."

"Thank God for music," I repeated.

He turned back to look at me and grinned. "You know, you should totally come into the city sometime. There are so many great CD stores, with stuff you'll never see anywhere else."

"That would be great." I tried to imagine Amy wandering through a cramped CD store, though, and realized that it wouldn't work. "But I don't know how much of that Amy would put up with."

"Oh. Well. I was thinking just you, you know? That's not really her thing."

"Yeah?" It was easy to imagine the whole day—Cameron showing me the campus, walking through cool CD stores, like I was already free of this life and onto the next. "That'd be great." It felt like we'd reached a natural break in the conversation, and I sensed it was time for me to say goodnight and go inside. I looked out the passenger window at my house, avoiding eye contact so I could stall the end of the night a little longer. At the far edge of our driveway was the well-worn, slightly bent basketball hoop my older brother had run around under for hours when we were younger. Maybe I should have played, too, even though the game never made any sense to me. Maybe if I had made more of an effort, Beau would have liked me more. Had it been all my fault, that we didn't get along?

When I turned to Cameron to say goodnight I was surprised to see he had moved closer. "I see you, too, you know." I'd wondered if he'd said the words out loud, or if I'd just realized how much I wanted him to say them. I wasn't sure until he moved his face towards mine, leaving me just enough time to think "He's going to kiss me" right before it happened.

There was a small mole, a tiny little circle, just above the right side of his mouth. I had never noticed before.

His lips were softer than I ever would have imagined, and when his hand reached up to graze my cheek the touch was light.

A caress.

I didn't resist, just let my head get slowly pushed against the headrest by the force of his kiss. For a long, quiet moment, I thought about nothing, my head completely clear. Had it ever been this clear before? When I watched him slowly pull away I decided this is what it must feel like, to get something you want before you even knew you wanted it.

There was another silence. The street I grew up on is so quiet, I thought, hearing only the Honda idling and Amy snoring. Will I miss this quiet when I leave?

"I'm sorry," he said quietly, shutting his eyes. "I've got a lot of weird stuff going on, Andy, and I shouldn't be screwing you up, too. I just thought." He stopped, and opened his eyes. "I mean, was it awful?"

I leaned into him, hoping that would be the answer.

Buzz. *lying faggot*

I sit at the kitchen table through a series of rapid fire vibrations from Amy, not responding to any of them. I send a message to Cameron instead: *what did u say* There's no answer for two minutes, just more Amy rants, so I try again. *i need to know what u told her*

> *sorry sorry sorry*
> *what did u say*
> *she woke up and saw u kiss me i was sure she was asleep*
> *so what did u say*
> *u made a pass i went along with it*

So he lied.

> *told her i didnt want to hurt u*
> *why didnt u just tell her the truth*

Amy has finally stopped writing nasty notes, so the phone is silent until he writes back: *i was afraid.*

I can't think of anything else to write, to either of them. Calling Amy with my explanation doesn't seem like it will do any good—I'm the outsider. She'll believe him. I want to fall asleep, right at the kitchen table, but the last thing I want to do is talk to my parents when they wake up in the morning. Will they take one look at me and know?

Jesus, Andy, did you kiss your girlfriend's brother?

And school. When I go back in two days I'll no longer be the fat Achenbach kid or the invisible kid or even that quiet kid who dates Amy Ferguson. I'll be that fag who screwed over Amy Ferguson. I won't be invisible anymore. Just wishing I could be.

I stare at my hands, holding the finally silent phone. So, is that really who I am? That fag who kissed my girlfriend's brother? Had I spent all this time trying not to be seen so no one would know who I really was? It's hard for me to even call myself the name in my own head, but I know I should get used to it. The whole world will be throwing it at me very soon.

Faggot.

My head throbs. I force myself to stand up and head to my room. The upstairs hallway seems out of scale, more narrow than I remember, and my door feels heavier as I push it open. I lie down on my bed in my clothes, and grab my Discman and headphones from my nightstand. The phone buzzes one more time: *im so sorry bet u wish u never met me.*

Do I? Never meeting him would mean never seeing the show tonight, not feeling that music press against me, not talking to Spider. Never kissing Cameron. That would make life easier, but would the price be worth it? So I can't be sure, lying in my bed, thinking about Cameron, that I would go back in time and make none of it happen.

I put the phone on my stomach. I'll write back, I'm just not ready yet. I slip the new Stackd Souls CD in and slip the headphones on my head. I imagine an alternate universe where the headphones don't exist, one of those tricks of temporary denial that can make me happier, by first making me sadder. Without them I'd have no way of hearing music at 3 a.m. without waking up my parents and my brother, no way for the music to completely wipe out the sounds of the world. It would be just me and the thoughts in my brain, and that can be a dangerous thing. As I adjust the headphones I'm more grateful than ever for their existence. How did Beau, the world's worst brother, the human who delighted in taunting me his entire life, manage to get me the best birthday present ever?

I hit play. Laying perfectly still, surrounded by the dark, I am as close to existing only within the music as I can ever get.

The first song starts. I'm more aware of the sound than the words, like I'm watching the layers fit together, organ on top of guitar on top of drums.

My entire body is focused on blocking any specific details from the night for as long as I can, especially all the mistakes I must have made, and my back grows tense from the effort. As the music continues, a series of snapshots slowly emerge, shaping themselves into a slideshow being broadcast on the back of my eyes. Amy emerges in pieces—her hair, when it falls across her eyes; her right hand, the shape it makes when it reaches out to touch my left elbow—but at least I continue to block out Cameron. It's hard to do, so hard I feel a physical pain in my spine. Because as much as I want to forget him, just for a moment, just so I can stop thinking about all the changes his existence will create, I also know he's probably surrounding himself with music right now, too.

Maybe even with the same CD. The copy I bought for him.

At the end of the bridge the bass and drums drop out, and it's just guitars and Spider's voice, singing "Ooh ooh ooh." It's what I imagine floating through the sky feels like, not knowing when or how you would land. Then the full band kicks in for the last chorus and I remember the physical force the music made at Brownies, the way Cameron and I both leaned into the sound, pushing back against that force so it would not knock us further from the stage. It jolts me as I sit up on my bed, uncoiling my back and freeing all the thoughts I'd been trying to keep locked away.

It's time to drop off the baggage
(There's no need for that now, I don't need that)
Time to see what's waiting for me
(It has to be there now, it has to be there)
Rolling into this next station
I got no expectations
Rolling into this next station
I got no expectations

I'm not afraid to remember the whole night, even the ending, now that the music is here with me. I breathe out slowly, aware of my arms opening and the muscles in my legs relaxing. I can't pretend things that happened did not happen, but as long as I keep listening I can pretend that I'm fine.

Fun with Jack & Jill

Barcelona, 2007

Spider learned early in his musical career that the halfway point of a tour is when the problems start. The early surge of adrenalin that carries band and crew through the opening weeks burns off, and the poor sleep, bad food, and inconsistent showering begin to take a toll on everyone. Two months into his four-month contract with Jack & Jill—that adorable married couple with a gift for catchy choruses, a platinum record (*Fun With Jack & Jill*, of course), and a stipulation that no band member directly address either one of them, unless requested to—he can feel the outer edges of his brain peeling away. The fact that he will make more money, in these four months, than he did any year he fronted one of his own bands, simultaneously lessens and increases the pain he feels playing the same awful songs every night.

The same songs. The same order. Sprinkled with the same carefully written banter.

As he walks on to the stage of Sala Apolo, a beautiful old theater in Barcelona, he feels the mid-tour sense of malaise soaking his bones. Jack & Jill's insistence that the band and crew appear at the venue by three p.m. on show days is not helping his mood. Warnings of an "intense soundcheck" are repeatedly issued: new songs to be learned, old songs to be fine-tuned, everyone expected to be on top of their game. And then band and crew sit around waiting, sometimes for hours, while the two stars sleep away the afternoon in their hotel suite.

Spider's roadie, Sammy, powers up his rig, and Spider begins to idly strum his old Gibson acoustic, the one piece of gear he brought with him. He's never been good at waiting. He feels like he's back in kindergarten, forced to stand in line while the nose-pickers and butt-scratchers did their thing. No recess or lunch or art until everyone is quiet and still? Really? What sense did it make, to make him wait for everyone else, when he was ready?

Spider starts to run through a melody he's been working on since they played Rome. It's too early to know if the sequence will solidify into a song, but it is beginning to feel like more than just a series of random chords. He's wondering if he should start with the last chord, and end with what's now the first, when Tiny walks over, unlit cigarette in his mouth. Most venues allow smoking in Europe, but Jack & Jill still ban it for the band and crew; chewing a Camel is Tiny's daily act of rebellion. "We gotta start a fucking pool on what time these assholes show up."

"Easy. 4:02."

"4:02?" Tiny pretends to write it down on an invisible pad.

"Yeah, so they can try and deny they were a full hour late. Even though they will be."

"I think you got a winner, my man." Tiny grins, his multiple silver and gold fillings flashing in the bright lights of the stage. A three-hundred-pound guitar tech who wears the same dark blue sweats every day, his presence on the tour has proven to be a mixed blessing. Even though he's Jack's guitar tech, Tiny has taken time to show the ins and outs of road life to Sammy, who'd never worked on such a long and large-scale tour. By the time they hit Germany, at the end of the first month, Sammy was handing Spider the right guitar before Spider even checked the set list to see what song was next.

It's all about not thinking. The less he thinks, the more he's able to endure being a side player.

The downside to Tiny's presence is the network of cocaine, amphetamines, and hashish dealers he's carved out in his years of traveling through Europe. Each time they hit a new city Spider reaffirms his vow to stop smoking, snorting, and drinking his per diems and paycheck; the whole point of working this crappy tour is to go home with a nest egg big enough to buy recording gear, make some demos, and start a new band of his own. But then Tiny shows up with some especially good weed or hash, or maybe a nice line of pure and shiny coke, and Spider puts off abstinence yet again: the would-be virgin unable to resist the allure of physical contact, always tempted to see how far things can go before she gets fucked.

"We just gotta hurry this shit up, one way or the other. There's a guy here in Barcelona with the real goods, know what I'm saying? Makes that stuff in Venice look like Pop Rocks. Spanish snow, my man, Spanish snow. Nothing like it."

Spider shakes his head. This is the day he is going to say no. "Not today, man. Once we're out of here I'm just gonna stroll La Rambla, look at some fine Spanish women, and eat a tapa or twenty."

"Say it ain't so, webslinger."

"It's so, it's so. I can't keep up with you young party animals. Need a night off."

Tiny gently places the back of his hand on Spider's forehead, as if checking for a fever. "I'm gonna swing by again later, in case this illness passes."

Spider watches Tiny waddle over to Kenny the drum tech and understands he's glimpsing one of his own possible futures. Many a fine guitarist has slid down the greasy pole from frontman to sideman to tech. At first they all convince themselves it's just a temporary phase, but eventually the pole becomes too slick to climb back up, and the rest of their time in the business is spent working for other players. You could usually tell how far gone they were by their weight. The heavier they get, the further away they are from their playing days. All Tiny has left is a steady diet of pizza, gelato, and cocaine. Spider has caught himself checking his own belly, to make sure he is not morphing from player to permanent roadie.

He wanders to the front of the stage, strumming the chords in his head in different permutations. Jack & Jill may not be playing the 10,000-seaters they fill in the States, but they're selling out theaters that hold 2,000. This one in Barcelona is particularly beautiful, much nicer than any of the places Monkeyhole or Stackd Souls ever headlined. With its ornate columns, plush red seats, and walls painted gold and silver, a building like this in the States would be embarrassing, some new venue trying to look old. In Europe, though, this style works because it's genuine—it looks old because it is old, not because it's trying to cover up some lack of history.

Authenticity. For Spider, there's no more important aesthetic. Jack & Jill will commit a crime when they play their faux songs on this stage, and he must accept the fact that he will be an accessory. Even worse: there are parts of the set he enjoys. Every show ends with the hit single, "How Much Fun?" The song drives Spider crazy for many reasons, from the way Jack & Jill hold out their arms wide during the chorus and then hug each other at the end, to the way it gets stuck in his fucking head. Most of all he hates the way he gets a rush from stepping to the front of the stage when he plays the lead break, the entire crowd on their feet by that point. The force of that crowd, cheering as his guitar solo blends into the final chorus, is stronger than anything he ever felt playing one of his own songs.

All of which are better than "How Much Fun?" Damnit.

Closing his eyes, he decides to put aside the chord pattern he's been working on, and starts scanning the continuously running layers of music in his head for something new. If he goes back home and writes a great record, an authentic record, then his crimes in Barcelona—and all the other cities on this tour—can be forgiven.

Just after 4:00 Foster, the annoying British tour manager, lets the band and crew know that Jack & Jill are "knackered" after a day of interviews with the adoring Barcelonian press. Soundcheck is cancelled. Everyone is free until the 8:00 stage call.

"Knackered," Spider says dismissively to Sammy. The two of them head out the back door together, though they will spend their free time separately; if you get too close to your tech, it's harder to treat him like an employee. "If anyone working for me ever said I was 'knackered' after bullshitting with radio dweebs, I'd have him fired." The line gets a smile from Sammy, but Spider wishes he had kept it to himself. Whenever he talks about what he'd do if he was in charge he risks sounding like an overly bitter has-been (never-was?), that drunk who corners you at a party and talks about the ways he was screwed out of his deserved fame.

When they get outside Sammy heads off with two other techs and Spider is alone, halfway between the stage door and the metal railing set up to keep the Jack & Jill devotees from harassing their idols. He looks toward the railing, trying to find the quickest way out before Tiny makes him an offer he can't refuse, and spots a pretty woman with her eyes locked on him, waving. The entire tour Spider has brushed off the few groupies who noticed him; now that he's a sideman, the girls who make themselves available tend to be larger, older, more desperate. There's a friendly glint in this one's brown eyes, though, and a face that registers more than a few steps above Drummer Level, so he smiles back and walks over to her.

"¿Estás libre?"

And with that simple question, spoken in a soft, heavily accented voice as those brown eyes widen just slightly, Spider is a goner. "Sí, estoy libre," he answers.

"Me gusta la música," she says, pointing to the club. "¿Tocas música?"

He can't tell whether she means she likes music in general, or Jack & Jill. At this moment, her face is so sweet he doesn't care. "Sí. Tódo el tiempo. ¿Como te llamas?"

"Miranda. ¿Y tu?"

"Spider." She looks confused, so he tries to remember the Spanish word for Spider. "Araña. Me llamo Araña."

"¿Araña? ¿De verdad?" She reaches out and rubs her palm over his fingers, the back of his hand, up to his wrist. "Pero... no te sientes como araña."

His Spanish is minimal, but he's pretty sure she just told him he doesn't feel like a Spider. For a thirty-five-year-old guitarist who's been sleeping in a bus for two months and hasn't had a real shower in days, that feels like high praise. He inhales deeply, pleased that she's wearing just enough perfume to detect. Perfume should work like a good bass player, he's always thought, and only get noticed if you pay close attention. He puts his hand on top of hers and says "Gracias" in the most seductive Spanish voice his accent allows.

She motions for him to walk around to her. He slips through an opening in the railing, almost forgetting to turn around to see if Tiny was out yet. As hard as he tries to ignore it, he can still hear the phrase "Spanish Snow" playing on repeat in some corner of his head. He's relieved when he only sees Foster by the back door, cellphone and coffee cup in hand.

He starts strolling down La Rambla with his new best friend, her arm wrapped naturally through his as she chatters away in Spanish. The throngs of people out on a beautiful September evening force them so close together that he can feel her hip press against the upper part of his leg, so what does it matter if he has no idea what she's saying? He's enjoying the way her voice changes pitch and tempo, the notes rising and falling faster, slower, and then faster again—it's as if she's performing her own take on *Sketches of Spain*. Her voice has a sweet, untrained tone, and her hand exudes a supernatural warmth as it gently slides up and down his forearm. If fifteen-year-old Spider Ebster had known that one day a beautiful European woman would lead him through the streets of Barcelona, high school might have been bearable.

He might have even finished it.

Miranda leans in closer. "¿Estás bien?" she asks.

"Sí, sí. Es una noche maravillosa," he says slowly, trying to remember if the Spanish word for "night" is masculine or feminine. She smiles, placing her head close to his shoulder as they walk. He can see now that she is younger than he thought at first—maybe mid-twenties, instead of early thirties. There's no good reason for her to approach him, which means there's probably an ulterior motive, but Spider chooses not to think about it. The best songs he's ever written are the ones he does not analyze as they emerge. Who's to say that he won't wind up in her bed, after the show?

After leading him down La Rambla for a long stretch, Miranda makes a series of rapid turns, into increasingly narrow alleyways. Spider begins to wonder if he should be trying to remember how to get back, but surely someone can give him directions to Sala Apolo. So he relaxes, thinking of his guide as a female Willy Wonka, leading him through a maze all the more beautiful for being so confusing.

After one more sharp right, Miranda announces, "¡Ya estamos!" Her arm points down a stairway to an apartment below street level. From the open windows Spider can hear music and loud conversation; when Miranda pulls him down the stairs and through the door, he's hit with a wild combination of scents—seafood, seared red meat, fried potatoes, and some very vibrant weed. The small kitchen is breaking all the laws of physics in order to hold at least a dozen people, pots bubbling and steaming on all four of the stove's burners. There's a loud hissing coming from somewhere, cutting through the babble of conversation, but no one seems to care. Bearded men with tight striped sweaters, surgically attached cigarettes, and deep voices, compete for metaphorical and literal space. Curved and smiling women, each one a different wonderful variant of brown, conduct multiple conversations while making rapid hand motions. It's like he's stumbled into an early Almodovar movie. Miranda issues a few quick pecks on the cheek to the group of people closest to the door, and then places her hand on Spider's shoulder. "This is my new friend, Spider," she says in a voice suddenly twice as loud as any she has used before. "But do not worry, I do not think he's to bite!"

Everyone in the room turns to stare. He smiles and waves, even as he wonders why Miranda has been talking to him in Spanish this whole time. His arm still wrapped in hers, they travel the perimeter of the kitchen, nodding hellos and accepting backslaps. Eventually the two of them squeeze behind a small table, and create some space for themselves on a crowded bench running along the back wall of the kitchen. More conversations can be heard down the hall behind them, and the stacks of empty plates and wine glasses scattered around the apartment make it clear the party has been going on for hours.

Spider is used to adapting to new surroundings and people—what is a tour, but a series of new surroundings you must make your own?—but it still takes him a few minutes to adjust to the frantic level of noise and activity. He is grateful for the chance to observe from the back corner, and even more grateful for the joints and plates of fried plantains and shrimp that quickly come his way. Miranda starts talking to a blonde on her left, while he marvels at the perfection of the tapa. Eaten in a few tasty bites, leaving your mouth no time to get bored. It's like listening to a really great radio station, he decides, and the comparison strikes him as so brilliant he needs to share it. When he turns to Miranda she's still talking to her friend, though. "Radio Tapas" starts playing in his head, to the tune of Queen's "Radio Gaga." He laughs out loud, and the sound of his voices makes him realize he is very stoned. Already. And for free!

He's still giggling as he bites into a tapa with chorizo and corn. This is his first meal of the day; he'd slept until it was time for soundcheck, after being awake for much of the overnight ride from Nice. Tiny had scored some good coke and he'd been up for hours, looking at recording equipment. Spider has been assembling his dream home studio as the tour bus wanders the highways of Europe, amazed at the way technology is changing music. Monkeyhole could barely afford a few days in a crappy studio for their first EP, and he's never been satisfied with the results. Even when they got signed to a major label, with what seemed like a ridiculous amount of money, he felt rushed to finish the album, and the results sounded incomplete. With Stackd Souls he wanted more control, so he decided they would record as much as they could on their own. He bought an expensive eight-track machine, but spent more time repairing it than using it. Then, as soon as everything was working, someone in the band would inevitably launch into a time-wasting drama. Long discussions over the best way to split the royalties they never fucking made. Monkeyhole had spoiled him; he'd assumed every band worked like a family. Annoying disagreements, occasional fights, and invisible grudges, yes, but also an understanding that all that shit got pushed aside when it came time to work. Stackd Souls taught him Tolstoy was right: every unhappy band is unhappy in its own way.

A man old enough to be Spider's grandfather passes him a joint with a knowing wink. Spider doesn't remember Miranda getting up, or this guy sitting down, but he looks pleasant enough, and the pot is strong. He inhales deeply, closing his eyes and feeling grateful for the good food, the free buzz, and the technology that will allow him to record everything on his own. No expensive studio or unreliable bandmates required. He just needs to focus on saving as much as he can the last half of the tour. Then he can go home, set up Pro Tools on a good Mac, and have unlimited tracks at his fingertips. He can make demos that sound better than anything Monkeyhole or Stackd Souls recorded, and just hire people to play it the way he wants it played.

"¿Cómo conoces Miranda?"

The question pulls Spider out of his daze. The man on his right, a bearded intellectual-type in a striped sweater, has poured them each a shot of something. How long has he been staring into space? The shrimp tapas have been magically transformed into a bowl of mussels, and the tequila burns a trail in his chest.

"¿Cómo conoces Miranda?" Intellectual Sweater repeats his question. He's also smoking a pipe, to complete the cliche.

"¿Música?" Spider feels like he's been talking in questions throughout this European trip.

"Ahhhh, música." Sweater nods slowly, and then turns to speak to a woman standing on the other side of the table. It suddenly hits Spider that Miranda really does have some connection to most of the dozens of people crammed into this apartment. He's not sure he knows this many people well enough to invite to a party, never mind people who like him enough to show up.

Spider reaches for another mussel, and looks up to see Miranda in front of him. She's standing next to a woman who looks like she could be Miranda's younger sister—darker hair, but the same sharp cheekbones and piercing eyes. Through the windows on the other side of the kitchen he notices that the sky is growing darker, and wonders if he should think about heading back to the venue; he'd been docked a day's pay when he was late in Amsterdam. He's trying to remember how to ask the time in Spanish when Miranda asks, in perfect English, for money, so she and her friend can make a Tequila run. Both women smile, and he thinks of how long it has been since he saw someone as beautiful as them naked. He opens his wallet to take out some money—after all he's eaten it only seems fair—but he feels a bit like a sitcom boyfriend when Miranda reaches down and grabs all his euros, blowing a kiss before she turns to talk away with her friend. He wonders if she would go to the show tonight, if he asked. As awful as Jack & Jill are, he long ago learned that women only really find him attractive if they get to see him on a stage.

Spider leans back and closes his eyes. A confused musical soundtrack—salsa into Astrud Gilberto into the occasional bit of American Top 40—blares from speakers he does not see.

He is pulled out of his waking nap when a different man in a too-tight sweater—why did every male in Europe wear clothes a size too small?—sits down on his left. On the other side of the man is a woman young enough to be his daughter, nibbling on his ear. "¿Cómo conoces Miranda?"

"Música," Spider says again, this time without the question mark.

"Ahhhh, música," he repeats, holding out his hand. "¿Americano, si?"

"Sí," Spider answers with a smile. "Estoy Americano."

"¡Perfecto!" The man turns to the woman and points at Spider. "¡La música, y los Estados Unidos!" Turning back to Spider he narrows his eyes and lowers his voice. "Is OK, I practice my English?"

"Yes, sure. Easier for me. Más fácil."

"¡Bueno! You like Barcelona?"

Spider nods. "Por seguro." If he really was in an Almodovar movie the man would start talking about sex, or religion, or religion and sex, but instead his new table companion lists tourist attractions Spider should visit. Some of it sounds interesting, especially the church and park that Gaudi designed, but the band bus will leave as soon as the gig is over. He's brainstorming ways to end the Tourism 101 conversation when he hears a Jack & Jill song playing. "How Much Fun," of course. Turns out a three-minute musical donut is more than enough fuel for a tour of Europe; there's even talk of hitting Japan in the fall.

First he has to not get fired, which means he needs to get to the venue. Soon.

Spider doesn't ask anyone for the time; knowing how late he is will just make him panic. All he needs to do is find his way back to La Rambla, as quickly as possible. He struggles to escape from behind the table, even as his would-be tour guide starts talking about the weather. "And summer, then? It is hot, in USA, in summer?" When Spider finally stands up his legs make their unhappiness clear, buckling twice before struggling to lock into place. How long has he been sitting there, anyway? And what has he been smoking?

He pushes his way through the kitchen, now even more crowded. At the doorway he sees Miranda, leaning against the sink next to a lanky blonde. Did she buy the booze and come back? Or never leave, just take his money? Leaving without offering to take her to the show, or even saying goodbye, means he's writing off his best chance to make love to a Spanish woman, but he reminds himself that a home studio will last longer than sex.

It's a sign of maturity, that he can make that calculation. Especially while stoned.

When he finally makes it out of the apartment he turns left on instinct, trying to convince his legs to move quickly. As long as he was there for the first song Jack would forgive him, though there'd be a long lecture about responsibility. He's faked his way through conversations like that since grade school, and long ago mastered the art of Nodding With Shame While Saying the Right Thing. The only problem will be finding the fucking club.

At the end of the block he takes another left, onto a cobblestone road that is narrower and darker than any he remembered from the trip to the apartment. The street is so poorly lit that he wants to turn around, but off in the distance he can see bright lights, lights he hopes are coming from La Rambla. He ignores his inner imaginings about what could be hiding in the dark crevices on either side of the alley, refuses to think about what the muted Spanish voices buzzing all around him might be saying—never mind where those voices were coming from, since all the buildings look like they've been abandoned. He focuses on walking at a steady pace, on the lights in the distance, telling himself the sense of foreboding crawling up his back is just the drugs. Just the drugs.

Maybe it's not foreboding he's feeling. Isolation? Desperation? How did he get to the point where his career depends upon a race back to a job he doesn't want but can't afford to lose, surrounded by people who don't speak his language? The metaphors unspool too easily, little rubber balls bouncing down a steep set of stairs. He really is all alone, in the dark. But he also doesn't know, as he stumbles down the alley, who he would have join him, if he could magically make someone appear. No one from Stackd Souls even talks to him. Certainly, none of his girlfriends would be much help. Each one—from Val in 8th grade to Emily, as she threw him out on the eve of the Jack & Jill tour—accused him of making them feel less important than his music.

He always wondered why they sounded so surprised. The primacy of music in his life was the one thing he never lied about.

Then it hits him: Danny and Paul. Of course. Danny would be panicking so much Spider would have to laugh, and Paul would be cracking bad jokes in fractured Spanish. He remembers a night in Minneapolis when they'd gotten lost on their way to First Avenue. It was below freezing, but when they left the hotel they were too excited to bother with coats: they were going to play a stage Prince had destroyed more than once. They were so busy bullshitting they missed their turn, and had to break into a run when Danny looked at his watch and realized they were supposed to start in ten minutes.

And then the three of them had stopped running, just as quickly as they had started. "We're the fucking band," Spider said, wrapping an arm around Paul and an arm around Danny. "Nothing's gonna happen without us."

"That's right," Paul agreed, putting on his best Italian mobster accent. Brando by way of Boston. "We're the motherfucking band." Spider wonders if he will ever be The Band again, or if he will only ever work for The Band.

By the time he makes his way to the end of the block he's too tired to be relieved that he has found La Rambla. A sinner on his deathbed, he's ready to give up all the drugs and booze for more paychecks from the Jack & Jill machine. If he can hang on for these last two months, he'll return with the money he's already imagined spending on new gear. Two more months, and he can turn the music in his head into quality recordings. He just needs to not get fired, and to not snort or drink everything he earns.

When he reaches the back door to the club he finally looks at his watch. It's just before 9:00. An hour late for stage call, but half an hour before showtime. He exhales slowly and nods at the doorman, but his hand is stopped before he can push the back entrance open. Surprised, he fumbles in his pocket and pulls out his ALL ACCESS pass. "Estoy con la banda," Spider says. "Jack y Jill."

The doorman motions for Spider to wait, and Spider wonders if he can blame some of this on this goon. I was stuck outside for ten, fifteen minutes, he imagines, fine-tuning his script. They'll still dock him for the day, but maybe the lecture will be shorter.

Foster returns with the doorman. In one hand is Spider's backpack, and in the other is his Gibson case. "I wanted to give the fucking guitar to one of the street kids, but Jack talked me out of it." Foster drops Spider's stuff on the ground and blocks the open door with his body.

"Come on," Spider says, glad no one's around to hear the pleading in his voice. "I'm not the first American to get lost in Barcelona."

"No, and you're not the only junkie who can play these songs," Foster says. "We'll find one who can damn well be on time. Fool me twice, blahdy fucking blah."

"Foster, man," Spider says, drawing out the words in hopes that if he can stall long enough he'll find the combination that will get him back inside. He can see Tiny with his back to the door, tuning a guitar, can hear the opening band wrapping up their set. And there, wearing a suit jacket and holding a guitar, is Sammy.

Replaced by his own fucking tech. And it sure looks like something they've been planning.

Maybe it's for the best, he tells himself as he turns away from the door. If you try to sell your soul but the devil turns you down, the last thing you should do is beg. He picks up his backpack and Gibson. If he had a pair of scissors he'd cut the fucking Jack & Jill tags off both of them, but all he wants now is to get away before anyone else sees him.

He walks toward the railing he'd met Miranda at, just a few hours earlier. Estoy libre, he thinks, wishing someone else could appreciate the joke.

Estoy libre.

The air smells different, like it's about to rain, and the background noise suddenly sounds louder, a track in a song that's been pulled forward in the mix. It's time for serious drinking to start, for tourists and locals alike. He wonders if he should try to make his way back to Miranda's apartment, but even if he could find it, what would happen? Indifference, or even worse pity, seems the mostly likely reaction to his reappearance, and he doesn't think he can stand either.

He reaches into his wallet to see how crappy a hotel room he'll be stuck with, but stops without even opening it. Miranda: he gave all his cash to her. Probably all she ever wanted, not his smile or American accent. Which means he's not just unemployed and homeless in Barcelona, but broke, too; before leaving for tour he'd used his advance to pay off his credit cards, and then cut them all up, a move that was supposed to inspire self-control.

As he starts to walk slowly down La Rambla, though, he remembers his emergency stash, buried in an inner pocket of his backpack. Some euros and some twenties folded into a tight little wad.

Enough money for a taxi.

When the cab drops him off at Parc Guell, Spider knows he's made the right decision for the first time all day. The colors and shapes and clots of people are so intense, so fantastic and alive, that he offers a silent apology to the man who'd bored him with sights to see in Barcelona. As he slowly walks up one of the trippy staircases at the entrance to the park, the sounds shift and twist; every time he turns his head he hears new strains of music and laughter, as if there was a drunken engineer moving levels up and down randomly.

God as a drunken soundman. There were worse possibilities.

For a long time he walks slowly from area to area of the Parc, pushed along in random directions by whatever flow of people happens to brush against him. Every corner he turns gives way to new treasures buried in plain sight, from brightly colored mosaics to impossibly curved columns to what appear to be bird nests built into the walls. It's as if Gaudi had as many streams of images floating through his head as Spider has channels of music. He finds himself moved by the idea that someone with such unusual visions had his work embraced by the world.

This insight makes him pause for a moment, and wonder why his own music has yet to receive even a fraction of that embrace. Maybe it's the colors, Spider thinks, watching so many different types of people happily wander through the surreal landscape. Maybe the bright colors make Gaudi's complex visions more appealing.

He starts walking again, drifting until he reaches one of the highest terraces. He takes a deep breath and decides to stay as still as he can for as long as he can. Far below, the lights of Barcelona shine brightly. Jack & Jill should be on their encores, by now. The sounds he's immersed in are much more satisfying—laughter, mixed with random drum circles and guitarists. He finds an open section of wall to lean against and takes out his Gibson, ready to be one more piece of musical driftwood, to play for no one but himself.

As he tunes he notices a pack of kids, half a dozen or so—guys in jean jackets and tight T-shirts, girls in loose blouses and flowing skirts. They seem to be in their late teens or early twenties, and watch him as he strums a few warm-up chords. They keep watching as he stumbles his way through Dylan's "Meet Me in the Morning," chosen because the melody is perfect for his tired voice. The words fit his mood, too, as Dylan's words often do. "They say the darkest hour/is right before the dawn."

As he finishes one of them breaks away from the pack and walks over, his own guitar in hand. He looks back to his posse a few times, and they urge him on. "Hola," he says when he's a few feet away from where Spider sits. "¿Eres Americano?"

"Sí, sí. Hola."

"¿Quieres tocar juntos? ¿Conmigo?"

Spider sits up a little straighter and motions for the kid to sit down. "Sí, por cierto."

"Me llamo Pablo."

"Hola Pablo," Spider says, deciding it's easier to just skip his name for now. Who knows, maybe before the night is over he'll have picked a new one.

As Pablo sits down next to him he motions toward the Jack & Jill decal, still hanging off the case of Spider's Gibson. "¿Jack y Jill?" His mouth breaks into a wide grin. "¿Conoces Jack y Jill?"

Spider also grins. Oh, I know those assholes alright, he thinks. "Sí."

"¡Bueno!" Pablo strums a chord, makes a quick adjustment to his D string, and then looks at Spider with an increased level of excitement. "Quiero aprender 'How Much Fun.'"

The broken English catches Spider off guard. "'How Much Fun'?"

"¡Sí, es mi favorito! ¿Me puedes enseñar?" Pablo hums a bit of the melody.

"¿Estás seguro?" Spider asks, hoping his tone of voice will cause his new friend to suggest something else. If there is one song in his life he is hoping never to play again, it's that one.

"¡Sí, sí!" Pablo motions to the kids he'd peeled away from and they walk over. "Voy a aprender 'How Much Fun.'"

"Si tu quieres," Spider says, looking up at Pablo's friends. Each has a cigarette in their mouth and a hand clasped around a beer bottle, the smooth skin of their youth making them appear as literal dolls, playthings equipped with matching accessories. One of the girls meets his eyes and then drops her gaze nervously, and he dares to dream she finds Aging Americans attractive. They all seem so eager, and... genuine. Is that a reflection of their European-ness? Or is this what it looks like, to be young and outside on a beautiful evening with some beer and your friends? It has been too long to remember ever feeling like that, if Spider ever did.

He turns to face Pablo, so the kid can watch him run down the chords. He tries to focus on the moment and not get distracted by all those bigger problems he will have to figure out soon. Like, where he is going to sleep? And how will he get home from Spain? That last question flashes across a back corner of his brain as he runs through the chorus for Pablo. What the hell, why dodge the even bigger question—where is home, anyway? His stuff is in storage, Emily done with him. Where is it he would return to?

The chords to the song, like the chords to any Jack & Jill song, are straightforward. After just a few minutes Pablo has the basic progression down. "No más," Spider says. "Es todo."

"¿Todo?" Pablo asks. "¿Estás seguro?"

"Sí, es todo."

Pablo looks at his friends and holds his hand out, so someone can pass him a beer. He takes a swallow, grins like an excited little boy, and then playfully slaps Spider on the knee. "¿Estamos listo?"

"Sí," Spider answers. He takes a swallow from Pablo's beer and then places it down on the ground between them. He plays the opening riff twice, and mouths "uno, dos, tres, cuatro," to let Pablo know when he should come in with the chords.

The boy plays a little anxiously at first, as if he's found himself behind the wheel of a new car and wants to get away before anyone notices. He quickly settles into the groove, though, and his smile grows wide. After they strum the chords to the chorus a few times Pablo motions with his mouth and nods at Spider, but Spider points at Pablo. "You," he mouths, "tu cantas."

And he does. "How much fun, how much fun is it," he starts softly, "how much fun, how much fun is it, how much fun to be with you?" When he reaches the second half of the chorus, his friends whoop encouragement and spread their arms as wide as they can, the way Jack & Jill do in their video. "This much fun, this much fun it is," Pablo sings, his accent becoming more pronounced as his voice strains for the notes, "this much fun and more, with you." Spider wonders if Pablo even understands what he's singing, but it doesn't seem to matter. The song is so free of irony that it translates instantly.

Pablo's friends grin and take long drags on their cigarettes as Spider and Pablo run through a verse. Pablo hums the melody softly, and Spider assumes he doesn't even know what the words to the verse are. He and his friends probably don't even know, or care, that Jack & Jill were in town that very night—the club seems too bourgeois for them. No, they only care about the chorus. The second time through, Pablo and his friends sing loudly from the start. "How much fun, how much fun is it?" Their young arms spread open wide; down below, the lights of Barcelona shine brightly, while around them the pockets of tourists and natives, friends past and present, blur happily into Gaudi's playground. "How much fun, how much fun, to be with you?"

When the chorus ends Spider repeats the intro riff, then makes a circle motion with his finger. There's no need to do the bridge, or even the lead guitar break that was the only moment he felt like a real guitarist, and not just a recording. Pablo's friends move closer to the guitar players, and they're so fucking happy Spider sings along, once again confronted by a truth he's spent so much of his life resisting: the world offers it warmest embraces to the simplest messages. This time he surrenders to that truth. His buzz fading, he no longer has the energy to fight.

Thirteen Ways of Looking

Amherst, 2008

After English I get cornered by Miss Conway, who wants to put one of my poems in the Senior Issue of *Camelot*, Kennedy High's Literary Magazine. We're standing so close I can tell that heavy perfume we all joke about is there to cover up the smell of cigarettes. She's talking about how great the poem is, so I guess I should be excited, but I'm too worried about the other thousand kids at Kennedy reading it. I just start nodding, though, mumbling "OK, sure," so I can get to lunch. No one ever reads *Camelot* anyway.

When I finally get to the cafeteria Tim, Charles, and Frog are already at our usual table, laughing so hard as I walk up that I start laughing, too. "Hey," I say, sitting down next to Frog. "What's up?"

Frog grins. "I Googled all the teachers last night."

I stare at my pizza, mad at myself for not thinking of such a perfect idea first. "What'd you find?"

Charles looks over at Tim and nods. They've been writing songs together since Thanksgiving break, so now they always act like they're speaking some secret language. It drives me crazy. "The best stuff," Charles says, "is about Mr. Cutrino."

I nod eagerly, like I can't wait to hear. We've got a running list of jokes to crack about all the teachers, and the ones about Mr. Cutrino revolve around the mug with the old Beatles Apple logo he always carries, or the way he says "History is everywhere!" *every* day. Nothing as bad as the jokes about Visinski's clothes or Greenberger's ass, but it still bothers me. I actually look forward to his class, even though it's the only one where I have to work hard for an A.

"Mr. Cutrino was in a band," Frog says, looking at me.

"A band? When?"

"Tell him the best part!" says Charles. "Tell him the name!"

Frog scrunches up his face the way he does when he plays drums, making his big eyes bulge out even more than usual. "Monkeyhole."

"Monkeyhole," Tim repeats, laughing as he unwraps a Twinkie. "Wonder why they didn't make it, huh?"

"He even played bass," Charles says. "Just like his favorite little student."

Cutrino's is the one class we all have together, and they're always kidding me about my good grades and the way I answer questions no one else will. "They put out records, and everything?" I ask Frog, ignoring everyone's laughter at Charles's joke.

"Yeah," he says. "At least one, anyway."

Mr. Cutrino in a band? For the rest of the lunch period, I keep trying to picture it. He seems so—regular? Much more like a regular person than any of the others, who must have been made at some factory that cranks out Oddball Science Geeks and Washed-Out-Jocks-Turned-Sadistic-P.E.-Coaches.

On our way to fifth period, Charles says, "You know what? I bet it's not even the same Cutrino."

"Uh-huh," says Frog. "Come over after school, I'll show you the web pages."

"Are there pictures?"

Frog shrugs. "I didn't see any, but he wouldn't look the same, anyway. Right?"

"No proof." Charles turns to Tim, who nods on cue. "How can you be sure it was him?"

I can't figure out why, but I can see from the look on Charles's face that this has become a big deal. He can get stuck in a loop, sometimes, hammering on some question until we all admit he's right—like whether "Planet Telex" or "Airbag" is a better opening track, or where we'd look coolest posing for our first band photos.

"It was the same name," Frog says, "and kind of seemed like the right age."

The four of us are standing right where three hallways converge, an intersection that's always clogged with students trying to get to class at the last possible minute. We linger here every day after lunch, bullshitting until the second bell rings and we split up. Before senior year I'd hated the time in between classes: hated pushing myself past the kids standing in my way and laughing loudly, hated wondering if they were laughing at me, hated myself for giving a shit if they were. Now that I'm in Time Capsule, I'm part of a cluster that gets in everyone's way. It's one of the best things about being in the band. Since Christmas break, though, I've started having these flashes, remembering what it felt like to be one of the kids trying to get past everyone else. Maybe I'm getting away with something by standing there as part of a gang; maybe I'm really supposed to be alone and my true self will soon be exposed.

Tim finally says we should just go to Mr. C.'s room after school and ask him. Charles thinks it's a waste of time but Frog thinks it's a great idea. I vote with Tim and Frog, because Charles isn't outvoted very often, so we all agree to meet outside Mr. C's classroom at the end of the day. When the first bell rings, Charles and Tim head off to chemistry, and Frog and I start jogging to photography. He's plotting ways to get into the darkroom at the same time as Jenny Muller, but I'm still wondering if it's true about Mr. C.

Freshman year sucked.

I'd actually been excited that last week of summer before school, convinced that high school would be some sort of new beginning. My optimism ended on the way to my very first class. Matt Haynes, an especially ape-like jock who'd tormented me since kindergarten, pushed me out of his way with a loud, "Watch it, faggot." Struggling to maintain my balance, watching the crowd of pathetic hangers-on Haynes always had with him laugh as my brand new three-ring binder slipped out of my hands, I suddenly understood. The same assholes from eighth grade would be in ninth grade. Nothing had changed.

Sophomore year and junior year sucked, too, but at least I'd stopped thinking school would ever *not* suck.

The summer before senior year I got a job at Safeway and worked as many hours as I could. I wanted to save money for whatever life I could start after graduation, but I also wanted summer to just disappear—for the first time in my life, I couldn't wait for school to start back up. The sooner the last year of high school started, the sooner it would all be over. Forever.

That summer, Frog asked if I wanted to join a band he was putting together. When I told him I'd never played bass, he waved me off.

"Excuses, excuses. You know more notes and chords than either of the guys playing guitar. Besides, all the bass has to do is hit the downbeat and stay out of the way."

Frog was my best friend, besides Lorrie, and one of the few people who knew I played piano. Music was this secret I had, a thing that I could do that no one else knew I did. When I came home to play after some shitty day, I felt like Superman must have when he went to the Fortress of Solitude. Listening to it, playing it, hearing it in my head—music was my survival trick. Bass was totally different, though, and I hated hanging out with new people. So I said no. A lot. Frog kept begging me to do it, just until they could find someone else, and said I could use his brother's bass and everything. I couldn't survive senior year without Frog, so I finally said yes.

And then everything about playing with Time Capsule surprised me. Playing bass came easily, playing with other people was much more fun than I'd ever imagined (once I stopped being afraid of making a mistake), and meeting Charles and Tim didn't feel awkward or weird. It felt like finally meeting people I should have known all along. Best of all, being in a band made me feel like I was wearing a bulletproof vest, even when I wasn't playing.

Joining Time Capsule even made life easier at home, at least for a while. It was just me and my father, ever since my mother had "wandered away," as my father put it, when I was in first grade. We got occasional post cards, usually from London or Paris, but I'd stopped asking when I would see her again, so Dad wouldn't have to lie about it anymore. At first he was thrilled by my new friends, and all the new reasons I had to leave the safety of my room: practice every weekend; trips to various record stores once or twice a week after school; getting together somewhere to listen to all those records. After Christmas break, though, his mood changed. He carefully examined every graded object I brought home, looking for some reason to limit my time for music. "Senior grades count, too," he kept saying. "You don't wanna screw things up for UMass in the home stretch."

My grades were better than ever, though, so my early acceptance to University of Massachusetts at Amherst was not in danger. What I didn't tell him was that the band wanted to move to Boston when we finished high school, to play in clubs and start making records. On New Year's Eve, we'd gotten Frog's brother to buy us a twelve-pack of Budweiser, and at midnight we'd made a drunken vow: everyone to Boston. No college, no fallback plan. No half-assed effort. We were all committed to being a Band, and nothing else. I'd raised my Bud like everyone else, the four of us slamming cans together hard enough to splash ourselves. It seemed impossible to me, like I'd just agreed to fly to the moon, or invade Russia, but I wanted to believe, even for just as long as the beer held out, that it could happen.

After photography with Frog, I have Lorrie with me in Mr. Coza's math class. Her presence is a good thing and a bad thing, the way it's been since second grade, when she introduced herself by tackling me on the playground. We sit in the back and pass notes. It kills her that I can do that and still pull down an A, while she barely holds up a C. And it kills me, to think about all the bad boyfriends I've talked her through as Loyal Confidant. Sometimes I even get frustrated enough to admit to myself I'll never be the guy she complains about to someone else.

The day Frog tells us about Mr. C., all Lorrie wants to talk about in math are the papers we're writing for history. Working on my own paper for Mr. Cutrino is the most fun I've had in high school. I'm writing about a minor figure from early in the school year, La Malinche. She'd lived in Mexico when Cortez the Conquistador landed, and was given to him as a slave. It turned out she was really good with languages, so Cortez made her his translator. She'd even had a child with him, though it was hard to tell whether she'd loved him or just been raped. Reading about her was like reading about two different people. Some Mexicans thought she was a traitor who sold out to the Spanish; others thought of her as the mother of Mexico. We only need to write a five-page paper, but I have enough research for one twice that long, and I'm still looking things up.

By the end of math class, I agree to "help" Lorrie. I know I'll wind up doing most of the work, but I don't mind. There'll be at least one trip to the library, maybe two, and I imagine us whispering as we walk around, looking like the couple we'll never really be.

When final period ends, I head to Mr. Cutrino's room with the rest of the guys. "Oh, look at this," he says when we walk in. "The Four Musketeers, come to get me."

"Well, we have something to ask you, Mr. C.," Frog says.

He leans back in his chair. "Sure."

We stand there not saying anything, until Charles raises his eyebrows and motions to Frog. "Were you ever in a band? Called Monkeyhole?"

"Now, there's a name I never expected to hear in this room." He grins. "But why do you all look so surprised? I keep telling you: everyone has a history."

So it was true. "Well, we're in a band, too," I say, a little louder than I'd planned.

"Yeah, and I gotta tell you guys—Time Capsule's not much of a name."

Charles frowns. He always brags about thinking up that name. "I don't think anyone in a band called 'Monkeyhole' can say anything."

Mr. C. laughs again. "Fair enough, fair enough. The name is pretty beside the point anyway—if you're good, it's a good name, if not..." He balances his chair on two legs, the way he always tells us not to. "So who plays bass?"

"Lucas," says Tim. He points to Frog, "Drums," then to Charles and himself. "Guitars."

He turns to me. "You know who the best bass player is, right?"

I stall, trying to think of a name that will impress him. "Um..."

"Exactly. The one you don't notice." He turns back to Charles. "So, what happens after you guys graduate?"

"Boston," Charles says. "We're gonna move to Boston."

"Yeah," I say. "Play clubs, make records."

"Your parents know about this?"

"Of course," Tim says. "It's what we're gonna do."

My head bobs up and down in rhythm to Charles's and Frog's. The other guys just assume I've told my father, and since they hardly ever see him and he hardly ever sees them, I've gotten away with that. Telling Mr. C. makes the lie more real, though.

"Well, OK then." After an awkward silence Mr. Cutrino rubs his chin, the way he does in class after making some complicated point, and says, "I'd offer you advice, but if there's one thing I never figured out, it's the music business. I hope it works out for you guys."

Charles is the first one to speak after we leave.

"Mr. Cutrino! Who woulda figured it?" He turns to hit Frog on the side of his head. "And I was sure you were wrong, Frog-man."

Tim shakes his head as we head to the parking lot. "God, can you even imagine? Him, actually, like, onstage?"

"Trying to play bass and hold that fucking mug at the same time," Charles says, laughing before he even finishes his joke.

The others start laughing too, joking about how ridiculous the whole thing is, but now that we know for sure, I'm seeing all the clues we missed. Mr. C. is always making musical references and reminding us we're his "audience." Once, when his lecture ended before the bell rang, he asked what he should do for an "encore." Most of all, he actually pays attention to you when you talk—he doesn't seem like he's just waiting for your mouth to stop moving, like most of the other teachers. The first thing I learned playing with Time Capsule is that I had to listen to everyone else, not just myself, for the music to sound any good.

By this time the students' parking lot is mostly deserted, except for the stoners hanging out in the far corner, car doors open and Led Zeppelin blaring: *"Been a long time since I rock and rolled..."* After Tim and Charles double-check plans for Friday's practice, I finally ask what I've been wondering since we'd left Mr. C.

"So, who wants to look for the CD?"

Tim stares at me. "What CD?"

"Mr. Cutrino's. Monkeyhole."

Frog scrunches up his face in excitement. "Man! How great would that be?"

Charles is shaking his head, though. "Why would we wanna buy his shitty CD?"

"I dunno. Hear what it sounds like."

Tim and Charles look at me like I'm crazy, and Frog suddenly doesn't seem excited. "Where would we even find something like that?" Charles asks.

I shrug. "On the web? Used, or something?"

"They probably sold, like, two copies, ages ago, so how could we ever find one? And why would we want to, anyway?" Charles looks over his shoulder as he starts walking to his Mom's minivan. "I mean, he's teaching. Here. Think of how much his band must have sucked."

"Teaching *here*, man," Tim echoes, pointing back at the school.

And that's it. So I laugh along, agree to call Frog about our bio homework, and get into my car. I put the key in the ignition but don't feel like following them out the way I usually do. Instead I sit in my car, fingers fidgeting with the key chain, and wonder if they noticed I am not moving.

After I finally leave, I drive around back roads, taking my time and listening to a mix tape I made Lorrie but haven't given her yet. I'm thinking about moving to Boston, and what college would be like, and what my poem will look like in print, next to other poems and stories. And Mr. C's band. It's almost six by the time I get home, and the sky is dark gray. The house seems even quieter than usual.

For as long as I can remember, Dad's worked a lot, picking up extra shifts at the pharmacy whenever he can. Money's one of those things we don't talk about, but lately I've been wondering if he started working so much when Mom left because he wanted to stockpile money for whatever crazy thing happened next. I know we're not rich or anything, that our house is smaller than the houses of everyone else in the band, but it's not like we've ever had the power cut off.

What his working so much really means is that I don't see a lot of him during the week. Most of my early after-school memories involve a series of babysitters, high school girls who put me in front of the TV and called their boyfriends. When I hit middle school I got my own key, thrilled to be in charge of myself. I used to go crazy with Pop-Tarts and old sitcoms, but now I barely watch TV at all—too much music to listen to. And ever since I got a computer in my room, I've started just heading there as soon as I get home, with Gatorade and whatever leftovers I can find.

When I search for Monkeyhole on eBay, I get three hits: all copies of a CD called *Behind Door Number Two*. None have any bids yet, and one is listed as "Buy It Now" for 99 cents, plus three dollars shipping and handling. I punch in my PayPal information, and then look for anything else I can find on the band. There's not a whole lot, but I do find some pretty positive reviews. I don't click on any video or audio clips, though; now that the CD is on its way, I want to wait. Frog teases me for still spending money on actual CDs, since he just downloads everything, but I like looking at the pictures and liner notes as I hit play for the first time.

Dad comes home a little after ten. Sometimes I go down and meet him, but usually I do what I do tonight: pretend to be asleep. I turn off the lights in my room, sitting in the glow from the computer screen as I listen to him move around. The house is so quiet I can follow his path. He starts by sifting through the mail I leave on the kitchen table every day, goes to the fridge to grab a beer, and then wanders into the living room and turns on the TV. He either leaves the sound too low for me to hear or watches it in silence. He never stays long, though, before he turns off the TV and heads up the stairs, so quietly I sometimes lose track of him until I hear his door gently shut.

I wonder if he's listening for my sounds as closely as I listen for his.

Tonight he comes upstairs pretty quickly. I surf old Radiohead setlists and wonder what Dad's thinking about, in his room alone. Does he ever think about Mom, like I do late at night? Does he imagine, sometimes, what the house would be like if she were still here? Would it be this quiet? We never talk about her, or why she never visits, or what life might be like in Paris. I know he must have some of the same thoughts and questions I do. I also know if he ever did want to talk about her, I wouldn't know what to say.

Mr. Cutrino's old band never comes up again. Tim and Frog get a copy of *Boston Phoenix* to see how much apartments and rehearsal spaces will cost, which makes us realize we're gonna need to find jobs, too. Frog's got a cousin in Boston who works for a lawn crew, but I can't imagine any of us cutting yards and planting bushes and stuff. Tim says finding jobs won't be hard at all, and Charles doesn't say much at all, because he's beginning to worry about graduating. I start helping him with biology, English, and even history. Mr. Cutrino may have been in a band, but it still looks like he might fail Charles.

At home, my father keeps asking me if I'd filled out the dorm room questionnaire UMass sent. I've looked at it a few times, but the long list of questions overwhelms me: Do I want to room with someone who stays up late or gets up early? Does sexual orientation matter? Religion? I don't want to deal with those questions in real life, never mind so some stranger could read my answers. I just keep sliding the packet back under my bed and hope Dad will forget.

I don't tell any of the other guys I ordered *Behind Door Number Two*, not even Frog. The last thing I want is to have them all listening to it with me for the first time, joking about how much it's gonna suck before I even hear it. It arrives after almost two weeks, in a battered brown envelope.

Grabbing some Gatorade and leftover pizza, I head to my room with the CD. It's a used copy, but the cover's in decent shape. Mr. C and the other two guys are on the back, trying to look tough, but everyone's hair is too big and puffy, and the shirts are a little too colorful. They all look young, too, maybe not that much older than we are now.

I take out the insert, put on my headphones, and turn the volume down low; if the record sucks I'll be disappointed and won't want to hear it too closely. Halfway through the first song I start over, this time with the volume up. It's loud and catchy, with lots of guitar and the drums way up in the mix and a really great singer. By the time the first song ends I have no idea how Mr. Cutrino wound up at Kennedy High. I listen all the way through, and as soon as the album ends I hit play again. It's so good I don't want the other guys to hear it. I'm pretty certain Charles would just say it sucks, even if he liked it. Besides, it feels kind of nice to have this secret thing to carry around.

Later that night, when I'm listening one more time before I go to sleep, I finally figure out why the guys didn't want to get the CD: they were afraid it would be good. Because then we'd have to worry about what happens if being a great band is not enough for us to make it.

After spring break the Senior Issue of *Camelot* comes out. "Thirteen Ways of Looking for Me" is on the last page. That bums me out, even though I wasn't sure I wanted it in there at all. I mean, how many kids even pick up a copy of the magazine, never mind read the whole thing? Frog tries to convince me it's cool, that I should think of all the great last songs on CDs, like "Videotape" or "On and On and On," but says nothing about the poem itself—and I'm afraid to ask. Charles and Tim don't say anything about it either, but with them I'm relieved. If they don't talk about it, they can't criticize it.

The whole week sucks. Lorrie is so worried about her boyfriend, some lunk on the basketball team who never texts back as quickly as she wants, that she doesn't do any of the math homework; we have to meet up before school so she can copy mine. And my father actually wants to talk at breakfast, not once but twice, when all I want to do is listen to the Monkeyhole CD and eat Frosted Flakes. I keep dreading that he's gonna bring up the UMass info packet again, the one I keep not filling out.

The idea of not being in the band seems crazier than ever, because looking forward to Friday's practice is the only thing that keeps my head from breaking open. Frog's parents have always been into the idea of the band, so they give us free run of the basement, and laid out old pieces of carpet Frog's father got from one of the hotels he works in. Tim hung some lights from the ceiling, so now it's possible to imagine we're playing at a real club; whenever I look around during practice and see everyone playing with their eyes closed I know that's what they're doing.

We take our breaks in the "finished" half of the basement, where there are a couple of old gray couches that smell like cats and a tiny refrigerator that almost keeps the Cokes cold. There's even cable, so we can make fun of everything on MTV. They barely even show videos anymore, but tonight we see Coldplay—again. They're our official "wimps of the week."

"Isn't it creepy, to have someone talk about 'fixing you'?" Charles asks. "Who buys this shit?"

"My sister," says Tim, opening a Coke.

"And my mother," says Frog. "She keeps asking why we don't sound like this."

"Tell her it's because we have balls," I said, a line good enough to earn me a slap on the back from Charles.

When we start practicing again, Charles says he wants to work on one he just wrote last night. Tim looks surprised, maybe even a little angry. As far as I know, they've only written together these last few months, so it's weird for Charles to have done one on his own. For a moment there's a tense kind of quiet, something we don't deal with too much. Frog can feel it, too, judging from the look on his face as he gets behind the drums. He burps twice, loudly, probably just to crack the silence.

"Is this Jam Band or Amadeus?" he asks. "Jam Band" is Frog's term for a song Charles doesn't have any specific parts for, one where the rest of us just kind of play around until we come up with stuff we like. "Amadeus" is a song where Charles hears all the different parts in his head, and knows what everyone should play—something Frog read Mozart used to be able to do.

"Kind of in between," Charles says, checking his tuning and strumming a few chords. "I have some ideas, but not for all of it."

"So, kind of a Jamadeus thing," Tim says.

The joke breaks the tension enough for Charles and Tim to share one of those knowing grins--still annoying, but better than having the two of them fight. I leave my amp off and finger the frets as I listen to Charles play the chords for Tim, my hands moving too fast because they're excited and nervous. Excited, because hearing a new song for the first time is like starting a new book, or watching a new movie: I have no idea where it's going to go, and I can't wait to see what happens. It's not like walking into Kennedy High, or my house, or even talking to Lorrie, where I usually know exactly what's going to happen. Nervous, because I always worry about not being able to play what Charles wants, or not being able to figure out something cool to add.

By the time Charles finishes showing him all the chords, Tim is strumming along, and I feel comfortable enough to map out the root notes. There's a kind of Radiohead vibe to the song, which doesn't surprise me considering how many times we've all listened to *OK Computer*, but I know it will sound different when we all play it. As Frog keeps saying, it's okay for us to try to sound like someone else. We'll never actually be able to do it, so it will wind up sounding completely different.

We play through the song twice, not stopping even if we screw something up, with Charles just calling out cues so we know when to switch from verse to chorus. He makes a few suggestions—everything a little slower, make the last chorus even louder—and then moves to the microphone. "OK, I'm gonna try and sing this thing now," he says, pulling a piece of paper out and putting it on the music stand we'd stolen from the band room.

"What's it called?" Tim asks, strumming loudly once to check his volume.

"'Thirteen Ways.'"

When I hear the title I resist the urge to look at Frog. After all, I took the "thirteen ways" bit from someone else, so maybe Charles did, as well. As soon as the song begins, though, I recognize my words.

> The world keeps getting smaller
> That's what they keep telling us
> Since the globe keeps shrinking
> Our lives are more dangerous
> But when I sit alone, on top of my roof
> The world seems too big for me to ever find you

It doesn't even sound like he's changed any words to make them fit with the music. I keep my brain focused on my fingers, to make sure that I can hit my marks with Frog, and by the end of the song I've almost forgotten that the words are mine; it just feels like a new Time Capsule song. Not fully formed, yet, and still stumbling as it moves around, but sort of alive.

When we're done I finally look at Frog, who's grinning as he stretches his back.

"I think it's gonna work," Tim says, running through the bridge chords as he talks. "Can't believe you just wrote it last night."

"Well, the words were already done," Charles says, and with that I finally look his way. "Lucas took care of those."

"You wrote those?" Tim says, looking at me.

"Yeah. I mean, it was just something for Conway's class. And then she wanted to put it in *Camelot*, or whatever."

"Why didn't you tell me?" Tim asks. "I never read that fucking thing, but I would have."

"And I only looked because Frog told me," Charles says. "What are you, publicity-shy already?"

I shrug. "I dunno. It was just a poem."

"Nah, it's lyrics. I could hear the music right away. Even if," he continues with a grin, "it should probably be called 'Lorrie, Why Won't You Suck My Dick?'"

Everyone laughs, but it doesn't feel like teasing. I kind of like the fact they all know I'm hung up on Lorrie, and that I don't stand a chance. And it's actually a relief, in a way, to know you can write a really sappy poem about your mother, and everyone will think it's just another song by a guy who wants to get laid.

As we roll through it again, I suddenly feel like everything they keep saying about Boston, about the four of us living together and playing shows and being a real band, could actually happen. Why not? We sound like a real band, like a band you think you've heard before even though you know you couldn't have. It feels like—sounds like—the place I belong.

I give Frog a ride home after practice. Usually we fight over who gets to hook their iPod up to the car stereo, but tonight we're too jazzed to do anything but talk. It's almost like what I imagine it would feel like to be a good athlete on a good baseball team, after a big win. Like you'll never lose another game again.

"And that new one, right? Charles has been on a roll."

"I know," I say. "The new ones have been so good they're all I want to play."

"I mean, tonight's—that's you and Charles, not you and Tim. And Tim looked pissed, that Charles had written something without him."

"I know. I'm glad he chilled out."

"Those are great words, too," he says, his voice getting a little quieter. He pauses, and then adds, "Even if they're not about Lorrie."

"What?"

"I mean, it's about your mom. Right?"

Frog's road twists and turns half a dozen times before his driveway, but I've been down it so many times—on my bike, and now in this car— that I can steer without thinking. It's not like it's a secret, or anything, that my mother is gone. Or even that the poem is about her. Thinking about it now, with my best friend in a dark and quiet car, it seems so obvious. That's why I was worried about it being published. I was sure everyone would figure it out, and be, like, sorry for me.

But only Frog got it.

"Yeah," I say as we get closer to his house. "I guess it is."

He nods, and doesn't say anything else until I pull into his driveway. He picks up his backpack from the floor and grabs the door handle. "Well," he says just before he gets out, "it's really great."

Lorrie used to ask me what I remembered about my mom. She gave up because all I could ever say was, "Nothing," but one night when I couldn't sleep I tried to list everything I really did remember. This was PTM (Pre-Time Capsule), but I still pull it out sometimes and look at it.

1. Her hair used to fall over her eyes when she was happy.

2. She smelled like baby shampoo.

3. She liked the Beatles. And Joni Mitchell.

4. She snorted when she laughed.

5. Her handwriting. That one's easiest to remember, because I still have the few postcards she sent. She wrote in script, and all the letters slant to the right, like the paper was held at an angle.

6. Her voice. When I wrote this list I could remember her voice, but I wish I'd written a description, because I don't remember it anymore. Which makes me worry about forgetting the few things I can remember.

The Thursday after that great practice, my plan—to never tell the band or my dad what I was going to do—collapses. I lose track of my father's footsteps when he reaches the top of the stairs, and the next thing I know he's standing in my open doorway, the hall light burning bright behind him. His face is hidden by shadows, but I look where his eyes should be and wait for him to complain about some chore I forgot to do, or how late I'm staying up.

"Hey."

"Hey," I mumble.

"First thing Saturday morning we're gonna fill out all that UMass stuff, OK? Together."

"OK." He can only know I haven't done it yet if he's been poking around under my bed and found the package, but I don't want to drag out our talk by accusing him of spying.

"Listen. I know that this is all harder, without her around."

I drop my eyes to the ground. Even as a pronoun, he hasn't made a reference to my mother in years.

"And if it's taken this long to fill the damn thing out, there must be something up. So I'm probably supposed to tell you something to make it better, like, don't worry, it's all gonna work out. Or, she'd be proud of you."

"It's OK," I say, staring at my hands.

"But. Truth is I never knew what she was thinking. So I don't know what the hell she would say now."

I can hear how hard it is for him to say all this, but I just want the conversation to end.

"I'm proud of you, though. You're smarter than me and her put together. And I should have told you that sooner."

I don't know what to say to that, but I figure I should at least look in his direction. I can't be sure if our eyes actually meet, since his face is still half-obscured by shadows, but this is the weirdest, most intense conversation we've ever had. I can't remember the last time he said something that surprised me.

"OK, then. Well. Don't stay up too late."

"Good night."

After he leaves I turn the computer screen back on and log into Yahoo. Lorrie's still up, of course. I try not to think about who else she's IM-ing with as I tell her about my father cornering me.

"fuck what r u gonna do?"

"I don't know," I type, trying not to be annoyed once again at the way she never uses capitals or punctuation when we IM. I mentioned it once and she said I sounded like her mother, so now I try to hear the words as if they'd been spoken in her voice, not typed in her poor grammar. I like to imagine the two of us sitting here, in the dark, in my room. Sometimes I let myself imagine even more, but not tonight.

"You should just tell him you don't wanna go."

"But I do."

"OK, so tell the guys you're going to college."

"But I don't want them to go without me."

"So do both."

"I can't do that either. The band's supposed to get all our attention. We promised each other."

"That's dumb."

"But otherwise it's like we're cheating. Like we're not really committed. Or something."

Her only response is to type in the keystrokes for a sad face.

"You're supposed to help me decide," I write. "What should I do?"

"Clone yourself."

"Haha."

"So fuck it all and come to UNC with me."

"Haha," I type again, wishing that really was a third choice. Maybe on some new college campus I could be someone else with her. Work out over the summer, sign up for all the same classes, and show up that first day as the funny and buff guy who helps her navigate the big, new world of college. For a brief moment I actually imagine applying to UNC, but the last thing I need is another choice, or to have to make another version of myself.

"Too bad you can't talk about this with your mother," she types.

My hands freeze above the keyboard. For the third time in a week someone's mentioned my mother to me, something that never happens. I get why no one wants to bring it up—the father's supposed to be the one to leave, not the mother. Every movie and TV show talks about a mother's love, and how it's the strongest fucking force in the galaxy. So what does it mean that mine could leave me and never come back?

It feels OK, though, to have Lorrie mention it. All week I've been wishing my mother was here. It might be that she was the kind of mom you'd never want to talk to about anything important, but there was a chance she'd be the kind of mom you could talk to about anything. "I know," I type back. She doesn't reply, but the chat window stays open, and I tell myself she's still there.

The next morning I stand at the kitchen counter and eat some cereal, desperate to think of some way to avoid having either of the conversations I'm supposed to have. I can fill out the paperwork to keep my dad happy, and then go to Boston with the guys when it's time. He might lose deposit money, though, and the idea of that would make me so guilty I'd just go to UMass.

And maybe that wouldn't suck. I imagine going to cool classes, and meeting a whole bunch of people as some new guy, but what if college is just like high school? What if the first day someone pegs me for a loser, and I never recover? Besides, I can't imagine the guys going to Boston and leaving me behind, the one group I belonged to disappearing. Not only disappearing, but continuing without me, like I'd never been all that important in the first place. Like the music didn't need me, after all.

On the way to school, listening to the Monkeyhole CD, I come up with a plan. I don't know if it will help, but having something to try gets me through the day. After last period I start walking out to the parking lot with the guys, but then I lie and tell them I have to go back and get my history book. We make plans to practice around seven and I head back, checking over my shoulder every couple of seconds to make sure they actually drive away.

The book's already in my backpack, and I take it out as I walk to Mr. Cutrino's room. He's still there, like I'd hoped, sitting behind a big stack of papers and sipping from that old Apple logo mug. When he sees me standing at the doorway I say, "Oh, hey Mr. C.," as casually as I can, like it's some weird accident I bumped into him.

"Lucas. You still hanging around?"

I hold up *America: Looking Forward, Looking Back*. "Yeah. Forgot this thing."

"I thought you'd have all the reading done by now."

"Almost." I let the book drop to my side. Deep breath. "Uh, you have a minute?"

"Sure. What's up?"

I walk into the classroom slowly, trying not to look as nervous as I feel. Sitting down on the chair next to his, I unzip my book bag and dig around for *Behind Door Number Two*, which I'd hidden at the bottom. As I'm looking Mr. Cutrino hands back my research paper.

"I'm giving these back Monday, but you can have yours now," he says.

I take *La Malinche, the Mexican Eve*, trying not to stare at the big red "A" on the front page, and slide it into my bag. "Thanks." I'm excited to see writing all over my pages—Mr. Cutrino's written comments are different than those of other teachers. All Conway ever does is point out comma splices and sentence fragments; Mr. Cutrino writes like the two of you are talking to each other on the page.

"You laid out all the different interpretations well, but what I liked most was the way you made your own case at the end. That's advanced, Lucas. Some people never learn how to do that."

"I have something for you to look at, too," I say as I take out *Behind Door Number Two*. "I got this off eBay."

His eyes widen as he takes the CD from me. "Wow, you actually found a copy." He leans back in his chair. "Man. I haven't seen this in years."

"Don't you have one?"

"Somewhere." He looks at the back, shaking his head when he sees the band photo. "It feels good to look at it again," he says, handing it back to me. "Thank you."

"So," I say, taking the CD back. "I listened to it." I start looking at the songs listed on the back so I don't have to watch him while I talk. "A lot. It's really, really... great." I look up again and he's staring right at me, like he actually wants to hear what I have to say about his music. I can't figure out whether I'm talking to him like he's a teacher, or another musician, or a regular person; it kind of feels like all three. "It's like I could tell how good it was gonna be," I say, "as soon as that first song began. I knew after, like, ten seconds, I knew I'd love the whole CD, that's how good the opening was. How right it sounded." The way he nodded told me he knew what I meant. "I love it when that happens."

"Me, too," he says. "*London Calling*."

"*OK Computer*," I say. "Though *London Calling*'s pretty good, too."

"I always wanted to make one of those records."

"You totally did," I say. "I mean, I'd like it even if I didn't know you."

"Thanks. It's nice to know it's still out there, being heard by anyone." He pauses. "Should I even ask what the other guys thought?"

I almost say they all thought it was great, but remember this is supposed to be a conversation where I don't lie. "They haven't heard it. I didn't tell anyone else I found a copy." There's another pause, and I wait for him to ask why I didn't tell anyone else. He doesn't ask, though, just waits for me to continue. I can hear the big metal doors at the end of the hall being pushed open and then slamming shut as I put the CD back into my book bag. "So what happened?" I say, finally asking the question I came to have answered.

"You mean, how come I'm here?"

"Yeah. The guys thought it must have been because your band sucked, but—" I stop myself.

He shrugs. "It's OK. I'd probably think the same thing. I mean, who would want to do this, right?"

"Do you want to do this?"

"Yeah, I do. I wouldn't have imagined doing it ten years ago, but I like it."

"So, what happened?" I repeat.

"Ah, it's a dull story, involving marketing, timing, and a French maid."

"A French maid?"

"Yup. They're easy to market, it turns out." He's staring out the windows along the wall of his classroom, the way he does sometimes in class when no one's coming up with the answer he's looking for. "It could have been all those things, or none of them. Truth is, sometimes not sucking isn't enough. I have lots of friends who didn't suck, who had to give up making music and make new lives."

"Does it bother you?" I ask. "That you didn't make it?"

He turns back to look at me. "Some days more than others. But I've been lucky enough to make a new life I like."

"But—if it had worked out, you'd still be playing, right?"

He nods. "Yeah, sure. It was fun, when it was going well."

Suddenly I think of Frog, doing his impersonation of the *Behind the Music* guy's voice. "Time Capsule didn't know it," he likes to say when we're doing something dull, like going to ShopRite for Cokes or walking into school on some crappy Monday morning, "but they were about to set America ablaze." If I dropped out of the band, would Frog even talk to me, anymore? "Are you still friends with the other guys?"

"Sort of? I mean, the three of us went through something only the three of us can understand, so we'll always have that. And we still message each other sometimes. Send along funny stories we think each other might get, or share random memories when they hit us."

"Oh. But you don't play together, or hang out, anymore?"

Mr. Cutrino shakes his head. "It's not the same as when we were all in the band together, no."

"Does any of this make you wish hadn't even tried, or anything?"

"No, I'm glad we tried. As soon as I joined the band, I knew it was worth giving up everything else for."

My lungs start to feel tight, because I know we just got to the part where I can ask the biggest question. "But how did you know?"

"How did I know what?"

"That the band was worth giving up other stuff for."

"Like, instead of, say, going to UMass or something?"

He's figured it all out, but I don't even care. I just want to know his answer. "Yeah, something like that."

He sits up straighter in his chair. "I was lucky. I was a pretty crappy student."

"You?" It seems impossible.

"I became a much better student in college," he says. "I never tried very hard in high school. All I wanted to do was play."

"Like Charles," I say.

"Yeah, I definitely see a lot of me in Charles." He lays his hands down on the desk and looks at me. "It's gonna be harder for you. You're a much smarter kid than I was."

I don't know what to say, just slide the strap of my book bag between my fingers.

"Have you talked to your dad about any of this?"

I keep my eyes focused on the strap. "He'd freak."

"He might not."

"He would. He's been talking about college since I was, like, six. It's pretty much all he's cared about since Mom left." I take a deep breath and look up.

"I can't tell you what to do. Or, that whatever you decide, it'll work out, because it might not." He pauses, and I can hear how quiet the school is on a Friday afternoon. "The thing is," he continues slowly, "you're gonna have to look for this answer yourself. The good news is, the world doesn't end if you don't know exactly what you're going to do for the rest of your life when you graduate high school. Or even five years after high school ends. We're not supposed to let our students in on that secret, but there it is."

"Uh," I say, "I don't think my father would believe that."

"He may not. But it's only important that you do."

I don't know what to say to that. Do I believe it? My father's life certainly didn't work out the way he planned it, and neither did Mr. C's, and they both made it. "That doesn't help me figure out what to do now."

"Nope. Sorry about that. But you'll figure it out. And when you do, come and talk to me again, OK? Because I can either help you pick classes for your first semester, or tell you ways to save money on tour."

"Deal." I stand up and shake his outstretched hand, a little bummed. I figured he was the one person who could tell me what to do.

I'm almost into the hallway when Mr. Cutrino calls out, "Hey, Lucas."

I turn around. "Yeah?"

"How much did the CD cost, anyway?"

I don't think he'd want to hear ninety-nine cents, but I don't want to say some amount so big that he'd know I was lying—that would be too weird for both of us. "Ten bucks," I say casually. "Plus shipping. You're lucky it didn't suck."

His smile is barely noticeable, but I can tell it's there. "Thanks for stopping by," he says, turning back to his papers.

"See you Monday," I say, stepping into the hall. The floors and walls are bathed in a soft gray glow, and the quiet has gotten so loud that I can hear my sneakers pull away from the linoleum. No one hangs out for very long after school on a Friday.

As I make my way across the empty parking lot I get the CD out of my backpack again, so I can play it in the car. I'm starting to feel better, even though Mr. Cutrino didn't have any sort of magic answer. It would suck a lot more if I had to choose between two things I'd hate doing, instead of two things I want to do. The hardest part is gonna be pissing someone off, but maybe that's something you have to get used to?

For a moment, just a split instant, I can imagine understanding why my mother did what she did.

When I get into the car I turn the key so just the battery comes on, slide the disc in, and skip to the title track. This time I focus on Mr. Cutrino's playing. His parts are just right: melodic, but not too complicated. Holding things up and pushing them forward, locked in with the drums, but never taking up too much space or attention. The best bass players are the ones you don't even notice.

It's the closing track, so when it ends the CD loops back to the beginning. As the drums that start the first song kick in, I sit up straight and turn the engine over. I'm the only one left in the student lot so I can drive out as slowly as I want, slicing across the angled lines of the parking spaces.

(A Dream Made of) Ice Cream

Atlanta, 2010

Atlanta wasn't supposed to be part of Paul's territory. Two more reps got laid off the day before his March sales trip, though, so it was added to his D.C. and Raleigh stops.

Paul ranted about the unfairness of all this to Julie when he got home. She had one of the twins in her arms, and he was ashamed to admit he didn't know whether it was Angie or Audrey—he still had trouble telling them apart, even when they were side by side. "I don't know how much of this crap I can stand," he said, waving his arms around. "Assigning me more territory, putting me on the road for longer stretches without even asking." Off in the distance he could hear the other twin start to cry, and he knew they had at least two hours of angry, hungry, dirty babies ahead of them. "I should just quit, right? Fuck it."

Julie swayed her body side to side while simultaneously swiveling her hips, the desperate dance she had developed to keep a child in her arms from waking up. A constellation of stains on her left shoulder, damp spots on the knees of her jeans: he couldn't remember the last time he had seen her in clean clothes. "You can't. God, how could you quit? I could sooner sprout wings and fly to London than find a job that pays what you make."

"You're right." He tried to sound deflated, but truthfully the only thing that sounded more painful than keeping the job he hated was not being able to escape the house for ten hours every day. He'd known all along quitting was not a realistic option—not with infant twins, an unemployed wife, and a stubborn recession—but wanted Julie to believe he was angry about being gone for longer than scheduled. "You're right."

As they stared at each other he knew that he could lay down right now, on their filthy kitchen floor, and fall asleep. Instantly. Was he going to be this tired until the twins went off to college? Would that be the next time he and Julie were alone? He wondered if they could ever recover from the changes the babies had brought to their relationship. When was the last time they talked about something that wasn't connected to the twins? And never mind sex—when was the last time they really kissed?

Three hours later Angie and Audrey were both fed and asleep. Julie helped him pack for what was now six days of travel instead of four, and then called her mother to come and help out. The next morning he was wrapped in the humming cocoon of a Delta widebody, nursing a venti latte and queueing up a *Fresh Air* podcast.

Paul hadn't been to Atlanta since the last Monkeyhole tour—1999? The city was more crowded and humid than he remembered, the traffic even worse. After spending an entire day in meetings in a downtown Marriott, surrounded by other men in other hotels having conferences about God knows what, he begged off the night's strip club run. He used to enjoy it when the band's record label took radio station reps out to watch naked women walk the runway, in a desperate attempt to get the band some airplay, but now that he had two daughters of his own the idea made his skin crawl.

Instead, he drove his rental car to Little Five Points, the hipster part of Atlanta that was home to the club Monkeyhole had played. The hippies clogging the sidewalks were still playing the same three Dylan songs— "Blowin' in the Wind," "Maggie's Farm," and "Tangled Up In Blue"—on the same out-of-tune Fenders. The stores were more geared toward the increased number of Yuppies, though, and the club Monkeyhole had played twice (one great night and one disaster) had been turned into a Vintage Clothing boutique.

The record store was still open, by some miracle. Both times Monkeyhole hit Atlanta, Paul and Spider and Danny had spent hours in Wax'n'Facts, amazed at the luck of having a record store next to the club. The stretch between the end of soundcheck and the start of the show was always the hardest part of the day. All they knew for sure was that something would happen—something amazing (great show, great crowd) or horrific (the reunited Beatles playing across town, no one shows up, band plays like they were in over their heads), or, most likely, something in between. Waiting to see just what the something would be was exciting and nerve-wracking, so browsing cool LPs and CDs had been a great distraction.

He'd dreaded those hours as he lived them, but missed them, now that they were gone.

It was toward closing time on a Tuesday, so he wasn't surprised the store was almost empty. Stepping into a space devoted to the physical form of music—rows of used vinyl, CDs crammed into glass display cases, posters all over the walls—was like stepping through a time portal. The promise of a trip to Pellet Records when the last bell rang had kept him sane in high school. To wander the rows of new and used records, buying something off someone's recommendation, or just on a whim, and then going home to crack the code of the new music: those were actions that made sense to him, in a way that dissecting frogs and solving algebraic equations never had. Now that the world had reduced music to waves, transferred by clicks of the mouse, it was reassuring to once again see and touch so much sound. To walk into a place where The Beatles hung next to Hendrix and Death Cab for Cutie, where slackers with long hair stood passively behind the cash register as *Houses of the Holy* played over the store's loudspeakers, was to come back to a world he'd known growing up. A world he'd never imagined disappearing.

He wandered casually, as if looking for something to jump out at him, but he knew where he wanted to go. After a quick browse of the vinyl, he went over to the display cases of used CDs. He went to the "M" section first, a habit he'd developed on tour, checking to see if the record company had actually gotten their record into the stores. He wasn't surprised to not find what he was looking for, but then he saw the box of "Recent Arrivals" on the counter. There, slid into the middle of the randomly placed CDs, was *Behind Door Number Two*. He took it out and flipped to the back; the three of them were trying to look so tough, but all he saw was three very young kids. And who ever thought those long bangs were a good idea? Paul couldn't decide whether he felt better or worse for having found it. Be careful what you look for, indeed.

He flipped open the slightly cracked jewel case and scanned the list of credits on the back of the front sleeve. There hadn't been as much space to thank everyone as they'd hoped for, since the label didn't want to spring for a big booklet—"not this first time," their manager had explained, promising to fight for a bigger production budget "on the next record." The three of them had agonized over squeezing in all the important names in the small space they'd had, especially their girlfriends: "And to Deb, Linda, and Rachel: thanks for sticking with us! Hold on for the ride!"

Spider had dumped Deb before the record even came out.

He'd lost track of his last copy when they moved, and it had been out of print for years, so he decided to buy it. A few could be found on eBay, and until recently never went for more than a buck or two. The sudden and surprising success of Spider's latest attempt to start his career, this time as Spider Webb, had changed all that—the thing could go for twenty dollars online, and this copy was ten. Was having one of your old bandmates find huge success without you affirmation of your talent or proof of your failure? Did Spider Webb's platinum record prove that Paul had been right to devote so much time working with him? Or was the success evidence that Paul and Danny had just been holding him back? Maybe that was another one of those questions he was happier not knowing the answer to.

As Paul headed to the cashier, Robert Plant's heavily affected voice urged him to "lock the door, kill the light." The girl in front of him was still stuffing her change into her Hello Kitty purse when the cashier, a stoner of indiscriminate age in a faded Who T-shirt, took the CD from Paul. "See, man," Stoner said to Hello Kitty Girl, shaking his head, "we just got this in and it's walking already. I told them to make it fifteen bucks."

Paul felt a quick flash of his old ego and pride, a single bolt of lighting across a desolate cornfield.

"What is it?"

"Monkeyhole. Some band that Spider Webb guy was in." Stoner Who Fan wrote down the name of the CD on the legal pad used to keep inventory. "You know... 'Got a dream made of ice cream, Got an ice cream dream.'"

Hello Kitty made a face. "The shit America buys."

Paul felt another twinge, a hard jolt of pain that pushed aside his pride. Spider's shift to country music was hard to watch, even if it was the move that finally led to the recognition he'd been expecting from birth. The man whose dreadlocks used to rattle when he shook his head now had a crewcut, tailored jeans, and a cowboy hat.

A cowboy hat.

Paul hadn't done more than exchange a few texts with Spider the last six months, as "(A Dream Made of) Ice Cream" exploded, and all of his teasing about the hat been ignored. And why not? Spider was wearing a big fucking cowboy hat, yes, but he was wearing it while he cashed some big fucking checks.

"Monkeyhole's actually nothing like that," he heard himself saying. Why did he care so much about what these kids—young enough to be his own, if he hadn't waited until his late thirties to procreate—thought?

Frog held out his hand for Paul's credit card. "So what're they like?"

Paul shrugged. As soon as you join a band people ask you what it sounds like, and the question never gets easier to answer. "Messier? A harder edge. Not a country band."

Hello Kitty took the CD from the counter and flipped to the back photo. "Three piece? Couldn't be all bad."

"Always liked trios myself," said Paul, watching her stare at the picture, wondering if she would recognize him. When she handed the CD back and pushed the door open without a comment he was disappointed, but not surprised. Too many years had passed, and he had aged more than he wanted to admit. He took the CD and credit card slip from Frog and stepped outside. Should he go back to the hotel, like he'd planned, or find a bar and have a beer? Which would be lonelier? Or should he drive around with the CD, listening to what his life had been like twenty years ago? For a man disappointed in the loss of the unexpected, he didn't feel ready to embrace the unknown.

Out on the sidewalk Hello Kitty Girl was standing under a streetlamp, staring at a pack of cigarettes in her hand. She turned to him when he stepped out of the store and smiled. "Got a light?"

He shook his head. If he'd lived *Mad Men*, instead of just watching it with his wife, he'd light them both a Camel, and then they'd have a witty conversation. The air would fill with puffs of smoke and double entendres. "No, sorry."

"It's OK." She stared at the pack, and then slipped it back into her overstuffed purse. "I'm trying to fucking quit, which is why I never have a lighter." She motioned to the CD in his hand. "So how'd you hear about these guys? They really worth listening to?"

He hesitated, wondering if there was a way to talk about his connection to Monkeyhole without sounding like he was trying to show off. Of course, the only reason to talk about it at all was because he felt like showing off, and why not? He was in town alone, giving presentations about high-tech medical devices to hospital administrators who spent most of their time on their iPhones. It had been a long time since he'd had a chance to talk to a pretty girl about his band. "We thought we were worth listening to," he said, aiming for charming self-deprecation, "even if we couldn't get many people to agree with us."

Her eyes widened. "That's you? No fucking way. Let me see."

Paul handed her the CD, and she examined it under the street lamp. He enjoyed watching surprise roll so openly across her face.

"Holy shit, it is you." She looked up, grinning. "Nice Barbie bangs."

"It was the nineties. Better hair than the eighties, but not by much."

"Well, I wouldn't know about that." Another grin, this one with even more of a sparkle.

"Of course you wouldn't," he said. He quickly did the math: twenty-two or -three, so born in... 1988? Right around the time he was first meeting Spider, she was learning to talk, an idea that made his head hurt.

She pulled a chain of comically large set of keys out of her purse, a hipster Mary Poppins with an impossibly large handbag. "I'm in a band, too."

"Really?" He smiled, thinking of the contest he and Spider and Danny used to play: who would meet more guys also in bands that night. "I love you guys" was often followed by, "Can I give you a tape?" Annoying, sure, but Paul had always been a little more inspired than cynical band banter allowed him to admit. All those people out there, convinced that they'd made a new and worthwhile sound. If even one percent of them were actually good, the world would be a little less shitty. "What do you play?"

"Bass. We're a trio, just like you guys. 3Way."

"That's great. We need more rock trios." An image popped in some distant corner of his memory, a flash of the beautiful brunette who'd played bass with him and Spider when they first started out. They both loved the way she looked with a Fender slung around her neck, the long strap she insisted on using keeping the bass low and her cleavage accentuated. Spider tried to hold off on replacing her with someone who could actually play until he'd slept with her, but he gave up when Danny came along.

In that same flash, Paul realized that Spider must have slept with her, and never told him.

"We don't have anything recorded yet, you know, just a few shit gigs, but we're good. You know, it's... real."

He could see the true believer look in her eyes, the enthusiasm of the young for something so important that everything else became secondary. He couldn't relate anymore, but he knew that he'd been that way, once—young and in love with his band. In love with being part of a band. "Be great to hear you sometime," he said, just as he used to when he met some eager musician in a club. A safe and bland thing to tell someone you'd never see again.

"Really?" Hello Kitty opened her eyes wide. "What are you doing now?"

"Right now?" He tried to read her face. "Not much. I'm just in town for a meeting, leave tomorrow."

"Fuck, that's fate, right? I mean, if I'd come here tomorrow night we wouldn't have met. And if you'd had a lighter I probably would have just lit up and been gone. Poof," she said, waving her hands dramatically across her face. She talked like a young woman who never settled for being told no. "But now," she continued, jangling her well-loaded key chain, "you can come over. Jam a bit."

How did their conversation jump from being asked for a light to being asked to play drums—something he hadn't done in at least two years. Had he ever been like that, able to give serious consideration to any random idea that entered his head? "Play? Now?"

"Yeah, of course. You won't be here tomorrow, right?"

The logic was as simple as the idea was crazy. "But—"

"It's perfect, man, I'm telling you, fate." As she repeated "fate," her fingers grabbed his forearm. "Our drummer's chasing after some girl in Athens, and who knows when he'll be back."

It was impossible to deny that he'd been thinking about playing from the moment he saw the Monkeyhole CD. His new life made it easy to forget that there was ever a Paul who didn't make sales presentations or try to get tiny babies to sleep. It was a big leap, though, to go from remembering his musical past to jamming with strangers. He'd made himself a decent drummer, but his best skill had always been figuring out the needs of individual songs, not grooving along while guitarists noodled. As he pulled out his phone to look at the time he lined up his mature, rational excuses: one more meeting tomorrow morning, followed by a flight to Raleigh for the next scene in Life of a Salesman; tired; need to check in with his wife.

Tired.

But as he listened to all those reasons bounce around his head, they all sounded like Old Man Excuses. Watching her face watch him, and feeling his fingers twitch to that distant soundtrack always playing in his head, he decided he did not want to be that old man. Not yet. And he did not want to say goodbye to the unexpected.

Not yet.

"OK, sure. What the hell."

Twice on the drive he was certain that he'd lost her; her ancient Honda took sharp turns with confidence, while his rented Dodge Neon struggled to maintain a speed over forty. Each time they got separated he thought, Good, now that's over, even as he strained to see any sign of her. The idea that he might not be able to play well was more depressing than the idea that he passed up a chance to jam with a pretty young girl to watch HBO.

He kept catching up to Hello Kitty Girl, though, and his relief convinced him that the only outcome worse than playing badly was not playing at all. Even if there was room to set his kit up in their much more crowded house, he couldn't imagine a time in the next two (or three or four) years when one of the twins wouldn't either be asleep or in the process of trying to sleep.

After a few final turns the Honda pulled up in front of a row of warehouses and Hello Kitty got out of her car. "Home sweet home on the range," she said. She slammed her door shut, flashed a smile, and bounded up the half dozen wide metal steps.

He hurried to keep up, trying to decide if she was just naturally much faster than the people he normally hung out with, or if he had just gotten that much slower. He caught the door just before it closed, and stumbled into a large, open space. White pipes ran along the top of the high ceiling, lit up by pale neon lights. On the right and left side of the room were folding walls of various colors, leaning inward; in the center, everything needed for a band to make noise: a tangled mess of cables and mic stands ringed by a guitar amp, bass rig, and nice-looking Gretsch drum set.

Hello Kitty Girl had disappeared, probably behind the hanging sheets serving as a kind of doorway at the back of the room. The warehouse smelled of stale beer, marijuana, and burnt rice—was there a kitchen somewhere? The space looked big enough for all three members to live in, and he wondered if it had been a mistake for Spider to live apart from Paul and Danny. Maybe it would have been harder for him to break up the band if they'd had some years together in the same house, if they'd more fully formed themselves into the makeshift family they always said they were.

"Who the fuck are you?"

He was surprised to hear a male voice coming from behind him. When he turned around Paul came face-to-face with a pale, skinny kid who looked to be in his early twenties, holding a bowl of cereal and wearing white boxers decorated with hearts. "Well?" Cereal Dude said. "Who the fuck are you?"

Paul wanted to say that everything was cool, he'd been invited, but he still didn't know Hello Kitty Girl's real name. "I'm with—"

"He's with me, Tommy."

Paul turned around and saw Hello Kitty emerge from behind the curtain. She'd changed into a purple skirt and a Flaming Lips T-shirt, an outfit made her look even younger. "There you are," he said. "So we gonna play?"

"Play? What the fuck is he talking about, Barnett?"

Paul turned to stare at Hello Kitty Girl, trying to attach "Barnett" to her face. Her last name? Some odd nickname?

"He's a real drummer," she said. "Made records."

"You can't piss in Atlanta without hitting a drummer. What's he doing here?"

"He's here to play."

Paul watched Tommy stare at Barnett for a long, silent moment. He couldn't tell if the tension between the two of them was because they'd slept together, or because one of them wanted to and the other didn't. As much as it looked like he wanted to say something, Tommy bit down on his spoon and disappeared behind one of the folding walls without saying a word.

"It's cool," Barnett said, walking over to Paul. "Surprises throw Tommy for a loop, but he'll be OK once we start playing."

"Good, good," Paul said, even if it didn't sound like she believed what she was saying. Now that he'd seen the nice Gretsch kit, he was even more anxious to play.

"Here," she said, handing him one of the two beers she was holding.

He took the Heineken gratefully. "Thanks," he said. He followed her to the aging leather couch randomly placed in the wide space between the front door and the musical gear.

"'Got a dream made of ice cream,'" she sang quietly as she sat down, her voice softer and sweeter than he'd imagined it could sound.

"God, don't remind me."

She smiled. "He was really in your band?"

"He was really in my band."

"Fuck. Does it drive you crazy, to see him doing so well? I think I'd hate it, if Tommy or Alan made it huge and I..."

Her voice trailed off—even this kid understood his story was sad. He stared at the beer bottle in his hands to avoid her look of pity. Spider's song was everywhere, and of course it drove him crazy. Not just because it was country, or because Spider sang it so convincingly, but because it was so fucking good. Even the easy-to-mock lyrics had more depth than you might expect. He could imagine Spider being proud, and rightfully so, of the "Might freeze my brain if I move too fast" line.

So why the fuck didn't get he get to play drums on it? The guy on the record was probably some overpaid Nashville hack, recording to a click in his basement and not doing anything Paul couldn't have done just as well. All Paul got, as far as he could tell, was a casual mention in a verse: "Left some friends behind/to get where I'm going." He wondered if he could get a royalty check for that, for being one of the people abandoned at the altar of Spider's success.

He looked back up at her. Yes, yes, it drives me crazy, he wanted to scream, but he was determined not to be Old Sad Loser Guy. "So what are we going to play?"

"Well, I really wanna work on this song I wrote. Usually Tommy does the writing, and me and Alan just throw in some ideas, but this one's all mine."

Paul was surprised. He'd expected they would just play bad cover songs. "That's great. I always wished I'd learned to play another instrument, so I could write songs."

"I've tried before, but this is the first time I, like, actually finished something." She drained the rest of her Heineken.

"So why haven't you guys worked it up yet?

"There's always been some fucking excuse." She lowered her voice. "First it was Tommy stalling, saying we had other stuff to do, and then Alan left to chase this girl he's never gonna catch, and Tommy just lost his shit."

"So why not get another drummer? I mean, Tommy's right, we're all over the place."

"It's complicated."

He felt a protective urge kick in: Monkeyhole had never really had any older bands to ask for advice, and he could look back and see a million times when it would have been helpful if they had. "So are you and Tommy an item, or what? None of my business, but..."

She blushed. "Not anymore. I mean, for a little while, at first. That's how Tommy hooked me up with the band, when they needed a bass player."

Paul again thought of that brunette bass player he and Spider had fought over. Shannon, that was her name.

"But then things got weird between me and Tommy, and then he and Alan started getting intense, but then Alan fell for this girl, so everything got fucked up between him and Tommy. And I'm just pissed because all this bullshit keeps us from playing."

She'd listed the changing romantic permutations in a steady monotone, her tone reminiscent of the sales rep from Dynamic discussing new catheters. The world was more advanced and more complicated than it had been twenty years ago; his own mother watched *Ellen* every afternoon now, perhaps forgetting how she'd insisted Paul switch art classes when rumors about Ms. Hirsch began to spread. Now Barnett could casually imply that the two guys hooked up, and that it was only a problem because it distracted them from the music. Was it easier or harder, to live with less black and white and more gray?

"It's driving me crazy that Alan's not around. I want to hear if the sound in my head, you know, is something that a band can really make. And now I wonder if there'll ever be a band to try it."

"Sure there will be. The hardest part is writing the songs... If you're doing that, you can always find someone to play them."

She smiled, but he could tell she didn't believe him. Your first band was like your first girlfriend or boyfriend: you can't imagine it not lasting forever, until it doesn't.

And then Tommy walked out from behind the same curtain Barnett had emerged from, dressed in jeans, T-shirt and faded brown sports jacket, keys in hand. Barnett pushed herself out of the couch and cut off his path to the front door. "Where you going? We're gonna play."

"I never said I was gonna play."

"But we have a drummer now. We can work on—"

"Alan's our drummer. We'll play when he gets back."

Barnett looked back to Paul, and then started dragging Tommy in the direction he'd come from. When they disappeared he could hear voices trying, but failing, to not talk too loudly. He decided to send Julie a quick message while waiting: *Stuck in one more mtg msg when back at hotel.* It wasn't a complete lie, though he certainly picked words that sounded like he was not having anything close to fun. He found himself doing that a lot when he traveled, worrying she would get jealous if it sounded like he was having a good time, while she was stuck with the kids. He understood why she'd react that way, but at the same time, it didn't feel exactly fair: was he supposed to turn down any chance for a good time?

Her answer, he knew, would be yes.

And he certainly didn't want to tell her he was waiting for a chance to play the drums again. By the time he started seeing Julie the role of music was fading from his life, and when the kids came along he stopped playing altogether. He didn't imagine she'd want to see that change anytime soon, either. What could playing mean for him, at this stage in his life? Not a career, or anything with a future—all she would see is one more reason for him to leave her alone with the twins.

The voices on the other side of the wall slowly grew louder, but he still couldn't make out what either one of them was saying. He stared at the Gretsch kit while he waited, relieved to see a bag of sticks underneath the floor tom, and a drum key on the snare. He used to have a drum key on his key chain—it was as important to be able to tune his drums as it was to unlock his house or start his car. When had he taken it off? Not when Monkeyhole broke up, because he'd assumed that he would find another band. He'd landed a few gigs pretty quickly, but nothing lasted. Or was even that much fun. And then he was over thirty and it seemed like he should get married, which meant it was time to find Something Else to do.

After ten minutes he decided to find out what was going on. It was getting late; if he was going to play he would hang out, but if everything was falling apart he'd go back to his hotel room. Crank up the AC, watch some bad TV. Sleep an entire night without hearing any children cry.

He pushed his way through the sheets. Tommy and Barnett were standing on the other side of one of the folding walls, in what looked like a communal bedroom: three narrow beds without headboards, close together, shaped into a kind of drunken triangle. Plates of various shapes and sizes, covered in hardened clumps of food, were scattered on the floor. It suddenly felt more like he'd stumbled into a hang-out for a small cult than a band house. Maybe the line between the two was thinner than he'd previously considered.

"Now you did it," Tommy said. "You made Dad come in."

Paul smiled, trying to play along. "You kids," he said. "With all the racket."

"I'm sorry, man." Barnett shook her head. "I thought this would all work out, that Tommy would miss playing as much as I do. Turns out he just misses Alan."

Tommy looked like he wanted to say something but stopped himself, just the way he had in the other room. If he made a habit of doing that, it probably drove the other two crazy.

"I wanna play, too," Paul said. He was trying to strike a balance between laid-back and excited, avoiding any mention of how long it had been since he played, or how much he needed to play, now that the chance was close. "Let's go."

"I'm going, alright." Tommy pushed his way past Paul, Barnett trailing behind. Alone in the crowded and filthy bedroom, Paul tried to remember how old he'd been, when he finally started washing dishes before the leftover bits turned into hard clumps.

The front door slammed shut, making a low rumble that bounced off the walls. Paul headed back into the main room, and found Barnett slumped on one end of the couch, her left arm draped over her eyes. When he slid his phone out of his pocket again, he was relieved there was no annoyed response from Julie, and surprised to see that he'd been there for less than an hour. Why did it feel like so much longer? Spider often talked about the way time, especially in music, could get caught in a vortex generated by nerves or drugs or crowds. A vortex that could either slow things down and stretch time out, or speed everything up and shorten time. When he sat down at the other end of the couch, Barnett opened her eyes, watching him with a softer look than he expected. "I don't even know your name."

"Paul," he said.

"Paul." She nodded, as if passing verdict. "I can see it." She patted the empty space on the couch next to her. "But if we're going to make out, you're going to have to move down here."

As he replayed the suggestion in his brain, making sure he heard her right, the echo of the words seemed to transform the air of the room. He imagined the temporary folding wall to his right being rolled away, revealing a studio audience of friends and family members. He realized in an instant that his confusion—make out? What are you talking about?—would ring false to everyone and the "LAUGHTER" sign would light up. He didn't remember any clues coming from Barnett, but that line of self-defense would be rejected by most courts in the universe. Why else would you follow this cute young lady? The Inquisitor would be harsh, face twisted like the trial judge in the movie version of *The Wall*. You really expect us to believe you just came to "play drums"?

Yes, he thought, turning to his left to peek at the drum set, suddenly needing to make sure it was really there. Yes, he just came to play.

Even if the studio audience wouldn't believe him, the look on his face made it clear to Barnett that he had not expected her move. "Fuck, oh fuck," she said, burying her face in her hands. "You don't even want to, do you?"

"No. I mean, of course I want to," he added quickly, trying to figure out which combination of words would be the least painful for her. "But I also want to be twenty years younger and thirty pounds lighter. And I'm not."

"Jesus, I'm pathetic." She slowly dropped her hands from her face. "I'm sorry. This is all more fucked up than I want it to be."

"It's cool, no worries," he said casually, wondering if he should move closer to offer comfort, or stand up to make it clear nothing was going to happen. Or should he move down to make out? Now that he knew it was on the table, it didn't seem like the worst idea in the world. He needed to say or do something, he knew that much, but talking to girls had never been his strong suit. Spider had his enigmatic genius schtick, and Danny had pretty hair he could flip innocently, but Paul had never been comfortable with women of any age.

He still barely knew what to say to Julie, after ten years of marriage.

Barnett was rubbing her head frantically, as if trying to dig a hole so she could pluck a piece of her brain out. He had a flash of the future, one of his own daughters sitting on some shitty couch, waiting for someone to say or do the right thing. He wanted to believe that if he could find a way to pull Barnett out of the kind of downward spiral you fall into all too easily in your early twenties, then someday someone would do the same for his own Angie or Audrey.

"Well," he said. "I came here to play drums, right? So let's play."

"Oh." Her hand slid off her head and she turned to look at the gear in front of her. "I don't know. I mean. No fucking guitar, without Tommy."

"Don't you play? I mean, how'd you write the song?"

"I wrote it on guitar. I can only fake the basic chords."

"That's all most guitarists can do. Let's go all White Stripes, drums and guitar."

"Black Keys." She almost smiled, as she said it.

"Now you're talking. Bass players are too fucking moody, anyway."

At that she did manage a complete smile, and for just a moment her face formed a look halfway between the tough girl she'd been outside the record store and the nervous and embarrassed girl sitting on the couch. It suited her beautifully, allowed her eyes to soften even as they narrowed to gauge the world before them.

They quietly moved toward the instruments. Barnett turned on the PA, then picked up a nice-looking Strat from its stand and began tentatively to tune it, while Paul finally got to sit down behind the Gretsch. He adjusted the height of the seat and snare, made sure the kick pedal wasn't too tight or loose, and moved the hi-hat to just the right distance: as long as he had those in place he could play any set. He found a matched pair of 5A sticks in the stickbag and nervously whacked his way around the kit, simple single stroke hits to get used to the spacing of the drums. He didn't want to play too much too quickly, surprised at how anxious he was to impress Barnett. That feeling of contact, as stick hit drum, that feeling of driving sound out into the world, was even more satisfying than he'd remembered. The force stung his wrists, but the feeling was not unpleasant. It felt like a bracing jump into a pool on a summer afternoon.

He turned to his right. Barnett looked great with a guitar slung over her shoulder, of course—Paul hadn't seen a woman yet who didn't look good wearing a guitar.

Barnett moved over to the microphone and tapped it, to make sure it was on. "Now what?" she said, left hand forming a chord, right hand holding a pick just out of range of contact with the strings.

"Now you show me this song," he said. "Run through the chords a few times, and then I'll work my way in."

"OK." She took a deep breath. "OK."

Even nervous, she managed to strum in time and generate a nice tone. Paul tapped a stick against his leg to feel the tempo, relieved as he watched her; a lot of people in the world said they could play an instrument, but maybe ten percent could actually do so in a way that did not cause him existential pain. After a few bars her hands seemed more in control, and the sound became fuller during the second series of chords. There was a vague Americana feel, like she'd been listening to a lot of Wilco, and there were much worse places for a new songwriter to start.

She ran through both chord sequences a second time, and he motioned with his hand for her to keep going when she looked over. As she circled back to the beginning again he came in with a downbeat louder and sloppier than he planned, but at least it was more or less in sync with Barnett. He kept the groove simple and stayed away from fills altogether, waiting until he found firmer ground. His arms were stiff and sore, surprised to find themselves moving in ways he had not asked them to in a long time, but they also began to loosen more quickly than he'd expected. He imagined the song as the Band would have worked it up, a loose Levon Helm groove rolling downhill. When he remembered to move his upper body as he played, he felt more comfortable and felt more confident about the groove, and the two of them began to sound like they were playing the same song.

By the time they reached the beginning again the song had a nice, middle-of-the-road tempo; fast enough to get there but slow enough to enjoy the ride, as Spider used to say. He closed his eyes, to try to see the music a little more clearly, and that brought to mind another of Spider's sayings: hearing a song for the first time was a lot like watching a woman undress. You could make guesses about what was going to come next, but you could never really be sure until everything was out in the open. Barnett was strumming with more clarity and command, and Paul could feel his arms moving more accurately. She made eye contact with him again and nodded, slowly moving toward the mic. Closing her eyes she began to sing, the words so mumbled and soft that it was hard to make out individual syllables. The melody caught him by surprise. It was more discordant than he expected, with an offbeat rhythm that fought the groove they had established. That tension worked, though, it made the guitar chords sound sweeter.

This time when they hit the chorus they attacked it, Barnett's wrist pushing the pick against the strings more aggressively. Paul opened up the hi-hat slightly and threw a few cymbal hits where he thought she was trying to accent, and his left hand started catching the edge of the snare for a nice crack. The song had morphed into more of a Stones feel, but there were worse places to go when you were trying to find a groove than the world of Charlie Watts. The Gretsch kit was old and warm, one of those kits that liked being whacked, and the warehouse created a deep and rewarding echo. Their noise grew more confident, even as it became sloppier, and Paul felt as though they had traveled an impressive distance together. They had learned the chords, and found the rhythm, and now they could search for the song itself. Buried under the noise was a beautiful sound, he was sure of it. That it was a sound he would probably never have a chance to hear again made him even more determined to enjoy it for as long as it lasted.

He wondered if she would still want to kiss him when the song ended.

Doin' Fine

New York City, 2012

"A baby. Let's have a baby."

"I thought that's what you said." Spider stares at Allison—naked, straddling his waist, long blonde hair drifting over her eyes as she leans down toward him—and has to concede that her beauty would offset the flawed genes he'd pass on to any child. Too bad everything else about the idea is ridiculous. "This... doesn't seem like the best time." He speaks softly, trying not to kill the mood for Pre-Tour Sex.

"There's never a 'best' time," she says. "We just have to pick a time and make it right. This time, right now?" She runs her finger down his chest slowly. "This could be perfect."

For a moment he wonders if he's just afraid. What if some great new opportunity is just on the other side of that fear? As she hovers above him, resting her weight on his hips, arms held out to her sides as if floating, he tries to imagine all the positive changes that could come from having a kid around. He has a whole list of things not to do all ready to go, developed while watching his own father screw up for years. And what a gift it would be, to have a chance to introduce music to a child—how amazing, to get to watch someone listen to the Beatles or Joni Mitchell or Miles Davis for the first time. Not to mention the benefits to his own work. The list of great songs written by musicians after they had kids was endless. Bowie's "Kooks," Lennon's "Beautiful Boy," and, Jesus God, Wonder's "Isn't She Lovely?" What if his masterpiece is hiding just on the other side of his pathetic fear?

Allison's broad smile tightens her neck muscles, her shoulders pushing down and back. Time stretches out as her hands rub his chest, pinkies drifting ever so lightly across his nipples—time becomes taffy, pulled see-through thin. It's like one of those great moments on stage, when the music and the crowd work together to create a new sound, a sound all the more powerful because it can never be recreated exactly the same way.

And then time snaps back into place, as it always does. He knows that a baby, if one were ever to arrive, is not likely to bring the two of them closer. At least, not for any extended period of time. He's leaving in less than twenty-four hours for rehearsals, preparing for a tour that could stretch on for months—hopefully longer, maybe even a full year—and Allison's been growing more and more resentful as departure day gets closer. He has this sense that she's waiting for him to decide she's more important than the music, and can feel her getting angrier each day that doesn't happen. Won't that anger grow, each time he misses a doctor's appointment or a school recital or a fucking birthday party? Before he knows what happened he'll be writing songs about divorce. Does he really want to live through the shit necessary to write "Brilliant Disguise" or "Here, My Dear"?

No.

He tries to joke his way out of the discussion, about it being bad luck to get someone pregnant right before you go on tour, but her face shifts so drastically and so quickly that he knows a fight has begun. She slides off his hips and onto the bed, releasing a series of well-worded arguments that she's probably been preparing for weeks, if not months. In a flash he sees the way the rest of the night will play out. There will be no sex, of course, just too much talking. They will be overly careful with their words at first, trying to find a way out of this dead end without breaking up. Then each will realize the other won't change their mind, and the tone will become harsher. The words will start to hurt as they come out, like voices run through a bad PA. That part of their night, the full-blown argument, will go on longer than it should, damaging what should be fond memories of the longest romantic relationship Spider has ever had. More than two years, he marvels, watching her wrap the sheet around her as she talks about her biological clock—about how everyone who's human wants to have kids, so it must be that he just doesn't want them with her. He hadn't seen the ending coming, but now that it's here he wishes they could walk away without unleashing all their pent-up grievances. Instead, they will have to play it out, the same way he has to finish sets even when they're not going especially well.

When they finally get out of bed and drift into the kitchen, tensely rummaging for leftovers, Allison wonders why he can't just fly home after gigs, the way she's heard other people do, so they can wake up with their families. That's when his frustration breaks out. "I'm not fucking Paul McCartney," he says, "and will never have my own fucking jet."

And that's when she packs up an overnight bag and heads to a friend's house.

It's after four by the time he falls asleep, so when his alarm goes off at nine Spider stares at it in anger and disbelief. He hits snooze twice before he remembers why he set it so early: Michael, his manager, begged him to make time for one more interview before leaving for rehearsals. "It's not just any website, Spider. *The Weight of Sound* is cutting-edge and normally only gives interview space to big indie acts. More than 300,000 visitors a day, man."

"Indie? I thought the whole point was to move me away from indie..."

"They cover it all, now, and the guy who started it loves Monkeyhole. He wants to talk about your whole career and run the piece the day before we drop, with what I'm assured will be a positive review for the new CD."

And that was the angle that sold Spider. Since no one paid any attention to anything he did before *Ice Cream Dreams*, this new one would have to battle the "One-Hit Wonder" tag. Talking about his previous bands gave him the sheen of a Career Artist finally experiencing some overdue success.

So he gets up and dresses, wondering if he should call Allison, or wait for her to call him. Seeing their bedroom in daylight makes last night's fight more real, though. He remembers how angry she was. She won't be calling. He probably won't even see her before his flight to Logan. Maybe that's for the best—there's nothing more depressing than the conversations you have right after a break-up. It's like making small talk at a fucking wake. Yeah, he had a good life, everyone says, eating cake and pretending death doesn't suck.

Shower first, he decides, even though his insides ache for coffee. The last thing he needs is to look as old as he feels.

He's glad he showered when the reporter who shows up is young and Jimmy Olsen-eager. Spider's first instinct is to shut the door and go back to bed, but instead he summons the energy to hold his hand out for the kid's extended shake. Showtime. "Hey, man. Thanks for coming."

"Andy Achenbach," the kid says, "and man oh man, it is a pleasure to meet you."

Spider steps aside to let him in. "I just made some coffee. You want some?"

"That'd be great, thanks." Andy starts to drop his messenger bag on the narrow white couch Allison picked out from Lazzoni, but hesitates.

"It's too fucking white, isn't it?" Spider had warned her people would be afraid to touch the thing.

"It looks great. I just don't want to, like—"

"No, go ahead, go ahead. I should just drop a piece of pizza on it and get it over with." Spider steps over to the kitchen's galley counter. At almost 800 square feet, the apartment is large by Chelsea standards, and feels even larger, thanks to Allison's insistence on knocking down the wall between the living room and the tiny kitchen. "Cream? Sugar?"

"Just black, thanks."

As Spider pours the coffee, he watches Andy cautiously sit down on the couch and take out a pad, a tape recorder, and three pens—a back-up for his back-up. "So I looked at your website," he says, carrying over their mugs. "I dug it, man."

"You did? Thanks."

Spider sits down in the dark red armchair next to the couch. Allison wanted something to contrast with the white couch and the white walls, but this morning the contrast is so sharp he feels trapped in an arty photo shoot. "Yeah. The biggest problem I have with anyone with a computer being able to start their own websites, where they can write whatever the hell they want, is that anyone can do it. Even people who can't write." He takes a sip of coffee, enjoying the aggressive brew. One thing that will get better with Allison gone—he can put the accelerator on the coffee. "But the writing on your site is solid."

"That's great to hear, because I'm with you. Don't get me wrong: democratization of the press made my life possible, you know? But when I see people putting out stuff with typos and bad grammar and stock photos, it bums me out."

"Democratization" and "bums me out." Spider wonders how long this kid's been out of college. A week? "Did you really start it when you were an undergrad?" Michael's first lesson of interviews: have information about the interviewer you can toss at them.

"Yeah. Nothing at college was really working for me, you know? And I'd always spent a lot of time online, talking about music with people." Andy shrugs. "I had a good friend tell me I should stop complaining about everyone else's websites and just put up my own. So I did. And you know," he continues, turning the small digital recorder on, "all this gets me to my first question, actually. You've been putting records out for almost twenty years now—"

Spider grins, both at the smooth segue and the way "twenty years" sounds like such a big chunk of time. Because it is. "Jesus. You're right."

"Do you think it's easier or harder for people to find good music, with so much of it getting put out there, every day? Used to be most musicians focused on getting a big label deal, but I think there's a new generation out there anxious to work outside the machine. So they just throw something on the web, and there's, like, only so much bandwidth in the world."

"I think you're right about the move away from labels, for sure. A guy sitting alone in his room with a laptop can record a song and have it online in a couple of hours. And that makes spending a few years, waiting for a big label to come and help you out, seem like a waste of time."

"Exactly. Which means a lot more music floats into the world. But does that just make it harder for the good stuff to get noticed?"

"It can." Spider sips his coffee and downshifts into his more deliberate talking pace. He's learned he gets in trouble when he talks too fast and says too much. The trick to a successful interview is to control what you reveal. Say just enough. "I mean, sometimes I poke around and waste time on some crappy song that takes three minutes of my life, and I get angry. But sometimes I stumble on something beautiful, or weird, or both, something that would never have been put out by a major label, or gotten on radio, and that one surprise can make my day. Without all this technology, there's a lot of great shit I never would have heard, which means we can't blame the technology, right?"

Andy nods. He picks up the notepad and one of his pens, and leans back into the couch. "I sure can't. High school would have been, like, fatal, without it."

Spider imagines Andy as one of those quiet kids high schools eat alive. The way he would have been, if he'd never gotten his hands on a guitar. Even with a guitar, he wouldn't have survived if he hadn't taken the GED the moment he turned eighteen. "I just wish all this crap had been around when I started out. Especially the recording technology—now you can make records in your basement that sound better than the ones we used to pay shitty studios for."

"Does it make you angry, thinking about how things could have worked out differently for you?"

"No, man. I don't have time for anger these days. Frustrated sometimes, yes." His phone buzzes: Allison, anxious to get the last word in. *And dont worry I never thought u were fucking McCartny.* The misspelling would strike him as endearing, if he weren't so tired. He looks up and sees Andy waiting for him to expand on his answer. "Especially," he continues, "thinking about people I played with who didn't make it, but should have."

"But no anger?"

"No, no." Spider finishes the last of his coffee in a single swallow. The rush of hot caffeine is the only real drug he has left, but when it's good, it's enough. "I mean, you're, what, twenty-two? Twenty-three?"

Andy laughs. "Twenty-six."

"OK. Still young. But I hope you're smarter than I was at your age, and have already figured it out: if you're going to actually succeed at whatever you're doing, right, you have to cut out all the distractions. The weed, the coke. The anger."

"Do you think giving up all the distractions is what led to your success with *Ice Cream*?"

Spider gets up to pour the rest of the French Press into his cup. A good host would offer it to his guest, but it's more important for him to be a good interview. "Maybe. I mean, I've been doing this twenty years, like you said, and I've learned that a percentage of your success, or lack of it, is... luck? Timing? Some combination of those two?"

"You think it's a big percentage?"

"No, maybe—two percent? But it's crucial." He sits back down. "It's like that moment in a bad suspense movie, when the hero is trying to download a key file on a flash drive, and everything crashes when it gets to ninety-eight percent. Our hero gets close, but not all the way—so he gets nothing." The kid watches him closely when he talks, writing the whole time. "That's what it felt like kept happening. And then I got lucky enough to have good timing, to get to 100 percent before the bad guys came in and shot me."

"Did the success catch you by surprise?"

"Surprise?" Spider smiles. "I should be humble, but no. I wouldn't have kept pushing the rock up the hill if I didn't think it would pay off someday."

"Did you expect moving to a more country sound would work so well?"

Spider takes a slow sip of coffee. He needs to pay particular attention to the way these words will look online—his switch from Indie Rock to Country can't be denied, even if you call it "Americana" instead. "(A Dream Made of) Ice Cream" featured pedal steel, a mournful tone, and an all-American metaphor, served up at a mid-tempo pace; the whole product was consciously country, as was the name change to "Spider Webb." Country stations were the ones that broke the song, the ones that made Top 40 eventually possible for Spider in a way the rock world never had. He's always been careful to make sure the switch doesn't come across as overly strategic, though, and that's even more important with the follow-up record. The biggest challenge they'll have is fighting the idea that Spider Webb is a carpetbagger, not "real country."

Of course, no one is "real country" anymore. Country Music is the new home for American Pop, which had drifted away—or been pushed away—from Rock and R&B, so the singers now wore cowboy hats and spoke with slight drawls.

But you couldn't say that out loud.

"It wasn't so much a conscious move, as much as... going where the songs led me."

"So the songs for *Ice Cream* felt different to you?"

"From the moment I wrote the first one."

"And that was '(A Dream Made of) Ice Cream'?"

Spider nods. As many times as he's told the story of writing his first million-selling song he's vowed never to sound annoyed or bored to tell it again. He's made the same vow about playing it in concert. He's fucked up a lot of things in his life, and the last thing he wants to do is fuck up his first hit; he hopes to be using it to close packed concerts for the next twenty years. The boy who found the chicken that laid the golden eggs would have been fine, if he hadn't cut the bird open to see how it worked.

At the time, he certainly hadn't imagined himself sitting down to write a hit. After being stuck in Barcelona for months, not writing anything, he'd accepted the fact he'd never write a song again. He told himself it was a relief to no longer struggle to pull the music out of his head and out into the real world. He was happy enough to become the American Jukebox, playing cheesy covers upon request at parties and bars, bartering his soul for whatever drinks and drugs he could get.

The days slid by, Spider spending most of his time trying to get as stoned and drunk as possible, while fine-tuning a few basic Spanish pick-up lines. He slept on various couches across Barcelona, initially working hard not to overstay his welcome in any one place. As the weeks stretched on, though, his attempts at finding a new tour to hook up with as an extra guitarist led nowhere—word of his time with Jack & Jill, and the way he'd been fired, must have spread. Even Michael, the one person in the industry who had remained loyal, stopped answering his e-mails. Soon he was worrying less about overstaying his welcome and more about eking out an extra night whenever he could.

Four months after Jack & Jill fired him, Spider found himself back at the first couch he'd stayed on. Luis, Matilde, and Pablo were three twentysomethings who'd taken pity on him when he wandered into Parc Guell, homeless and broke. They'd invited Spider to their cramped apartment, and everyone spent several weeks having stoned and drunken sing-a-longs. When he returned to that first apartment, nine couches later, everything felt different. The place was cleaner, Luis was gone, and Pablo and Matilde were in a committed and happy relationship. He rolled a welcome back joint the first night he was there, sharing the last of his own stash as an act of kindness (and hoping to benefit later from the large quantity of great weed Pablo always kept on hand). He was surprised when Pablo took only a perfunctory hit. Matilde passed completely, instead offering Spider a look muy lastima.

Pity. He was getting pity from a young insurance secretary living with a slacker boyfriend who still couldn't play barre chords.

Matilde and Pablo explained, as they headed to sleep at ten fucking thirty on the first night he returned, that Pablo had to get up early, since he now had an apprenticeship at one of Barcelona's most cutting-edge architectural firms. Burning the roach by himself, Spider could hear the two of them speaking quietly in Spanish, and he didn't need to translate to guess what the discussion was about. In the few months between his first visit and this visit he had morphed from American Rock Star to Loser on Their Couch, and they were ready for him to go.

The next morning he woke up at noon. The apartment was empty, Pablo and Matilde all grown up and off to work. He drank the dregs from the French Press, borrowed Pablo's guitar, and headed to the tiny balcony off the living room. He planned to work up enough cover songs to book some gigs in some of the local bars and cafes. Maybe if he started sliding Pablo a little dinero he could stay with them until he figured out whatever the hell was supposed to happen next.

And before he knew it he was playing a new chord progression. Later he would say that the song was written in ten minutes, start to finish; it took closer to an hour, but it was still one of his most quickly written songs. He played it a few times, unsure if it was brilliant or a comic mistake. It had been too long since he'd pulled something new off the loops of music playing in his head; his internal editor was still sitting in a bar in a galaxy far, far away. He took a break, struggling to find a buzz in the previous night's roach. Watching the old people on the street below—men in faded white T-shirts who spent their days sitting on rickety folding chairs, talking loudly, and drinking tiny cups of espresso—he wondered if should he should accept his fate and join them. Was it time to start spending the rest of his life talking about the things he almost did when he was young?

When he played the song again he slowed it down, pleased with the way the words had more room to slide around at this new tempo. For the first time he decided it could actually be good. When he played it for Matilde and Pablo he knew their praise was amplified by their eagerness to have him out of their lives, but it still felt good. That night Pablo showed him how to work up a demo in GarageBand, and before Matilde was done cooking dinner, the music was recorded. He sang the vocals the next day after they went to work, and e-mailed a copy to Michael. Within twenty-four hours Michael had written back, asking to hear more new songs. By the end of the week they'd talked on Pablo's cellphone, Spider having long ago lost the ability to afford his own. Then Michael bought Spider a ticket back to the States.

"So all it took to have a hit was being homeless in Barcelona?"

Spider shrugs. "Maybe? But I don't think it's an exaggeration to say that song saved my life. Not just my musical life, either. Without it I may not have made it back to the States, and I certainly wouldn't have gone into rehab."

If he hadn't come back to the U.S., he would have worn out his welcome at Matilde's and Pablo's, and officially been out of options, couch-wise. He closes his eyes and makes a mental note: "No More Couches To Crash," future song title. He looks to his left, at the wonderfully open space

Allison could somehow imagine creating the moment they walked into the cramped apartment. "This one," she'd said with a forceful authority. "This is our new home." Without that song, written on that balcony in Barcelona, he wouldn't have made it here.

"I gotta admit," Spider continues, trying to pull himself out of one of those memory death spirals that never leads anywhere good, "I was a little surprised when I found a review of *Ice Cream Dreams* in your archive. Your site mainly takes on rock, right?"

"Yes and no. I mean, that's how it started, but I've been trying to make us a bigger kind of filter. A place people to go to find worthy music, no matter what kind it might be."

Spider smiles. "What good record stores used to do."

"Exactly. It'd be great if everyone had a place like Other Music in their neighborhoods, but they don't." Andy leans forward to pick up his coffee mug, pen still in hand. "The site was just beginning to really take off when we got an advance copy of *Ice Cream*. We were getting so many CDs we had interns putting them into Yes, No, and Maybe piles. Sometimes I'd poke through the rejects myself, you know, in case there was something I wanted to check out, even if it didn't work for the site." He pauses dramatically for a sip of coffee. "And there it was: Spider Webb."

"So I was a No?"

"Yeah, sorry, man." Andy puts his mug down. "But, come on. The cover, the name—doesn't scream Indie Rock, right?"

Spider shudders remembering those first few weeks of the *Ice Cream* promo tour—solo acoustic shows with a new cowboy hat, one roadie, and twenty or thirty people in the clubs. He was being put in a lot of No piles. He'd only kept from losing all hope because he knew it was his last chance. It couldn't fail, because the question of what he'd do next was too impossible to even consider.

And Allison: his first post-rehab relationship, helping him through what could have been his last record launch.

"So why did you take it out of the No pile? The cool cowboy hat I was wearing?"

"To be honest, the hat made me want to put it back down. But come on, how many guys named Spider could there be? I needed to see if this was the same Spider that was in Monkeyhole."

Spider grins. "Michael told me you were a fan of that record, man. Good to hear."

"Well, I mean. Jesus. If I wanted to embarrass us both I'd start telling you how much that record meant to me, in high school."

"Hadn't it disappeared by then?"

"Not disappeared. Just kind of slid underground. I heard about it online, talking to other tortured music geeks."

Hearing that people talked about that record, keeping it alive long after the world tried bury it, is like hearing life had been found on Mars.

"I even followed the Stackd Souls stuff, man. Saw you at Brownie's."

This is even more surprising. Monkeyhole comes up in most interviews longer than fifteen minutes, but very few people mention Stackd Souls. And no one ever said they'd actually heard anything. "Brownie's? No shit. I remember that show, too. That was one of our better nights."

"I thought you'd make it for sure that time. And then you kind of disappeared."

"Yeah." Spider drains his coffee and places the mug down. Allison bought fancy coasters, but they're buried in a drawer on the other side of the coffee table, and she's not here to complain. "That band made me appreciate just how easy and rewarding it was to work with Paul and Danny, because Souls was a fucking train wreck. Our own worst enemies."

"That's too bad. Man, that was such a good show. My first time in a club, and just, that wall of sound..." Andy shakes his head. "Anyway, I had to know if Spider Webb was you. I couldn't tell from the picture, or the credits, so I grabbed the CD and listened on the way home."

"When did you realize it was the same guy?"

"First moment of the record. I mean, it opens with your voice, and I recognized it immediately. Older-sounding, if that's OK to say? But still you."

Spider nods. "It's OK to say. Considering how hard I pushed my luck, I'm glad to hear my older-sounding voice."

"And even with the country production touches, I recognized the songs as yours. Something about the words, and melodies, connected it all to your earlier records. As soon as I started listening I knew we had to review it for the site."

"Thanks. Though I was hoping for more than an 85."

"Yeah, one of the side effects of starting this as an undergrad was the grading system. Once I started, couldn't really change it." Andy grins. "But an 85 is pretty solid—we give lots of C's. If everything gets A's and B's the site loses its value."

"And you're gonna review the new one?"

"Of course. I gave it to my Americana guy, he wrote a rave. I wanted to write the review for the *Behind Door Number Two* reissue. It's fantastic, that more people will finally hear it."

"I hope they do. I'd just about given up getting the rights back, but sometimes things work out."

"Timing."

"Timing." Spider grins. It's been almost an hour, which is when Spider had planned to end things, but he's grown a lot fonder of the kid since he mentioned Stackd Souls. "And I'm fucking hungry. You mind if we move this somewhere I can get something to eat?"

"Yeah, no problem," Andy says. He begins to put away his pad and pens, but leaves the tape recorder out. "And I know we haven't even talked about the new album yet, but first I want to hear what it was like, playing with Paul and Danny again."

"Weird. Really fucking weird." Spider grabs his keys and picks up his iPhone. There are several new texts lined up, waiting for him. *Why didnt u just tell me the truth* reads the last one. He grabs his coat off the hooks they'd had put in by the front door—score another one for Allison—and slips the phone into the pocket. "I know it's become this thing, where any band who ever broke up seems to get back together. But we made one record that bombed, another that never came out, and then I fired the two of them. So I was pretty sure we'd never play together again."

It was Michael's idea to film the original three members of Monkeyhole playing together in the studio, and use some of the footage for the promotional video for *Doin' Fine*. Spider had been skeptical from the beginning. "What if we suck? Couldn't the whole thing seem a little Spinal Tap?"

"We just need a couple of minutes of decent-sounding footage, with a few shots of the three of you talking bullshit from the old days."

"Won't that make me sound old?"

"You're thinking of this all wrong. It makes you sound like a guy who's had a career, a guy who's been writing songs and making records for twenty years."

Spider wanted to believe him; after all, Michael was the one who had saved Spider's career, by convincing him "Ice Cream" should be produced like a country song. If he wanted to be dramatic, Spider could even credit Michael with saving his life, when he convinced Spider to enter rehab. And to go back twice more, until it finally worked. While things were less tense with Paul and Danny than they had been in years, thanks to the easy banter instant messaging made possible, he didn't think either one would ever fully forgive him. The only reason they might say yes was the chance to make some money off *Behind Door Number Two*. Michael had gotten the rights to reissue it, and it would be available as a download for the first time.

"You're worried about them still being angry." Michael leaned back in his custom leather office chair, his big indulgence after *Ice Cream Dreams* went platinum.

"Of course."

"But it's their legacy, too, remember. This is a chance for people to finally hear this record. So we offer to fly them up here, put them in nice hotels, and try to finally make money off *Number Two*. They'll be all over it."

Michael was right, of course, the way he was a solid seventy percent of the time. Two months later he, Spider, and Spider's favorite engineer, Eggo, waited together at The Cutting Room. They'd booked an afternoon to film and record the band playing "Gardenia," the Monkeyhole song Michael thought most likely to have crossover appeal.

Danny arrived first. He looked startled by the cameras, as if he'd forgotten that their session would be filmed. Spider hadn't been as close to Danny when they were in the band, but now he chatted online with him more than he did with Paul. His bassist had mellowed over the years, and played the aging hipster well, complete with receding hairline and thick-framed glasses a young Costello would have worn.

"Is this the right spot for the auditions?" Danny asked. He threw a grin in the direction of the cameras. "And which way do I look for the cue cards?"

Spider offered the requisite man-hug with double back-pat. "You worked those jokes up ahead of time, didn't you?"

Danny's stories about teaching high school, and Spider's about hanging with various country music stars, kept the vibe loose, in spite of the camera crew. Things only got a little awkward when Danny wondered if there was any beer, and Michael whispered something to the bass player Spider had gotten drunk with hundreds—thousands?—of times.

"They tried to get me go to rehab, and I said no no no," Spider sang directly to the camera, trying to bring back the lighter mood. "Until I finally said yes yes yes." It worked. He and Danny spent the rest of the time they were waiting for Paul walking around the studio, marveling at how far technology had progressed since they'd made their records.

The atmosphere changed again when Paul arrived, though. He'd been hit harder by the break-up of the band, and a year ago Paul and his wife had gotten divorced. The bitter edge that had always been present in Paul's messages and e-mails had gotten even sharper. From the moment he arrived he was more guarded than Danny, acting as if this really was a stressful audition, and he didn't want to give too much of himself away too quickly.

Or maybe, Spider thought, noticing a bit of red coloring Paul's nervous eyes, he was just stoned.

Time passed slowly, the three of them making awkward conversation with Michael and Eggo. Every now and then Spider's long-time tech, Jimmy, Monkeyhole's former tour manager, would pop his head in to ask a question about gear requirements. The whole scene reminded Spider of an awful club gig, when forty-five minutes could stretch into what felt like four hours. The extra people milling around the studio didn't make it easier: four cameramen, three roadies, two engineers—Monkeyhole had played entire shows to smaller crowds.

Spider hoped everyone would relax when they started playing, since it was the way the three of them always worked best. And when they first headed into the studio there were some good laughs, jokes about creaky backs, nicer instruments than they'd ever had when they were a real band, and Spider's inability to remember just what that weird chord was in the bridge. But everything was too different. There was a tech to make sure Paul was comfortable with the kit, a tech to make sure Danny got handed a perfectly tuned P-Bass, and Jimmy obsessively checking Spider's tuning on his Les Paul. All in front of cameras trying so hard to stay out of the way that they were constantly in the way.

Finally, Eggo signaled that he was ready in the recording room, and the cameras began to roll. After a quick nod to Paul and Danny, Spider strummed the opening chord. He closed his eyes, as if to will himself back to their 1996 club tour, but he was so worried about his adrenalin speeding things up that he started too slow. When he tried to fix the tempo before the opening drum fill, he just made things worse, so Paul had trouble finding the downbeat and Danny had nothing to grab hold of. The song disintegrated before they even hit the first chorus.

"Well, that's a wrap," Jimmy said sarcastically. "You guys are just as good as I remember."

During the fourth run through they made it to the instrumental break. That section always sounded a little empty live, with just one guitar, but Spider pulled off the minor vocal riffing he used fill the gap, and he began to think they might complete a decent take. The breakdown verse was a disaster, though, breaking down so completely that the song collapsed in on itself, like a building that had been rigged for explosion. Paul tried to pull them all back into the last chorus with an extra-loud fill, but he started it too early.

Or too late? Spider couldn't tell what was wrong; he just knew very little was right. He didn't start pointing fingers, though, just kept making sure the guys could hear OK, trying to be as polite and supportive as possible. The fifth time through they made it from start to finish, playing as carefully as a nervous Holiday Inn band. And sounding no better than that.

Spider looked at Paul and Danny as the last chord faded out. He could tell they felt it, too. "To be fair," Danny said, wiping his face with the towel his tech handed him, "this song was a bear when we were still a band."

Spider handed his guitar to Jimmy. "Why don't you guys go take ten."

The techs and cameramen headed out off to the catering room, and Spider turned to face Danny and Paul. "So why is this sucking?"

Danny shrugged. "Maybe we're not the kind of band that can take fifteen years off."

Stretching as he stood, Paul slowly stood up behind the kit. "That. And maybe I shouldn't have had that joint."

"You came here stoned?"

"Jesus, don't go all teacher on me," Paul said to Danny.

"But why?"

Paul grabbed a Coke from the cooler as he walked out from behind the kit toward Danny and Spider. "Are we gonna get share-y now?" he asked. "If we are, I'm a need another fucking joint."

"I could tell when you showed up," Spider said. "You eyes always get so fucking red."

"Yeah, Bad Paul smoked a joint. Come on—how many shows did we all played fucked up, one way or the other?"

"I know, I know," Danny said, "It's just been so long since I've smoked. Didn't even occur to me."

Paul took a long swig of Coke. "Jealous?"

"I am," Spider said.

"Yeah, I'm sorry, Rehab Man," Paul said. "I smoked outside, at least. 'Cause *People* magazine told me all about your problems with addiction." He looked back and forth between them and added, "But don't tell me I'm the only one who was a little stressed about this."

Danny nodded. "Of course. It's been a long time since I played."

"Oh, come on," Paul said. "Don't leave out the part about hanging with the big star who fired us way back when."

Spider exhaled. Would he eventually have to apologize to everyone he was an asshole to in twenty years of making music? Because he didn't have the energy for that. "I said I was sorry, Paul. Shit happened, and I just—"

"Needed a new start, blah blah. I remember." Paul held up a hand. "We're not here to rehash all that, right? But I do want Danny to admit it."

"So now I need to get all share-y?"

"Sherri, baby," Paul sang in a Frankie Valli falsetto.

"OK, yeah, it sucked. A lot of things have sucked in the last twenty years."

"This was up there, though, right?"

"Oh, yeah. Top ten, for sure."

Spider felt like they were turning the corner from bitching to riffing, but it had been so long since the three of them sat in a room together he couldn't be sure. "I was hoping for top five," he said, testing the waters.

"Jesus, you rock stars and your fucking obsession with the charts," Danny said.

"Uh, rock star?" Paul pointed to Spider.

"Excuse me," Danny said. "Country star."

"Yeah, maybe that's it," Paul said. "I was so fucking nervous about jamming with Spider Webb, I had to take the edge off with a joint."

"Which is kind of a shitty thing to do, around an addict."

"It's OK, really," Spider said. He appreciated Danny's support, but he didn't want Paul to feel attacked, especially just as the mood was beginning to lighten. "I mean, I have rules on the road about shit that goes on around me, but there are times I'm around everything I can't have. I've had to learn to deal with it."

"How long has it been since you—" Danny suddenly stopped, as if he'd decided it was a rude question to ask.

"Since I did anything? Two years, eight months, five days. The scotch and the pot—those are still the hardest. In fact," Spider continued, shaking his head as he remembered that first intake interview, "when I entered rehab, I asked them to just leave me the weed. You know, help me get rid of the coke and the booze, and just let me get stoned every now and then. That was my first swing and miss."

"First?" Danny asked.

"I swung and missed twice, but the third time worked."

"See, sharing can teach us all something new." Paul drained the rest of his Coke, swallowed, and burped. "And can we all just admit how weird it is, to have this record come out again? It's like having twenty-year-old me back in my life. Maybe I don't want him around."

"Especially if everyone hates him again," Danny added.

Spider shook his head. "Nah. The world is ready for our twenty-year-old badasses now."

"I sure hope so," Paul said. "That would mean some checks. Divorce is not cheap, people. In case you were wondering." He paused, burped again. "Or fun. In case you were wondering."

Was the divorce the reason Paul looked ten years older than everyone else? Spider couldn't believe Danny was the one he'd worried about. There was an awkward pause, and he wondered if Paul really wanted to talk about it, because that would really fuck the mood. Luckily, Danny changed the topic.

"I don't think the weed is the only reason we suck. I mean, it's a pretty weird scene, right? All those cameras and techs? It was always harder to play for ten people than a thousand."

"I didn't think it would come right away," Spider said. Had Danny always been so good at steering conversations? "But I thought once we started playing it would get easier. Instead we just suck more each time."

"Law of diminishing returns," Danny said.

Paul pointed at Spider. "To be honest, man, I think you're the biggest problem."

"Me? The stoner points at me?" Was Paul determined to find a way to drag things down? Spider wondered how long he had to pretend this could work before he could pull the plug. He could just tell them the last one is good enough—they did make it all the way through, at least—and send them on their way. Maybe they could sync the audio from the CD up to whatever footage they had. "I mean, guys, I'm sorry, but one of us has kept playing all these years, and he's not the one fucking up."

Paul laughed. "If he's talking about himself in the third person, then he's pretty fucked up."

"It's not your playing," Danny said. "It's you."

"But—"

"You're being so fucking nice," Paul said, reaching out to smack Spider on the arm.

"Nice?"

"You always told us when things sucked, and told us how to fix it. But today it's like you're, I don't know, Bambi or something."

"That was great, guys!" Danny says in a high-pitched voice, waving his hands too excitedly. "So, let's, uh, do it again!"

"Jesus, man. Did they cut your balls off in rehab?"

Spider had always hated admitting when they were right, but he did feel lighter as he exhaled, as if he'd just been told he could take off an uncomfortable suit jacket. "I guess I didn't want you to feel bad, coming here, and..." He let the words drift off, unspoken.

Paul finished. "Coming here and seeing how fucking good you have it?"

"Yeah. I guess."

"College done taught me how to add," Danny said. "Once I saw people buying your fucking CD in Target, I figured you were making money."

Spider almost added a comment about not enough money, about all the ways his income gets reduced by all the people he has to pay so he can make all that money, the vicious, self-eating circle of capitalism—but realized how whiny that would sound. "I admit it. I went into a few Targets, on the road. Just to see myself there, next to Britney Spears."

"Not Hank Williams?"

"Nah. Usually filed under Spider. Like Cher."

More laughs, followed by another pause. This time it felt natural, though, not like a strained moment of funereal silence.

"OK, Cher." Danny stood up. "Time to go make some alimony money."

"Sweet Jesus, yes please." Paul started to move back to his kit. "But I kind of wish it could just be us."

"We need footage for the promo video." Spider looked through the glass wall separating the tracking room, where they were playing, and the engineering room, where a few of the techs and cameramen were waiting, sandwiches in hand. Jimmy was the friendliest face, someone who had been with the band in its brief period of almost-glory, on the road with the money and support of a major label. "OK. How about Jimmy comes in to film, and everyone else stays out?"

The mood was completely different with just Jimmy in the room with them. They were used to ignoring him, after all the gigs he'd hung around the stage. The best call of the day, though, came from Paul. After he whacked the snare a few times, looking for the sweet spot, he smoothly segued into the opening beat of "Pay Me Now." Something about the sound reached Spider in a way he didn't think a song from that part of his life still could. It felt like he was in a movie, swept up in a wall of CGI effects and dropped onto the stage of a packed club, full of confidence and energy.

He threw Danny a look and the two of them hit the downbeat together. The next three minutes passed effortlessly—everything was a bit too fast, and the last chorus almost ran away from them completely, but when Spider pushed to hit those final calls to "listen again," Danny screaming away into the mic next to his, the ending had as much force as it had on their first club tour. Just when the plane felt like it might not land safely the wheels slammed into the ground, everyone still alive.

Spider grinned at Danny and Paul and then turned to Jimmy. "You got that, right?"

"Of course, dude. Been sitting here all day waiting for something worth filming."

For the first time that afternoon Spider felt sweat on the top of his head. Even Paul looked more like the Paul he remembered, not the stoned ghost that had been trying to play the drums. How much had they all been holding back before? "Well, then," he said, checking his tuning as he talked, "I think we're ready for 'Gardenia.'"

He finishes the story of the Monkeyhole reunion as he and Andy walk into Le Grainne. It's a perfect time of day to be there: only a few morning stragglers remain, no lunch crowd yet. He nods at Catherine, the hostess, and heads to his regular table in the back corner.

"So, have you stayed in touch, since playing together?"

"With Paul and Danny? A little, but it's hard." He pauses, so he and Andy can both order coffee and chocolate croissants. The truth is, he and Danny have messaged each other a few times a week since then, but all he's heard from Paul is a request for an advance on royalties. There's no reason to say any of that, though; the band's code of silence should live on, even after the band is dead.

The interview shifts to the more common topics of other pre-release interviews: *How happy are you with the new record? What's different/similar about the new record?* And the classic, *How did you handle the pressure of following up such a successful record?*

"You know, people started asking me about pressure the moment *Ice Cream* hit. But I've been writing songs since I was in high school, and nothing I'd ever written had ever made anybody any money. That, that's real pressure, man—wondering if you're going to even get the chance to even make another fucking record, which is the only thing you know how to do. Or want to do."

"Sure, but you're a business now, right? Layers of people counting on you for their living. I can't believe that you didn't get pressure to consciously write some. . . "

"Hits?"

Andy nods, and there it is: the implication that he is somehow selling out. It's a conversation he's had in his own head, when he imagines a twentysomething with unwashed dreads staring at his current self in disbelief. He always tells his younger self he's not "selling out," that selling out would mean making music that isn't his own. When he finished "Doin' Fine," he knew it was catchy enough to be the first single, and had enough personal meaning to be the title track for the new record, but, most importantly, he knew it was his own. Michael had begged for a single that had "a fast, happy chorus," and Spider had met that request—then balanced the choruses with darker verses.

So he tells his younger self to relax and enjoy the attention for as long as it lasts. He's still tapping into the streams of music playing in his head, like he's been doing since he was thirteen. He's more selective about which streams he dips into, and dresses the songs up with certain sounds, but the music is still his.

"I figured I'd get at least one swing, right?" He takes a bite of croissant. "Radio would spin the first single to see if I'd gotten lucky again, and critics would listen to see how much I'd blown it. And the fans have been great, but I also know I was still the new kid, for a lot of them, and I needed to prove I was worthy of more attention. So I wanted to take a swing with a song that meant something to me."

"I dug it the first time I heard it. I love the organ, and that Zydeco feel, but it's the verses that really hit me. You're singing about a failed marriage, an absent father, someone who lost his chance to be a father... Heavy stuff, but laid on top of this barn-burning groove."

"Huh. List the verses like that, and it sounds like I'm singing about mid-life crisis shit."

Andy smiles at him. "Well. . ."

"Yeah, I know, I know," Spider says. "Twenty years of making records, twenty years old when I started, do the math. I am mid-life."

"And are those things you're thinking about? Fatherhood? Lost chances?"

"I guess? Like most things I write, this one's based on my life but also completely made up." Spider has a flash of Allison reading this part of the interview. She'd accuse him of always knowing he wouldn't have any kids and withholding that information from her. Would she believe him, if he explained that sometimes his music brain figures out parts of his life before his regular brain does? He also thinks of his own father, holding on in his retirement home but fading fast ever since his mother died. He eats the last of his croissant, wondering if flaky-butter-drenched pastries will be the next thing he has to enter rehab for. "Like, that part where the singer is talking about his 'old man.' For the record, my father made a lot of mistakes, but at the end of the day he played *Revolver* for me when I was five, and changed my life."

Andy nods, flipping through his notes. "As great as the title track is, though, you don't start the record with it, the way you did last time."

"No, I wanted 'Doin' Fine' to be last. I think it sums up everything that came before it."

"What made 'The Limited Patience of the Wilco Fan's Wife' a good opener?"

"I've always loved playing with record sequences, you know? Still do, even though I know not everyone listens to records start to finish, anymore. I always like first songs that set the rest of the record up well, sonically and lyrically."

"It does, with the acoustic and lap steel at the top, and your voice coming in so quickly. I also think it's the most direct combination of what you're doing now and what you were doing in Monkeyhole."

Spider nods. It's always satisfying when the interviewer has really listened to the music. "I think that's well put, man. To me, it kind of points to where I've been and where I'm going."

"And every music geek ever lucky enough to have a girlfriend will imagine her in the song."

"Oh, yeah," Spider says. "And that one, that one for sure came out of my own life—I wrote it because anyone I ever dated accused me of not understanding what it was like for them, to have to share me with music. I could never really apologize, because the truth is, I can't be sorry for what music means to me. But I did want to at least try to imagine what it'd be like, to date someone who is also in love with something else—some thing she can't compete with."

"To date someone in love with Jeff Tweedy, then?"

"Yeah. Or, at least, Tweedy's songs. Tweedy's world."

"Were you dating someone at the time? And did she dig the song?"

Spider remembers playing the demo for Allison, the two of them sitting side by side on the couch. "She thought it was funny," he says, still able to see the look on her face as she realized what the song was about.

How many times had she asked him, directly, or with subtle tests, whether she was as important as the music? When he was younger he used to be honest, he used to admit the music would be more important than anything, or anyone, else in his life. He wanted to act more like a grown-up with Allison, so he said she was more important. He thought he was doing the right thing; he thought couples had to each say what the other needed to hear, even when you both knew it was a lie.

"So the single's been out a few weeks, doing pretty well at radio, and the album drops next Tuesday. Tour starts later this month. You must feel everything, like, picking up speed." Andy closes his notepad and places it next to his empty plate. "Does it feel like it's all going to happen again, with as much success?"

"Yes. Maybe. I think?" He finds the willpower to wave off the waitress offering a refill. Another sign of middle age: his bowels can only handle so much caffeine per day. "A friend of mine once compared this stage of the record's life, when things are just getting started, to what a ski jumper must feel like, having just shot off the ramp." Spider closes his eyes, remembering the conversation clearly: backstage at Webster Hall with a friend who should have entered rehab himself. "You're in the air, no going back. All you can do is wait to see how far you can fly, and how smoothly you can land." He opens his eyes back up. "The thing is, your landing— whether you're going glide smoothly to a first-place finish or crash and burn when you hit the ground—has already been determined by the speed and angle of your take-off. Your fate is already set. So you might as well enjoy the view while you're floating."

Andy turns off the tape recorder. "That seems like a good last image, doesn't it? Spider Webb, in the air, waiting to land."

After saying goodbye to Andy, Spider looks at his phone. There's only one new message: *Dont wry I will come n get things after u leave for boston shoud i leav key on countr?*

He needs to answer but can't think of anything to type but "Yes." He knows that such a short response will just piss her off, that she's waiting for him to apologize. But he can't do it in real life, any more than he could do it in a song.

Exhaustion hits as he stands there on the sidewalk. The idea of gearing up for a tour does not make him more tired, though—in a way, the kind of tired he feels now is something he suspects will fade only when he starts working again, just as there used to be mornings he could only wake up if he had a joint. He should go home and pack, maybe even play guitar for a bit, but walking into the apartment, and seeing all of her clothes and things left behind, will be too fucking depressing. He's never been the one to stay after a break-up; he's always been the one to leave, the feral musician some nice woman had failed to domesticate, headed back to the streets. It will be much harder to be the one who stays behind, who keeps finding stray bits and pieces of the disappeared.

So he decides to take a walk on the High Line. He visualizes the rehearsal space they rented for the next few days, with its deli trays and freshly cleaned road cases, roadies and musicians, and that air of anticipation, and he decides to embrace that pre-tour optimism, that sense that something great is going to happen.

No astronaut climbs into the rocket because they expect to burn up in the atmosphere.

Finally at the stage of his career where he can pick and choose each player, Spider has assembled his dream band. Remembering what it was like to play with Paul and Danny again, though, he's aware of what this new kind of band is missing. There's none of the banter, or fighting, generated by musicians who know each other, really know each other, as people, not just as musicians. He always told himself all he really needed was the music; after forty years of waiting, he was about to find out if that was true.

Walking the stairs up to the High Line he feels the pull of the rip cord in his chest, the one that holds in place all the missing pieces of his life. Everything tumbles out for him to examine. Moments like this were always a good time to push his brain out of his body with some sort of chemical additive, so he could avoid looking at anything too closely. Now all he has left to distract himself is himself, as he waits for the opening to reseal. It has always closed back up, at least so far.

So far.

He reaches the top of the metal staircase and steps onto the path. It's a sunny day, the blanket of the early fall chill taken off for the first time in weeks, and maybe for the last time before winter. The crowd is thick, layered with tourists and baby-wearing moms and businessmen taking phone calls. His first instinct is to turn around and go home, but instead he breathes in deeply and steps into the flow of human traffic making its way east. The force of the crowd gently pushes him forward. As he walks he turns down the half-heard conversations of people he will never know and turns up one of the streams of music in his head, wondering where it will take him next.

Acknowledgements

This book would not have been possible without all the years I spent traveling the country in a Ford Econoline Van, meeting people who love to play, listen to, and talk about music. I may have forgotten some of the names, but bits and pieces of the stories we shared made their way into these pages. Those years made me who I am today, and I thank all of you.

When the match is a good one, touring with another band is like traveling in a bulletproof limo, offering private mini-bars and protection against challenges great and small. I was lucky enough to spend many a late night and early morning with the members of Trip Shakespeare, Semisonic, the Verve Pipe, Matthew Sweet, Drivin' N Cryin', Robyn Hitchcock, the Black Crowes, Sheer Thursday, Three Merry Widows, 86, Ben Folds Five, Right as Rain, the Skylarks, Big Fish Ensemble, and the Reivers.

Riding in the bulletproof limo with me: Matt and Jeff and Bill. A real band is a very, very particular and special thing.

The accompanying soundtrack (see this book's copyright page for how to get your free copy) would not have been possible without Theme Music. In the credits you can find the impressive list of performers, most of whom I met through this online community. Please be sure to visit the websites of my co-writers, so you can enjoy more of their creations. Everyone involved worked relentlessly on this, recording in home studios on their own time, helping with arrangements, and answering e-mails from Hassle Man. They did not do this for promises of riches; they did it because they're beautiful people who love music, and I'll be forever grateful for the way they expanded the Monkeyhole Universe. I need to include extra loud shout-outs to Lee Flier, who recorded most of the drums and provided help with the direction and shape of the soundtrack, and Paul Melançon, who gave voice to Spider.

It is fitting that Wax'n'Facts plays a crucial role in the book, because they played a crucial role in my musical past. Danny Beard gave Uncle Green a home on his beloved dB Recs, and Steve Pilon worked tirelessly to promote our albums. Thanks to all store employees, especially Sean Bourne, for making it possible to shoot the cover there one Sunday afternoon. Also thanks to Angela Georges, for taking the perfect photo, and Erin Dangar, of Dangar Design, for laying it all out.

Early versions of all these chapters were read by members of my Writing Group. Beth Gylys, Jessica Handler, Sheri Joseph, and Susan Rebecca White are patient, encouraging, and, when necessary, ruthless; their thoughtful comments made the finished product better by a degree I cannot calculate. Bob Fenster read the whole thing more than once, offering valuable advice each time, and Jill Melançon offered some fresh eagle eyes at the last moment, as did Laura Seebol. Kim Ware proved to be an engaged and supportive reader, as well as a charming lunch companion. Halley O'Malley, Jacob Slichter, and Carey Anne Farrell were all kind enough to read chapters along the way. The whole book was lovingly examined and sharpened by my amazing editor, Tess Hoffman; reading the before and after versions of the manuscript is like listening to a song before and after a mixer with great ears has worked on it. And I wouldn't even be writing these acknowledgements if not for Mark Doyon, who was not only an early and enthusiastic reader—he was also crazy enough to be excited by the idea of releasing a book and a soundtrack at the same time.

I'll end with a special thanks to my family. My mother and sister offered encouragement through all my creative ramblings, including many visits to rock clubs of dubious quality to watch me play. Finally, and most importantly, thanks and love to Bruce & Olivia & Teagan, who have made my life much richer than I ever dreamed it could be.

74766746R00127

Made in the USA
Columbia, SC
06 August 2017